A RATION BOOK DAUGHTER

Cathy was a happy, blushing bride when Britain went to war with Germany three years ago. But her youthful dreams were crushed by her violent husband Stanley's involvement with the fascist Blackshirts, and even when he's conscripted to fight she knows it's only a brief respite — divorce is not an option.

When a telegram arrives declaring that her husband is MIA, Cathy can finally allow herself to hope — she only has to wait six months before she is legally a widow. So she advertises for a lodger, and Sergeant Archie McIntosh of a Royal Engineers bomb disposal squad turns up. He is kind, clever and thoughtful; their mutual attraction is instant. But with Stanley's fate unclear, and bombs raining down, will Cathy ever have the love she deserves?

JEAN FULLERTON

A RATION BOOK DAUGHTER

Complete and Unabridged

MAGNA
Leicester

First published in Great Britain in 2021 by
Corvus
an imprint of Atlantic Books Ltd
London

First Ulverscroft Edition
published 2021
by arrangement with
Atlantic Books Ltd
London

A catalogue record for this book is available
from the British Library.

ISBN 978–0–7505–4889–2

Published by
Ulverscroft Limited
Anstey, Leicestershire

Printed and bound in Great Britain by
TJ Books Ltd., Padstow, Cornwall

This book is printed on acid-free paper

For all NHS and Care staff, who while I was at home writing Cathy and Archie's story were on the front line in a world-wide pandemic saving lives.

1

Standing among the rails of donated clothing, Cathy Wheeler, neé Brogan, ran her eyes over the various boys' coats. Spotting a green tweed one towards the end of the rail, she grasped it and pulled it out.

'I only unpacked it yesterday. It was in one of the new Canadian Red Cross parcels,' she said, turning it around and holding it up. 'But I think this might fit your little lad, Mrs . . . ?'

'Prentice. It looks a bit big,' said the young mother with tired eyes.

'Why don't you get him to try it on, Mrs Prentice?' Cathy said, giving it to her.

Cathy waited as the young woman fitted the donated coat on her son.

It was Friday afternoon and, as always when she did her stint at St Breda and St Brendan's ARP Rest Centre, she was dressed in her forest-green Women's Voluntary Service uniform. Three and a half years ago, before the war started, the room she now stood in had been used by the local community for wedding receptions, dances and the youth club. Now the main hall of the church's Catholic Club was the first port of call for those who, after a night in an air raid shelter, arrived home to discover a pile of rubble where their house had once stood.

The second-hand clothing section of the WVS's rest centre, which Cathy was responsible for, was located in the back corner of the main hall. Opposite her was the canteen area, from where a faint smell of hotpot

1

drifted across. Behind the serving hatch, half a dozen of her fellow volunteers were preparing an evening meal for families and ARP workers alike. The massive Bush wireless belted out tunes as the women worked. The rest of the hall was taken up by the dozen or so rows of camp beds with striped tick mattresses. On each bed was a neatly folded grey blanket with a pillow resting on top, ready for the next unfortunate occupant. However, fog had been blanketing the London Docks, just a stone's throw away, for the past week, which meant the Luftwaffe was unable to use the Thames's reflection to locate London, and so the emergency beds hadn't been needed.

It was the first week of November 1942 and Cathy had taken over the running of the second-hand clothes section at the end of the summer from her mother, Ida. They had joined the WVS together a couple of years before to help with the war effort. She'd been carrying Peter at the time and after he'd been born she hadn't been able to help out as much, but when he turned eighteen months last Christmas, Cathy decided to take advantage of the rest centre's nursery. So now, while Peter had fun with Auntie Muriel and Auntie Pat, Cathy did her bit to fight Hitler.

'I still think it's a bit on the large size,' said Mrs Prentice, studying her son all buttoned up in his new coat.

Cathy's gaze flickered over the youngster.

'It's got a bit of growing room, I grant you,' she said. 'But you only have to tack up the sleeves an inch or two and you'll get a lot of wear out of it.'

The woman sighed. 'I suppose you're right. I'll have it then. And I've got a couple of gymslips my girl's grown out of.' She delved into the shopping basket at her feet. 'Can I swap them for a bigger size?'

She offered Cathy the navy garments.

'Thank you,' the woman said, as Cathy took the dresses from her.

Unfortunately, as always when there was something on offer for free, people took advantage. There had been a spate recently, especially when word got around that a new consignment from the US or Canadian Red Cross had arrived, of people turning up at a rest centre pretending to have been bombed out. They'd take the pick of the new clothes, plus household items like crockery and linen, which then turned up a few days later for sale on market stalls. Thankfully, although Cathy had never met her before, Mrs Prentice was obviously a genuine case.

'How old is she?'

'Ten.'

Cathy, tucking a strand of light brown hair behind her ear, moved to the school uniform rail and sifted through the line of assorted skirts, blazers and trousers.

'Here we go,' she said, dragging out two pinafores. 'Gladys!'

A young girl reading a comic at one of the canteen tables looked up.

'Come and try these on,' called the young mother, beckoning her over.

Cathy caught sight of the clock over the door at the far end of the hall.

Almost four thirty already!

Leaving Mrs Prentice to deal with her daughter, Cathy tidied the hangers and straightened the piles of newly washed and pressed men's shirts set out on the trestle table, neatly ordered by collar size.

3

'How are we getting on?' she asked, turning back to her customer.

The mother looked her daughter up and down.

'They'll do until Easter, I expect,' said Mrs Prentice, bending to tug the hem of the navy gymslip straight. 'Go and change back into your clothes now, Gladys,' she instructed her daughter.

'I have some navy school knickers, too,' added Cathy. 'They're new if you could use a couple of — '

'Thanks,' the young mother cut in, opening her purse and pulling out her pink clothing ration book.

'They've been donated as second hand so you won't need coupons, but if you want, you can drop a couple of coppers in our Spitfire jar instead.' Cathy indicated the sweets jar on the refectory counter. It was half filled with coins and had a picture of the fighter air-craft mid-flight stuck on it. 'We'd be grateful.'

'I'll see if I've got a bob or two,' Mrs Prentice replied. 'But what with these two eating me out of house and home and the prices in the shops going up every day, I've barely got two ha'pennies to rub together at the end of the week.'

'I know what you mean,' said Cathy, thinking of the handful of coppers in her own purse.

'I thought it would get a bit better when the Yanks joined in last year but now you can't get petrol, sweets for the kids are down to just a couple of ounces and they've even put biscuits on ration,' Mrs Prentice went on. 'I don't know how the blooming government expects me to keep a roof over my head and feed two kids on a couple of quid a week from the army.'

Cathy gave her a sympathetic smile. 'I know, but we all have to support our brave boys.'

'I suppose.' Mrs Prentice heaved a sigh. 'Still, I'd

better get on. Thanks again for the knickers.'

Gathering her children and their newly acquired garments, Mrs Prentice headed towards the door.

Taking the clothing ledger from the table, Cathy sat on the chair next to the rack of shoes and took her fountain pen from the top pocket of her jacket. After logging Mrs Prentice's items in the 'taken' column and listing the two gymslips under 'donated', she closed the book and stood up.

Once she'd pushed the three rails full of assorted jackets, dresses and children's wear back against the wall, she covered them with dust sheets ready for when she arrived the following morning.

'Ain't you got no home to go to?'

Cathy turned around to find Mary Usher, wearing the same WVS uniform as Cathy, standing behind her.

A petite brunette, Mary had spent the afternoon in the yard outside bundling up scrap paper and cardboard for recycling; now she had the red cheeks and windswept hair to show for her hard work.

She'd been a few classes above Cathy at Shadwell School and had lived over her parents' shoe repair shop in Salmon Lane, which was where she was living now with her two children, because her merchant seaman husband was somewhere in the frozen North Atlantic ferrying armaments to Murmansk for Britain's fickle ally Russia.

'Just finishing off,' Cathy replied, flapping the cover over the boxes beneath.

'Honestly, you're always the last one here,' continued Mary. 'It's a wonder you have time to get yourself fed and watered before you have to head off to the shelter.'

5

'I put a hotpot in the oven on a low light before I came out and that'll be ready to dish up when I get in,' Cathy replied. 'Unless the air raid sounds, the doors to Bethnal Green station shelter don't open until five thirty, so I've plenty of time, and my mum's always one of the first through the door so she'll make sure no one takes my spot.'

'It seems daft to go traipsing all the way up Cambridge Heath Road when the Tilbury shelter's only five minutes away,' said Mary.

'My brothers go to Parmiter's School, behind the museum,' Cathy replied, 'so it's not so far for them to get to school in the morning. You in tomorrow?'

'No, I've got to go and queue up for the Ration Department at the Town Hall and try to get Dad a replacement ration book for the one he lost a week ago,' said Mary. 'Mum's going spare as she's trying to feed all of us on quarter ra —'

The rest-centre doors crashed back against the walls as Wilf Ingles, the ARP warden for Sutton Street, burst in.

'Have you heard?' he shouted, waving an *Evening News*. 'Monty's bloomin' well done it!'

'Done what?' asked someone.

'Beat the bloody Hun,' Wilf replied, his lined face alight with excitement.

The room erupted into clapping and cheering. A couple of two-tone whistles cut through the air as people slapped each other on the back.

'Where?' someone shouted above the noise.

'Some place called El something or another,' Wilf replied. 'It's all here in the early edition. It calls it a 'Great and Glorious Victory', and says our lads have captured thousands of Wop prisoners and hundreds

6

of tanks. And now they're driving Rommel and his gang of Nazis into the sea.' He shook the newspaper again. 'You can read if for yourselves.'

People crowded around the elderly warden, looking over his shoulders and craning their necks to read the account.

'Isn't your Stan in North Africa, Cath?' Mary asked, turning to face Cathy.

'Yes,' Cathy replied flatly.

Mary laughed. 'Well, your old man must have been right in the thick of it. I bet you're doubly pleased to hear it's our boys that have won the day.'

Noticing Cathy's tight expression, Mary placed her hand over hers. 'I know, luv, it's ruddy hard not having them around, isn't it?'

Cathy didn't reply.

'And it's not just the . . .' She gave Cathy a bashful look. 'You know . . . but the little things. Like how their eyes light up when you put their favourite dinner in front of 'em, nights in front of the fire listening to the wireless together when the kids are in bed.' She laughed. 'I even miss my Ted's blooming snoring.'

'There'll always be an England,' sang a male voice above the throng.

Others in the room took up the tune.

'I'd better collect Peter and get home,' said Cathy, raising her voice to be heard. 'See you when I see you.'

'Not if I see you first,' Mary shouted back.

Cathy turned, and, weaving her way through the crowd of singing people, she left the main hall and headed for the door at the far end of the corridor.

Catching a faint whiff of carbolic, Cathy walked into what had been the caretaker's storeroom and was now the organiser's office. Wall charts and stirrup pumps had replaced the mops and buckets, but the smell lingered on.

The woman sitting behind an old schoolmaster's desk at the far end of the room looked up and gave Cathy a weary smile.

'You finished for the day then, Mrs Wheeler?' she asked.

In her late fifties, with steel-grey hair and a sparse frame, Miss Edith Carpenter had lost her fiancé in the previous Great War and had never found another. As the only child of the chief surgeon in St George's Hospital, she was blessed with a private income, so instead of using all her energy and talents to run a home and family, Miss Carpenter poured herself into good works. It was natural, therefore, that when the WVS was founded a year before Hitler marched into Poland, she was one of the first to volunteer.

Although the WVS — or Women of Various Sizes, as their founder Lady Reading often called them — didn't have an official management hierarchy, in truth, in every canteen or rest centre Cathy had ever visited, it was the wives of professionals and well-to-do businessmen in the area who took charge.

'Pretty much,' said Cathy, closing the door. 'Have you heard the news?'

'Yes, Peggy Wilson popped her head around the door a few moments ago to tell me,' Miss Carpenter replied. 'Marvellous. Your husband is serving in North Africa, isn't he?'

'Yes.'

'Well, no doubt you'll have a letter from him soon telling you all about it,' the older woman said. 'And how he misses you, too, I'm sure.'

Cathy gave a tight smile but didn't reply.

'I hear your mother's had her baby,' said Miss Carpenter.

'Yes, two nights ago, in the middle of an air raid,' said Cathy. 'A little girl; six pounds, thirteen ounces.'

Miss Carpenter's fair eyebrows rose. 'Goodness. Is she all right?'

'She's fine,' Cathy replied. 'Her waters went just before lights-out at ten and the midwife delivered the baby at three thirty.'

'Have your parents chosen a name yet?' asked Miss Carpenter.

'Victoria,' said Cathy.

The rest centre organiser's pale eyebrows rose. 'That's unusual.'

'That's what everyone says,' Cathy replied.

'Well, it must have been a bit of a shock for her discovering she was pregnant again at her time of life,' said Miss Carpenter.

'It was,' Cathy replied. 'I think it was more of a shock for my dad, though.'

Truthfully, it had been a shock for the whole family, especially after the falling-out her parents had had the year before.

It was a long story, but when Ida's old friend Ellen arrived with ten-year-old Michael and they found out he was Jeremiah's son, it didn't take much to imagine what Cathy's mother's reaction was. To be honest, she and her sisters Mattie and Jo had refused point-blank even to speak to their father when they found out, but as her mother had wholeheartedly forgiven him, Cathy had to as well.

'Well, give her my regards when you see her,' said Miss Carpenter. 'And I'll see you in the morning.'

Wishing the older woman goodnight, Cathy left her

to her paperwork and headed towards the smaller hall at the back of the building.

Pushing open the half-glazed door of what had been the large committee room, Cathy walked into the nursery to a boisterous chorus of 'Ee-I-Ay-Di-O', as the two dozen or more children holding hands sang at the tops of their voices.

Cathy's eyes scanned the laughing children for a moment before they rested on her son Peter, and love swelled in her heart.

Although he was only two and a half, Peter was already an inch or two taller than most of the boys his age. She had her side of the family to thank for that, but his thick, sandy-coloured hair and broad features were down to her husband Stan.

Peter was on the far side of the circle between two little girls but, seeing her, he broke free and hurried towards her, scattering wooden bricks and tin soldiers in his path.

Cathy put on her brightest face and, crouching down, held out her arms.

'Hello, young man,' she said, as she enveloped him in her embrace.

'Mummy,' he replied, hugging her tightly.

Cathy closed her eyes and hugged him back.

Feeling the heaviness that was always hovering just over her shoulder and threatening to descend, Cathy gave him a last squeeze and then let him go.

Forcing a smile on to her face, she straightened up and took his hand. 'Let's get your coat and then we can go home.'

★ ★ ★

Within a few moments of leaving the rest centre, Cathy reached Commercial Road.

Before the war, the main highway between Gardiner's corner and Limehouse had been barely passable because of the cars whizzing past in both directions. However, since the abolition of civilian petrol rations a few months before, only lorries and buses and the occasional horse and cart now trundled along the wide road.

'Look, Mummy,' said Peter, pointing a chubby finger at a Charrington's dray rolling along on the other side of the road.

'Yes, Peter, it's a black horse,' she said, manoeuvring his pushchair across the road.

Turning east, she walked past Arbour Square and then left into Head Street and left again. Pausing by the gates of Senrab Street School, Cathy's eyes rested on the neat rows of three-storeyed houses running along either side of the street.

The last few people were shutting their doors for the night as Winnie Master, the street's part-time ARP warden, finished her early-evening round, ensuring Cathy's neighbours were complying with the blackout regulations.

Tightening her grip on the pushchair handle, Cathy headed down the street and turned into the side alley beside the red door halfway down. Reaching the end, she unlatched the side gate and walked through.

Unlike her parents' home half a mile away in Mafeking Terrace, the houses here had reasonably large back gardens. At the outbreak of war, most of Cathy's neighbours had dug up their lawns and planted an Anderson Shelter instead of spring bulbs in their flowerbeds.

11

Her corrugated refuge was buried under a great mound of earth, which looked as if the lawn was about to give birth. Unlike some, it had proper drainage and two good-size bunks. Her husband Stan had dug it for her and his mother to shelter in, but Cathy never used it.

The weight surrounding her threatened to press down on her shoulders again, but Cathy lifted her chin, opened the back door and rolled the pushchair into the kitchen.

The kitchen straddled the width of the house with a window next to the door. On one side of the room was a porcelain sink with an integrated draining board set into a white enamelled stand. At the far end of the room was a built-in dresser with long cupboards on either side of a central section with a pull-down work-top, which sat over a set of drawers. The room also housed two other items that, as far as she knew, no one else in the street or even the area had: a washing tub, with internal paddle and mangle, and, tucked in the corner on its squat little legs, a refrigerator.

Stan had refitted the kitchen before he'd brought her home as his bride, and, in truth, most women would give their eye-teeth for a kitchen such as the one she was standing in. But for Cathy, there was a coldness about it that had nothing to do with the temperature outside.

The smell of her shin of lamb hotpot wafted over to her, making her stomach rumble.

Kicking on the pushchair's brakes, Cathy took off her coat. Then, setting Peter on the floor, she unwrapped him from his winter layers.

'Is that you?'

Cathy took a deep breath. 'Yes.'

She pulled a smiley face at Peter.

The little boy laughed but then his attention shifted to something behind his mother and his happy expression disappeared.

Cathy turned to see her mother-in-law standing in the doorway.

Wearing the long-ago fashions and muted colours of the Edwardian age, Violet Wheeler looked a decade older than her fifty years.

'Now that the clocks have gone back and it gets dark so early, you might have come home sooner,' said Violet, her pale lips drawing into a sullen line.

Tying her son's Noddy and Big Ears bib around his neck, Cathy didn't reply.

'Still,' continued Violet, putting on her hard-done-by-little-old-lady expression, 'after all this time, I should have known you don't care about my poor nerves.'

Cathy crossed to the dresser and pulled out the cutlery drawer. 'I've been busy all afternoon, so I was late getting away.'

'Busy!' scoffed her mother-in-law. 'Is that what you call gossiping with those do-gooding friends of yours at that centre?'

'Busy helping families who've lost everything in the bombing,' Cathy replied.

Violet's thin face pulled into a sorrowful expression.

'And what about my poor little Stanley?' She ran her bony hand over her grandson's fair hair and the boy looked up. 'Were you left all alone, my poor darling, while your selfish mummy was enjoying herself?'

'His name's Peter,' said Cathy, collecting the knives and forks from the dresser. 'And you know full well

Peter was in the nursery playing with the other children.'

Her mother-in-law's eyes narrowed. 'And if that's not bad enough, you dump him on your mother every Wednesday to go gadding around,' Violet added.

'I'm taking typing and shorthand classes at Cephas Street, not dancing the night away in the Lyceum,' Cathy snapped back.

'Evening classes,' sneered her mother-in-law. 'What do you need evening classes for?'

'To better myself,' Cathy replied. 'Perhaps I'll get a little job when Peter gets older.'

'You've got a job as a wife and mother and looking after me as you should. And if you think you're going to get yourself a swanking job in an office somewhere then you'd better think again. My Stan won't have you showing 'im up by letting people think he can't provide for his family.'

Turning her back on her mother-in-law, Cathy started to wash her hands.

'I'll be writing to him tomorrow, to tell him just how you treat me,' continued Violet, speaking to the back of Cathy's head. 'Mark my words. He'll sort you out good and proper when he gets back.'

Graphic memories of her brutal and fearful life with Stan flashed through Cathy's mind and panic fluttered in her chest.

'And it'll be no more than you deserve,' added Violet.

Reminding herself that her husband was two thousand miles away in North Africa, Cathy pushed the unsettling thoughts aside.

'I suppose you'll be off to the shelter with your mother in an hour,' Violet said.

14

'I will,' said Cathy.

'I don't know why you don't just go straight there,' said Violet.

Cathy said nothing. Stretching up, she went to take two dinner plates from the rack.

'Don't bother,' said Violet. 'I got fed up waiting for you, so I've had mine.'

Placing her and her son's plates on the table, Cathy picked up the tea towel from the hook by the cooker. Winding it around her hands, she crouched down.

A blast of hot air hit her face as she opened the oven door and lifted out the enamel casserole dish. Placing supper on the table, she lifted the lid.

Cathy stared at what was supposed to be her and Peter's supper for a moment then raised her head.

'What?' asked Violet, with barely concealed malice glinting in her pale grey eyes.

'What do you mean, what?' snapped Cathy, pointing into the bowl. 'You've had the lot.'

'No I haven't,' her mother-in-law replied, giving her an airy look. She glanced into the dish. 'See.'

She pointed at the couple of potatoes, the handful of carrot slices and the bits of gristly meat at the bottom of the dish. 'That's more than enough for Stanley.'

'And what about me?' Cathy asked. 'That was part of my weekly meat rations, too.'

Violet shrugged. 'Well, had you been here you could have said something, but as you weren't, hard lu —'

The door knocker echoed down the hall.

'Who's that?' said Violet.

Again, not answering, Cathy wiped her hands on the tea towel and went through to the hallway.

'It'd better not be any of your bog-trotting family,' shouted Violet, as Cathy reached the front door. 'I

15

won't have them under my roof, do you hear?'

Patting her hair into place and straightening the front of her blouse, Cathy opened the door.

Standing on the step was a post office messenger dressed in a navy uniform with red piping and a pillbox cap. He was about thirteen or fourteen, with the shadow of his first moustache on his top lip and acne sprinkled across his forehead. His bicycle was propped up on the kerb.

Gathered on the pavement on the other side of the road were Cathy's neighbours, all with pitying expressions on their faces.

Cathy's heart leapt into her throat.

'Mrs Stanley Wheeler?' the boy asked, his Adam's apple bobbing up and down as he spoke.

'Yes.'

Diving into the bag slung across him, he pulled out a telegram and handed it to her.

'I'm sorry.'

Touching the stiff peak of his cap, the lad climbed back on his bicycle and cycled away.

Cathy stared at the envelope in her hand for a moment then went back inside, closing the door behind her.

'Who is it?' bellowed Violet.

Cathy walked back into the kitchen and the blood drained from her mother-in-law's face when she saw the telegram.

Cathy broke the seal and unfolded the page.

'Is it my Stanley?' asked Violet as Cathy's eyes tried to focus on the lines of tickertape that were dancing about on the page.

'Is he injured?'

Cathy didn't reply.

'Tell me,' screeched Violet. 'Tell me if my son's all right. Tell me!'

Violet snatched the paper from Cathy's hand. Her hard eyes darted across the page for a moment then she looked up at Cathy.

'Missing in action,' she shouted. 'How can he be missing in action? I only got a letter yesterday.'

'That's what it says,' Cathy replied.

Peter toddled over and grabbed Cathy's legs, so she lifted him up and slid him into his highchair.

'What are you doing?' asked Violet.

'Giving Peter his dinner before we go off to the shelter,' said Cathy.

Her mother-in-law looked at her in disbelief. 'But your husband's missing! Doesn't that mean anything to you?'

'Of course it does,' said Cathy, placing Peter's plate in front of him. 'If he doesn't turn up or appear on a POW list in the next six months, I'll be a widow.'

2

Although the damp from the London clay he was lying on was seeping through his khaki battle jacket, Sergeant Archie McIntosh barely noticed the discomfort. It was now mid afternoon on the first Friday in November and he had more important things to worry about. The main one being the 1,500-kilo German bomb, known ominously as a Satan, that he was lying alongside at the bottom of a ten-foot trench.

On the other side of the bomb, hunkered down on his haunches, was Lieutenant Monkman, the officer in charge of North East London Bomb Disposal Unit's D Squad. He was chewing the side of his thumb and, despite the chilly air at the bottom of the wood-clad shaft, Archie could see perspiration gathering on his senior officer's forehead.

'Can you see the number on the fuse yet, McIntosh?' Lieutenant Monkman asked, the steam of his breath visible as he spoke.

'No, sir, there's too much muck,' Archie replied.

With thin Brylcreemed brown hair and elongated features, Nicholas Ernest Monkman was a bit younger than Archie's thirty years. Although Monkman's officer's uniform was tailor-made rather than standard issue, the jacket still hung loosely from his shoulders and had plenty of room across the chest. According to Tubbs Croker, the mess sergeant who dealt with the officers' lounge and bar, Monkman was the younger son of some earl. Growing up in Maryhill, Archie hadn't had too much to do with the aristocracy or their offspring, but two years of serving under Monkman had given him a practical understanding of the words 'entitled' and 'condescending', and had confirmed to Archie why he was a card-carrying member of the Labour Party.

Taking the cloth tucked inside his jacket, he wound it around his finger and, reaching across, gently wiped the mud from the circular disc in the fat belly of the explosive.

The cavity made by the ten-foot-long bomb as it had ploughed its way underground after impact had been discovered by the local ARP warden earlier that morning while he was inspecting the damage of the previous night's air raid. As the unexploded armament had come to rest between the three storage tanks of the St Pancras Gasworks and the mainline station itself, the control room at Islington Town had immediately phoned through to Wanstead School, where the bomb disposal unit was based. Archie's team were on first call that morning and they had been sent out immediately. That was just after nine, and the men had been digging down for the past five hours to uncover the bomb.

With his heart thumping against the inside of his chest, Archie gently cleared away the last few smears of mud. Taking his torch from his breast pocket, he flicked it on.

'It's a seventeen,' Archie said, as the beam illuminated the number in the centre of the disc. Inching forward, he placed his right ear on to the dirty metal. 'And the wee bugger's ticking.'

Fear flickered in Lieutenant Monkman's close-set eyes and he scrambled to his feet. He glanced at the ladder leading up to the surface and, for one

19

brief moment, Archie thought his senior officer was going to make a bolt for it, but then Monkman's eyes returned to him.

Holding the other man's gaze, Archie stood up.

'Chalky!' he yelled up the shaft without taking his eyes from the man opposite.

'Sarge?' Corporal White shouted back.

'It's a Satan with a number seventeen fuse, so the lieutenant will be needing the clock stopper and the stethoscope,' Archie bellowed up.

'Right you are,' White yelled back.

'And have the drill and steamer ready to go once we've stopped it ticking,' Archie called.

The lieutenant took his handkerchief from his pocket.

'What in the devil's name is taking them so long?' he asked, mopping his brow and casting anxious glances at the bomb at their feet.

'Dinna fret, they'll be here presently,' Archie said.

'I'm not fretting,' snapped the lieutenant. Taking a packet of cigarettes from his trouser pocket, he sneered, 'I just don't want them *aping* around, that's all, Sergeant.'

Archie held Monkman's mocking gaze.

The officer took out his lighter, a silver one with his initials stamped on the side.

'Good God, man,' he said, flicking it, 'it's not too much to ask that they get a shift on, is it?'

'No, sir,' Archie replied.

'I bet they wouldn't be *monkeying* around if they were standing next to a sodding ticking bomb,' said Monkman, frantically flicking the lighter cap to get a flame.

Irritation flared in Archie's chest.

20

Chalky and the lads had finished their shift the previous night at ten, after cleaning and reordering the equipment and loading it back in the truck, a full three hours after Lieutenant Monkman and a couple of his fellow officers had disappeared up West for an evening out. Today, the lads had already shovelled out several tons of mud and set the shaft props in place before Lieutenant Monkman arrived, pulling up at the scene in his sports car just after lunch.

Stifling his resentment on his men's behalf, Archie took a deep breath to steady his pulse.

At last a flame flickered, illuminating Monkman's thin face in an orange glow. However, as he held the tip of his cigarette to the flame, he lost his grip on the lighter and it clanged on to the bomb casing.

Fear flashed across Monkman's narrow face and he froze.

Archie's eyes locked with his and both men held their breath.

The dripping water from the oozing mud counted down the seconds for what seemed like an eternity then Archie bent down and picked up the lighter.

'Allow me, sir,' he said.

Stepping forward, Archie offered his senior officer a light.

Monkman's hands shook as he held the tip of his cigarette into the flame.

Archie gave back the lighter and the officer forced a laugh.

'Damn cold. Freeze the balls off a brass monkey, wouldn't you say?' he asked, his thin moustache lifted in a smirk.

Archie's eyebrows raised a fraction but he didn't reply.

21

They stood in silence for a moment then a two-tone whistle echoed down the shaft.

'Mind your heads,' Chalky called.

Archie looked up to see the cradle with the equipment in it being lowered down the shaft. Stepping carefully around the bomb, he reached up and guided the mesh box down.

'About bloody time, too,' muttered Lieutenant Monkman as he joined Archie.

The clock stopper was a two-foot-wide, four-inch-thick device that stopped the fuse's internal mechanisms by means of a magnetic current. The earlier versions resembled a horse collar; however, the one D Squad now used was square with handles. Monkman tried to lift it out of the cradle but hit the metal sides instead, sending a loud clang back up the shaft.

'Perhaps it might be best if you let me position the clock stopper, sir, while you listen in with the electronic stethoscope,' Archie suggested, taking the solid ten-pound piece of equipment from his senior officer's hands and moving it clear of the bomb.

Ten minutes later, with Lieutenant Monkman crouched opposite him with his earphones on, listening to the fuse mechanism and puffing on the last half-inch of his cigarette, Archie tightened the last bolt on the clock stopper's metal strap.

He looked at Monkman, who nodded.

Turning on the balls of his feet, Archie switched on the handheld generator and block battery attached to the clock stopper by two leads.

A low hum signalled the cumbersome equipment's response to the electrical charge passing through it.

Holding his breath, Archie looked across at his senior officer again.

Monkman gave him the thumbs-up, indicating the ticking had stopped, and Archie's shoulders relaxed.

Rising to his feet, he pressed his hands into the small of his back to relieve the tightness, then cupped his hands around his mouth.

'Chalky!'

Corporal White's apple-round face appeared over the edge of the parapet. 'Sarge?'

'You, Mogg and Ron get yourselves and the drill down here pronto, and tell Arthur to fire up the steamer,' Archie called.

'Yes, Sarge,' his corporal shouted back. 'And, Sarge! Guess what?'

'The Andrew Sisters are dropping into HQ to entertain us all over a spot of tea?' Archie yelled.

'No,' his second-in-command bellowed. 'One of the coppers up here just got a copy of the Evening Standard, and splashed across the front page is the news that old Monty's gone and kicked Rommel's fat German arse in some place called El-Armin or sum-mink.'

'Well now, while I'm right pleased for General Montgomery, Chalky, you'll forgive me if I dinna go too wild with joy just at the moment, due to the fact I'm standing alongside 1,500 kilos of high explosives. So if you don't mind . . . ?'

'Sorry, Sarge,' said Chalky.

'And fetch us down a slug of water, will ya?' Archie shouted back. 'Ma mouth's as dry as the bottom of a budgie's cage.'

Chalky hurried off to do his sergeant's bidding.

Flicking his cigarette butt into the corner of the damp pit, Monkman stood up.

'Well, McIntosh, I'll get out of your way while you

and the chaps get the drill and steamer going.'

'You'll nae be hanging around to oversee the operation?' asked Archie.

He shook his head.

'Too many cooks and all that.' He grinned and slapped Archie's upper arm. 'Good work, Sergeant.'

Turning, he practically bounced up the ladder and was gone.

There was a scuffling above and Archie looked up to see Chalky and the three squaddies he'd asked for climbing down the ladder with the drill and rubber hosepipe from the steamer.

Chalky, a solid individual with sandy-coloured hair and a ready smile, stepped off the bottom rung of the ladder and sidled over.

'I see our commanding officer has done his usual,' he said, handing Archie a water bottle. 'Well, at least wiv him gone, we've got a decent chance of getting out of the stinking pit in one piece.'

Uncorking the canteen, Archie's mouth lifted slightly by way of reply. He took a swig of water and then hunkered down.

'All right, me bonny lads,' said Archie, picking up the discarded headphones and putting them over his ears. 'You know what to do, so let's get on with it.'

* * *

Hooking his towel on the peg, Archie stepped under the stream of water pulsing out of the chrome shower head a few inches above him.

Resting his hands on the white tiled wall in front, he hung his head and let the warm water trickle down his aching body.

24

It was already dark by the time he and his men had arrived back at the depot half an hour ago. Thankfully, drilling through the outer casing of the bomb had been pretty straightforward, as had the removal of the explosives. It hadn't taken long to emulsify them using the steamer. Although, even without the fuse, the explosives could still blow you to kingdom come, Archie had decided that it would be better to get the whole thing up top so he could disarm the fuse in the daylight. Unfortunately, as the bomb was smack bang in the middle of two buildings vital to the war effort, they'd had to transport its carcass, with the clock stopper still attached, to the safer location of the bomb graveyard on Hackney Marshes.

They'd arrived there just as the blackout started at six, so in a tarpaulin blackout tent under the glare of two spotlights, Archie had finally detached the fuse with his spanner and made it safe before heading back to base.

The army's bomb disposal squad was housed in what had been Wanstead High School for Boys. With most of its pupils evacuated elsewhere, the school had been converted into the North East Regional Head-quarters, housing ten sections, comprising of half a dozen men apiece. Each squad was headed up by a sergeant and, in theory, were under the command of any of the dozen or so lieutenants. In reality, with a few notable exceptions, the lieutenants did little work, leaving it to experienced sergeants like himself to manage the day-to-day business.

Archie's D Squad was located on the second floor of the old school building, along with E and F Squads. The classrooms had been converted into barracks, but, although it was cheaper to live on site, Archie, like a couple of the other non-commissioned officers, had found himself a billet close by, just east of Bow Bridge. The officers made their own arrangements and rented houses if they had families or took lodgings if they were single.

Of course, by the time he and his team had returned, soaked to the skin and ravenously hungry, the officers were already celebrating the news from Egypt, knocking back large Scotches in the mess as if they'd been the ones who'd routed Rommel.

Archie was now standing in what had been the boys' changing room, and around him were the six men that made up D Squad, all vigorously scrubbing the day's filth off them with slivers of carbolic soap.

'Oi, Archie!'

He looked around at Fred Wood, the driver and tea maker, lathering himself under the shower opposite.

'Me and some of the boys are going to the Regal later to raise a glass or two in Monty's honour, fancy joining us?' asked the private, who'd been a bin man in Doncaster before he was called up.

'Yeah,' said eighteen-year-old Private Tim Conner, rubbing his hands across his hairless chest. 'There'll be plenty of totty.'

'The boy's right, Archie,' said Mogg Evans — the Swansea Mangler, as he was known in amateur wrestler circles. 'Wild they are since those Yanks arrived. Coming down to London from all over looking for a bit of fun.'

'Yes, I tell you, I just flashed the old bomb squad badge last week at the Ilford Palais and I was swamped with girls who wanted to show a hero of the Blitz their gratitude.'

Archie smiled. 'I wouldnae want to cramp your

style, lads.'

''Ark at 'im,' laughed Ron Marchant, who'd been a stevedore in the Royal Docks. 'The UXB's very own Casanova.'

They all laughed, and Archie joined in.

'Come on, Archie,' urged Arthur Goodman, who at thirty-eight was the oldest in the squad. 'You need to get out a bit.'

'Yeah, come on.' Chalky glanced down at Archie's bare crotch. 'Give your todger something to do for once.'

Archie smiled. 'Thanks for the offer, pal, but I've already got a date. And don't enjoy yourselves too much: we're back on duty at six.'

This brought forth the usual groans, expletives and rude gestures.

Archie's smile widened, and, throwing his towel over his shoulder, he headed off for the changing room.

In the steamy atmosphere, each one of his squad's naked bodies looked much the same as the other. Only he looked different. And not just because at six foot two he towered over the other men. He looked different because, despite his Glaswegian accent and Highland name, while they were pale pink all over, he was the colour of milky coffee.

27

3

As everyone was keen to read the full account of the 8th Army's rout of Rommel in North Africa in the Sunday papers, Fieldman the stationers, at the bottom of Watney Street Market, was doing a brisk trade by the time Cathy reached them. Crunching through the thin layers of ice on the pavement puddles, she turned into Chapman Street.

It was just after eight thirty and a little over a week since she'd received the telegram about Stanley.

A train rattled along on the viaduct above, leaving black smoke and the smell of coal dust in its wake. As Cathy walked past the archway of her father's removal and delivery business, her thirteen-year-old brother Billy tore around the corner with twelve-year-old Michael just a step behind. As always on a Sunday morning, they were both in their school uniform.

Known to friend and foe as 'the Brogan boys', they were in fact chalk and cheese as far as appearances went. Billy was stocky, with a mop of sandy-coloured hair, while Michael, with his black curly hair and lanky frame, looked so much like Cathy's older brother Charlie it was uncanny. Michael's face lit up as he spotted her.

'Can't stop, Cath, or we'll be late,' he shouted as he shot past her.

'I guessed as much,' Cathy replied.

'See you at church,' added Billy as he sped by.

Cathy watched them for a moment or two then continued on towards the turning they'd just come from.

Mafeking Terrace, where her parents Ida and Jeremiah Brogan lived, was a couple of turnings down the road, so within a moment or two Cathy swung the front wheels of the pushchair into her parents' street and headed for the house with the green door.

The street — just a hop, skip and a jump from London Docks — was part of the Chapman Estate. Like dozens of others in the area, the Victorian cottages that lined both sides of the thoroughfare opened straight on to the cobbled street, with just a narrow pavement in front of them. There had been mutterings about the council condemning them as unfit for human habitation. And truthfully, with damp in the walls, windows rattling in their frames and an unreliable sewage system running beneath, you'd have a hard time arguing otherwise. However, with half the houses in the area just piles of rubble and families living in one room, it wasn't the right time to start bulldozing what was still standing, no matter how ramshackle they were.

Within a few moments, Cathy was at her family home, but instead of knocking on the front door, she headed down the narrow alleyway between the houses towards the wooden gate at the end. Flipping the latch, Cathy wheeled the pushchair through into the backyard.

Her father Jeremiah had taken over from his father as the local rag-and-bone man when he'd come back from France the first time the country was at war with Germany. However, under the War Act the Government now bought all scrap metal at a fixed rate, so he had had to branch out. Now Brogan & Son no longer dealt in old mangles, misshapen pots or bedsteads, but was, instead, a removal and delivery firm, with a second-hand furniture business on the side.

Where discarded household items had once been stacked, there now stood a barrel with potato leaves spouting out of the top and next to that was a row of old china sinks planted with carrots and onions to go alongside whatever cut or kind of meat her mother managed to prise out of Ray Harris, the butcher they were registered with. However, the most notable change at the back of the family home was the chicken coop straddling the back wall.

Spotting the hens pecking around in the dirt as Cathy wheeled him into the yard, Peter stretched his arms towards them.

'Chick chicks,' he said, waggling his mittened hands and looking excitedly at his mother.

'In a minute, Peter,' Cathy said, and smiled. 'Let's see Nanny and the baby first.'

Knocking the pushchair's brake on with her foot, Cathy lifted her son out and tucked him on to her hip. As she opened the back door, the smell of porridge and toast filled her nose.

Her parents' kitchen was as familiar to her as her own face in the mirror, and it was the welcoming heart of the house. Although none of the chairs around the scrubbed table matched, there were enough seats for everyone, plus a spare or two for visitors. There was always a cuppa to be had and, rationing permitting, often a slice of her mother's cake to accompany it. At the far end was a massive dresser that housed all her mother's mismatched crockery, alongside the odd beer glass or two; that was also where Ida now kept Cathy's brother Charlie's battered school satchel containing all the family certificates and her Prudential saving book, ready to take to the shelter.

'Only me, Mum,' shouted Cathy, closing the door

behind her.

'Hello, luv,' her mother called back from the parlour. 'There's a fresh pot if you fancy a cuppa, and could you bring me another while you're at it. I'm parched.'

'Right you are,' Cathy shouted back as she took off her son's coat and scarf.

Free of his outerwear, her son toddled off into the lounge and after pouring herself and her mother a mug of tea, Cathy followed.

Like the kitchen, the back parlour also reflected her father's trade and was furnished with an odd assortment of easy chairs, with a three-seater leather sofa along the far wall. The south-facing window that looked out on to the narrow passageway at the side of the house provided some light. Standing on one side of the fireplace was her father's pride and joy: a floor-to-ceiling bookcase. There was also a shiny Bush wireless in the corner, and new metal frames around the family photos; with people having to find new accommodation and furniture after being bombed out, her father's business was clearly prospering.

Cathy's mother was a few months short of her forty-sixth birthday and had the same light brown hair and hazel eyes as Cathy. She was wearing the navy maternity dress with the white collar Cathy had found when she'd been unpacking one of the Red Cross packages a while back.

She was sitting with her feet up on the sofa and although she looked tired, as well she might with a ten-day-old baby, she had the contented glow of a new mother.

On the floor beside her was one of the drawers from her parents' tallboy, which had been emptied to be

31

used as a makeshift crib.

Peter had pulled out the toy box from behind the sofa and was sitting on the hearth rug rummaging through.

Crossing the room, Cathy placed a cup of tea on the table beside her mother and gave her a kiss on the cheek.

'Hello, Mum, I thought I'd pop in before church to see how you're getting on?'

'All the better for seeing you,' Ida replied. 'I'm still a bit sore, but now my milk's come in at least I haven't got two rocks on me chest.'

'Is she still feeding well?' asked Cathy.

Her mother nodded. 'She'd put on another three ounces when the nurse weighed her on Friday.'

'I've just passed the boys dashing to church,' said Cathy, as she sat at the other end of the sofa.

Her mother nodded. 'It's going to be a special commemorative service for the victory at El-Alamein. Father Mahon wants to make sure the altar servers and choir know what they're doing.'

'And behave themselves,' said Cathy. 'Where's Dad?'

'He did an extra duty at the fire station so he's upstairs having a kip,' her mother replied.

Cathy's gaze shifted down on to the improvised crib next to the sofa.

Her new sister looked very different from when Cathy had first seen her, red-faced and mucus stained, the day after she'd been born. She had plumped up and the dark hair that had been plastered to her head had turned to soft downy curls. Weighing in at six pounds thirteen ounces, the new baby Brogan was no lightweight, but nestled in among the white and lemon knitted blankets, with her fists clenched, she looked tiny.

Cathy drank her tea as her mother went through how many times Victoria had woken her in the night, how it seemed strange after all this time to have a new-born and how she was going straight down to the Town Hall's ration department to get Victoria her ration book as soon as her two weeks' lying-in was over.

Finishing her last mouthful of tea, Cathy put the cup on the sideboard.

'Can I have a little cuddle?' she asked, watching the infant's almost transparent eyelids flicker as she dreamed.

'Of course you can, luv,' her mother replied.

Cathy gently scooped up her new-born sister.

Looking down at the infant slumbering peacefully in her arms, Cathy's heart ached; she would never know the joy of motherhood again.

'Has the official letter arrived from the army yet?' her mother asked softly.

Cathy nodded. 'It came in the second post on Friday. Stan was officially listed as missing three weeks ago on the twenty-second of October, so I'll be free of him on Good Friday.'

'You've counted,' said her mother.

'Why wouldn't I, Mum?' Cathy replied, enjoying the feel of the baby in her arms.

Reaching across, her mother took her hand. 'Oh, Cathy, if we'd only known what Stan was like your father would have nev —'

'I know, Mum,' cut in Cathy.

'And to think how he came between you and Mattie,' added her mother.

33

The cloud of sadness that was always there when she thought how Stanley's involvement with Mosley's thugs had stopped her talking to her eldest sister Mattie for over two years descended.

'I shouldn't have been so blind to what Stan really was.' She gave Ida a plucky smile. 'And at least now I've got it in writing that he's missing in action the bank will let me have access to Stan's savings, so I'll have something to live on other than Stan's grudging army allowance from the Post Office each week.'

The baby gave a little sigh. Cathy kissed her sister's peach-like forehead.

'Anyway,' she said, giving her mother a bright smile, 'let's forget about Stan. Tell me how's the baby been otherwise?'

'The sweet darling's been a pure angel, so she has, and there's none who'd say otherwise.'

Cathy looked around and found her grandmother standing in the hallway door.

Slightly built, Queenie Brogan would have had to stand on her tiptoes to make five foot. She was in her mid-sixties and looked as if a strong gust of wind would have her off her feet. However, her wiry arms put the family's washing through a cast-iron mangle each and every Monday, and her sparrow-like legs could outpace a woman half her age from one end of the market to the other.

Although on every other day of the week, her gran wore a faded wraparound apron, which was probably older than Cathy herself, today, as she would be going to Mass soon, she wore her best maroon dress with the crochet lace collar, freshly laundered lisle stockings, and her hair was neatly styled into a tight bun. Also, as it was the Lord's day, she'd popped in her false teeth.

Seeing his great-grandmother, Peter stood up and, clutching a rag book in his hand, toddled across, arms outstretched. As he reached her, Queenie swept him effortlessly up into her embrace.

Cathy glanced at the clock on the mantelshelf. 'You've got half an hour yet, Gran. I can squeeze one more out of the pot, if you fancy one.'

'Thank you, no,' Queenie replied, setting Peter back on the floor. 'I thought I might get there a bit earlier as I'm mighty worried about poor Father Mahon. For wasn't he coughing fit to rip his soul from his body at confession on Friday? So I want to see how he's faring. He's been a martyr to his chest since he was a boy. It's damp today so I hope he's remembered his scarf.'

'I'm sure Mrs Dunn would have reminded him,' said Ida.

'Mrs Dunn,' scoffed Queenie, opening the door and retrieving her ankle-length black coat and Sunday hat from the stand in the hall. 'Don't talk to me about the so-called housekeeper at the Rectory. She let him go out last week in the rain without his umbrella.'

'I don't know, Queenie,' said Ida, 'the way you fuss over Father Mahon.'

'Sure, haven't I known the man all my life?' Queenie replied. 'And, tell me if you will, who's to watch over him if I don't?'

She turned towards the door but as she did, she spotted Cathy's empty cup.

Quick as a light and before Cathy could stop her, her gran's bony hand shot out and she grabbed it.

Throwing the grouts into the aspidistra's yellow and green majolica pot on the sideboard, Queenie peered into the mug.

Unhappiness pressed down on Cathy again. She didn't need the tea leaves to show her what her future was because until she found out if Stan was alive or dead, she had none.

However, as Queenie studied what remained inside the china teacup, a blissful smile lifted the old woman's thin lips and the long-forgotten feeling of hope fluttered in Cathy's chest.

'What?' she asked.

Her grandmother raised her head.

'Oh, nothing,' she said, her coal-black eyes dancing with delight.

★ ★ ★

As Fred pulled on the 3-ton Austin K5 handbrake, Archie opened the cab door.

Straightening his field cap, he banged on the side of the truck then strolled to the rear. The canvas curtain flapped back as the tailgate dropped down.

'Come on, bonny lads,' Archie shouted as half a dozen men scrambled out. 'We havenae got all day.'

'But it's Sunday, Sarge,' murmured Mogg, stifling a yawn. 'And we ain't had no grub yet.'

'Aye,' Archie agreed, 'but I'm afraid a category-A bomb won't wait until you jessies have had your Day of Rest or filled your bellies.'

'I bet the officer ain't been dragged out of bed,' said Ron.

'Too true, boyo,' said Mogg. 'One law for the toffs and another for the rest of us.'

Truthfully, there should have been an officer on duty, but after seeing it was Monkman chalked up on the duty board, Archie had decided to take the report and reconnoitre the place himself. It wasn't the first time he had done so and, having been in bomb disposal since the word go, he had twice the experience of nearly all the lieutenants assigned to the North East London Unit.

'Never you mind about the officers, Evans,' said Archie.

'But, Sarge,' said Ron Marchant, giving him an artless look, 'I thought you were a socialist. I thought you said all men are equal and all that.'

'Aye, they are,' Archie replied. 'So I'll be sure to keep an eye on you so you shovel as much muck as everyone else today.'

The squad laughed.

'Now, away,' said Archie, suppressing a smile. 'And make sure you and the lads look lively if I give you the nod. Chalky, get them in order.'

'Yes, Sarge,' the corporal replied.

Leaving the crew to unload, Archie went and stood next to the Shadwell Social Hall and stared down a deserted Johnson Street. On the viaduct above his head ran the railway from Tilbury that carried almost all the goods unloaded from every dock east of the City, and just half a mile away was the entrance to the Blackwall Tunnel, one of only two river crossings east of Tower Bridge. Both the tunnel and the railway were vital to the war effort.

Being close to the docks and railway, the whole area had taken a pounding the night before, as the brickwork, shattered glass and personal effects strewn across the cobbles testified. Most of the houses at the far end of the street had had their roofs blown off, while the last two were missing their side walls. A lamp-post lay at half mast, its mangled light mantel touching the paving stones as if executing a very low bow in the early-morning chill.

Seeing him, the elderly ARP warden, with a knitted balaclava under his helmet, shuffled over, blowing on his hands as he rubbed them together.

'Morning,' said Archie.

'And you,' the warden replied, giving him the surprised look his dark features usually engendered.

The warden's watery eyes shifted to the three stripes on his upper arm then back to his face.

'Where's the little beauty, then?' asked Archie.

'Her, over there' — he indicated a stout woman in a navy ARP warden's uniform and tin hat standing under the stone arch of St Peter's porch — 'thinks there's a UXB behind the Three Tuns, but I say it's already blown.'

'Why?' said Archie.

'Well,' the old man's droopy grey moustache moved from side to side as he chuckled, 'you only have to look around to know the answer to that!'

He was right, of course. The whole street looked like the morning after the Sack of Rome but . . .

'Do you mind if I take a look?' asked Archie.

''Elp yourself,' said the warden.

Archie gave a two-tone whistle and Chalky, who was leaning on the truck's red wheel arch, looked around.

Archie nodded and then set off, his corporal soon falling into step alongside him.

'But don't blame me if you find sod all,' the warden shouted after them.

Archie raised his hand in acknowledgement.

'And keep an eye out for kids,' the warden added. 'Little buggers are forever popping up where they

38

oughtn't.'

As he and Chalky headed towards the public house, Archie told his second-in-command what the warden had said.

'So he thinks we're wasting our time,' said Chalky when he'd finished.

'Aye,' said Archie. 'But if three years of hunting and destroying German armaments has taught me one thing it's never say never.'

Skirting down the side of the drinking house, Archie lifted the latch to the yard and wandered in.

'What d'you think, Sarge?' asked Chalky.

Archie looked around.

'Well, although they're cracked, the windows aren't all blown out, so whatever destroyed the front was to the south, closer to the river,' he said.

His gaze travelled over the upturned crates strewn across the cobbled yard until he spied a piece of distorted metal poking out from behind a barrel by the wall.

Archie walked over and, reaching down, dragged out a tail fin just short of a foot across.

He held it out. 'Two hundred and fifty kilograms?'

'I'd say so,' Chalky agreed. 'But where's the entry point?'

Archie looked around again then noticed the bricks in the back wall were buckling out of line.

He kicked one of the toppled barrels nearer to the wall. Grabbing the rim, he set it upright and, using an old tin brandy keg as a stepping stone, jumped up on to the barrel.

He peered over into the next garden. Archie found himself looking down into a cavity some five feet wide, double that depth, and with recently disturbed soil in the middle. This was the reason why he'd had to drag the squad from their pits so early that morning.

Smiling, he jumped down.

'You found it, then?' said Chalky.

'Aye,' Archie replied, rubbing the dirt from his hands. 'So now let's dig the bugger out.'

The squad were leaning on the truck, smoking, but when they saw the two men emerge they stood up.

'Right. Safety point around that corner, Ron,' he said, nodding towards the shop at the bottom of the street with the shutters locked down. 'And get the kettle on. The rest of you start digging, Chalky will show you where while I go and find us some grub.'

★ ★ ★

Ten minutes later, having gathered all their billy cans into a haversack, Archie strolled north towards the main road in search of something to fill his squad's bellies. Despite it being Sunday, there was likely to be a Jewish baker or perhaps a café open. Skirting around the heavy-rescue teams that were still digging out a collapsed building, the mobile ambulance and the kitchen table that had been set up as an ARP information point, Archie reached the main road. Although the scene here was a little calmer, in the wide thoroughfare there was a burnt-out trolley bus with its cable dangling from above and the tarmac had bubbled, the result, no doubt, of an incendiary bomb dropped during the previous night's bombardment.

Looking around he spotted a Morris van with the letters WVS painted on the side. It was parked by the side of a Victorian church and standing by the van's open back doors was a handful of women serving breakfast to a dozen or so ARP personnel.

Archie's stomach rumbled, so, adjusting the haversack on his shoulder, he set off at a brisk pace towards the van, but as he reached the front gates of the church one of the bell ringers in the tower let go the treble, setting off a joyous round of bells. As the ringer in the bell tower started their second round, other churches nearby joined in.

Caught up in the country's jubilations, Archie stopped and raised his face to the icy blue November sky. Taking a deep breath as the sounds not heard for over three long years rolled over him, something collided with his leg.

He looked down to see a small boy of about three, with sandycoloured hair and dressed in his Sunday-best coat, looking up at him.

'Hey there, pal,' said Archie, smiling down at the toddler. 'Where did — '

'Peter!'

Archie looked up to see a young woman wearing a becoming cobalt-blue coat dashing towards him down the path, her rich corncoloured hair glistening in the sun as she ran.

The child, seeing his mother heading towards him, started off again, but before he'd taken a second step Archie swooped him up.

'Thank you,' the woman said breathlessly as she reached them.

'Nae problem,' Archie replied, settling the boy on his forearm. 'I know what they're like at this age.'

'Yes,' she agreed, her pale hazel eyes filled with relief. 'Turn your back and — '

'They're off.'

41

'Like a streak of lightning.' She laughed.

Archie smiled and handed the boy back to his mother.

Her eyes flickered on to the emblem on his sleeve.

'You're in bomb disposal,' she said, tucking her son on to her hip.

'Aye,' he replied, noting the curve of her cheek. 'We've found one down the end of Johnson Street.'

'Oh,' she replied. 'I'm just at church.'

'So I see.'

'They're ringing the bells,' she said, raising her voice to be heard over the noise.

'For El-Alamein.'

'Yes, for El-Alamein,' she replied.

'Cathy!'

They both looked around.

Standing in the church porch was a woman with dark hair wearing a black ambulance service uniform. The young mother in front of him nodded at her and the dark-haired woman went back in.

Cathy looked up at him. 'That's my sister Jo. I expect they're starting the service, so I'd better go.'

'Aye, me too.' He adjusted the haversack strap on his shoulder. 'I'm supposed to be getting the lads their breakfast.'

She laughed and put her son back on the ground. Holding the toddler's hand, she turned to walk away but after only a couple of steps, she turned back.

'Thanks for catching Peter and good luck with the bomb.'

Giving him half a smile and a shy glance from under her eyelashes, she walked inside the church, Archie's eyes following the sway of her hips and her shapely legs all the way.

42

As she disappeared from sight, Archie stood staring after her for a long moment then, dragging his mind back from where it had wandered, he continued with his task.

★ ★ ★

As the Reverend Eustace Paget, followed by his curate and the ten-strong choir, processed out to the vestry, Violet clasped her hands in front of her and begged the Almighty once again that Stanley would soon be found.

The army and others might say otherwise but, in her heart, Violet knew that her son, who loved her more than anyone in the world, was just missing and not dead.

It was just after ten thirty and, as always on Sunday, she was in St Philip and St Augustine's, having completed her week's obligation to God. Around her in the frigid church, wrapped up in scarves and gloves, were the fifty-plus congregation.

In common with all the Anglican places of worship in the area, those attending St Philip and St Augustine's were the sober, respectable and upright members of the neighbourhood. Unlike the drunks and ne'er-do-wells clogging the pews in the Pope-worshipping Catholic churches, her daughter-in-law and her hateful Irish family included.

Feeling the anger rise in her chest, as it always did when she thought of Cathy, Violet weaved her fingers together and closed her eyes.

As she did each morning when she woke and each night before bed, she reminded God of Stanley's many virtues and prayed earnestly for his swift return.

She also assured God that although as a good Christian she couldn't wish anyone ill, should part of His divine plan include her daughter-in-law's demise, she wouldn't question His great wisdom.

Waiting until the last note of the organ died away, Violet crossed herself and, leaning heavily on the seat behind her, stood up.

Hooking her handbag over her arm, she left the pew and made her way towards the side entrance, but she'd only got as far as the end of the aisle when Elsie Weston and Dot Tomms stepped out in front of her.

'Any news?' Elsie asked, her close-set eyes heavy with sympathy.

'Not yet,' said Violet for the umpteenth time that morning.

Dot placed her hand on her arm. 'Well, you mustn't give up hope.'

'I haven't,' said Violet. 'And I know he's probably been captured trying to save others because my Stanley's brave like that.'

'I'm sure you're right,' said Dot, her eyes appearing abnormally large as she looked at Violet through the thick lenses of her spectacles.

'Oh, yes, you mark my words,' continued Violet, imagining her son striding tall and proud across the desert sands, 'my Stan was never one to hold back from a fight. Nineteen thirty-three East London heavyweight champion, he was. I've still got the cup in pride of place on the mantelshelf.'

The two women looked impressed, as they should, and murmured their admiration.

'And he's such a wonderful son. So mindful of my feelings. Nothing is too much for him as far as I'm concerned,' she continued, warming to her subject. 'I

44

got a letter each week without fail and I'm sure he'll write to me as soon as he can.'

'How are you, Violet?' asked Ruby Wagstaff, who had sidled over to join them.

'Very well,' she replied.

'No news?' asked Ruby, her round face a picture of sympathy.

'Not yet,' repeated Violet.

'How's your daughter-in-law holding up?' asked Dot.

Violet's mouth pulled into an ugly line. 'As far as she's concerned my poor Stanley's dead and buried.'

'It's a disgrace,' said Ruby, and the others nodded their agreement.

Basking in their sympathy, Violet delved into her handbag and pulled out a handkerchief.

'It almost broke Stanley's heart the last time he was home.' She dabbed her eyes. 'When he saw how she treated me.'

'She ought to be ashamed of 'erself, especially seeing as how you help keep a roof over her head and food on the table with your late 'usband's pension.' Elsie patted her arm.

Violet didn't comment.

'Mrs Wheeler.'

Violet turned to find Marjory Paget, the vicar's wife, standing behind her.

In contrast to the Reverend Eustace Paget's somewhat rotund figure, his wife was just an inch or two shorter than her husband's stocky five foot ten and elegantly slim. With an oval face, cool grey eyes and her dark brown hair smoothed back into a French plait, Mrs Paget wouldn't have looked out of place on the front cover of *Vogue* or *Harper's Bazaar*.

45

Her family owned some manufacturing company near Birmingham, so she wasn't short of a bob or two, as the expensive navy suit and silk blouse testified. The low-heeled court shoes and the handbag hooked over her arm probably cost more than a docker earned in a week and, although it invited gossip given her husband's position, Mrs Paget was never seen without a powdered nose and a lipstick-reddened mouth.

She was in her early forties and had dutifully presented her heavenly minded husband with two boys who were in the army and air force respectively. She subscribed to the view that while her husband had been called to serve God, her vocation was to rule the congregation.

'Good morning, Mrs Paget,' the women around Violet muttered.

The vicar's wife acknowledged them with a cool smile then her attention returned to Violet, who put on her holiest smile.

'I thought your husband's sermon on Sodom and Gomorrah was very thought provoking,' she said.

'I'll be sure to tell him, Mrs Wheeler.' A small frown creased Mrs Paget's brow. 'From what I understand, Piccadilly and Mayfair are not too dissimilar to that wicked city since the Americans arrived in London.'

The women nodded their agreement.

'I'd just like to say how sorry I am to hear your news, Mrs Wheeler,' said Mrs Paget. 'Both Eustace and I will remember you in our prayers. And you must have faith.'

'Thank you, Mrs Paget.' Tilting her head, Violet gazed at the high altar. 'And where would we all be without it?'

The three women put on their Sunday faces and

nodded piously.

'Indeed,' agreed the vicar's wife.

'Will we be seeing you at Mothers' Union on Tuesday?'

'Sadly not,' replied the vicar's wife. 'I've just had another three of my regular volunteers at Smithy Street rest centre move to other centres, so I've been to HQ to ask them to find replacements.'

'You do seem to be very unlucky with your volunteers,' said Violet.

'Indeed, I am, Mrs Wheeler,' agreed the vicar's wife. 'The WVS is a uniformed service, after all, so why the women baulk at the least bit of discipline is beyond me. After all, there is a war on.' She glanced at her watch. 'Goodness, is that the time? I should be getting back to the vicarage to supervise.'

'Supervise?' asked Violet.

'Yes.' Mrs Paget sighed. 'Since our char Mrs Fowler had to go to tend her sick sister in Southend, I've got a new one, a Mrs Levin or Levi or something, and yesterday she served the reverend his afternoon tea in a coffee cup! We've got the archdeacon for luncheon so I want to ensure she doesn't lay out dessert spoons for the soup!' She gave them her Sunday-morning smile. 'I trust I'll see you in church for midweek communion.'

'Of course,' said Elsie.

Violet gave a sweet smile. 'It's the highlight of my week.'

Adjusting the handbag hanging on her arm, the vicar's wife turned on her expensive heels and marched back across the hall towards the door.

Violet watched her go for a few moments then turned back to Elsie. 'And I'll tell you something else that good-for-nothing daughter-in-law of mine said . . .'

* * *

As Sunday evening crept towards midnight, and with the fog from the River Lea swirling around the front wheels of Archie's Triumph Tiger motorbike, he finally reached the dull brown door halfway down Wise Road where the hard-pressed billeting officer had allocated him digs.

Like the dozens of streets running off the Romford Road in Stratford, Wise Road comprised two-storey terraced houses with bay windows. The small area in front of each house was separated from the pavement by a low wall with evenly spaced puncture holes running along the top of the brickwork, showing where they had once held ornamental wrought-iron railings, which were probably now part of a fighter plane or battleship.

As a scabby-kneed kid growing up in a one-room tenement, the solid respectable houses lining both sides of Wise Road, with running water and their own toilets, would have been considered palaces where he came from.

Yawning, Archie switched off the motorbike's engine. Taking hold of the handlebars, he wheeled his bike down the arched alleyway between the houses.

Lifting the gate latch, he rolled it into the handkerchief-sized backyard. Under the mound of earth, safe in their Anderson shelter, Mr and Mrs Charlton, his landlord and landlady, snored the night away.

Careful not to kick the troughs sprouting carrots and turnips, or knock the zinc bath hanging on the

48

wall, Archie guided the front wheel of his Triumph to the far side of the garden and heaved it on to its stand, then secured the tarpaulin over it.

Satisfied his motorbike was protected from the elements, Archie nipped into the brick-built toilet by the back door. Leaving the cistern to rattle into a flush, he retraced his steps back to the street and, retrieving his key, opened the front door.

Closing it and the blackout curtain behind him, Archie switched on the hall light and spotted a six-by-three brown parcel next to the telephone. His name was written in bold letters across the middle and it had 'Glasgow PO' stamped over the array of colourful postage stamps in the top right-hand corner. There was also a scribbled note from his landlady apologising for not leaving it out yesterday when it arrived.

Slipping his key back into his pocket, he picked up the parcel and, with his feet feeling like lead, trudged up the stairs.

The Charltons' house had two decent-size bedrooms at the front, one of which Mrs Charlton insisted was her son Malcolm's, and which, she was at pains to tell him, wouldn't be touched until Malcolm returned, so Archie had been given the smaller bedroom on the turn of the stairs. Although it was half the size of the other upstairs rooms and sat over the scullery, Archie was more than happy with his billet because it faced full south and had good light from sun-up to sunset, even now in the winter.

Flicking off the hall light, Archie opened the door to his room.

He'd left before dawn that morning and Mrs Charlton hadn't been in to sweep, so the blackout curtains were still drawn. Turning on the bedside lamp, Archie shrugged off his sheepskin airman's jacket and hung it on the back of the door.

With just a single wardrobe, three-drawer chest and freestanding oak vanity washstand with a flowery bowl in the corner, it was pretty basic, but Archie didn't mind.

The sparse nature of the room suited him perfectly. It gave him plenty of space to store not only his kit but also his collapsible fisherman's stool and paint-splattered easel, which slid easily under the bed and out of the way, while the lack of furniture meant he had the whole wall opposite the window against which to lean his stretched canvases and art-grade cardboard without fear of them being knocked over or damaged. The stoneware jars with his brushes were kept under the vanity unit, while his paint box, with his mixing palette inside, sat on a folding card table in the far corner of the room.

Loosening his tie, Archie sat on the bed, the rusty springs creaking as they took his weight. Weariness stole over him, but he shrugged it off and picked up the parcel.

Breaking the sealing wax, Archie untied the knot and unwrapped the brown paper. As he opened the last fold, a three-page letter and two boxed tubes of Winsor & Newton block paints, wrapped in another sheet of paper, fell out.

Archie smiled.

Yellow ochre and indigo, just what he needed.

Archie stood up and crossed the bare boards of his bedroom floor. Lifting the paint-box lid, he placed the unopened tubes alongside the half-squeezed, twisted ones lined up in colour order in their balsa-wood slots.

Closing the lid, Archie unfolded the sheet of paper

50

the paints were wrapped in and he smiled again.

It was a picture, drawn in multicoloured crayons, of a woman with yellow hair and a little girl with long black plaits, standing side by side. They both had smiling red lips and were waving. The words 'love to Da' were carefully written above the figures, while at the bottom of the page it read 'Kirsty McIntosh, age 6 ¾'.

Archie glanced up at the picture of his daughter, all pigtails and freckles, sitting on the mantelshelf. It was a studio photo taken a few months back, and she was smartly dressed in her school uniform. As his tired eyes took in the image yet again, Archie's heart ached to hold her.

His gaze lingered on her laughing face for a second or two, then his attention shifted to the image of Moira sitting in a deckchair with a six-month-old Kirsty on her knee. He'd taken the photo with the second-hand box Conway camera Moira had bought him for his birthday a few weeks earlier. They'd been on a day trip to Largs, and for once the sun had shone. They'd spent the day pushing their baby daughter's pram along the esplanade and stopping at cosy little tea shops from time to time, enjoying ice cream, fish and chips and the good weather, before catching the train back to Glasgow as the sun sank into the western sea. Studying his wife's smiling face, Archie's heart ached again for a very different reason.

When, with twenty-month-old Kirsty in his arms, he'd stood and watched the undertakers lower Moira's coffin into the grave on that damp winter's day, Archie thought the pain of losing her would never go away. It hadn't, not completely, but now, after all these years, it was like an old scar that ached from time to time but no longer shaped his life.

As his gaze shifted back to his daughter, the image of the little boy he'd apprehended dashing from church that morning flitted through Archie's mind.

Actually, if the truth were told, it was the attractive young woman chasing the boy that Archie remembered vividly.

Hoping her husband, whoever he was, appreciated his good fortune, Archie sighed and then, putting the memory of his early-morning encounter aside, he picked up a drawing pin from the little dish on the chest of drawers and pinned the picture to the back of the bedroom door facing the foot of his metal-framed bed.

Sitting down, he unlaced his boots and kicked them off then, without undressing further, lay his head on the pillow. He studied his daughter's artwork for a moment longer then opened the three-page letter that accompanied the package.

4

Jimmy, the shop's assistant, was already unhooking scraggy-looking cuts of meat from the metal rail in the window outside Harris & Son when Cathy parked Peter's pushchair outside.

It was just before three and, having finished her Tuesday-morning stint in the rest centre, Cathy was picking up a few midweek groceries in Watney Street Market.

The sun had almost disappeared behind the building opposite and, thanks to the cloudless skies above, there was already a layer of ice on the puddles. However, clear skies would mean more than just slippery pavements and popped milk-bottle tops in the morning to worry about.

The fog of the previous weeks had lifted and the weather had been clear and bright since the weekend, allowing the Luftwaffe to take full advantage of the unimpeded view of London from above. Spurred on, no doubt, by the drubbing the British Army had just given them at El-Alamein, the Nazi pilots had unleashed wave upon wave of bombers on the city for the past four nights.

South of the river had taken the brunt of the attack for the previous few days, but every day Cathy had walked past newly burnt-out houses and destroyed factories as she went about her business. Each morning the first-aid station set up in the Old Dispensary in Cable Street was crammed with casualties, while the heavy-rescue crews dug out others from piles of rubble that had once been homes. Even though it was the afternoon, the air around Cathy was still filled with the smell of charred wood and spent phosphorus from the night before.

'Be a good boy,' she said, securing the brake with her foot. 'Mummy won't be long.'

Peter gave her a solemn nod.

Leaving her son to watch the stall-holders close down their displays, Cathy went inside the butcher's, scattering dirty sawdust under her feet.

Ray, who was the 'son' on the shop's sign, was gathering up the last few handfuls of liver and preparing to deposit them back in the fridge. He looked up as she walked in.

Being the size of a brick outhouse, with a wiry red face that could be described as lived-in, Ray hadn't been all that lucky in love before the war but now, along with every other butcher in London and beyond, he was more attractive than Gary Cooper.

'Hello, Caff,' he said, wiping his hands down his blood-streaked apron. 'What can I do you for?'

Cathy eyed up the trays in the glass cabinet. The pork chops with the layer of plump white fat under the skin looked tempting but they were marked up as 1/3p a pound. Reluctantly, her gaze moved to the tray of tripe.

'Thruppence' worth of tripe, please,' Cathy said.

'Right you are,' said Ray. Licking his fingers, he removed a square of white paper from the pile in front of him and slid it on to the scales. Leaning into the cabinet, he pulled the spiked price ticket from the tray of tripe and jabbed it into another part of the display. He lifted out a portion of quivering white flesh in his claw-like hand and slapped it on to the sheet of paper.

Ray dropped a couple of metal weights on to the other side of the scales. He took a few bits off the meat until the upright needle settled in the middle.

Satisfied, he wrapped it up and placed it on the counter in front of her.

'Anything else?'

Cathy ran her eyes over the trays again.

'How much is the stewing steak this week?' she asked.

'A tanner a pound,' he replied.

Cathy pursed her lips as she considered the half a crown and couple of coppers she had in her purse.

'I tell you what,' said Ray, seeing her hesitation, 'seeing as how your mum's always been a good customer and your gran let me have a couple of eggs on the old QT last week, I'll throw in a couple of ounces of kidney, too.'

'Oh, all right, I'll take a half-pound,' said Cathy. Delving into her handbag, she pulled out her purse. 'If I add carrots and potatoes, it'll stretch for two days. How much?'

'Nine pence in all.'

Cathy handed over a silver florin.

'You all right for lard?' Ray asked, indicating the half a dozen waxed tubs on the end of the counter.

Cathy nodded. 'But keep some by for Friday when I come for my weekend meat, will you?'

'Right you are.' Ray threw the coin in the wooden drawer below the counter. After rummaging around, he gave her thruppence back then handed her two parcels of meat wrapped in newspaper. 'See you Friday.'

Cathy left the shop and went to collect Peter from outside, where an old woman was leaning over the handle of his pushchair and making faces at him.

She looked up as Cathy stowed her basket in the tray beneath the seat.

'Oh, hello, dear,' the woman said, grimacing as she straightened up. 'Such a handsome boy. I'm Mrs Wagstaff,' she added, seeing Cathy's puzzled expression. 'Your mother-in-law's friend from St Augustine's.'

'Yes, I remember,' said Cathy, doing nothing of the sort.

'They grow up so quick, don't they?' said Mrs Wagstaff.

'They do,' Cathy replied.

'He'll be in long trousers before you know it,' the old woman continued.

'Well, I've got a good few years before I have to worry about that,' Cathy replied.

The older woman's gaze shifted on to Peter, wrapped up against the cold, and a sentimental look stole across her face.

'And he looks just like your husband,' she added. 'Don't you, Stanley?'

'His name is Peter,' said Cathy.

Mrs Wagstaff looked confused. 'But Violet calls him Stanley.'

'I know what my mother-in-law calls him, Mrs Wagstaff,' said Cathy, 'but my son's name is Peter. That's what he was christened and that's what he's called. After my grandfather.'

The woman beside her sighed. 'Well, you're his mother, dear, so I suppose —'

'Nice to see you,' said Cathy, grabbing the handle and kicking off the brake.

Without waiting for Mrs Wagstaff to respond, Cathy bounced the pushchair off the pavement and headed towards the top of the market, the wheels rattling over the cobbles.

Cathy had calmed down from her encounter by the time she reached the top of the market; she turned right at the hollowed-out shell that had been Christ Church and headed towards Limehouse.

Within a few moments she was outside the solid double-fronted Victorian building of the Trustees Savings Bank. Parking Peter's pushchair alongside the railings, Cathy unclipped him and lifted him out. Settling him on the pavement, she gripped his hand and guided him between the two neoclassical columns either side of the entrance and up the handful of steps into the bank.

Pushing open the brass-plated door, she walked into the high-ceilinged interior filled with the sounds of typewriters pounding and telephones ringing. There were only a couple of people in the queue, so Cathy joined the end to take her turn at one of the two positions that had a clerk sitting behind them.

The walls were a light shade of grey and running the length of the public area was a highly polished counter. A mesh barrier separated the customers from the public, who spoke to the counter clerks through arched hatches set at regular intervals.

A woman stepped away from the far position and the clerk, a young woman with her ginger hair trimmed into a bob, looked expectantly at Cathy.

'Good afternoon,' Cathy said, scooping Peter up and sitting him on the counter. 'My husband Stanley Wheeler has a savings account with you, and a few days ago I received this from the army telling me that he's missing in action.'

A look of professional sympathy spread across the

clerk's round face.

'Let me express the bank's deepest condolences, Mrs Wheeler,' she said, in an affected voice that couldn't quite cover her cockney twang.

'Thank you. However, life must go on.' Cathy unclipped her handbag and pulled out the official notification. 'I believe he has left instructions with you that if he was missing or killed, the money should be transferred to me.'

She handed the letter to the young woman, who regarded it through the round lenses of her gold-rimmed spectacles.

'If you would be so good as to wait, I'll go and check his account file.' Holding the letter aloft, she walked over to the solid wooden filing cabinets that lined the back wall. Having found the W drawer, she pulled it out and retrieved a manila wallet.

Resting it on the open drawer, she lifted a few papers out and read them. Giving Cathy an odd look, she hurried across the room to a man sitting behind a solid-looking desk. She handed him the manila wallet and said something to him.

He nodded. Rising from his seat, he tucked the wallet under his arm and walked to the far end of the counter.

'Is something wrong?' asked Cathy as the young woman returned.

'Mr Curtis, our accounts manager, will explain. If you would be so kind as to follow me.'

Hauling Peter off his perch, Cathy walked to the other end of the counter where a middle-aged man in a well-worn navy suit was waiting for her.

'Good afternoon, Mrs Wheeler,' Mr Curtis said, as she stopped in front of the opening at the far end of the counter. 'You've come to apply for access to your husband's bank account as he's missing in action?'

'Yes,' said Cathy. 'I understand before he shipped out in April that Stan came down to fill out the required forms in the event of him going missing or being killed in action. I know you need the official notification, which is why I brought it with me.'

'I'm so sorry, Mrs Wheeler,' said Mr Curtis. 'I'm afraid in the file I have a solicitor's letter, signed and witnessed, from your husband stating . . .' He hesitated.

'Stating . . . ?' asked Cathy, looking incredulously at the manager.

'Stating that we transfer the money in your husband's savings account into his mother's account.'

★ ★ ★

Cathy kicked the back gate so hard it bounced against the wall behind her and sprang back, glancing against her arm and shoulder as she wheeled Peter's push-chair into the backyard.

Slamming on the brakes, Cathy unclipped Peter, hauled him out and sat him on her hip. Taking her shopping bag from the tray beneath, she stormed through the back door.

Dumping her shopping on the table and setting Peter on his feet, she took off his outer clothes. Throwing them on to a chair as she passed, Cathy stormed through to the back parlour with Peter trotting behind her.

Violet was sitting in her usual chair by the fire with her feet up on the pouffe, listening to *Forces Fanfare* as she cradled a cup of tea in her hand.

Seeing Cathy's furious face, a smug expression slid across hers. 'Been to the bank, have you?'

'You've got a bloody nerve,' shouted Cathy.

'No, I've got my Stanley's hard-earned savings and,' she took a sip of tea, 'I'm going to keep them safe until he gets home.'

'I suppose it was your idea, wasn't it?' said Cathy, as her son clung to her legs.

'I did suggest it to Stanley, yes,' her mother-in-law replied. 'He thought it was a good idea after the way you treated him when he came home on leave last time.'

'How I treated him!' said Cathy. 'I was the one who couldn't show my face in the market for a week because of his fist.'

'Well, it's no more than you deserved,' Violet replied. 'Cheeking me and giving him a lot of old lip. Who'd blame him for wanting to put his money somewhere safe to stop the tinker slut he married squandering it.'

'Squandering it!' Cathy placed her hand on Peter's sandycoloured curls. 'I suppose you mean keeping a roof over my son's head and food on the table.'

'You've got more than enough to do that,' Violet replied. 'When I ran this house, Stan had meat in his lunchbox every day and a hot dinner to sit down to when he came in from work, all on two pounds a week.'

'Yes, but now the rent is five bob more than it was then,' said Cathy. 'An onion costs more than five pounds of potatoes, if you can find one. The bacon and butter rations have been cut again, and all a shilling's worth of meat ration buys you some weeks is a bit of shin or a scrag end of lamb.'

Violet regarded her coolly.

60

'It's not my fault if you're a bad housewife,' she said, taking another sip of tea. 'And before you ask, no! I'm not giving you any more than half a crown a week. In fact, you're lucky to get that. My dear Norman didn't slave over a desk for fifty years at the Eastern Gas Company just so you can live in luxury. If you don't like it, you can sling your hook back to your mother's. It's my Stanley's army wages that pays for everything and after the way that poxy sister of yours and your Irish tinker family have treated him, you' — she jabbed her finger at Cathy — 'ought to be grateful he gives you anything.' Her mother-in-law gave her a syrupy smile. 'Now, if you don't mind, I'd like to drink my cup of tea in peace.'

Maintaining her sweet expression, Violet reached across and turned the volume dial of the brown Murphy wireless and 'Chattanooga Cho Cho' blasted out.

Cathy glared at her for a moment then, sweeping her son up from the floor and into her arms, she turned and marched back into the kitchen, running through some of her gran's more colourful curses in her head.

* * *

'I was hoping Hitler had forgotten about us in East London,' said Sergeant Mills, rain dripping from the peak of his helmet. 'But no such luck.'

Archie gave a mirthless laugh. 'Well, he's got to take his temper out on someone, I suppose.'

'You mean with the Russians holding out in Stalingrad?' asked the officer.

'Aye,' Archie replied. 'You can't call yourself the master race and then get your arse whipped by people you've mocked as peasants to your adoring followers, can ye now?'

It was just after midday on the last Tuesday in November and Archie was standing in Dock Street, just a stone's throw from the Tower of London and St Katharine Docks. Behind him, sitting in the comfort of the van that was tucked safely behind one of the high warehouse walls, was D Squad. They were passing the time by playing cards, scoffing plate loads of sandwiches and knocking back gallons of tea, supplied by the grateful café owners in Cable Street.

Smudger, the clerk from the control room, had handed Archie the ticket for a Cat-A bomb almost the minute he'd walked into the depot that morning. After gathering the men together, he'd set off on his motorbike, leaving the rest of them to follow.

That was five hours ago, but for once they hadn't been digging their way through London clay because the bomb they had been sent to defuse was dangling from its parachute. This time it was tangled around the signals at the western end of the Minories-to-Blackwall railway, which ran along the viaduct at the other end of the street. In fact, as it was a sea mine, it wasn't even really their bomb.

Early in the war, when the first bomb disposal units were scraped together from the Royal Engineers and Tunnelling companies, there had been a bit of a tussle among the army and navy top brass as to who should be in charge of the whole shooting match.

Understandably, the population, with bombs raining down on them night after night, was more interested in the unexploded bombs being made safe and less concerned about who did it. So, in the best of British compromises, it was agreed that the army's bomb

62

disposal units should grapple with German land bombs while the navy's bomb disposal units should deal with naval mines, which is why Archie was now standing in the pouring rain behind a rope with a yellow rag tied on it denoting a police cordon.

Behind them, other than the odd ARP warden checking that everyone who had been told to evacuate had left, the street was deserted.

'They're taking their time, aren't they?' said Sergeant Mills, looking at his watch.

The A Squad's grey-haired section sergeant had a figure that put considerable strain on his uniform jacket's silver buttons and belt. Archie and the good sergeant had been standing around long enough for him to discover that although the officer had completed his twenty-five-years' service in the capital a month after war broke, he'd volunteered to stay on to do his bit by plugging the gap left by younger men who had signed up.

'As you said yerself,' Archie replied, 'it was a busy night last night.'

Reaching under his rubberised cape, Sergeant Mills pulled out a five pack of John Players. Flipping it open, he offered one to Archie.

'That's good of you, but no,' said Archie.

Sergeant Mills shook the pack. 'Go on, I've another pack back at the station.'

Archie shook his head. 'I'm grand.'

'Where you from, lad?' the sergeant asked.

'Glasgow,' said Archie.

'No, I mean originally, like?' the officer asked as he lit his cigarette.

Archie raised an eyebrow. 'Where did I get my lovely tan?'

The officer nodded.

'My father was from Trinidad,' Archie replied. 'Why?'

'My mate Jacob's old man comes from Jamaica,' the officer replied.

An engine roared behind them. Archie turned to see a five-ton Bedford lorry bouncing over the cobbles towards them. It screeched to a stop a little way behind them and a naval lieutenant in a flat cap and sea boots jumped out of the cab on the passenger side.

Spotting them, he gave Archie the usual curious look and then strode over, the rain forming dark spots on the thick fabric of his camel-coloured greatcoat.

Archie stood to attention and saluted.

'Lieutenant Unwin,' the officer said, returning his salute. 'Right, Sergeant . . . ?'

'McIntosh.'

'Right, McIntosh. What have we here, then?'

'Looks to me like a Luftmine B 1,000-kilo dangling yonder,' Archie replied.

The officer, six inches or so shorter than Archie, raised his weather-roughened face and followed Archie's gaze.

'Shall we check?' He strode off.

Archie caught up with him in half a dozen strides. They walked abreast to inspect the eight-foot-long metal tube packed tight with high explosives that was hanging by its nylon guy ropes above them.

They stopped beneath it and, taking off his peaked cap, the naval officer looked up.

'You're right, Sergeant,' said Unwin, scratching his head through his sandy-coloured hair. 'It's a Luftmine B. And you're all bally lucky it hasn't gone off.'

'Triggered by the rail's magnet fuse, you mean?'

'Yes,' said Unwin. 'So we'd better get a shift on and defuse it.' He raised an eyebrow. 'I'm surprised it still has its parachute.'

'I don't believe in the spoils of war, Lieutenant, so there's no pilfering from my lads,' Archie replied flatly.

The officer's pale eyes studied Archie's face for a second then he saluted.

'Good work, Sergeant,' he said. 'We'll take it from here, so you and your boys hop off and get something hot down you.'

'Thank you, sir,' Archie replied, returning his salute.

Leaving Lieutenant Unwin to get his crew organised, Archie marched back to the Austin where his squad were sheltering. Going around to the rear, he lifted the tarpaulin cover aside.

A cloud of cigarette smoke escaped, revealing D Squad sitting on the side benches huddled in blankets and cradling enamel mugs of tea.

'All right, lads,' Archie said as he leaned over the tailboard, 'the navy's taking over so we've to stand down.'

There were murmurs of 'about bleedin' time', 'what kept them?' and 'fank gawd' as the men started packing away their kit.

'It's all right for you, little pets. Some of us have been standing out in this,' he said as rain lashed against his face.

The men laughed and a couple of them blew him noisy kisses.

Archie grinned.

'Away with you, you ugly bunch of Sassenachs,' he said. 'I'm for getting meself something to fill me belly so I'll meet you back at the base once I have.'

Fred climbed over into the driver's seat and turned

on the engine. Archie banged on the backboard and then stepped away.

'And try to keep yourselves out of trouble for once,' he shouted after them as the lorry rolled away.

'You not going with them?' asked Sergeant Mills as the vehicle disappeared around the corner.

Archie shook his head. 'I'm going to get myself some grub first. Can you point me in the direction of a decent café or something?'

'Well, there's a British Restaurant around the corner from St Dunstan's Church, but I'd recommend you try the WVS canteen in St Breda and St Brendan's Rest Centre,' Sergeant Mills replied. 'It'll only be a few moments from here and as it's Tuesday you'll be able to enjoy Mrs Lipman's lamb stew and dumplings.'

Having retrieved his bike from Bassington & Co's loading bay, where the dispatch manager had allowed him to store his Triumph, Archie pulled up outside the rest centre just as the rain started to ease. Anchoring the waxed cover over his seat with a couple of elasticated straps and chaining his front wheel to one of the upturned cannons that served as bollards, Archie strolled in.

Judging by the full-width stage and sprung floor, the hall had clearly been the social hub of the area. It still was, but now it served a different purpose for those who'd once enjoyed themselves beneath its arched roof.

As Sergeant Mills had predicted, the delicious smell of lamb filled his nose as Archie walked through the double doors into the hall.

Naturally, as it was just after one, the canteen area, which was situated at the opposite end of the room

66

from the stage, was a sea of khaki and navy and was packed with ARP wardens and members of the Home Guards, plus the odd fireman and ambulance driver sprinkled among them.

The other uniform colour very much in evidence was the forest green of the WVS women, who were busily serving meals, sorting out clothes and household items ready to be given to families who had been bombed out or helping fraught mothers with children. There was even a group of more mature volunteers helping younger women with their knitting and sewing.

Taking off his field cap, he stowed it in his right epaulette then started for the serving hatch. However, he'd only taken a few steps when a woman's throaty laugh made him look around.

He stopped dead. There, bending over to admire a little girl's rag doll, with a soft smile lifting her full lips, was the woman who had run out of the church after her child a few weeks before.

Cathy! That was her name. Cathy.

He wondered in passing why he should remember her so clearly. After all, they'd only exchanged a few words, but oddly he had. Vividly, too.

However, although his memory had been right about her shapely legs and her slim figure, it hadn't fully registered her pleasing curves. Also, now he could see her corn-coloured tresses were plaited into a figure of eight and secured low on the back of her head, which set him wondering how far down her back her loose hair would fall.

There was something else. He'd thought her easy on the eye, which she certainly was, but it was her lovely open smile that set her eyes sparkling that now had his total attention.

His hunger forgotten, Archie just stood there, mesmerised as she talked to the child. He studied her for a moment or two then, pulling down the front of his jacket, he made his way towards her.

* * *

'So, what did you ask Father Christmas for, Ruby?' Cathy asked the eight-year-old girl.

'A new doll. But now the letter's gone with everything else,' replied Ruby.

'Don't worry, sweetheart,' said Cathy, smoothing a stray curl of light brown hair from the child's forehead. 'Father Christmas knows, so I'm sure he'll have one in his sack for you. Now I can see your mum's at the front of the dinner queue, so why don't you go and join her?'

Ruby gave her a brave little smile then trotted over to the canteen area.

'We meet again,' a deep voice said behind her.

Cathy turned and found herself staring up into the light brown face of the soldier she'd met outside church a few weeks before.

He smiled. 'I don't know if you remember me but I — '

'Stopped my son's dash for freedom.' Cathy laughed. 'Yes, I remember.'

How could she not? Even without his brown skin, standing well over six foot and with eyes the colour of cornflowers and lashes any woman would envy, this bomb disposal sergeant wasn't a man you could easily forget.

He glanced around.

'Don't worry,' added Cathy, studying his strong square jawline, 'I promise you won't have to sprint after him today. He's with Auntie Muriel in the nursery.'

They stared at each other for a couple of seconds then he spoke again.

'So, you're in the WVS.'

Cathy glanced down at her uniform. 'What gave it away?'

He laughed. 'Just a shot in the dark.'

Cathy laughed too, feeling oddly light-hearted.

'I volunteer here most days,' she replied. 'I deal with the secondhand clothes usually, but at the moment I'm also in charge of sorting out the children's Christmas party. It's only four weeks away and we've got about thirty kids coming, so I'm trying to make sure Father Christmas has a toy for every child. Which reminds me, I must make sure I label up a doll for Ruby Freeman. She's the little girl I was talking to when you came over. Her family were bombed out two days ago and they are staying with relatives nearby.'

'Poor lass.' A sentimental expression softened his angular features. 'She's about the same age as ma Kirsty.'

Cathy smiled. 'So, what brings you here, Sergeant?'

'A parachute mine in Dock Street,' he replied. 'I've been keeping an eye on it since first light but have finally handed it over to the navy fellas. I've sent the lads back to base, but I'm looking for some grub.'

'Well, you've come to the right place because they're just dishing up,' Cathy replied. 'It's lamb stew today.'

'I know, it was a recommendation that brought me here.' He glanced at the canteen area. 'It's filling up.'

'Yes, Mrs Lipman's lamb stew is famous,' Cathy

replied. 'You'd better get in the queue before it's all gone.'

'Aye, I'd better,' he replied, not making a move to do so. 'Well, nice to see you again.'

'And you,' said Cathy, conscious of her friends sorting the clothes sending her curious glances.

'I'm Archie, by the way.' He offered his hand. 'Archie McIntosh.'

'Cathy Wheeler,' she replied, taking it. 'Mrs.'

'Nice to meet you, Mrs Wheeler,' he said.

As his fingers curled around hers, a little ripple of pleasure started up her arm, but she cut the feeling short.

'You too,' she said, taking her hand back. 'I hope you enjoy your dinner.'

'I'm sure I will,' he replied. 'And perhaps I'll see you again sometime.'

Cathy smiled.

He smiled back, then turned and headed for the canteen.

Cathy watched him stroll across to join the queue.

She shouldn't really be eyeing him up, of course, but a woman would have to be dead from the neck down not to find herself studying how his broad frame stretched the shoulders of his battle jacket or the way his khaki trousers fitted snugly around his long legs.

Dragging her mind back to the pile of clothing waiting to be sorted, Cathy made her way back to the bench on the other side of the hall.

'All right,' said Maureen Morgan, who was a year or two older than Cathy and lived in King David's Lane just off the Highway, 'spill the beans, Cathy, who was that dusky dreamboat you were talking to.'

'Oh, no one really,' said Cathy, tucking her skirt

70

under her as she sat. 'Just someone I — well, actually Peter — ran into a few weeks ago.'

She told them how Archie had stopped Peter running into the road.

'Lucky you,' said Doris. 'Is he from the West Indies?'

'Well, half of him obviously is,' said Sadie.

The women laughed.

'He's Scottish, if you must know,' said Cathy.

'I don't care where he comes from,' said Maureen. 'I wouldn't mind passing the time with him in the blackout.'

'Me neither,' said Coleen.

'Well, I think we're out of luck, girls,' added Maureen, casting her gaze around the women at the table. 'Because from where I'm sitting, it looked like our Scottish sergeant only has eyes for Cathy.'

Cathy forced a light laugh.

'Honestly, you lot are blooming man mad,' she said, trying to ignore the fluttering in her chest. 'And if you must know, he's married with a little girl.'

There were mutters of 'shame' and 'lucky woman'.

'Your sergeant might be handsome, but that don't make it right,' said Edie.

'What?' asked Doris.

'Mixing the races,' Edie replied.

'Don't be daft,' said Cathy. 'We're all different colours around here, from jet black to freckled ginger, and all shades in between. And where would we be without the Jewish bakers on a Sunday?'

'And the Italian cafés,' said Maureen.

'Don't forget the Greeks who run the fish and chip shops,' added Coleen.

'Yes, well, that's different,' said Edie.

'I don't see how?' said Cathy.

'Because they're more like us,' Edie explained. 'You know, in colouring. And I'm sure you wouldn't want any of your daughters married to a darkie.'

From nowhere an image of Stan looming over her with belligerent beer-glazed eyes and clenched fists flashed across Cathy's mind and fury rose up in her chest.

'I haven't got a daughter, Edie,' she said, her eyes narrowing as they fixed on the other woman. 'But if I did, I wouldn't care if she married a man with black, white, red, blue, green or yellow skin, or even a combination of them all, as long as he loved her.' Pushing herself away from the table, Cathy stood up. 'And as for Sergeant McIntosh, I don't care what colour he is, where he comes from or who his parents are. Because not only did he stop Peter ending up under the wheels of a bus, but he spends every day digging out German bombs and then defusing them to keep all of us and our families from being blown to kingdom come. Now, if you'll excuse me, I've got to add Ruby Freeman's name to the toy list for the Christmas party.'

Turning around, Cathy headed for the door but halfway across the hall her gaze returned to Archie McIntosh as he stood in the queue.

He would have been counted as good-looking for his square jaw and strong cheekbones alone, but add in his ice-blue eyes and, well . . . goodness me. He was handsome.

The woman in front of him was holding a grizzling child and he was pulling a funny face to amuse it while the mother was getting served. Then, having put in his own order, he carried the woman's dinner to a nearby table for her before returning to collect his own meal.

72

He handed over his money and, taking his plate, squeezed himself between two elderly matrons who greeted the newcomer with motherly smiles.

Who cared what colour any man was? What mattered was that they were kind and caring, considerate and gentle, but above all they had to love you totally.

She didn't know if Archie McIntosh was a man like that, but it didn't matter if he was because she was not free to find out. Not yet, anyway.

★ ★ ★

With the barrage balloon hovering over the dock shining pink in the dying rays of the sun, Cathy pushed Peter, wrapped up to his ears in his coat and woolly scarf, in his pushchair towards Watney Street Market.

She'd left the rest centre just half an hour ago and, although it was only just after four, the blackout would be starting in half an hour. The shops on both sides of the thoroughfare already had their blackout blinds down and the last few shoppers gathered their purchases before the daylight disappeared completely.

Arriving at the back door, Cathy lifted the front wheels of the pushchair over the step and into the kitchen.

Her mother-in-law, standing by the stove in her candlewick dressing gown and curlers, looked around as she walked in.

'Don't you scrape my cabinet doors with those spokes,' she said, indicating the pushchair wheels with a nod.

Lifting Peter out of his seat, Cathy didn't reply.

She unwrapped her son and he toddled off to explore the bucket and brushes behind the curtain that hung from Violet's posh integrated enamel sink and draining board.

Dressed for her night in the shelter, Violet watched Cathy for a moment then a crafty expression spread across her face.

Pulling a buff-coloured envelope with 'final demand' stamped across the top in red from her pocket, Violet placed it on the table.

'This came in the afternoon post,' she said.

Cathy picked it up. 'You've opened it.'

'Of course I opened it,' said Violet. 'It's addressed to Mrs Wheeler.'

'Yes, to me, Mrs S. Wheeler. Not N. Wheeler,' said Cathy, waving the envelope at the old woman.

Violet shrugged. 'So, I made a mistake. But it doesn't alter the fact that you're behind with the rent.'

Giving Cathy another hateful look, her mother-in-law turned, and clutching her green rubber hot-water bottle, walked out of the back door, slamming it behind her.

Cathy stared after her for a moment then placed her hands on the table and hung her head.

'Mummy.'

Forcing her brightest smile, Cathy looked up at her son.

'Right, Peter, do you want some din-dins?' she asked, taking his bowl from the table.

Her son nodded in reply.

Retrieving the casserole dish from the oven, she portioned out the mutton stew she'd left in there before going to the centre and put it into their bowls.

Placing a bowl in front of Peter, she sat down next to him and offered him a teaspoon. 'There we go, young man. Eat it all up and then we can go to the shelter to see Nanny and the boys.'

Peter took the spoon and his soft cheeks lifted in a smile.

She smiled back and ran her fingers lightly over his fair hair. There was no denying he looked like his father, but, despite him being a living reminder of her husband, Cathy loved him utterly.

5

'There you are, get your smackers around that,' said Chalky as he handed Archie a fresh pint of bitter.

Closing his fingers around the chilled glass, Archie raised it high.

'Cheers,' he said to his squad, who stood alongside him at Stratford Town Hall's long mahogany bar.

They responded in kind, then turned as one and surveyed the crowded dance floor.

It was the last Friday night in November and if the clock over the door was correct it had just gone ten thirty. For once Archie had given in to the men's cajoling and joined them for a night out. And why not? Plus, he had all weekend to finish the painting he had on his easel, so beer and perhaps a dance or two wouldn't do any harm. After all, didn't all work and no play make Jack a dull boy?

Being the end of the working week, the Town Hall's main function area was a sea of khaki and navy, with a smattering of air-force blue worn by Brylcreemed boys who'd travelled in from their Essex bases. Dotted among the uniforms were brightly dressed girls with smiling red lips and swirling skirts, as determined as their dance partners to live for today. The seven-piece band was surprisingly good, and added to the fun of the evening by energetically working their way through the most popular tunes of the day.

'I spy with my little eye, lads,' said Mogg, his pint poised in front of his lips.

Archie followed his gaze across to the other side

of the room where half a dozen girls, all with bouncy curls, high heels and colourful dresses, gathered together on the edge of the sprung dance floor.

Sensing they were being watched, the girls glanced over and started whispering together.

'Mine's the redhead,' said Fred, raising his glass to them.

Tim gulped a mouthful of beer and set down his glass. 'I'll have the blonde on the left.'

Ron straightened the front of his battle dress. 'I'll take that saucy brunette next to her with the big Bristols.'

''Ang on, lads,' cut in Chalky. 'Let Archie get a look-in.'

'Yeah,' agreed Fred. 'What one do you fancy, Sarge?'

Archie's gaze drifted across the dance floor. The bevy of girls eyeing them up were pretty enough but . . .

'Dinna fret about me, lads,' Archie said, shifting his attention back to the drink in his hand. 'I'll fend for myself when I've a mind.' He sipped the froth off the top of his pint. 'But I'll nae spoil your fun.'

Grinning, the men smoothed their hair with their hands, straightened their ties and then, glasses in hand, strode across the dance floor.

Leaning his elbow on the bar, Archie took another mouthful of beer and watched the dancers gliding around the dance floor.

Something red flashed at the edge of Archie's vision. 'Hello.'

He turned to find a tall blonde with mud-brown eyes standing behind him.

'Hello,' he replied, noting her pointed chin and slightly offset mouth in passing.

77

'You got a light?' she asked, brandishing a cigarette between her fingers.

Sliding his hand in his trouser pocket, Archie pulled out his lighter. 'Sure.'

He flicked it into flame. Cupping her hands around his, she drew on her cigarette.

'Thanks,' she said, blowing a thin stream of smoke out of the side of her cherry-red lips. 'I'm Rose.'

'Archie.'

'And' — she lay her hand lightly on his arm just below his unit's embroidered flaming bomb insignia — 'a sergeant in the Bomb Disposal, I see.'

He smiled. 'Can I get you a drink?'

'That's very kind of you,' she replied. 'Gin and it.'

Archie beckoned the barman over and gave him her order.

'You 'ere by yourself, Archie?' she asked.

He shook his head.

'I'm with that bunch of jessies.' He indicated his men skylarking about on the other side of the crowded room.

She glanced over. 'They seem to be enjoying themselves.'

They were. Fred was already in a clinch with the redhead he'd singled out, Tim was sitting with his arm around the blonde, while Ron was smooching his well-endowed brunette on the dance floor.

Rose's drink arrived and she took a sip.

'You from up north?' she asked.

'Scotland,' he replied. 'Glasgow, in fact.'

'Funny,' she giggled, 'you don't look Scotch.'

'Well, it's a bit draughty for m' kilt tonight,' he replied.

She laughed again and then leaned into him.

78

'Is it true you don't wear nuffink under it?' she asked, the smell of sweet perfume filling his nostrils.

His smile widened. 'It's a closely guarded secret that I can't tell a Sassenach.'

Pressing against him, Rose gave him a lavish look. 'Well then, Archie, I shall have to find out for myself, won't I?'

Downing another mouthful of beer, Archie put his glass down on the bar. 'You fancy a dance, Rose?'

Placing her drink alongside his, she smiled. 'I thought you'd never ask.'

Taking her hand, Archie walked her on to the dance floor. The band struck up for a quickstep so, drawing her into his arms, Archie stepped off.

'You're a good dancer,' Rose said, as they passed the band on the stage for the second time.

'Thanks,' he replied. 'You're mighty nifty yourself.'

She wasn't but then he was also a gentleman.

'And you've got lovely blue eyes,' she added.

Archie smiled. 'So I've been told.'

Tucking herself closer into him, Rose ran her hand slowly up his back.

'You know,' she said, gazing adoringly up at him, 'I spotted you as soon as I walked in.'

'I shouldnae wonder at it,' Archie replied, with a low laugh. 'I'm the only brown face in the place.'

'No, not just that, you daft apeth.' She pressed her thigh into his, promptly igniting his interest. 'Rose, I thought to myself, that chap over there is something special.'

'Did you?' Archie replied.

His arm tightened around her and excitement flashed in her eyes.

'Do you fancy going somewhere a little quieter?'

79

she asked, nuzzling closer.

'Where did you have in mind?'

'Well, me and my friend share a room in a house in Windmill Lane.' She winked and rubbed her thigh against his again. 'And, well, she's on a night shift so I have the place all to myself.'

Archie's gaze ran over her notable cleavage, her tightly fitted red dress and her peep-toe high heels.

Why not? After all, it had been a while. And wasn't he forever telling himself that it was time to move on?

'Have you?' he replied, wondering if there was a French letter machine in the Gents.

Smiling, she pressed her cheek against his.

'Yes, all night,' she whispered, her breath hot on his skin.

He turned to look at the woman in his arms.

Her red lips were moist and open, her full breasts pressed into his chest and her hips were rocking against his hardened penis.

With her heady perfume wafting over him, Archie lowered his head, but before his lips closed over hers, the image of Cathy in her forest-green uniform talking to the little girl flashed into his mind. Her golden hair, grey-green eyes, curvaceous body and dazzling smile . . .

Archie stopped dancing.

'I'm sorry, Rose,' he said, removing her arms from around his neck.

Confusion clouded her face.

'What's the matter, Archie?' she asked. 'Did I say something?'

'Nae, you didn't,' Archie replied. 'Nice to meet you, Rose, and enjoy the rest of your evening.'

He turned, and weaving his way between the

dancers and drinkers, Archie made his way out of the hall.

★　★　★

Archie had only got as far as Stratford Market station when the air raid siren on top of the Town Hall started its mournful wail, so by the time he'd reached Wise Road some ten minutes later, the drone of the approaching aircraft was almost overhead.

Strolling down the side of his digs, Archie took the keys from his pocket and let himself in to the house. He made himself a cup of tea and then went up to his room.

Archie regarded his easel for a moment then lifted off the calico covering the painting beneath. Draping the fabric over the back of the chair, he took a sip of tea and studied the canvas.

It was an image of Chalky, Tim Conner, Mogg Evans and Arthur Goodman at the bottom of a shored-up trench, bent double over a bomb. He'd started it over a month ago, and had managed a few hours here and there in the last couple of weeks. Now, with a full weekend in front of him, he hoped to progress the work enough to take it to his art class on Wednesday, but at the moment he had something else he needed to get down on paper.

Throwing the calico back over the painting, Archie picked up his foolscap sketchpad that was resting against the wall.

As he grabbed the Oxo tin that held his pencils, the first bomb hit the ground, about half a mile away to the south of him, judging by the vibrations through the floorboards.

Archie sat on the bed and, after unlacing and removing his boots, swung his legs up on to the patchwork counterpane. Shuffling back, he rested against the wall.

Another explosion set the light above him jumping for a moment or two. Propping the pad on his thigh, Archie opened the battered tin box and selected an HB pencil.

Flashes of red and gold from exploding bombs forced their way through the sides of his blackout curtains but the image of a pair of hazel eyes filled his mind and, oblivious to everything else, Archie started sketching the stunningly beautiful face that had blighted Rose's bald-faced advances an hour before.

★ ★ ★

'It's a bit odd, isn't it?' said Cathy, as she looked down at the sleeping baby.

'What, you mean Victoria being our sister?' said Jo, who, dressed in a pale blue suit and matching pillbox hat, was looking over the ivory-coloured handle of the Silver Cross at the newest member of the Brogan family.

'Not so much odd as strange,' said Mattie, standing on the other side of the pram dressed in her Sunday best, with her son Robert on her hip.

It was the last Sunday in November, Advent Sunday, in fact, and she and her sisters were in the Catholic Club bar on the first floor, having just returned from their baby sister Victoria's christening at St Breda and St Brendan's.

Whether for family weddings, birthday celebrations, Christmas parties or funeral wakes, Cathy had been in and out of the Catholic Club for as long as she could remember.

Situated above the WVS rest centre where she helped each week, the large square room had a long mahogany bar at one end and a small stage at the other. Despite the fine mesh and the gummed tape criss-crossing the high windows, protecting the glass from stones thrown by local lads and, more recently, from bomb damage, they let in enough of the chilly winter sunlight to save switching on the cluster of upturned lamps hanging from the ceiling. The faded photos of past club presidents and other notables that had once lined the walls had long been taken down and replaced by government posters urging people to Dig for Victory and Buy War Bonds.

The dozen or so tables and chairs that were usually dotted about the place had been squashed together against the side walls to accommodate the trestle table where the tea, sandwiches and cake were laid out.

Naturally, as with all boys of their age, Billy and Michael both had hollow legs and had been hovering by the spread ever since Cathy and her sisters set it out. However, now they'd eaten their fill of sardine and spam sandwiches and eggless fruit cake, they were loitering around on the other side of the room with their bottles of lemonade and a couple of their choirboy chums.

The place was full of friends and neighbours, all there to celebrate Victoria's initiation into the Church and to congratulate Ida and Jeremiah on the arrival of their daughter. The proud parents themselves were standing together by the small stage. Ida, thanks to a couple of safety pins, had managed to get into the skirt of her navy suit, while Jeremiah was resplendent in a wide-lapelled pinstripe suit and floral waistcoat.

Reaching down, Cathy straightened the knitted blanket over the newest member of the Brogan family.

'But she is very sweet,' she said.

'And very unexpected,' said Mattie. 'Who'd have thought it?'

'At their age, too,' laughed Cathy.

A sad expression flitted across Jo's pretty face. 'Lucky them.'

Cathy put her arm round her youngest sister's shoulders. 'Don't worry, I'm sure you and Tommy will have happy news soon.'

Jo glanced across to the bar where her husband was raising a glass with Mattie's other half, Daniel.

Both men were dressed in their army uniforms, which in Tommy's case was the Signal Regiment and in Daniel's that of the General Staff. Daniel had major pips on his epaulettes rather than his brother-in-law's sergeant stripes but, unusually, they were both stationed in London and were doing something vitally important that no one spoke about. Despite the long hours and the occasional day of unexplained absence, Jo and Mattie enjoyed some semblance of a normal married life.

'Cathy's right, Jo, and in the meantime,' Mattie winked, 'you'll have to just keep practising.'

'And what are you three up to?'

Cathy turned to see her ebony-haired Italian sister-in-law Francesca standing there, her swelling stomach pushing out the front of her emerald- green maternity dress.

'Nothing much,' said Mattie, who'd been Francesca's best friend since they were in school. 'We were just saying it's a bit peculiar having a sister who's younger than our own children.'

'I suppose it must be,' said Francesca. 'But at least when she gets a bit older, she'll have five small playmates.'

'Have you heard from Charlie?' asked Cathy.

Francesca nodded. 'I had a letter yesterday.'

Mattie's son started to wriggle.

'How is he?' she asked as she set Robert on the floor.

'Fed up with sand and flies and missing home, but otherwise fine,' Francesca replied. 'He said he's still getting a lovely tan looking for his friends but at least he has plenty of water close by, so I'm guessing his regiment is mopping up the last bits of German resistance as they push on to the Mediterranean. Plus, I had a whole paragraph telling me not to run around after Patrick too much, and to make sure I get enough rest and eat properly.'

'What do you think you're having?' asked Jo.

'Oh, I don't know,' she said, gazing down and running her hands over her bump. 'As long as he or she is healthy, that's all I care about.'

Out of the corner of her eye, Cathy saw Queenie coming towards them. She was also wearing her Sunday best and was dressed in a long maroon dress with a knitted cardigan, lace-up shoes and a wide-brimmed felt hat. She'd dug out a long string of pearls from somewhere, strung in three rows around her neck, and, in honour of the occasion and because it was Sunday, she also had her teeth in.

'Is the fair darling still asleep?' she asked, as she gazed into the pram.

'Like a baby, Gran,' said Mattie.

A sentimental expression softened the old woman's

coal-black eyes.

'May Sweet Mary above love and protect her,' she said, crossing herself.

Cathy and the other three girls did likewise.

'I'm going to get Tommy to get me a top up,' said Jo. 'Anyone else?'

'No, I'm fine,' said Mattie.

'Me too,' said Francesca.

'Perhaps in a minute,' said Cathy.

Her sister left and headed towards her husband at the bar.

Peter, who'd been jumping about on the dartboard oche with Francesca's son Patrick and a couple of other toddlers, trotted over.

Actually, Patrick was Francesca's stepson from Charlie's first marriage. However, if Stanley was in hell just now, he wouldn't be alone, because her brother's first wife, Stella, would be right there alongside him.

Picking up her son, Cathy kissed him and settled him on her hip.

'Mummy, see Gran's chick chicks?' he asked, wriggling his chubby hands at his great-grandmother.

Queenie caught his outstretched hand and kissed it. 'Your mammy will bring you around soon, my sweet angel.'

Cathy kissed her son's soft cheek again. 'He so loves the chickens.'

'That he does,' agreed Queenie. 'Just don't let him know it'll be one of them that'll be gracing our plates at Christmas. Oh, and cease your wondering: you're carrying a girl,' she added, looking at Francesca.

Victoria gave a little cry.

Jeremiah, who'd wandered over to the bar to chat to

a couple of old friends, put his half-drunk pint down and came over.

Although his wife had insisted he wore a tie for the ceremony, he'd ripped it off as soon as he'd walked out through the church doors, so now his blue shirt collar was undone, as was his tapestry waistcoat, revealing that his Sunday trousers were being held up by a pair of bright red braces.

Jeremiah Brogan was a few years older than his wife, but he was still a force to be reckoned with. Rumour had it that in his younger days it would have taken three or four policemen to take him into custody, but Cathy could never recall him laying a hand on her or any of her sisters and brothers. He didn't need to: his disapproval was punishment enough.

There were a few streaks of grey threaded through his wavy black hair, but it was still abundant and his grey-green eyes were bright and soft as they rested on her.

'Is she awake?' he asked, looking down at his newborn daughter.

'I don't think so,' said Cathy.

The tiny infant sneezed.

'I'm thinking she may be,' he replied.

Squeezing between Cathy and Jo, their father reached in with his beefy hands and lifted his three-week-old daughter out of her lemon and white knitted blanket nest.

'You'll spoil her,' said Mattie.

Jeremiah grinned. 'That I will; for sure, isn't it one of the joys of being a father of girls to spoil them rotten?'

Pressing his lips into his daughter's mass of dark hair, Jeremiah settled her into his arms and strolled back to the bar.

Ida went over to join her husband, who held their daughter effortlessly in his safe embrace. She and Jeremiah gazed down at their sleeping offspring for a moment then exchanged a look of love and joy that twisted Cathy's heart.

Watching her parents' devotion to each other, Cathy wondered, not for the first time, how, with an example of such a happy marriage to guide her, she had got it so very wrong.

Something behind Cathy caught her grandmother's eye and anxiety flashed across the old woman's face.

She looked around to see what had caused it and saw Jo helping Father Mahon into a seat.

'I thought he was looking a mite weary,' said Queenie.

'Well, I suppose it's to be expected,' said Mattie. 'He's had three Masses today and Father Mahon must be knocking on a bit now.'

'How old is he?' asked Cathy.

'Sixty-seven in September,' Queenie replied. 'The thirtieth.'

'Goodness, he should have retired years ago,' said Cathy. 'But, Gran, fancy you remembering that.'

Queenie scowled. 'I'm not doolally yet, you know.'

'I didn't mean that, Gran,' she replied. 'I just meant — '

'It's his chest,' her gran interrupted, her attention fixed on the red-faced old priest. 'Martyr to it, so he is. Just like his mother and the rest of her family. I'm just glad your . . . she, his mother, didn't pass it down to the rest of the family.'

Cathy looked confused. 'I thought you just said — '

'I'd better make sure the poor man's all right,' cut in

88

Queenie.

She hurried over.

'What on earth . . . ?' Cathy stared after her for a moment then caught sight of her sister's face. 'What?'

'I don't know if I should say,' Mattie replied.

'Say what?' asked Cathy.

'It's only something that Daniel said ages ago and . . . well . . . ' Mattie glanced over her shoulder then leaned forward and whispered, 'He thinks that Father Mahon is Dad's real father.'

'What!'

'Shhh, keep your voice down,' said Mattie.

Cathy laughed. 'Honestly, Mattie. He must be pulling your leg.'

'I thought so, too,' Mattie said. 'That is, until a couple of years ago when I saw Dad and Father Mahon together one time. And the more I think about it, I'm beginning to wonder if he might be right.'

'But he's a priest,' said Cathy.

'Well, he wasn't when he and Gran were youngsters together, running barefoot through the meadows back in Ireland.' Mattie gave her a wry smile. 'And he wouldn't be the first priest to father a child. Think about it, Cathy. I know old ladies of the parish like to mollycoddle their priest, but don't you think Gran's just a little bit too concerned.'

Cathy looked back at Father Mahon in his black cassock and dog collar, and her gran in her best Sunday hat.

The old priest seemed to have recovered from whatever it was that had set him coughing so Jo had gone to rejoin her husband Tommy. Now, with just Queenie to tend to him, they sat in the same easy companionship that she had seen them enjoy together so many

89

times before.

She was just about to dismiss Mattie's notion all together when her gran's dark eyes softened and she gave the elderly priest a look that caused yet another lump to form in Cathy's throat.

6

The old woman standing in front of Cathy, huddled in a worn coat and with a scarf wrapped around her head, shuffled forward. Moving Peter on to her other hip, Cathy did the same and noted that she was now third in the queue.

It was just after ten on Monday morning, the day after Victoria's christening, and she was crammed into the waiting area of the Arbour Estate's offices in Smithy Street and had been for the past hour and a half. She'd known it was going to be a long wait as soon as she'd turned the corner of Jamaica Road and seen the queue already snaking down the street. However, although it meant she'd be late for her afternoon session at the rest centre, there was nothing for it but to park Peter's pushchair alongside the half a dozen others and get to the back of the line.

She'd finally made it inside the building twenty minutes ago, where the line divided into those paying rent and those poor souls who, thanks to the Luftwaffe, were seeking accommodation.

In truth, the offices were the downstairs rooms of a terraced house much like Cathy's and, having squeezed through the door, she was squashed in what had once been the front parlour. There was a wide, dark-wood counter across the width of the room with a grille that reached to the ceiling. A woman sat behind the counter dealing with enquiries.

As it was now a place of work rather than the centre of a family home, the fireplace had been bricked up and the space had no rugs, just bare boards. The wallpaper had long since faded into various shades of brown, with the occasional darker square denoting where a picture had once hung. As there had been a bomb in the street behind a few nights before, the bay window was still boarded up, which added to the gloom, as did the solitary 40-watt light bulb hanging from a flex above.

The old woman moved forward again, and Cathy did too.

'I'm going to have to put you down,' she said to Peter as she lowered him to the floor. 'But don't you run off.'

He laughed and ploughed into the old woman's legs as he tried to dart away.

The woman glanced around.

'Sorry,' said Cathy as she caught him.

The woman's worn face lifted in a kindly smile.

'Don't worry, duck,' she said. 'I've had seven of my own, so I know they're a full-time job at that age.'

'They certainly are,' agreed Cathy, giving her son a fierce look.

'And, of course, it don't help that they haven't got a father's hand to pull 'em in line, neiver,' the woman added. 'He your only one?'

Cathy nodded.

'I suppose your old man's in the army,' the old woman asked.

'Yes,' said Cathy. 'North Africa.'

'Ah well,' sighed the woman, 'let's hope now Monty's given Rommel a right pasting they'll be coming home soon and then perhaps your boy'll have a little brother or sister.'

Cathy gave a tight smile.

The man at the counter moved away.

The old woman stepped forward to take her place at the counter, leaving Cathy to quell the sheer panic the old woman's words had set off in her chest.

As Peter swung on her arm, Cathy took a couple of deep breaths to calm her thundering heart. Thankfully, after a moment or two, the old woman concluded her business. Scooping Peter up in her arms, Cathy stepped up to the counter.

The thin-faced clerk behind the counter looked up.

With a powdered face, rouged cheeks, heavily mascaraed eyes and two ridiculously large victory rolls at her temples, the Arbour Estate's representative was a little overly made up for taking tenants' hard-earned money. Cathy judged she was a few years older than her own twenty-three years, but by the look of the tailored pale blue suit she wore, plus her earrings and pearls, she had not needed to stretch a cheap cut of meat over two days.

'Name?'

'Mrs Wheeler,' Cathy replied, settling Peter on the counter.

The woman on the other side of the counter ran her red-painted fingernail down the cut-out index at the side of the page then flipped it open to the 'Wh' page.

'Address?'

Peter lunged at the pen sticking out of the inkwell, but Cathy caught his hand. 'A hundred and three Senrab Street.'

The clerk's hazel eyes skimmed down the page.

'Ah yes,' she said. 'Mrs Wheeler. I see you owe us some rent.'

'I do,' agreed Cathy. She pulled the crumpled envelope from her pocket. 'But it's only one week so why have I been sent this?'

Peter thrust his arm through the cubby hole to touch the pages of the ledger with sticky fingers, but Cathy pulled him away.

'It's our new policy,' said the clerk, giving the boy a disapproving glance.

Cathy gave her a querying look. 'Policy?'

'I'm sure you'll understand that, as you can see' — she pointed to the people crowded around the clerk at the other end of the counter — 'with the increased demand for accommodation, we can't afford to have tenants who don't pay their rent.'

'But it was only one week,' said Cathy, gripping on to Peter as he tried to squirm off the counter.

'Yes, and in future, anyone who misses a week's rent will get a final demand and if it's not paid within three days then I'm afraid we'll have to take action.'

'Action?'

'You'll be evicted.' The clerk's crimson lips lifted at the corners in a condescending smile. 'There's a war on, you know, and — '

'There are plenty of people cashing in on it,' cut in Cathy.

A flush coloured the clerk's throat, but she maintained her chilly smile. 'In addition, from the first of January the rent on all our properties will be going up by five per cent.'

'How much?' asked Cathy.

'Nine pence,' the clerk replied. 'Now, have you got the rent?'

'Yes, I have.' Opening her handbag, Cathy pulled out her purse. 'There you are.'

She slid the white pound note and a brown ten-shilling note from her emergency fund through the

94

mesh hatch.

'That's what I owe, and this is this week's rent, too,' she said, placing it in front of the patronising clerk.

The woman scooped up the money and, pulling out a deep drawer beneath the counter, deposited the cash. 'Have you got your rent book?'

Taking the brown book with 'Arbour Estate' printed across the top from her handbag, Cathy pushed it through the grille.

Picking up the pen, the clerk tapped off the excess ink and noted payment in the ledger then on the book, before sliding it back through to Cathy.

'Thank you.'

Cathy slid it back into her handbag, and the clerk's disdainful smile returned.

'Not at all, Mrs Wheeler.' She placed the pen back in the inkwell. 'But I'd advise you to keep our new policy in mind in future.'

'I'm hardly likely to forget it, am I?' Cathy replied.

Holding Peter under the arms, she swung him off the counter. At the same time his chubby hand shot out and grabbed the pen, knocking over the inkwell.

It rolled haphazardly around before tipping off the edge of the counter and into the clerk's lap.

The clerk's powdered face took on an expression of horror as she stared down at the black stain spreading across the pale fabric of her skirt.

Taking the pen from her son's hand, Cathy placed it on the counter then, with him tucked on her hip, she left the choking atmosphere of the waiting room. Back out in the chilly street, Cathy wended her way between the parked prams until she found hers.

Lifting Peter off her hip, she gave him a noisy kiss on the cheek.

'Nice shot, Peter,' she said, as she placed him in his pushchair. She looked at her watch. 'Let's go and see if Granddad's back in the yard after his morning rounds.'

★ ★ ★

Cathy was relieved to see that the double gates of her father's scrap-metal yard were wide open when she turned into Chapman Street some thirty minutes later. Her father's business was situated halfway down the row of arches between a Brittans motor repair shop and Rodin's the cooperage. Bouncing Peter over the cobbled street, Cathy crossed the road and walked into her father's yard.

With people donating their spare pots and pans to the war effort instead of selling them, her father had started a removal and delivery business buying and selling second-hand furniture.

So now, instead of being confronted with rusting metal machinery and twisted spokes, the place was filled with double wardrobes, chests of drawers, rolled-up rugs and mismatched chairs, along with smaller items like scrubbing boards and zinc tubs.

Her father was nowhere to be seen so, wheeling Peter's pushchair past the green Bedford lorry with 'Brogan & Sons' painted in smart gold lettering on the side, she headed for the office at the back.

Well, 'office' was a bit of a grand name for it, as her father had hammered together a random selection of front doors and inserted what had been someone's front window in the middle of one wall to let in some light. Although he came home each night with his cash box and ledger tucked under his arm, the office had a desk and a set of beaten-up filing cabinets where he locked his order sheets and the essentials for any successful business: his tea, biscuits and mugs.

Parking the pushchair next to a washing mangle, Cathy unclipped Peter and, holding his hand, she opened the door and walked in.

Jeremiah, who was sitting at his desk writing in the foolscap diary in front of him, looked up.

'Hello, luv,' he said, a broad smile lifting his unshaven face. 'And Peter, too. This is a grand surprise on a dreary day. But I thought you were at the rest centre this afternoon.'

Cathy sat down and unwound Peter's scarf. 'I am, but we thought we'd pop in and see Granddad before we went, didn't we, Peter?'

'See Gangad,' Peter repeated.

'No, Peter,' Cathy said, as he stretched out his hand towards the small paraffin stove in the corner. 'It'll burn you.'

Peter retracted his hand.

'There's a good lad,' said Jeremiah. 'If you sit on your mum's lap, I'll give you a bickie.'

Peter clambered up and, reaching into the drawer behind him, his grandfather pulled out a custard cream.

'Where on earth did you get that?' asked Cathy, her eyes practically on stalks as she looked at the rare luxury.

'The fairies left a packet of them in your mother's cupboard it seems, just after my ma returned from some egg bartering,' her father replied, with a raised eyebrow.

Cathy laughed. 'Have you had a good day?'

'I have,' he replied. 'There were half a dozen notes

sitting in the letter box this morning, all wanting me to shift people or to deliver something. To be honest, I'm fair rushed off my feet, especially now your mother can't man the yard in the mornings. She says she'll start doing the odd morning once Victoria's weaned and she can leave her with a bottle, so I'll struggle on until then. I'm also going to get Billy and Michael down here after school a few days during the week and on Saturdays to help me with deliveries. I was on my father's waggon when I was ten and Charlie did the same when he was their age, so it won't do them any harm to see the sort of graft it takes to earn a crust.'

'Good idea,' said Cathy. 'And perhaps after Christmas I could pop down a couple of times a week and help in the yard, just until Mum's ready to come back.'

'What about Peter?' asked her father.

'Well, Francesca's giving up work in a few weeks and I'm sure she wouldn't mind having him as it would be company for Patrick. And now I'm doing office skills at evening classes, it would be good to get in some practice working in a proper business.'

'Well, although Brogan & Sons is no rival to Pickfords just at the moment, I wouldn't mind a bit of help with the paperwork. Especially the government stuff. Saints alive, there's enough of it to sink a battleship and sure aren't they the ones who are after telling us not to waste paper.'

'Also,' Cathy took a deep breath, 'I went to the bank last week and . . .'

She told him about her conversation at the bank.

'The scheming old cow,' said her father, when she'd finished. 'Is there nothing you can do?'

Cathy shook her head. 'At the end of the day, it's

Stan's money. All two hundred pounds of it. And even if I tried to take her to court, it would probably cost me the best part of it to challenge it.'

Her father's eyes opened wide. 'Two hundred quid. I thought he was a porter at Spitalfields not a bank robber.'

'I was a bit surprised myself when the bank manager told me what was in the account, but however he came by it, it's Violet's now,' said Cathy, repositioning Peter on her lap. 'Plus, in the solicitor's letter it states that as long as Stan's name is on the rent book, she can't be asked to leave. Which means that although as his wife I have to pay the rent to keep a roof over our heads, Stan's mother is entitled to stay. My problem is that Stan only signed over the minimum amount of his army wages to me, which is topped up by the Army's Family Allowance, but in six months' time, Stan's wages will stop and all I'll get is a widow's pension, so my money will be cut in half.'

'Well, you know me and your mum will always help you out if you're short,' her father said.

'I know,' said Cathy. 'But I'm a grown woman now and I have to stand on my own two feet. That's why I signed up for secretarial evening classes — when Peter is a little older, I can get a job to support us both. But that's a few years off, so I'm going to do something about my situation now rather than wait until Easter when Stan is officially declared dead . . . ' She took a deep breath. 'I'm going to take a lodger.'

Peter grabbed at her father's keys that were lying on the desk. Jeremiah gave them to him.

'What do you think Violet will say?' her father asked.

'Probably raise merry hell, but I don't care,' Cathy replied, already imagining the argument. 'And that's another reason why I've popped down to see you. I need a double bed with a decent mattress, a wardrobe, chest of drawers, a washstand and bowl and a small desk. I might need a cot, too, or a child's bed if a mother and child take the room.'

Her father scratched his head. 'It might take me a week or two to get them, luv.'

'That's all right,' said Cathy. 'I'm not going to advertise the room until after Christmas. And as I'm going to put them in the downstairs front parlour, would you mind helping me shift things about in the house.'

'Of course not,' her father replied. 'Just tell me when and me and the boys will be down.'

A sad expression stole across his face.

'You know, luv, me and your mum are so proud of you taking everything on your shoulders, and glad as I would be to see you free of that bastard' — reaching out, he laid his hand on her forearm — 'perhaps we should keep in mind that Stan may yet turn up.'

An image of Stan's belligerent features and his bruising hands flashed across her mind as the bitter taste of bile stung the back of her throat.

Hugging Peter closer, Cathy pressed her lips on his soft curls. She closed her eyes for a moment then raised her head and looked at her father.

'I know, Dad,' she replied, forcing her words out despite the fear that gripped her chest. 'But even if he is alive, it won't change anything, because I swear by the Virgin Mary and all the saints above that, no matter what, I'll never live under the same roof as Stanley Wheeler ever again.'

7

'Are you sure it's not too much for you, Mum?' asked Cathy, as her father stopped his lorry alongside the kerb.

'Of course not,' her mother replied, putting her free arm around Peter, who was sitting between them. 'He's never any trouble, and the boys can help me.'

It was just after five thirty on Wednesday, two days after she'd been to the rent office.

Jeremiah, dressed in his auxiliary fire brigade uniform, was at the wheel of his Bedford lorry, while Cathy, Peter and Ida, who held four-week-old Victoria in her arms, sat alongside him in the cab. Billy and Michael were sitting in the lorry's cavernous rear and had been holding on to the two prams while the truck had bounced along the two-and-a-half-mile journey to Cephas Street School.

Although the blackout had started over an hour ago, the early December night was clear. There was an almost full moon overhead and even though he was driving on muted headlights, her father could see his way clearly.

Of course, it was because of the brightness of the moon that they were all in the van. After another week of fog so thick you couldn't see across the street, an icy blast from the North Sea had dispersed the area's protective shield. It was for this reason that Ida, like many others who'd enjoyed several nights safe in their own bed, was trekking down to the shelter again. Cathy would join her there after her evening class.

'Well, as long as you're sure,' said Cathy.

'I am,' said her mother. 'Now run along.'

Giving Peter a quick kiss on the cheek, she opened the cab door and climbed down.

'Be a good boy for Nanny,' she said, taking her basket from the floor. 'And I hope you have a quiet night, Dad.'

'From your lips to God's ears,' said her father, smiling across at her. 'Now off with you before you get a hundred lines for being late.'

Grinning, Cathy slammed the lorry door and stepped back to avoid the exhaust fumes as Jeremiah pulled away.

Hooking her basket over her arm, she turned and walked through the arched entrance to the school's playground to join the few dozen people also making their way into the building.

Cephas Street Secondary School, which was a ten-minute walk from Bethnal Green station, was one of the many solid three-storey, brick-built schools the Victorians had commissioned in a drive to educate London's poor, although the building was now empty of pupils as many had been evacuated at the beginning of the war. Crunching across the gravel, Cathy headed for the main entrance and pushed open the half-glazed doors, which had protective tape pasted across the panes of glass. Making sure she'd closed the door behind her, she moved the blackout curtain aside and stepped into the corridor.

The St John's Ambulance had set up a casualty station on the ground floor, so the hall in front of her had a dozen or so hospital beds lined up neatly along the far wall. The beds were divided by screens and were used for caring for the more seriously injured.

Patients with bumps and bruises were treated in one of the chairs positioned next to stainless-steel trolleys. The staff, in anticipation of a busy night, were busy rolling bandages and decanting surgical spirit into smaller bottles ready for use.

Although the ground floor of the school had been given over to war work, the upper two floors were still used for lessons and meetings.

Turning right, Cathy joined the crowd of people heading up the stairs to the top floors where the Workers' Education Association had set up evening classes.

Walking past the refreshment area on the first floor, where a number of people who'd come straight from a day's work were having their evening meal, Cathy carried on to the top floor, where the practical lessons were taught. Passing the tailoring class on her right and the cookery class on her left, she headed for the classroom at the end of the corridor.

Miss Browne, a thin woman wearing a tweed suit and gold-rimmed glasses, was already standing by her desk on the raised area at the front of her class, the double blackboard behind her, when Cathy entered.

The classroom's thirty desks were arranged in neat rows facing the front, and on each desk, draped with a canvas cover, was a typewriter.

Hanging up her coat on the row of pegs by the door, Cathy wove her way between the desks to her place in the third row, greeting her classmates as she went. Taking her place behind the desk, she took the dust cover off the black enamel Imperial typewriter and tucked it away on the shelf below. As the last few members of the class came in, Cathy reached into her basket on the floor beside her and pulled out her *Pitman's Intermediate Typing* book. Placing it on the desk, she delved back in and took a sheet of foolscap paper from her folder and loaded it into the typewriter's carriage. After ensuring it was straight, Cathy adjusted her chair to avoid getting cramp in her shoulders, then looked ahead.

As the large hand on the white-faced clock above her head reached the number twelve, Miss Browne cleared her throat.

'Good evening, class,' she said. 'As you all did so well in the speed and accuracy test I set you last week, this evening I'm going to move on to typing detailed reports. Essential for those of you who aspire to jobs in local government or in legal firms.' She placed her hand on the large stop clock beside her on the desk. 'If you could turn to exercise nine in your books, we'll begin.'

There was a rustle of paper as the class turned to the appropriate page. Propping the book to the left of her, Cathy placed her fingers lightly on the middle row of keys and waited.

'You have three minutes,' said Miss Brown. 'Starting now!'

The clatter of metal typewriter letters striking paper filled the room. Cathy, her eyes skimming across the top line of the text, set her fingers flying across the keys.

★ ★ ★

'Well done, girls,' said Miss Browne, beaming at them through her spectacles. 'You've all worked very hard tonight. Next week we will look at the particular requirements needed when typing legal documents, so I'll see you all then.'

Cathy arched her back to ease the tightness in her spine and neck caused by almost two hours hunched over a desk.

Pulling the paper out of the typewriter's carriage, she placed it carefully back in the manila wallet. She'd only used one side, and as a quire cost 2/3p in Woolworths — and that's if they had any in stock — unless every inch of it had been used, Cathy squirrelled it away for later. Centring the old typewriter's carriage, Cathy fitted the cover back over the machine. Then, stowing her pens, rubber and sharpener back in her old school pencil case, she tucked it and her textbook back in her basket and stood up. She hooked the basket over her arm and, collecting her coat as she passed, filed out of the classroom behind her fellow pupils.

Thinking of nothing in particular, Cathy headed towards the stairway and joined those making their way down. However, as she reached the floor below, she was confronted by two men carrying a table. Stepping back to let them pass, she looked across the open expanse of the first-floor's central hall and her heart did a little quickstep.

There, talking to a group of men and with a hint of a frown, was Archie McIntosh.

Although he was in uniform, his tie was loosened and he had his hands in his pockets.

She should have looked away, but she couldn't. Instead, Cathy's eyes took on a life of their own as they drank in Archie's broad shoulders and chest before moving lower to his slim hips and long legs.

Almost every man she met wore one uniform or another, but none looked as good in it as Archie McIntosh. Although his khaki battle jacket and combat trousers were army issue, they fitted him as if made to measure.

Despite people bustling around her, Cathy was rooted to the spot, her gaze fixed on the unbelievably good-looking bomb disposal sergeant.

Perhaps she should pop over and say hello.

But what if he didn't recognise her? It would be so embarrassing.

Wouldn't matter; after all, she was only being polite.

Blast, she was wearing slacks and a favourite jumper, would he . . . ?

Cathy pulled herself up short.

What on earth was she thinking?

She turned to go but then his serious expression changed in an instant and he laughed. A great, chest-rumbling, unguarded laugh that, even at this distance, Cathy felt as much as heard.

Her eyes ran over him again and then, adjusting her grip on her basket, she made her way towards him.

★ ★ ★

'I'm serious, Archie,' said Ted Inglis. 'You really should enter your
    stuff into the 'Images of Defiance' exhibition.'

Archie smiled. 'Maybe.'

Ted shook his head. 'There's no maybe about it.' He slapped Archie on the upper arm and grinned. 'Your stuff is good, really good.'

The art instructor's hooded eyes shifted off Archie's face and on to a point behind his right shoulder.

Archie turned and found himself staring down at Cathy Wheeler's beautiful face.

'Hello,' she said, that smile of hers lighting up her face. 'I don't know if you remember me, Sergeant

106

McIntosh — '

'Aye, I do,' he cut in. How could he forget? 'But what are you doing here?' he asked, his heart thundering in his chest.

'Secretarial and typing classes upstairs,' she replied.

Caught in her hazel-eyed gaze, Archie's mind went blank for a second then he remembered the man standing next to him.

'I'm sorry, Ted, I — '

'That's all right, Archie.' Ted looked from Archie to Cathy then back again and he smiled. 'The rest of the class and I will be in the Queen's Arms.'

Taking a long multicoloured knitted scarf from his pocket, Ted wound it around his neck and sauntered towards the exit.

Archie looked back at Cathy.

'Er, the canteen's still open, so can I get you a brew?' he asked.

She glanced at her watch. 'I should really be getting to the shelter.'

'Just a wee one,' he added. 'Ma treat.'

Cathy pressed her lips together for a second then shook her head. 'I really just popped over to say hello and I ought to be getting to the Bethnal Green shelter.'

'That's just around the corner from here, isn't it?' he said.

'Yes, about a ten-minute walk up Cambridge Heath Road.'

'Then let me keep you company,' he replied, not liking the thought of her walking along the dark road in the blackout.

Her brow furrowed into a delightful frown. 'But the Queen's Arms is in the opposite direction.'

'I could do with the exercise,' he replied, patting his stomach.

'If you're sure it's no trouble,' she said.

'After you,' said Archie, ridiculously pleased she'd agreed.

Cathy headed for the staircase, allowing Archie to appreciate how the navy slacks she was wearing hugged her in a very pleasing fashion. Very pleasing indeed.

Within a few moments they were outside in the playground. Switching on their muted torches and shining them at their feet, they walked side by side towards the school's main entrance.

'So what were you doing tonight?' Cathy asked, her breath turning to steam as she spoke.

'I'm taking art classes here.' Archie smiled. 'It keeps me out of the boozers and trouble.'

She gave him a little smile and they walked on past a pile of rubble on the other side of the road that had once been someone's home.

'How's your little lad?'

'Full of mischief,' she replied. 'But he seems to have a new word every day. What about your daughter?'

'Aw, she's grand,' Archie said, feeling the familiar ache for Kirsty. 'Got ten out of ten, she did, for her spelling test.'

They had reached the main road, so they turned and walked along the side of Bethnal Green Gardens. Two policemen with canvas respirator bags strapped to their chests strolled by as a bus trundled past, its internal blinds pulled down and the slit cover on its headlamps casting a blade of light on the road in front of it.

'So, you're learning to type,' he said, as they joined

108

the last few stragglers heading for the shelter of the underground station.

'Yes,' she replied. 'I'm going to get a job when Peter's a bit older, and as I'd rather work in an office than a factory, I thought I ought to learn to type.' In the dim light an odd expression crossed Cathy's face. 'If I'd known then what I know now, I would have done it at school, but . . . ' She looked sad for a moment. 'Also my big sister Mattie's got her matriculation and I want to prove she's not the only one who's a brainbox.'

'Have you got any other brothers or sisters?' he asked.

'Three brothers,' she replied. 'And three sisters. My brother Charlie is . . . '

She told him about her family.

'It sounds to me like your ma and pa had a full-time job keeping you from tearing each other apart,' he said.

Cathy laughed. 'It was like that sometimes, but although some days us kids had potatoes for breakfast, dinner and tea, we survived, and I can never remember going to bed hungry.'

'Aye, not many like us can say that,' he said. 'I'm an only child so I envy you being close to your brothers and sisters.'

'I know. I'm very lucky but,' she raised an eyebrow, 'it wasn't always peace and harmony, I can tell you. Sometimes Jo and I would fall out, and then it would be Jo and Mattie, and always about something stupid. But I'd be lost without them both. I really would. What about your family?'

'There's not much to say really. My ma's family moved to Glasgow from Argyll half a century ago.

Her father kicked her out when he found out she was pregnant, so she had to go to the nuns in St Nazareth House. They took her in, but when they tried to force her to give me up she snuck out one night.'

'Couldn't your dad help?' said Cathy, aching for any woman in such a situation.

'He'd long gone,' Archie replied. 'Ma doesn't talk about him much, but he was a sailor called Marcus. From what I gather, they'd planned to get married but one day he sailed away and never came back. She found out she was expecting a couple of months after she'd waved him goodbye.'

'How did she manage to survive alone with a baby?' asked Cathy.

'To be honest, I really don't know, but she must have scrubbed every office floor in Glasgow in her time,' he said. 'Still, there was always food on the table and coal in the grate. Despite the falling-out with her father, Ma was close to her brother George. He worked in the Yarrow shipyard so, despite my being a Catholic, he got me an engineering apprenticeship when I left school.'

'It must have been tough for you growing up,' said Cathy, thinking of her safe childhood home.

'It wasnae too bad. There were other kids in the school with West Indian or Indian fathers,' said Archie, as memories of being 'that darkie or sambo kid' flitted through his mind.

'It's a bit like that in my school,' said Cathy. 'We had a few from Limehouse with Chinese fathers. What about — '

'I think we're here,' Archie cut in, indicating the low-roofed entrance with the corrugated tin roof behind her.

She glanced around.

'So we are,' she replied. 'Thanks for keeping me company.'

'My pleasure.' He smiled down at her. 'I'll see you again sometime.'

She laughed. 'We do seem to keep running into each other, don't we?'

'Aye, we do,' he replied.

They stared at each other for several heartbeats then she glanced around again.

'I'd better go,' she said.

He nodded. 'Me too. Goodnight.'

She gave him a little smile then walked away, but as she got to the entrance of the shelter she turned and waved to him.

Archie waved back and then she disappeared into the crowd.

He guessed she'd been about to ask about his wife, which is why he'd cut across her.

It wasn't because he didn't want to tell her. He did. He wanted to tell her about the heartache of losing Moira. And he would tell her, not on a pavement on a cold winter's night but holding her in his arms.

★ ★ ★

Cathy followed the crowds making their way from the ticket hall down the hundred or so steps to the two platforms of Bethnal Green tube station below.

'Evening, Cathy,' said Bob Mitchel, the grey-haired veteran of the last conflict with Germany, who was now one of the shelter's wardens.

'Evening, Mr Mitchel,' she replied. 'You're busy tonight.'

'Do you wonder at it?' he replied, as people nudged into them as they shoved past. 'There's not a cloud in the sky and I reckon the Luftwaffe will be keen to pay us a visit, especially now Monty's shoving Rommel's lot into the sea.'

'My dad says much the same,' Cathy replied.

Bob nodded. 'I saw your mum with the boys and your little lad earlier. He's getting big.'

'I know,' said Cathy. 'I can't believe he's three in June.'

'They grow up too quick, they do,' Bob replied. 'My little lad was twenty-eight two weeks ago and floating about somewhere in the middle of the Atlan — '

The two-tone wail of the air raid siren that had punctuated their lives for the past three and a half years cut across Bob's words.

On hearing the ear-jangling warning, those coming down the stairs surged forward again.

Someone jostled Cathy from behind and she missed her step.

'There's no need to push!' bellowed Bob.

He took his whistle from his pocket with his old campaign ribbon stitched on and blew three short blasts.

'Stop bloody pushing,' he shouted over the boom of the ack-ack guns in Vicky Park and the sound of women screaming.

Cathy continued down the stairs and turned right on to the westbound platform. Well, that's to say it would be the westbound platform when the war was over.

The sound of the shelter choir singing 'Holy Night' in preparation for the underground carol concert drifted over the chatter.

Passing the people sitting next to the row of three-tiered bunkbeds, Cathy headed towards her and her mother's spot.

In addition to those who had a ticket and an allocated place each night, the shelter also housed a number of passers-by who, when the air raid siren went off, sought refuge. They often had to squeeze into any place they could find, including between the train rails.

However, they were quite safe because although the work of extending the Central Line from Liverpool Street through to Woodford in the wilds of Essex was complete, before they'd been able to set the trains running along them, war had broken out and the plans had been shelved, so trains had yet to run along the rails. The work hadn't gone to waste, though, as the Ministry of War had taken over the section of tunnel between Leytonstone and Gants Hill and the electrical firm Plessey had been relocated there and were now making equipment for the army, while the platforms in Bethnal Green station were used as air raid shelters.

So, unlike people sheltering on platforms along the Northern, Piccadilly and Bakerloo Lines, who had trains rattling past and people stepping over them until midnight, those bedded down at Bethnal Green station had an undisturbed night — well, except for the bombs crashing all around them, that is.

In the early days of the war, her mother and Cathy had taken Billy and Michael, plus Charlie's son Patrick, to the Tilbury shelter. At first the conditions were truly appalling, but it didn't take long for the strong-minded East End women like Cathy's mother to bring order to the place. They'd forced the council

113

to install proper toilets rather than a handful of buckets, stopped the Cable Street prostitutes plying their trade in the dark arches at the back and organised a ticket system for billets. They'd probably still be there now if Michael and Billy hadn't been offered places at Parmiter's Boys' School. They'd started in September, over two months ago now, and, as the Bethnal Green shelter was just a stone's throw away from the grammar school, Ida had applied for and got them a family ticket. They had been allocated bunks towards the far end of the platform, which was convenient for both the toilets and the WVS canteen in the stairwell.

Smiling a greeting to people as she went, Cathy finally reached the Brogan family's three-tiered bunk. As always, Ida was sitting in her folding chair and knitting.

'Hello, Mum,' said Cathy. 'How are you?'

'Better now madam's asleep,' she said, indicating Victoria bundled up in the bunk beside her.

'Did Peter go down all right?' Cathy asked, stretching up to look into the top bunk where her son lay curled up with Mr Bruno.

Kissing the tips of her fingers then placing them lightly on his forehead, Cathy sat on the lower bunk.

'Like a dream,' Ida replied. 'Michael took him to listen to Storytime in the library on the other platform while I fed Victoria, then after his warm milk I put his night nappy on him and he was asleep almost as soon as his head touched the pillow. Did you have a nice time tonight?'

The image of Archie McIntosh smiling down at her with those lovely blue eyes of his materialised in Cathy's mind and her heart did a little double step.

'I'm up to thirty words a minute,' she said.

Her mother looked impressed.

Cathy sighed. 'I wish I'd been a swot like Mattie and worked a bit harder at school.'

Her mother reached out and squeezed her hand. 'You're doing it now, that's the main thing.' Slipping her wool over her needles, her mother gave her a considered look. 'Are you sure about taking a lodger, luv?'

'I am,' Cathy replied. 'It's the only way I can think of to keep a roof over mine and Peter's head now that Violet's got all Stan's money and refuses to give me any more housekeeping.'

'What about you and Peter move back home?' said Ida.

Cathy laughed. 'Don't be daft, Mum. You've barely got room as it is without us trying to squeeze in. Besides, I'll be damned if I'll let that old witch drive me out.'

'But having strangers in your house,' said Ida.

'I'm not just taking any old body,' Cathy said. 'They'll need references, naturally, and I'm going to put 'suitable for mother with one or two children' on the ad.'

'Well, that might be all right,' her mother replied. 'And I suppose it's a Christian kindness to offer a home to a mum and kids. But it — '

'Mum, it'll be fine, honest,' Cathy cut in.

Her mother gave her a dubious look and was about to argue but then, after looping a strand of wool over her needle, her gaze returned to the knitting pattern balanced on her knee.

Taking in a lodger would be fine because, with prices going up day by day and the threat of eviction hanging over her head, it had to be.

8

As she came through the rest centre's door, Polly Nugent's pale eyes darted around the hall until she spotted Cathy, then she hurried across to her.

It was just after three on the second Thursday in December and over a week since Cathy had seen Sergeant McIntosh after her evening class. She and the other women sitting around the table were putting together the Christmas gift packs for the Merchant Navy.

'Cathy,' Polly said, a little breathlessly, as she came to a halt. 'Someone told me you were here. Mrs Crowther from headquarters is in the office and wonders if you've got a moment?'

'Of course,' said Cathy.

Polly left them.

Maureen, who was pairing socks, looked at her questioningly.

Cathy shrugged. 'Search me.'

'Well, go on then.' Maureen nodded towards the door. 'Find out.'

As Cathy walked between the neatly laid-out camp beds, she was joined by Olive Freeman, who oversaw the knitting circle, and Dora Black, who looked after the salvage collection.

They gave each other a baffled look. Stopping outside Miss Carpenter's office, Cathy knocked on the door.

Someone on the other side called out, 'Enter.'

Cathy opened the door and the three women piled

116

into the former caretaker's storeroom.

Mrs Crowther, the area organiser, was sitting in Miss Carpenter's place behind the desk. Beside her stood a very slim woman, and the contrast between them couldn't have been starker.

Taller by a head than every woman squashed into the small space, Mrs Crowther could best be described as strapping, and Cathy could easily imagine her in a gymslip, studded boots and brandishing a hockey stick having just scored the winning goal. Straining the seams of her WVS uniform to their limits, the straight cut of her steel-grey hair to just below her ears merely added to her combative appearance.

The woman beside her had been fashioned in a very different mould. Thanks to her heeled court shoes, she was an inch or two taller than Cathy and as slender as a wand. With flawless make-up and her light chestnut hair combed into a French plait, she looked as if she'd stepped off a catwalk. Unlike Cathy, who'd had to take in the waist, let down the hem and turn up the jacket sleeves of her off-the-peg WVS uniform, the newcomer's perfectly fitting forest-green suit had made to measure stamped all over it.

There was a small smile on the woman's cherry-red lips that didn't quite make it to her cool grey eyes.

'You wanted to see us,' said Cathy as the door closed behind her.

'Yes, I do.' Mrs Crowther cleared her throat. 'I'm sorry to pull you all away from your vital work, girls, but I'm afraid I bring bad news. Sadly, Miss Carpenter, who has overseen this rest centre for the last three years, was killed in last night's air raid — '

There was a gasp as the women, wide-eyed with shock, put their hands over their mouths.

'I'm afraid her house in Bow Common Lane took a direct hit,' continued Mrs Crowther, with a glint of moisture shining in her eyes. 'Although she was in her Anderson shelter, the damn blast flattened the houses either side of her and their gardens to boot. I understand from the ARP warden chappie in charge of that area that the heavy-rescue boys are still using all their muscle to recover bodies from the site.'

Feeling tears gathering, Cathy crossed herself, as did the others. Dora started to cry.

The area organiser cleared her throat again. 'However, there's a war on and so we cannot let sentiment interfere with the vital work you do at St Breda and St Brendan's Rest Centre. To that end, Mrs Paget here,' she indicated the woman beside her, who inclined her head, royalty-like, 'will take charge until further notice, for which we are all bally grateful. Her husband is the Rector of St Philip and St Augustine's and she has led the WVS team at Smithy Street Rest Centre for the past two and a half years. With Christmas just around the corner, I know you'll put your shoulders to the wheel as you did for Miss Carpenter.'

'We will, Mrs Crowther,' said Cathy.

Mrs Crowther cast her gaze around as the women nodded their heads and muttered their assent. Her ruddy face lifted in a head-girl smile.

'Good show. I'd be grateful if you could all let your sections know as quietly as possible so as not to disrupt the work and then if you, Mrs . . . ?' She looked at Cathy.

'Wheeler,' she replied. 'Cathy Wheeler.'

'Well then, Mrs Wheeler,' said Mrs Crowther, 'once you've given your team the sad news, I wonder if you

118

wouldn't mind giving Mrs Paget a quick tour and a rundown of the centre.'

★ ★ ★

'And this is the cupboard where we keep all the spare toys,' said Cathy, pointing at the shelves laden with die-cast soldiers, wooden trains and dolls of various sizes, most of which had both eyes.

It was all of forty minutes since Mrs Crowther had departed and Cathy and Mrs Paget had started their tour of the centre. Cathy had introduced St B & B's new organiser to the girls in the kitchen, the bandage-making team, her own second-hand clothing section and all the other groups of women who were knitting, stitching and packing in the hall. They had even looked in at the nursery, where the bigger children were having story time while the babies had their afternoon nap.

They were now standing on the stage at the far end of the hall, where all the equipment the ARP divisions didn't have room to store in Cable Street Mixed Infant School — where the Wapping and Shadwell ambulance service, heavy rescue, fire service and communication centre were all based — was stacked.

'And this is the baby equipment that we loan out,' continued Cathy, indicating the handful of battered pushchairs, ancient prams and wicker cribs parked alongside the spare canvas stretchers, stirrup pumps and boxes of first-aid equipment.

'And how is that allocated?' Mrs Paget asked, giving it a cursory glance.

'Just as people need it,' Cathy replied. 'And we write who's taken it in the loans book, which is kept in the office.'

Mrs Paget gave her a tight smile but didn't comment.

'And now, last but not least, I'll take you to meet our elves,' said Cathy.

One of Mrs Paget's carefully pencilled eyebrows rose half an inch. 'Elves?'

Cathy smiled and indicated the half a dozen steps leading off the stage. 'After you.'

Holding the rail and with her metal-tipped heels striking the wooden struts, Mrs Paget made her way back down to the floor of the hall.

Sidestepping between the table of ARP crew and the Local Voluntary Defence personnel having their afternoon cuppas, Cathy lead Mrs Paget across to the double doors at the end of the hall and into the corridor. The sound of men's voices drifted down the stairs from above.

'What's up there?' asked Mrs Paget.

'That's the Catholic Club's bar,' Cathy replied. 'The club used to have all sorts of organisations, like a Brownies, Cubs, Girl Guides, Scouts, who all used to meet at the club before the war. But when the war started the club's committee donated the downstairs space so we could set up the rest centre, but they kept the bar.' She laughed. 'Well, they had to leave us somewhere to have wedding receptions and funeral wakes.'

Mrs Paget gave her another stiff smile.

'And here,' said Cathy, grasping the brass handle of the small meeting-room door just in front of them, 'are our elves.'

She opened the door and Mrs Paget walked in.

Sitting around the central table were half a dozen women, with silver thimbles on their fingers and needles in their hands. In the centre of the table was a

120

cardboard box with 'OMO' stamped on the side, which had assorted dolls and teddies spilling out of it.

Cathy went around the table slowly, introduced Mrs Paget to the women. 'They're helping me and a couple of others with the children's Christmas party.

'Ladies,' Cathy went on, smiling at them all. 'This is Mrs Paget, who will be taking over the running of the centre for the time being.'

The women said 'hello' and 'pleased to meet you' as they plied their needles through fabric.

Mrs Paget stepped nearer and peered into the box.

'What are you doing?' she asked Dot Buckle, who was threading the arms of a plastic doll through the sleeves of a knitted dress.

'These toys have been donated from all over the country for children made homeless by the blitz,' Dot explained. 'We're making sure the toys are in good order so they can go into Santa's sack. In the case of the dolls, we're ensuring they all have a new dress and a pair of knickers before the party.'

'Never mind knickers,' said Lottie Perkins, the grandmother of ten, as she pulled a naked doll from the jumble of legs and arms. 'This one needs a full wardrobe.'

The women around the table laughed.

Mrs Paget's tight smile returned. 'Thank you, ladies. I'll let you get on with your task.'

She turned and swept out of the room in a waft of expensive perfume.

The women looked at Cathy and she gave them a little encouraging smile then followed Mrs Paget out.

'Well,' Cathy said, when she joined Mrs Paget in the hall, 'that's about it. I hope you've got the general idea about how things are run.'

'Indeed I have, Mrs Wheeler,' Mrs Paget replied, as her cool grey eyes held Cathy's hazel ones.

'Please call me Cathy,' she said. 'Mrs Wheeler makes me sound like my mother-in-law.'

'I prefer Mrs Wheeler,' the vicar's wife replied. 'However, I did notice several toys still in their boxes, including a Tri-ang fire truck, a bridal doll and what looked like a Crown Potteries Happy Children tea set.'

'Yes, the Houndsditch Warehouse kindly donated a box of toys for our party,' said Cathy.

'How very generous of them,' said Mrs Paget. 'But perhaps in view of their quality, they might be better suited somewhere more fitting, like Belgravia, so perhaps we —'

'The toys have been donated to the children here,' said Cathy.

'I know,' said the vicar's wife, 'but surely it would be better to give them to children who know how to care for them properly.'

Cathy fixed her with a hard stare. 'As I said, all the toys have been donated for the children here, in St Breda and St Brendan's Rest Centre, most of whom have been bombed out of their homes. Many have seen friends and family members killed, and they've had to sleep in shelters for the past three years. So, Mrs Paget, if any of the 'quality' toys go missing, I'm sure you would report the matter to the police at Arbour Square and I'm certain they will take a very dim view of anyone stealing toys intended for our East End children.'

Above the pristine white bow at her throat, a crimson blush spread up the other woman's throat.

'Now if there's nothing more,' continued Cathy, 'I

have some Canadian Red Cross parcels to unpack.'

She turned and, with Mrs Paget's eyes boring into the space between her shoulder blades, walked back into the hall.

* * *

'I think I can spot someone just leaving,' said Jo, picking up the tray with two bowls of hot stew and mugs of tea.

Handing over her money to the woman behind the white marble counter, Cathy looked around. 'You grab it and I'll catch you up, Jo.'

It was just past midday on Saturday and they were in Cooke's pie and mash shop opposite Stratford Town Hall. Cathy and Jo had jumped on the number 25 bus at Stepney Green on the dot of eight thirty. Stowing Peter's pushchair under the stairs, they'd found themselves a seat downstairs for the three-mile journey over the old cast-iron Bow Bridge to Stratford. After reaching their destination they'd had a quick cup of tea in the market café then, like dozens of other women, they'd started their usual Saturday-morning forage for bargains in Stratford Market before heading for lunch.

Cathy transferred her shopping bags to one hand and took her son's hand with the other. She guided him to the corner where her sister had found them a table.

If she had a penny for every time she'd eaten in Cooke's on a Saturday lunchtime, Cathy would be a rich woman by now. Like many of its kind to be found in the highways and byways of East London, the shop had floor-to-ceiling white tiles, table and chairs bleached white with decades of scrubbing and a floor strewn with sawdust to soak up spillages. The menu, if it could be called that, was simple: stewed or jellied eels or the more popular choice of beef pie and mash. The pies were baked in individual tin dishes and served upturned on a plate. They were accompanied by a pile of mashed potato and smothered with parsley sauce. However, the liquor, as the sauce was universally known, was like no other sauce you've ever tasted because it was made from the water used to cook the eels and had a distinctive flavour and faint green tinge. That said, it was the nectar of the gods for any true East Ender.

'Goodness,' said Jo as Cathy reached her, 'I've never seen it so packed.'

'Are you surprised?' she replied, lifting Peter on to a chair. 'With less than two weeks until Christmas, people are desperate to find something to put under the tree.'

Jo placed their plates in front of them and sat down. 'I don't know what on earth to buy Tommy. Blooming men, they're so difficult.'

Taking a bib from one of the bags clustered around her feet, Cathy tied it around Peter's neck.

'Perhaps you can get him a Parker fountain pen in Boardman's,' she suggested, as she scooped up a lump of potato from her plate and offered it to her son.

'Maybe,' her sister replied. 'But I was hoping to get him something a little more personal, like a set of cufflinks. I did see a set I liked in Spiegelhalter's but they cost an arm and a leg so I had to scrub that idea.'

'Still, at least we've both got something for Mum,' said Cathy, cutting into her pie.

'Yes, thank goodness,' said Jo. 'But only because

124

you managed to grab the last set of embroidered handkerchiefs and I spotted the bottles of scent in the chemist's window. All we need now is to find something for — ' Jo jumped up. 'Mattie, Fran!' she called, waving frantically. 'Over here.'

Cathy looked across to where their elder sister and very pregnant sister-in-law, Francesca, were waiting in the queue.

Mattie waved back and then said something to Francesca, who took the bags Mattie was holding and waddled over.

'Thank goodness,' said Francesca, as she sank into the chair next to Jo. 'My feet are killing me.'

'I bet,' said Cathy. 'Where's Patrick?'

'I left him with Dad,' said Francesca. 'He follows him everywhere, so I left him helping his 'Nonno' lay the tables for breakfast.'

'What about Mattie's two?' asked Jo.

'Daniel's got them for the day,' Francesca replied.

Holding the tray high, Mattie wove her way through the jam-packed shop and then placed her and Francesca's midday meals on the table.

Cathy lifted Peter off his chair and on to her lap so her sister could sit down.

'Thanks, luv,' said Mattie. 'And how's my favourite nephew named Peter?' she asked, giving him a wide smile.

Peter replied by wriggling his hand at her.

Mattie grabbed it and kissed it noisily, then picked up her knife and fork.

'If Fran and I had known you two were going to Stratford today, we could have all come together,' said Mattie.

'We only decided yesterday when Jo switched shifts,'

125

said Cathy. 'How long have you been here?'

'Since about ten,' Francesca replied. 'I think we're more or less done, but I've got to get my dad something and Mattie's still looking for a present for Daniel, so we'll probably have another look around once we've had lunch. What about you?'

'We caught the bus at eight thirty so we were here when the shops opened,' said Jo. 'We've been mooching around the market ever since and . . .'

She told them what they'd bought that morning.

'. . . so there's just Gran, but I'm hoping I'll be able to get her a couple of lily-of-the-valley soaps nicely wrapped in a box when we get to the Co-op,' said Jo.

'Of course, that still leaves the boys and the baby,' said Cathy.

'I've knitted Victoria a matinee jacket with rabbit buttons and matching leggings.' Balancing Peter on her knee, she took a mouthful of tea.

'So what's everyone been up to?' Jo asked.

As the four of them ate their dinner, Francesca told them she was looking forward to giving up work after Christmas and that the midwives at Munroe House were almost certain the baby was head down, which all of them agreed was a relief. Mattie told them Daniel was off to somewhere in Dorset in a few days for something he couldn't talk about, while Jo mentioned Tommy might be going to Bletchley Park after Christmas for a week or two to train some new recruits to do whatever it was they did up there.

'What about you, Cathy?' asked Francesca. 'What have you been up to?'

'Oh, nothing much. You know. Just running around after this one.' She gave her son a squeeze. 'The evening classes are going well and Miss Browne says if I carry on making progress, I'll be ready to take my level-three in both typing and shorthand in June.'

Mattie, Jo and Francesca looked impressed.

'And, of course, we're snowed under at the rest centre, what with Christmas and kitting out people now the Luftwaffe have been visiting again. I told Jo on the way up but . . .'

She told them about Miss Carpenter's demise, Mrs Paget taking over and their conversation about the toys.

'Blooming cheek,' said Mattie when she'd finished.

'That's what I said,' added Jo, through a mouthful of potato.

'Did she believe you, do you think, about going to the police?' asked Francesca.

'I hope so, because I will,' said Cathy. 'In fact, before I left that afternoon, I made a list of all the new toys in boxes and I've made sure she's seen me checking them every day.'

'Well, good for you, Cathy,' said Mattie. Her attention shifted to her other sister. 'It seems strange to see you out of uniform, Jo.'

'Yes, I have a whole weekend off,' Jo replied. 'And so has Tommy, so,' a cheeky smile spread her lips wide, 'we've decided to spend the whole day in bed tomorrow.'

'You hussy,' laughed Mattie.

Jo pulled a face. 'You're just jealous.'

'I blooming am,' Mattie agreed. 'Most mornings the children have us up before the milkman's horse comes around the corner. I can't remember the last time the two of us had a lie-in.' A dreamy expression spread across her sister's face. 'What I wouldn't give for a couple of undisturbed hours under the sheets with Daniel.'

'Will you two give over,' said Francesca. 'At least your other halves are stationed in London. Charlie's a thousand miles away in North Africa and the saints alone knows when he'll be back.'

'But think how keen he'll be when he does.' Jo winked. 'Sure, you'll have to suck a lemon to get the shameless look off your face.'

Mattie and Francesca laughed.

From nowhere an image of Archie McIntosh sprang into Cathy's head. She tried to push it away, but her imagination retaliated by stripping him of his shirt and laying him on a fresh white sheet. In her mind's eye, she saw a look in his blue eyes that started something very unfamiliar but very pleasant swirling in the pit of her stomach —

'Cathy?'

The vision evaporated.

Cathy blinked and looked up to find three pairs of eyes regarding her oddly.

'What?' she said.

'You tell us,' said Mattie.

'You've got a very funny look on your face, Cathy,' said Francesca.

'Have I?'

'Yes, and you sighed,' added Jo.

'I never did,' said Cathy.

'You'd obviously drifted off somewhere,' said Francesca.

'Yes,' said Mattie, scrutinising her face closely. 'So, come on, Cathy. What were you daydreaming about?'

'Nothing really, you know, the centre, shopping, the usual stuff,' Cathy replied, feeling suddenly very warm.

Mattie arched an eyebrow. 'Really?'

Cathy held her sister's gaze for a moment then Mattie picked up her tea and took a sip.

'Well, from now on, girls,' said her older sister, 'when we are missing our men, perhaps we should try thinking about shopping, as it seems to have brought a contented smile to Cathy's face.'

★ ★ ★

As the organist played the final bars of the processional piece, Violet crossed herself and, leaning heavily on the flat wooden seat behind her, heaved herself to her feet. Stowing the kneeler on the hook, she sidestepped out of the pew, genuflected towards the altar and then, with her handbag hooked over her arm, made her way out.

Having shaken the Reverend Paget's hand at the door and assured him, as she always did, that he'd delivered a lovely sermon, Violet headed across the frost-whitened strip of garden surrounding the church and made her way to the hall at the back.

In contrast to the icy air outside, the room where the after-service tea was being served was comfortably warm, thanks to the enormous hundred-year-old boiler in the corner.

Surveying the high-ceilinged space, Violet grimaced as she spotted Madge Stone pouring the teas and making a fuss of Father Silas, St Philip and St Augustine's wet-behind-the-ears curate.

Greeting acquaintances and giving Madge a frosty look as she collected a cup, Violet glanced around. Dorothy Michel and Hattie Fallow had a spare chair at their table, so Violet went to join them, but before she'd got halfway across the hall, Mrs Paget, wearing a tweed coat and a chilly expression, stepped into her path.

'Good morning, Mrs Paget,' said Violet.

'And to you,' said the vicar's wife. 'Is Mrs Cathy Wheeler any relation of yours?'

'She's married to my son,' said Violet, giving the other woman a wary look.

Mrs Paget's mouth pulled into an ugly line.

'I'm sorry to hear that because . . . ' She paused and took a deep breath. 'Due to the untimely demise of Miss Carpenter three days ago, I was asked to take over the running of the St Breda and Brendan's Rest Centre. Your daughter-in-law was tasked to show me the ropes and, well . . . I've never been spoken to in such a rude manner in my life.'

Violet's face screwed into a mortified expression.

'Oh, Mrs Pa-Paget.' She pulled a handkerchief out of her pocket and dabbed her eyes.

'Please, Mrs Wheeler, do not distress yourself,' said Mrs Paget. 'I do not regard your daughter-in-law's total lack of civility as any reflection on you as — '

'Oh, Mrs Paget,' sniffed Violet, squeezing a tear. 'I've tried, honestly I've really tried, but . . . ' She glanced around then leaned towards the other woman. 'Blood will out,' she whispered.

'What do you mean?'

'Well, I'm not one to judge,' said Violet, 'but everyone knows her family, the Brogans, are nothing but a bunch of Pope-worshipping, Irish tinkers. Let me tell you. Her father styles himself as a house removal and delivery man, but he's nothing more than a grubby totter and a ruddy Paddy one at that,' she continued. 'My Stanley, he had a good job and a nice home, so you can see why *she* set her cap at him. So I overlooked everything about her family and welcomed her like the daughter I never had into my home, but . . . ' She dabbed her eyes again. 'I tried to warn my Stan not to get involved with her, but he wouldn't listen. Much too good for her, he is, but she caught him good and proper.'

Mrs Paget's eyes flew open. 'She was in the family way?'

'She wasn't,' said Violet, 'but only because I brought my Stan up as a good Christian. I'm sure if it were left to her, little Stanley would have been born months earlier. And if that isn't enough to make your hair curl, neither of her so-called brothers are her mother's.'

'They're not?'

'The ginger one, Billy, is the brat left in the workhouse by Cathy's loose-knickered aunt,' Violet replied. 'And the other one, Michael, he's her father's sprog by some woman who pegged it and then dumped her bastard on the family.'

'You mean both of the Brogan boys are illegitimate,' said Mrs Paget, her face a picture of incredulity.

Violet nodded.

'Have they no shame?'

'They don't know the meaning of the word,' said Violet, with relish. 'And her oldest sister just got the ring on her finger before they had to call the midwife.'

Mrs Paget's pale lips pulled into a tight bud.

'And I didn't mention,' Violet continued, 'that her other sister's husband has a convicted criminal for a brother. He's in prison for manslaughter.'

'My goodness,' said the vicar's wife.

'And then there's Queenie.'

Mrs Paget looked puzzled.

131

'The gran, she lives with them too,' Violet explained. 'She's completely barmy and ought to have been locked up in a loony bin long ago. Pretends she talks to the spirits and tries to let on she can foretell the future by reading tea leaves.'

The colour drained from Mrs Paget's face. 'But that's witchcraft and condemned by the Church,' she said, with a slight tremor to her voice.

'As I said, bad blood,' said Violet. 'I begged my Stan not to marry her, but . . . well, you can see what she looks like, and men, even the best of men like my dear son, can have their heads turned.'

'It's true,' agreed the vicar's wife. 'Men are particularly susceptible when it comes to the temptations of the flesh. Mrs Wheeler, I don't know what to say.'

'It's hard to believe, isn't it?' said Violet, extracting her handkerchief from her cardigan sleeve and dabbing her eyes again.

'He didn't have to go, you know, my Stanley,' Violet added. 'As he was chairman of the local branch of the Britons for Peace Union, he could have become a conchie. Lots of them did, but not my Stan,' said Violet. 'He said, 'Mum, as much as I don't want to go, this is my country and I must do my duty.' And now my poor boy is missing.'

'Well, Mrs Wheeler,' said Mrs Paget, a sympathetic expression lifting her thin features, 'we all have our crosses to bear.'

'We do.' Violet heaved a sigh and then placed her hand on the other woman's arm. 'But it will give me great comfort to know that while everyone thinks my daughter-in-law is a blessed angel from heaven, you know what she's really like.'

132

9

'Now, Terry Adams, there's no need to snatch,' said Cathy, giving the eight-year-old boy a severe look. 'There are plenty of pilchard sandwiches and, Linda Spelman, you've already had two so put that fairy cake back.'

It was just before three o'clock in the afternoon on the Wednesday before Christmas and the day of the children's party.

Although the air raid siren had gone off just after the blackout had come into force the night before, mercifully, just a handful of enemy aircraft had flown over, and having dropped their bombs south of the river, they'd headed back to their bases in Northern France. In view of this, and the fact that the all-clear had sounded before Cathy had had a chance to gather herself together and head off to the shelter, she'd allowed herself the luxury of a full night's sleep in her own bed.

Violet, regardless of there being a raid or not, spent every night in the shelter so, after putting Peter to bed, Cathy had spent a cosy hour in front of the fire listening to 'The ENSA Half-Hour' on the wireless.

It was just as well she'd had a restful night as she'd been on the go since she'd arrived at the rest centre at nine o'clock that morning.

Along with Dot, Lottie and other members of her Christmas team, she had been flat out putting up decorations, shifting benches, buttering bread for sandwiches and making sure there were sufficient toys for all the children they knew were coming and any that might turn up unexpectedly. As Christmas paper was as rare as hen's teeth, they'd wrapped up the fifty-plus presents in sheets from old comics, which were at least colourful if not festive.

They'd even managed to make a grotto by covering both legs of a tall stepladder with red and green crêpe paper and then sticking bits of cotton wool all over it. That was tucked into one of the corners ready for her father, whom she'd persuaded to play Father Christmas.

Jeremiah had arrived some twenty minutes ago and was now in the small committee room changing into the costume Mattie had run up for him.

The children had been told to bring their own plates, cups and spoons, and these had been set out on the half a dozen trestle tables in preparation for the Christmas tea. Meanwhile, the children had played Pass the Parcel, What's the Time, Mr Wolf?, and other party games, while their mothers sat along the sides of the hall watching their offspring dash about, shouting and laughing.

Having almost exhausted themselves and the helpers, Cathy had called order and, after they'd been marched out to wash their hands, the children had sat down to enjoy the spread she and the rest of the team had set out that morning.

Cathy's gaze roamed over the table where girls in bright dresses with ribbons in their hair and boys in their school uniforms and long grey socks were happily chatting and eating. She was just calculating that she'd be able to call her father through in about fifteen minutes when the rest-centre door swung open and Sergeant McIntosh stepped in.

134

Before she could stop it, her heart did a little dance.

Evening classes had stopped for the Christmas holiday the week before, and although he'd dropped into the centre again for a cuppa last week, she'd been up to her ears sorting out three Canadian Red Cross parcels, so they'd only had time for a quick hello.

He stared across the hall at her for a moment or two then, with his blue eyes locked with hers, he smiled and walked over.

'Hello,' he said, as he reached her. 'I thought I'd gatecrash the party.'

Cathy gave him a wry smile. 'I think you're a bit big to sit on Father Christmas's knee, don't you?'

His laugh rumbled over her. 'Aye, probably so. But the wee 'uns look like they're enjoying themselves.'

'They are,' she said, smiling at the children polishing off the last few sandwiches and cakes. 'It's nice to see them forget about the destruction all around them and just be children again.'

Cathy turned back to find herself looking up into his strikingly handsome face.

He opened his mouth to say something but before he could, Maureen came hurrying over.

'How long shall I get Mrs Drummond to wait until she fetches in the nursery children, Cath?' she whispered.

'About a quarter of an hour?' said Cathy. 'Once they're in I'll fetch Dad.'

Maureen nodded and left them.

'He's Father Christmas,' Cathy explained.

'I'll leave you to it and get myself a brew,' he said.

'Good idea,' said Cathy.

'Can you join me?'

She glanced around. 'Well, I'm not — '

'Please,' he added, his gaze capturing hers. 'It is Christmas.'

She smiled.

'All right,' she said, feeling suddenly very light-hearted. 'But let me sort my dad out first.'

He smiled, then made his way towards the serving hatch at the far end of the hall.

Cathy watched him for a moment then hurried out of the hall and across to the small committee room.

* * *

Archie had just put a saucer on the top of Cathy's cup to keep her tea warm when a clanging bell heralded her return as she followed

Father Christmas, with a bulging sack slung over his shoulder, into the hall.

With a strapping physique, white beard, red costume and firemen's boots, Cathy's father certainly looked the part.

'Yo ho ho,' he shouted as he strode across the hall.

As you'd expect, the children sitting around the table screamed and bounced on their chairs as Cathy led him across the room to the improvised grotto.

She then helped boys and girls down from the table and ushered them into a haphazard line. Father Christmas took his seat under the crêpe paper and Cathy stood aside while a couple of other WVS volunteers guided the children forward to receive their presents.

Everyone was focused on Father Christmas. Everyone, that is, except Archie, who was looking at Cathy.

He shouldn't, of course. Even though he'd long since dispensed with religion, organised or otherwise, there were still things he regarded as wrong. And desiring another man's wife definitely fell into that category.

But he couldn't help himself. She was one of those women who took your breath away but didn't know it. Her figure was slender but womanly and although she barely wore make-up, she didn't need to. Her complexion was clear enough, her eyes bright enough and her lips red enough without artificial enhancement.

He guessed she was probably a handful of years younger than him, but she was not a giddy-headed girl. In truth, despite her soft smile and bright eyes, there was a sadness about her. Perhaps it was just the sadness of a wife missing her husband, but Archie sensed it was something deeper and he wished he could fathom it.

As the children moved forward, Cathy glanced across at him.

He smiled and she smiled back.

After saying something to another woman in a forest-green uniform, Cathy made her way towards him.

As she approached, he stood up and pulled out the chair opposite for her.

She gave him a grateful look, then tucking her skirt under her, she sat down, and Archie returned to his seat.

'There you are,' he said, taking the saucer off the top of the cup and moving it in front of her. 'I hope it's as you like it.'

'I'm sure it is.'

Smiling, she took it and as she did her fingers slid across his, awakening his senses in an instant.

Picking up her cup, she blew across the top. 'Thank

you.'

Archie smiled at her like a loon for a moment then found his voice.

'The young 'uns seem to be having fun with Father Christmas,' he said, as the next child stepped up to receive their present.

Glancing around, Cathy laughed. 'I think my dad's having more fun than any of them. Big kid that he is.'

She turned back and Archie studied her face as she took a sip of tea.

Considering he'd done it from memory, the sketch he'd made of her when he'd got back from the dance was pretty good, but each time he saw her he noticed something more.

'I popped by Monday, but I didnae see you around,' he said, taking particular note of her long lashes.

'Peter was running a temperature, so I couldn't come that day,' she replied.

'Is your lad all right now?' he asked.

'Yes,' she laughed. 'It was just one of those twenty-four-hour things. But you can't be too careful.'

'No, you canna,' he agreed, remembering the worrying nights he'd spent cooling Kirsty's fever with a flannel on her forehead.

The hall door opened again, and a motherly middle-aged woman led the group of toddlers two by two into the room, with another member of the WVS bringing up the rear.

'And here he comes now,' said Cathy, half turning towards the newcomers.

The little boy who'd collided with Archie's legs a few weeks before was near the front of the crocodile, holding hands with a little girl.

He spotted Cathy and waved.

She waved back and then watched as he took his place in the line waiting to talk to Santa.

'I hope he doesn't spot that it's his granddad under all that clobber,' said Cathy.

Love filled Cathy's face as she watched her son stand solemnly in front of Father Christmas.

Sadness tightened around Archie's heart, knowing Kirsty would never remember her mother looking at her that way.

Father Christmas said something to Peter, who nodded. Delving into his sack, Santa pulled out a present and handed it to the little lad.

The woman in charge of the children moved him aside, then, clutching his wrapped parcel, he turned and ran to his mother.

He stopped in front of her and held up his gift.

'Is that what Father Christmas gave you, Peter?' Cathy asked.

Peter nodded.

'Oh, shall we see what it is?' she added.

He handed it to her then scrambled up on to her lap. Taking back the present, the lad started tearing at the paper, but the string tied around it held fast.

'Here, let me give you a hand, son,' said Archie.

Peter looked uncertainly at his mother.

'It's all right, Peter,' said Cathy. 'Sergeant McIntosh is a brave soldier like Uncle Charlie.'

Peter offered him the parcel. Taking it, Archie unpicked the knot and handed it back to the boy.

With eager fingers Peter unwrapped the pages of the comic to reveal a bright red wooden train engine, with yellow wheels and a green funnel.

'Cho tain,' he said, happiness written all over his face.

Cathy's large hazel eyes opened in surprise. 'Oh, Peter. Isn't that what you asked for?'

'Tain,' repeated Peter.

He held it out to Archie, who looked suitably impressed. 'You mustae been a rare good boy for your ma all year.'

'He has.' Cathy pressed her lips to the lad's soft cheek. 'He's the best boy in the world.'

Peter wriggled out of her embrace and slid off her lap. Sitting next to her feet he started rolling his present back and forth on the floor, making chuffing sounds.

Cathy watched the lad for a moment or two then her gaze returned to Archie and she took another mouthful of tea.

'Are you going home to see your family for Christmas?' she asked.

'I am,' he replied, feeling the familiar ache in his heart at the thought of them. 'I got a travel pass this morning and I'll be catching the train from Euston tomorrow so I'll be home ready for when Kirsty wakes up on Christmas morning. In fact, that's why I spent this afternoon buying Christmas presents.'

Cathy laughed. 'Why do men always leave it so late?'

'Because we're such dafties at it,' he replied.

She pulled a face. 'Dafties?'

'Useless.'

She laughed again.

'But this year,' he delved into the top pocket of his field jacket, 'I think I've come up trumps because I've got this for my daughter.'

He pulled out a flat square box and handed it to Cathy.

She took it and opened the lid.

'It's beautiful,' she said, admiring the silver St Christopher he'd paid a full two guineas for.

'My ma bought her one a while back but the chain broke, and it was lost,' he continued. 'The last time I drove down Mile End Road I spotted that little jewellery shop squashed between what looks like two halves of a department store.'

She smiled. 'Oh, you mean Spiegelhalter's.'

'That's the place,' he said. 'I thought I'd see if I could find her another.'

'Lucky you were passing by today,' she said.

'Yes, wasn't it?' he replied.

They looked at each other for a second or two then Cathy closed the lid and handed the box back. 'I'm sure she'll love it.'

'I hope so,' he replied, putting it back in his pocket. 'In fact, I managed to get my ma a brooch, too.'

'What about your wife?' Cathy asked. 'I hope you got her something or you'll be in tr — '

'My wife is dead,' Archie replied.

Cathy's sunny expression vanished in an instant.

'I'm so sorry. Was it recent?' she asked.

He shook his head. 'Five years last month. It was a real peasouper of a day and she was waiting for the tram in Union Street. There was a rush as it arrived, and she and another woman stumbled in front of it. They were killed instantly so that was a blessing but . . .'

'Your poor daughter,' she added. 'She couldn't have been more than a baby when she lost her mother.'

'Kirsty was just shy of her second birthday,' he replied, as the memory of holding his daughter in his arms as her mother's coffin was lowered into the

141

ground flooded back. 'She lives with me ma now. And I'm mad to see her. I bet she's grown another inch since July.'

'And I'm sure she feels the same.' Cathy frowned. 'It's so hard for children having their father disappear for months, even years on end.'

'Hard for wives, too, I imagine,' he added.

'Yes,' she replied, in a tight voice.

'Well, I hope, Mrs Wheeler, it won't be too long before your husband's home again,' he said, thinking, not for the first time, what a fortunate man he was.

'Perhaps,' she replied. 'But he's missing in action.'

'I'm sorry,' Archie replied. 'But I'm sure the Red Cross will find him before too long so don't give up hope.'

A desolate expression flashed across her face, but she forced a plucky little smile.

They looked at each other for another moment then she glanced around.

The women of the WVS were starting to clear away the remnants of the sandwiches, cakes and jellies as the last few children collected their presents from Father Christmas.

Turning back to face him, Cathy swallowed the last mouthful of her tea.

'I ought to go and give a hand,' she said, putting the cup down.

She rose to her feet and Archie did the same.

Looking up at him, her captivating smile returned. 'It's good to see you again, Sergeant, and I hope you have a wonderful Christmas at home with your family.'

'You too,' he said.

Scooping her son and his train off the floor, she settled him on her hip and walked back to join the rest of the volunteers.

Waving at Peter, who was studying him over his mother's shoulder, Archie watched her go.

He wanted to call, 'See you in the New Year', but he bit back the words.

Although the pain of Moira's death would always be there, he knew he was ready to love again; but perhaps, as she was a married woman, for both their sakes it might be better to let Cathy believe he was still mourning.

*　*　*

'Well, that went well,' said Olive as she scraped uneaten crusts into the pigswill bin.

'Yes, it did,' Cathy replied. 'We've even got half a dozen presents left that can go to East London children's hospital.'

'And,' Olive winked, 'I see your handsome sergeant dropped by again.'

Although her heart did a little dance as Archie flashed through her mind, Cathy set her face into a deadpan expression.

'Firstly, he's not my sergeant and secondly, he just happened to be in the area.' Picking up another used plate, Cathy put it alongside the others in the enamel bowl. 'Now, I'll just take these through to the kitchen,' she said, lifting the pile from the table. 'Leave the rest stacked at the end and I'll come back for them once I've washed this lot.'

'Right you are,' Olive called after her.

Elbowing the door open, Cathy carried the dirty

crockery into the kitchen. Passing Dot and Lottie, who were setting out the plates and cutlery ready to serve up macaroni cheese for those wanting a ration-free meal before heading home, Cathy went to the deep butler sink at the far side of the room.

Taking the dirty plates from the bowl, she lowered them into the sink and turned the tap on the Ascot heater. She picked up the pack of Oxydol from behind the cold tap and sprinkled soapflakes under the steaming water as it covered the crockery.

She'd just grabbed the washing-up sponge when the kitchen door opened, and the elegant figure of Mrs Paget walked in.

Glancing around, she spotted Cathy.

'Ah, there you are, Mrs Wheeler,' she said, striding towards her. 'If I could have a word.'

Cathy turned off the hot water and plunged her hands into the soapy water.

'Is there a problem?' she asked, running the sponge over the surface of the first plate.

'Possibly,' said Mrs Paget. 'Who was that darkie soldier you were talking to?'

'If you mean Sergeant McIntosh,' said Cathy, stacking the plate on the draining board, 'he's part of the bomb disposal division at Wanstead, why?'

'I noticed you and he seemed very friendly,' she replied.

Cathy looked puzzled. 'Did we?'

'Yes, you did,' said the vicar's wife. 'A little too friendly, to my mind.'

Placing another plate on the draining board, Cathy turned to face her. 'We were just having a cup of tea and talking.'

'Were you?'

144

'Yes, we were,' said Cathy. 'Talking about the present he'd just bought for his daughter.'

A flush darkened Mrs Paget's throat. 'He's married?'

'Widowed.'

'Nonetheless,' said the vicar's wife, 'that isn't an excuse to be as familiar with him as you were. I tell you, I wasn't the only one who noticed.'

'We were just talking, that's all,' said Cathy. 'And anyone who says otherwise has the wrong end of the stick.'

Mrs Paget's cool eyes studied her for a moment then she spoke again.

'Very well, but let me remind you that the Women's Voluntary Service is a respectable organisation and I expect those who work for it to keep that in mind. I would therefore be grateful if you would tell your half-caste sergeant and any of his coloured friends to find somewhere else to take their meal breaks.'

★ ★ ★

With the glow of seeing Cathy still swelling his chest, Archie rode along Mile End Road, but just past the old workhouse the ear-jangling wail of the air raid siren cut through the cold crisp evening air.

In the distance he could see the tell-tale red glow in the sky indicating the Royal Docks and the factories by Barking Creek were taking the brunt of the raid. Probably the Luftwaffe planes dropping their remaining bombs as they turned around and headed back to their bases in Northern France. Thankful that Cathy and her son would be safe from this raid at least, Archie opened up the throttle and sped on towards his billet some mile and a half away.

With the ominous hum of enemy aircraft overhead, he continued eastwards to his destination. However, as his front wheel rolled on to the bumpy surface of Bow Bridge, the first bombs fell just south of where he was, close to the entrance of Blackwall Basin and Tunnel.

Others fell almost immediately, rocking the ground beneath his rubber tyres and sending red and gold flashes across the sky. They were still south of where he was but getting closer, much closer, probably following the nearby River Lea to target the factories along its banks and the Stratford railway shunting yards just beyond.

The ear-splitting clamour of falling bombs was joined by the whistles of ARP wardens, police claxons and fire-engine bells.

Navigating past buses that had stopped so their passengers could seek shelter, Archie slowed down. He had just crossed Bow Bridge when a bomb found its target behind him, landing almost in the river and sending a fountain of water skywards. The vacuum of the explosion sucked at his clothes and hair, causing him to slow down even more as he lowered his feet to skim the tarmac. With the acrid smell of scorched munitions and sulphur in the air, Archie motored on past the paint factory towards his billet.

Swerving to avoid a block of masonry lying in the middle of the carriageway, he turned left into Wise Road.

However, as he rolled to a stop, he stared wordlessly at the quiet residential street.

A bomb, probably a 500-kilo one judging by the depth of the crater and spread of the damage, had landed on the neat row of terraced houses, flattening them like a foot on a sandcastle.

The impact had pulverised four or five houses on both sides of the street, leaving smouldering rubble where cosy homes had stood only a few hours before. Unsurprisingly, the blast had punched out every window in the street and there was glass and shattered wood everywhere. Although not totally obliterated, the houses just outside the initial blast area were damaged, too, and one of them was Mr and Mrs Charlton's house where he lodged.

The three-bedroom terraced house looked as if someone had taken a large carving knife and sliced off the outside wall, which lay with barely a brick disturbed on the rubble. Exposed to the elements, for all to see in the glow of the burning buildings, was Mr and Mrs Charlton's brass bed minus its sheets and blankets, which were hanging from an exposed beam like a patchwork flag.

The tallboy hadn't escaped and all its drawers had been forced out by the blast, allowing Mr Charlton's long johns and his wife's corset to spill out. Downstairs, the sofa had been shoved across the parlour with the force of the explosion and it lay against the upright piano, while on the carpet his landlady's extensive collection of china figurines lay headless and armless among the shimmering shards of glass.

Drawing to a halt outside what had been the front door, Archie pulled his bike on to its stand as the all-clear sounded. Seeing the street's ARP warden knocking on doors a little way down, Archie strolled over.

'Do you need a hand, pal?' asked Archie.

The warden, an elderly man with a walrus-like grey moustache, looked around.

Confusion flashed across his face for a second then he spotted Archie's regimental insignia and he chuckled.

'You know, for one minute there, mate,' he said as Archie reached him, 'until I saw your badge, I was wondering what one of those Negro GIs was doing strolling around Stratford. And thanks for the offer, but I think we're all right,' he replied. 'A couple of the heavy-rescue lads are just checking the garden shelters while the rest of them dig out a couple trapped in their Anderson at number twenty-eight, but other than that I think everyone is more or less accounted for. You billeted here?'

Archie nodded. 'Number seventeen. Look, just so you know, I'm not looting; I'm going to pop in to fetch some of my stuff.'

The warden's moustache shifted back and forth on his top lip. 'I don't know, the house's been badly damaged. It could be unstable, and I wouldn't want you falling through the floorboards.'

Archie grinned. 'I dinna want to do that maself; I'm on fortyeight-hour leave tomorrow.'

'Off you go then, lad,' said the warden.

Archie turned and walked towards what was left of his billet.

'And watch where you put your size tens,' the old man called after him.

Archie raised his hand in acknowledgement.

Taking out his torch, he crunched over the front door, which now lay flat on Mrs Charlton's hall runner, and headed for the stairs. Keeping close to the solid wall adjoining the house next door, he made his way upstairs to his room.

Like the other two bedroom doors, his had been

148

blown off its hinges by the blast and now lay at a forty-five-degree angle against the end of his bed.

Stepping carefully over it, Archie entered the room and shone the beam around.

His easel was on the floor with the watercolour painting he was working on beneath it. The brush pots had shattered, scattering the brushes all over the rug, and his paint box was on the floor. Thankful that he'd remembered to secure the lid properly the day before, it was still closed tight, and the half a dozen completed paintings and newly stretched canvases alongside them were still propped up against the far wall.

Relieved to find his painting equipment more or less intact, Archie balanced the torch on the top of the dresser. Grabbing his kitbag from the floor, he pulled open the drawstring and propped it up against the chair. He went to his chest of drawers, scooped out his underwear and socks and threw them into the bag, then went back and did the same with his three laundered army shirts. He picked up the frames with Kirsty and Moira's photos in and placed them carefully on top of the folded clothes, then he piled his civvy clothing in, before throwing in his wash-bag. Putting his paint box and brushes on top, Archie pulled the threaded cord tight and secured it. Leaving his haversack by the door he then pulled out his large portfolio case from beneath the bed, slid his paintings and canvases in and fastened the zip.

Looping the kitbag cord across him and pulling a dangling string free from the smashed venetian blind, Archie picked up the portfolio case, hooked his easel over his shoulder and retraced his steps downstairs.

As he stepped out into the street he came face to

face with his landlady, with a head full of curlers, and her husband in his tartan dressing gown, their faces ashen as they looked up open-mouthed at what remained of their home.

Putting down his portfolio, Archie put his hand inside his airman's jerkin and pulled out his wallet. Opening it he took out a brown ten-bob note.

'Mrs Charlton,' he said.

Dazed, she looked at him.

'I've taken ma gear,' Archie said. 'And here's next week's rent.'

He offered her the money.

She stared at him for a moment then took it. 'Thank you.'

'I'm away then,' he said, nodding towards his bike parked nearby.

She nodded but didn't speak.

He held out his hand. 'Mr Charlton.'

The other man took it. 'Sergeant McIntosh.'

They shook once then Archie picked up his portfolio again.

Mrs Charlton's face crumbled.

'Oh, Ernie,' she sobbed.

Her husband put his arm around her, and she buried her face in his shoulder.

Archie gave them a sympathetic look then turned away.

Having secured the portfolio on the passenger seat of his motorbike with the cord from the blind, he kick-started the Triumph. As the two-stroke engine ticked over, Archie balanced his kitbag on his back and then, with his easel over his left shoulder, he grasped the handlebar and swung his leg over.

Rolling the bike off its stand, he kicked it into gear

and pulled on the throttle. Wending his way between the fallen masonry, shattered glass and broken bricks towards the Romford Road, Archie realised he'd forgotten to wish them Merry Christmas, but under the circumstances it was probably just as well.

★ ★ ★

The puddles were just starting to get a thin layer of frost on them by the time Archie roared into Wanstead High School's gravel yard some three-quarters of an hour later.

The half a dozen canvas-covered lorries belonging to the various bomb disposal teams stationed at North East London BD base were parked neatly against the back wall of the playground, and although many of the officers' cars had already gone from the yard, he noticed Monkman's and Captain Moncrief's vehicles were still there.

Steering his bike past the pile of sandbags on his left, Archie drew to a halt under the shelter of the old bike racks.

Putting his Triumph on its stand, Archie untied his portfolio and, shouldering his knapsack, strolled towards the main building.

It was a long cold ride to Glasgow, so he'd swung around via Euston station earlier in the week and booked himself a seat on tomorrow night's mail train.

Stepping through the blackout curtain, the smell of boiled cabbage wafted over him from the canteen in the main hall opposite. Through the half-glazed window he could see the unlucky crew designated on duty over Christmas eating their evening meal under the paper chains and Chinese lanterns that the kitchen staff had put up the week before.

To his left, the rhythmic tick, tick, tick of the clerks bashing away at typewriters echoed out from the main office, while further down the hall Bill Willis was stretching high on the cork noticeboard pinning up a fresh set of Ministry of Defence regulations about mislaying personal kit, the correct filling out of meal chits, or some such trivia that no one even looked at let alone took notice of.

From a wireless somewhere, a brass band played 'God Rest Ye Merry Gentlemen'.

Standing to awkward attention for a moment as two of the newly arrived lieutenants walked past on their way to the officers' mess, Archie then headed upstairs to where the squads were billeted.

Ron and Tim, who were lounging on their bunks smoking, looked around sharply when Archie walked in.

'Where is everyone?' asked Archie.

'Chalky's phoning his missis and Mogg caught the midday train to the Valleys; the rest are down the pub,' Ron replied. 'But what are you doing here, Sarge?' he added, swinging his legs around and sitting up. 'I thought you'd be getting ready to head off to Scotch-land.'

'Aye, I would've been had it not been for Fritz dropping a whacking great five-hundred-kilo right next to ma digs,' Archie replied.

He told them about the damage to Wise Road and how he'd rescued his personal items.

'You were bloody lucky,' said Tim when he'd finished.

'Aye, that I was,' Archie replied. 'But sadly, lads, and although it pains me to have to do it, I'll be having to slum it with you scurvy rabble until I can find somewhere else. I'll take the spare bunk in the corner.'

Tim grinned. 'You'll be nice and warm there, Sarge, cos Ron next door farts all night.'

Archie gave him a pained look and strolled over to the narrow single bed in the corner of the old class-room.

Resting his easel against the bed, Archie placed the portfolio with his canvases in it on the khaki blanket then put his kitbag down on the floor.

Hunkering down, he reached under the bed, pulled out the metal box provided for stowing personal belongings, then slipped his easel alongside it. Add-ing his paint box, Archie pushed it back under the bed then hung up his shirts in the narrow locker beside the bed. He was about to slip his portfolio under his bed when Tim piped up again.

'Let's have a gander, Sarge.'

'They're nothing special,' said Archie.

'Come on,' said Ron.

Archie looked between them for a moment then, unzipping the portfolio, he pulled out the painting he'd finished a couple of days before and leaned it against the headboard.

'It's called Digging Out,' Archie added, stepping back so they had a clear view.

Ron and Tim stared wide-eyed at the image of the three men at the bottom of a shaft as they crouched beside a Satan.

'Cor, Sarge, it's bloody good, ain't it?' said Tim.

'Bloody is,' agreed Ron. He pointed at the figure in the front of the picture. 'Is the one with a shovel Mogg?'

'Aye,' said Archie. 'The local war committee is put-ting on an exhibition called 'Images of Defiance' at the Whitechapel Gallery in March and I'm thinking of submitting it, and this one, too.'

He pulled out another image of the squad, dirt-splattered and dishevelled, hauling up bags of mud on the winch.

'It's called *Just a Few More Feet*,' Archie added.

Tim laughed. 'Look, Ron, that's you there in the background having a quick fag. And Chalky.'

Ron's face creased in a smile. 'I don't know nuffink about la-di-dah art like they have up West, Sarge, but even a blind man could see you're a dab hand at the old painting lark. You should put them both in.'

Archie smiled. 'Thanks.'

'Ron's right. Seriously, Sarge,' said Tom, 'you definitely should.'

'Well, Sergeant, I am surprised,' Monkman's cultured tone said from behind him.

Alarm shot across the two men's face. They snapped to attention and gave a sharp salute.

Archie turned and found the lieutenant leaning on the doorframe with a smirk across his narrow face.

Resting the painting in his hand next to the other one, Archie drew himself up to attention and saluted too.

'Naughty, naughty, Sergeant,' Monkman continued, wagging his finger at Archie. 'I ought to call the Military Police.'

Standing away from the doorframe, Monkman marched a little unsteadily into the barrack room and stopped in front of Archie.

'You know, don't you, Sergeant,' he said, looking up into Archie's face, 'that looting is a hanging offence?'

'Aye, I ken, sir,' Archie replied. 'But these paintings are mine.'

'Don't be ridiculous,' scoffed Monkman, the smell of spirit wafting up as he spoke. 'On your pay you couldn't afford a damn seaside postcard never mind original artwork.'

'You misunderstand my meaning, sir,' said Archie, looking him in the eye. 'They are mine because I painted them.'

An incredulous expression crept across the lieutenant's face. 'You painted them?'

'Yes, sir.'

Monkman's gaze shifted from Archie to the images on display and back again.

He studied Archie for a moment then resentment twisted his mouth.

'I thought the only thing your kind painted was their faces,' he said. 'You know . . . ' Raising his hands, he wriggled his fingers at Archie. 'Oooooh, to scare the white man.'

Giving the man in front of him a glacial look, Archie didn't reply.

The lieutenant's bloodshot eyes held Archie's for a moment then he looked away.

'What are you doing here anyway, McIntosh?' snapped Monkman. 'Aren't you supposed to be on leave?'

'Aye, sir, from tomorrow,' Archie replied. 'But my billet's been bombed so I'll be bunking in with the lads until I find somewhere new. If you've no objections, that is, sir.'

Monkman chewed the inside of his mouth. 'Very well. But make sure you hand over your ration book to Willis in the main office.'

'I will,' Archie replied.

They eyeballed each other for a moment then

Monkman spoke again.

'Carry on.'

Archie and his two men straightened up and saluted.

The lieutenant gave Archie another bitter look then marched back across the wooden floorboards, but as he reached the door, he turned.

'And just so you don't start getting any grandiose ideas about yourself, McIntosh. When I referred to those,' he nodded towards the paintings propped up on the bed, 'as artwork, I was being sarcastic.'

Archie raised an eyebrow. 'Yes, sir.'

Monkman's close-set eyes flickered over him again then he turned and stomped out.

'You know what?' Archie said to the men standing behind him. 'I'll take your advice and enter them into the exhibition.'

10

'I have to say, Ida, me darling, you've gone above and beyond, so you have, this year,' said Jeremiah, pushing away his bowl with nothing but a couple of crumbs and a smear of custard in it.

'Are you sure?' said Ida. 'I mean, apple and prune tart isn't any substitute for a proper Christmas pudding.'

It was just after two and Cathy was at her parents' house, where the family had just finished their Christmas lunch. The easy chairs and sofa had been pushed back to allow the table to be extended to its full length, but even then it was a tight squeeze. The only member of the family not gathered around the table was Victoria, who was in her pram, sleeping under the new pink blanket her Auntie Francesca had given her.

'It was lovely, Mum,' Cathy said. 'Wasn't it, Peter?'

Peter, who was sitting next to her, nodded.

'Well, we have Gran to thank too,' said Jo, who, wearing a tartan pencil skirt and red cowl-neck jumper, was sitting across the table from Cathy.

'Yes, bit of luck that, eh, Queenie,' said Tommy, nudging his wife. 'Two birds getting sick like that just before Christmas.'

Queenie's almost invisible eyebrows rose as an angelic expression settled on her wrinkled face.

''Twas a gift from the saints above, to be sure,' she replied. 'And no more than a kindness to put them out of their misery.'

'And in the oven,' added Jo.

Everyone laughed.

Although Cathy's gran maintained her saintly countenance, a mischievous twinkle crept into her eyes. 'And that's what I'll be telling that eejit inspector from the Ministry of Food, should he inquire.'

To go with the juicy birds, stuffed with oats and chopped cooking apples, Queenie had peeled almost her own body weight in spuds on Christmas Eve before going to Midnight Mass, while Ida, working alongside her in the kitchen, had made short work of the two heads of cabbage and five pounds of carrots she'd staggered home from the market with that morning.

'Is there any more custard?' asked Billy who, like Michael, was sitting at the far end of the table where their father could keep an eye on them.

As it was a special day, both boys were wearing their school uniforms.

Ida picked up the china jug and peered in. 'A couple of dollops. If you and Michael pass your bowls, you can have half each.'

Licking his spoon clean, Billy held out his bowl and Cathy passed it to her mother. Using the battered dessert spoon standing up in the jug, Ida scraped around the inside then plopped a blob of thick, bright yellow custard in the middle of his bowl. Cathy passed the bowl back then took Michael's and handed that to Ida, who repeated the process.

'It's a shame Mattie and Daniel aren't here this year,' she said, handing Michael his dessert.

'Well, they've been with us for the past two years, so it was only right they visit Daniel's family this time,' said Jo.

Ida sighed. 'It doesn't seem the same somehow,

especially with Charlie away, too.'

Jeremiah gave his wife a soft look. 'Perhaps he'll get leave next year.'

Ida nodded. 'Please God it might even be all over by then.'

'Well, I don't want to pour salt on your strawberries, Ida,' said Tommy. 'We might have the Germans on the run in North Africa but I reckon it'll be a few years before we'll be able to do the same in Europe.'

'Tommy's right, Ida,' said Jeremiah. 'I don't think they'll be shipping our Charlie home any time soon, but you'll see Patrick tomorrow when Francesca comes over, so cheer up.'

'And you'll have another one soon,' added Jo.

'Yes, I know, it's not long until March,' said Ida, a fond smile spreading across her face.

'And another little soul will be joining us by next Christmas, too,' said Queenie. 'I feel the innocent spirits of them hovering close.'

Ida rolled her eyes. 'Well, you hardly need the spirits to tell you that, do you? What with Mattie talking about having another and Jo and Tommy just married.'

A bleak expression flashed across Jo's pretty face.

She stood up. 'Shall I put the kettle on?'

'That's a grand idea,' said her father. 'We'll listen to the King's address then me and Tommy'll get stuck in with the washing-up, won't we, son?'

'After such a meal, it's the least we can do,' agreed Tommy.

Jo gave a tight smile and hurried for the kitchen.

'Do you want a hand with the tea, Jo?' Tommy said, looking anxiously after her.

'It's all right, Tommy, I'll help,' said Cathy, rising to

her feet.

Gathering together some of the dirty crockery, Cathy followed her sister out and found Jo standing with her hands resting on the sink, her head hanging down.

'Are you all right?' asked Cathy.

Jo looked around.

'Not really,' she replied, with tears shimmering in her brown eyes.

Putting the crockery on the table, Cathy crossed the space between them and put her arm around her sister.

'Oh, Jo,' Cathy said, drawing her into her embrace.

Her sister rested her head on Cathy's shoulder for a moment then straightened up.

'It's not fair,' she sniffed. 'I've been married for six months and I still come on each month as regular as clockwork. And it's not as if me and Tommy aren't . . . you know. Busy.'

'These things take time,' said Cathy, as she refilled the kettle.

'So everyone says,' Jo replied. 'But Daniel only has to hang his trousers over the end of the bed and Mattie's pregnant. Charlie and Francesca only had one night, one blooming night, before he shipped out and now she's like a beached whale. And then there's Mum and Dad — they still managed to have Victoria even though they are practically ancient!'

Cathy smiled and lit the gas.

'Honestly, Jo, six months is nothing,' she said. 'And they do say worrying about it can stop it happening. Just enjoy being 'busy' and, for all Mum saying otherwise, Gran's normally right about such things.'

Taking out a handkerchief, Jo looked up.

160

'I suppose you're right,' she said, carefully dabbing under her eyes. 'Has my mascara run? Because if Mum and Gran see I've been crying they'll give me the third degree.'

Cathy laughed. 'No, you look fine. Now, don't just stand there, set the cups on the tray.'

Jo gave her a small smile and went over to the dresser.

Cathy made the tea while her sister laid out the tray and fetched a fresh bottle of milk from the stone keep in the yard.

After rinsing the old leaves out of the tea strainer, Cathy put it and the teapot, covered in its red, white and blue knitted cosy, on the tray.

'You take it through,' she said. 'I'll put the plates in to soak then follow you in.'

Jo picked up the tray and headed for the door.

'You're probably right about the baby thing,' she said, as she elbowed the handle down. 'After all, it took you months to fall for Peter.'

Nudging open the door with her hip, Jo went back into the parlour.

Cathy stared after her for a moment then picked up the stack of plates and took them to the sink. Lowering them in, she turned on the tap and shook in some Fairy soap flakes then rested her hands on the edge as they dissolved into bubbles.

With the smell of the family's Christmas dinner still lingering in the air, Cathy gazed around the familiar room, and happy childhood memories came flooding back to her.

She, Mattie and Jo had fought like cats in a sack on a daily basis and had fallen out with each other as regularly as the mantelshelf clock struck the hour, but each night, the three of them had snuggled together under a pile of blankets in the creaky old double bed in the front bedroom, warm, happy and surrounded by their parents' love. And although her big brother Charlie had sensibly kept out of their girlie squabbles, he'd been quick to step in between them and playground bullies. Billy had slotted in from the start and, although a latecomer to the Brogan brood, Michael now seemed as if he'd always been one of their number. Soon Victoria, too, would find her place among them all.

And that had been Cathy's dream when she'd walked down the aisle on her father's arm just three short years before: a happy family with a handful of children and a loving husband.

Jo wasn't quite right. It hadn't taken Cathy long to fall for Peter — just two weeks. Two weeks of Stan climbing on and climbing off her in the dark, with barely a word and never a kiss. Of pain too, even when he spit on his hand and rubbed it on her as he entered. Hardly the stuff of Hollywood.

It was her fault, of course, that it had all ended up as dust under her feet. She'd seen only the dream of the family she yearned for but had been blind to the man she'd foolishly chosen to build it with.

Swallowing the lump in her throat, Cathy stood up and collected the mugs from the dresser, but as she did she caught her jumper on the corner of the drawer.

Annoyed at her clumsiness Cathy looked down at her clothes.

Like Jo, Cathy had put on something special for the day. In her case, it was the skirt from her plum-coloured suit with her ribbed cream sweater. It was the jumper she'd been wearing the night she met Archie McIntosh after her typing classes.

An image of Archie's eyes as they flickered over her flashed through her mind and a sensation her husband had barely disturbed throbbed through her.

A little smile lifted the corner of Cathy's mouth.

Perhaps the dream of a loving marriage and a large family wouldn't be lost after all.

★ ★ ★

With the mellow tones of the Band of the Grenadier Guards playing 'We Three Kings' drifting over him, Archie pressed his lips on to Kirsty's soft curls.

He was in his flat on the second floor of a double-fronted Victorian mansion, which had been divided up to make a two-bedroom dwelling on each floor. It was situated in Drumchapel, an area that was definitely a step or two up from where he'd grown up. Although truthfully, with water running down the wall when it rained, bedbugs and cockroaches, not to mention the not infrequent murder of a neighbour, anywhere was a step up from the tenement block where he'd started life. He and Moira had moved to the flat just after Kirsty was born, as Yarrow shipyard ran buses from there for workers, which saved him thruppence a day in fares.

Although the flat looked much the same as when Moira was alive, his mother, who had moved in after his wife died, had added some bits of her own. He didn't mind, it was her home, too. In fact, when he and Moira had married, he'd asked her to join them but she'd said that newlyweds needed time to work out how to live together, and although it had been terrible circumstances that had finally brought her to live under his roof, he was glad she was there for all sorts of reasons, not least so Kirsty was being looked after by someone who loved her as much as he did while he was away.

Archie kissed his daughter's forehead again. She didn't stir. He wasn't surprised, she'd been up since first light to see what Father Christmas had left.

Having saved his sugar ration for two weeks, along with a set of coloured pencils, a new drawing pad and an orange his mother had found from goodness knows where, Kirsty had woken up to discover a bar of Fry's chocolate in the grey school sock that she'd hung at the end of her bed.

Despite her gran's insistence that she wash and dress first, Kirsty had put on the St Christopher Archie had bought her as soon as it was out of the box. She'd thanked him with a noisy kiss and a choking hug, so he guessed it was a good choice. She'd given him a multicoloured scarf. It was her first attempt at knitting and although it was a bit short, with a couple of holes, he'd assured her he'd wear it, and he would, too, every day.

That was twelve hours ago and now, with just the washing-up from their Christmas lunch to do, they were relaxing by the fire listening to the BBC Forces Service.

'So will you be looking for other lodgings?' asked his mother, Aggie, sitting knitting in the other fireside chair.

She, like Kirsty, had been up since dawn, but in her case it was to prepare their Christmas feast of rabbit stew, swedes and potatoes and treacle tart. Now, the day's work done, she had removed her apron

164

and, dressed in her Sunday-best frock and slippers, was having a well-earned rest with her feet up on the pouffe.

'I'll have to,' Archie replied. 'D Squad are grand lads, right enough, but there's hardly room to swing a cat in the barrack room, let alone set up an easel. I'll start looking once I get back, and I've been thinking . . . We talked about you and Kirsty coming down to join me a while back and you weren't too keen, but I'm wondering if you've had any more thoughts on the matter, Ma?'

'Well now, son, it's a big step for me; I've never been to England, never mind London. And Mr Carr at the munitions factory's been good to me and I wouldn't want to let him down.'

'I know, Ma,' said Archie, 'but there's plenty of work in London if you want it, plus, it wouldn't have to be in a factory either — there are plenty of jobs in offices, shops and with the local council.'

'I can't say it wouldn't be nice to come home smelling of something other than engine oil,' said Aggie.

'And now your brother George has moved to Falkirk, it's not as if you've got family keeping you here,' said Archie, pressing home the point.

'That's true,' his mother agreed. 'And I've not heard from Moira's sister since their mother passed on three years ago.'

'And if we were all together under one roof you could drop down to part-time hours and ease up a bit,' added Archie.

'I hope you're not saying I'm getting old, Archie,' she said, looking over the rim of her spectacles at him.

He grinned. 'No, Ma, I wouldnae dare.'

'I'm pleased to hear it,' she said, 'but you may have

a point, and a nice little job in a library or chemist does sound mighty tempting. Perhaps with the world upside down it would be better for all of us to be together.'

'Shall I start looking for a place after Easter?' Archie asked.

She nodded and then her eyes flickered on to her granddaughter snuggled in Archie's arms. 'She should be in her bed.'

'Aye, she should,' Archie agreed, kissing his daughter's forehead again. 'But I'll be gone in the morning.'

'True.' Her gaze shifted back to the sleeping child in his arms and a soft expression lifted her face. 'I can't tell you, son. Every morning for the past week she's told me, 'It's just five, four — or whatever the number was — days until Da's home, Gran.''

Archie smiled. 'I've been doing the same myself. I said as much to Cathy.'

His mother looked up at him. 'Cathy?'

Archie laughed. 'Well, I should say Mrs Wheeler. She helps at one of the rest centres in East London. I dropped into the party she was organising.'

His mother raised an eyebrow.

'I know what you're thinking but it's nothing like that,' Archie laughed. 'I stopped her son dashing into the road a few weeks back and I've run into her a couple of times since. That's all.'

'If you say so,' Aggie said.

'I do,' he replied, giving her a firm look.

She regarded him steadily for a moment or two then reached for her cup of tea, which was resting on the table next to her chair.

Adjusting his sleeping daughter in his arms, Archie leaned his head back and let the music wash over him.

166

With the warmth of the front room surrounding him and the soft harmonies filling the air, Archie's mind wandered off and, as always, his thoughts headed in the direction of Cathy Wheeler.

What was she doing? Was she at home with Peter or at a large family gathering? Perhaps she was listening to the same wireless programme as he was or maybe she was gathered around a piano with friends and family having a sing-song.

His imagination conjured up an image of her not in her WVS uniform but in the slacks and figure-hugging cream sweater she'd been wearing when he'd met her after the art class at Cephas Street School.

A smile crept across his face as he pictured her mouth and imagined it under his.

'She's pretty, then?' said his mother from what seemed like a long way off.

'More beautiful than pretty,' he replied. 'With lovely hazel — '

He opened his eyes to see his mother smirking at him.

He raised an eyebrow. 'Very clever, Ma.'

'Well,' she said, picking up her knitting and looping a strand of red wool over her needle. ''Nothing like that'! Do you think I was born yesterday? When a man mentions a woman's name it's always 'like that' and has been since the world began. And truthfully, I'm right glad to hear it. I know losing Moira hit you hard. And why wouldn't it? But she'd be the last person to expect you to mourn her for ever, and she would want you to be happy if you found someone else to love.'

'I know, Mo was a grand woman, but it's awkward with Cathy,' Archie replied.

His mother gave him a level look. 'She's married,

167

is she?'

'Yes. No. That is, her husband's missing in action,' said Archie. 'And if he's still alive . . . '

'Does she like you?'

'I don't know. Perhaps I'm reading too much into things and she's just being friendly, but . . . ' An image of Cathy laughing floated into his head and a smile lifted his lips. 'She's funny and kind. Straight too and doesnae put up with any nonsense. And she's bright, although she doesn't think she is.' He sighed. 'But what does it matter? As I said, she's happily married.'

'Is she?'

'What?' he replied.

'Happy,' said his mother.

Archie stared at her as the question rattled around in his head.

Dragging a length of wool from the ball on her lap, Aggie spoke again.

'Not everyone's as merrily married as you were, Archie,' said his mother. 'And I'll tell you plain, there's many a woman around these parts praying each day that her husband won't be back.'

Kirsty stirred and Archie adjusted his arm to accommodate her. Glancing down at his sleeping daughter, his heart ached.

If he did nothing else with his life, she was his greatest achievement, but he'd always imagined Kirsty would be the eldest of three or maybe four children. That dream had been shattered the day the police had knocked at his door and told him about Moira.

For five long years he'd fought through the grief of her untimely loss and he'd buried his desire for a large family. Rightly or wrongly, since Cathy had run into his life that Sunday morning six weeks ago, the dream of holding the woman he loved in his arms and having more children had blossomed again. But was she happy?

The memory of Cathy's son struggling with his present from Santa returned to his mind for some reason. What had she said? What had he missed?

Archie ran through their conversation again and then he remembered. She'd told Peter he was a soldier like his uncle not his father! In fact, he didn't even know her husband's name because she'd never mentioned him once.

Hope and possibility washed over Archie as the dream that had died under the wheels of a trolley bus suddenly burst into life once more.

11

'And,' said Violet, as she surveyed the middle-aged women looking intensely at her, 'Stan's commanding officer finishes, 'although I know the news of Stanley is a great blow, Mrs Wheeler, I hope you'll find comfort in knowing that because he volunteered to stay at his post and single-handedly held back the enemy, he was instrumental in saving the lives of dozens of his comrades, and for that reason I am recommending him for the King's Bravery Medal. In short, Mrs Wheeler, your husband is a hero.''

'A hero!' muttered someone.

'Awarded the King's Medal,' said another.

'Saved dozens of lives,' whispered yet another of Violet's audience.

It was just after eleven thirty on the Tuesday after Christmas and she and a half-dozen other widows of the parish were having a warming cuppa in St Philip's church hall after mid-week communion. They needed it, too: due to the shortage of coal, the church's heating had been switched off. It was the miners' fault as they had downed tools again. They should be shot, the lot of them, the filthy communists, for denying decent Christian people a little comfort while they prayed.

'Why did his commanding officer call Stan your husband?' asked Elsie.

Violet rolled her eyes. 'Because the top brass has to write to the wife.'

'Oh, I see.' Elsie's rounded face lit up. 'It was good of your daughter-in-law to let you bring it along to show us today.'

Violet gave a tight smile but didn't reply.

'She must be very proud,' said Bettie.

'Proud!' sneered Violet. 'The only army letter she's looking out for is the one telling her my poor son's officially dead.'

'No!' said Rose Winters, her shocked expression matching the rest of Violet's audience.

'I tell you, she's counting the days, but,' Violet folded her arms, 'her nose is going to be right out of joint soon because my Stan's not dead.'

A couple of the elderly women glanced at each other.

'He's not,' repeated Violet.

'You're right, Violet,' said Rose. 'We shouldn't give up hope.'

'No, we shouldn't,' said Peggy Watson sitting next to her. 'Your son may well turn up somewhere.'

'He will,' said Violet. 'I can feel it in my bones.' She caught sight of the clock. Swallowing the last of her tea, she stood up. 'Now, I must get on so, God willing, I'll see you all on Sunday.'

★ ★ ★

Forty minutes after saying farewell to Elsie and the rest of her Mothers' Union acquaintances, Violet reached the top of Jubilee Street and then turned left on to Oxford Street. It usually took her half that time to get this far, but a bomb had landed at the end of Sidney Street the night before. It had blown away a row of houses, two pubs and the corner shop. Those houses not destroyed were badly damaged and, for fear that they might collapse, the area had been cordoned off.

There'd been a couple of ambulances standing by while the heavy-rescue crew dug for survivors.

Of course, she thought, as she strolled towards St Dunstan's between the piles of rubble that had once been homes and businesses, if people had listened to that nice Mr Mosley, none of this would have happened.

But no. Men who wanted to avert war with Germany, like Stan and his friends at the British Peace League, patriots who had this country's best interests at heart, weren't listened to. And that's why things were in such a mess now. Who knows, with his brains and charm, Stan could have been an important person in Mosley's government by now, but instead he was so-called missing in action.

The fury that was always bubbling just under the surface in Violet flared up again.

And why, why is my poor boy stuck in the middle of the Godforsaken North African desert in the first place instead of at home where he belongs? Because of Cathy Brogan and that bloody family of hers, that's why.

Reaching the Clare Hall public house, Violet waited until a convoy of army lorries with squaddies sitting in the back passed, then she crossed the road into Diggon Street.

Nodding her head to neighbours in acknowledgement as she passed, Violet marched into her own street.

As was usual for this time of day, the scrubbed white half-circles on the pavement outside every front door were shining in the dull winter light. Every front door but one, that is: hers, which was open. Parked in front of it was a lorry piled high with furniture and with the words 'Brogan & Sons' painted in gold on the side.

Pressing her lips together, Violet marched up the street and arrived at her house just as Cathy's father, dressed in old corduroy trousers, a leather jerkin and a red scarf tied at his throat, stepped out into the street.

'What are you doing here?' she snapped.

'And the top of the morning to you, too, Mrs Wheeler,' he replied, doffing his cap.

Violet scowled. 'I said, what are you doing — '

'My dad's delivering some furniture and helping me shift a few pieces around,' said Cathy as she stepped out on to the street.

Although it was one of her days at the rest centre, she wasn't dressed in her WVS uniform. Instead, she was wearing an old dress with a wraparound apron over it and her hair was pinned up beneath a scarf turban.

'Furniture?' asked Violet. 'What furniture?'

Curling his fingers in his mouth, Cathy's father let out a two-tone whistle and his two boys hurried out. The bastards, thought Violet, a sneer twisting her lips.

'Give us a hand with this, Michael,' Jeremiah said, heaving a washstand from the back of his van. 'And, Billy, you bring the bowl and jug.'

Lifting the painted wooden frame between them, Jeremiah and Michael carried it into the house while Billy, flowery china bowl under one arm and matching pitcher in the other hand, followed them in.

Violet watched them trudge their boots into her house then her attention returned to Cathy.

Folding her arms, a hint of amusement flitted across her daughter-in-law's face.

'I gave you a chance to pay your fair share,' said Cathy. 'But as you won't, I'm taking in a lodger to keep a roof over our heads and food on the table.'

'You're doing what?' asked Violet, thinking she couldn't possibly have heard right.

'Mind your back.'

Glaring at Cathy, Violet stepped back as Cathy's father strode out of the house carrying Peter's old crib on his shoulders.

'I'm taking in a lodger,' Cathy repeated, as her father marched back in the house. 'I'm putting them in the downstairs front parlour. That no one goes into from one year to the next.'

'You can't,' said Violet, itching to smack her hand across her daughter-in-law's smug face. 'And what about my furniture?'

'I've moved it into other rooms, that's all,' Cathy replied.

'That's all?' screeched Violet, as her temples pounded. 'That's all, you say. You've moved all my expensive furniture out of my best room so a stranger can move in and you say that's all.'

Cathy gave her a mocking look then turned and went back into the house.

Violet followed her.

After almost being knocked sideways by Cathy's scruffy brother as he tore past her, Violet found her daughter-in-law making tea in the kitchen.

'Where's Stanley?' Violet asked.

'Peter's at my mum's,' Cathy replied, turning her back on Violet as the kettle on the gas started to whistle .

Violet stared at the point between Cathy's shoulder blades and imagined plunging her best carving knife between them.

'I don't suppose you're interested, but a letter from

174

Stanley's commanding officer arrived this morning,' she said.

'I guessed as much when I found an empty envelope addressed to me in the dustbin,' Cathy replied, as she poured out three mugs of tea.

'Well, do you want to know what it said?' asked Violet.

Picking up the tea, Cathy gave her a sweet smile.

'Not really,' she replied as she swept out of the room.

'It said Stanley's a hero . . . ' Violet shouted after her.

Without breaking her stride, Cathy walked through the front door.

With her lips pulled into an almost invisible line and with her fists clenched, Violet glared down the hall after her hateful daughter-in-law.

Having given her father and brothers their hot drinks, Cathy returned. Striding past Violet again, she went to the pantry and pulled out the old one-handled shopping bag where she kept the potatoes. Plonking it on the draining board, she took a pot from the rack and, after filling it with cold water, placed it alongside.

Violet unclipped her handbag and extracted her son's letter.

'It says Stanley is a hero.' She flourished the sheet of paper at Cathy. 'Do you hear? A hero.'

Selecting a knobbly spud, Cathy picked up the kitchen knife and started peeling the brown skin.

'He sacrificed himself,' Violet continued, 'to save hundreds of soldiers' lives.'

Cathy cut the potato into quarters and dropped them into the pot.

'And on top of that, he's going to be given a medal.

The King's Bravery Medal.'

Pausing in her task, Cathy stretched out and turned on the wireless on the window sill.

'The King's Bravery Medal,' shouted Violet above Edmundo Ross and his orchestra. 'Do you hear? My Stanley is a hero — '

'Hero!' Cathy swung around. 'You don't have to tell me what kind of man your precious Stanley is, Vi, because I know, believe me, I know,' she said, pointing at her with the vegetable knife. 'He's a Nazi lover, who terrorised our Jewish neighbours by putting dog shit through their letter boxes, smashing up their shops and setting fire to their homes. So you can tell all your cronies at the Mothers' Union what a bloody wonderful hero Stan is, but remember I — and plenty of other people — know different.'

'You mean your poxy sister and her husband, who made up lies about Stanley,' snapped Violet.

'Yes, my dearest sister Mattie and her husband, both of whom nearly died stopping your Stanley and his chums landing Nazi spies in London docks.'

A claw of fear gripped Violet's chest at the memory of the police officers standing on her doorstep, informing her that Stanley had been arrested for treason.

'So, remember, Vi,' Cathy's voice continued from what seemed like a long way away, 'your Stanley was lucky he was paroled into the army for his crimes and not left to swing at the end of a rope.'

★ ★ ★

Waiting for a number 254 heading for Hackney to pass and careful to avoid getting the pushchair's wheels caught in the tramlines, Cathy crossed Whitechapel Road.

'Grangrad,' said Peter, pointing a mitten enclosed finger at a couple of auxiliary firemen standing by their red-painted fire wagon in front of the Blind Beggar to the right of them.

'That's right, Granddad's a fireman,' said Cathy, smiling at her son, who was wrapped up like a knitted parcel against the icy wind.

'Aunnie Fran,' said Peter, pointing at the steamed-up windows of Alf's Café on the corner of Brady Street.

'That's right,' said Cathy. 'You can tell Auntie Fran and Patrick all about the firemen when we get there.'

Peter nodded.

Not wanting to navigate the pushchair between the tables crowded with ARP personnel and shoppers eating their midday meal, Cathy continued past the café's main entrance to the side door which led to the living quarters at the rear.

Stopping in front of it, Cathy knocked, then, pulling on the handle, pushed it open.

'Only me,' she shouted through the blackout curtain, which had been pulled across the doorway to stop the draught getting in rather than the light getting out.

'We're in here,' her sister-in-law Francesca shouted back.

Manoeuvring the front wheels through the door, Cathy parked the pushchair in the square hallway. Lifting Peter out, she unwrapped him and set him on his feet. Knowing where he was, her son trotted off in search of his two-and-a-half-year-old cousin.

Taking off her coat, Cathy followed him into the parlour behind the shop.

Like her family home in Mafeking Terrace, Francesca's living room had a cast-iron fireplace with an over-mantel mirror above. There was an old-fashioned one-armed sofa against the wall with a tartan blanket draped over it, two chairs either side of the fireplace and a fringed circular rug covered the terracotta tiles. An ornately inlaid wooden cabinet under the window displayed half a dozen sepia photos of men and women dressed in their village costumes and standing against painted mountainous backgrounds.

Pride of place among the old photos was the tinted portrait of Francesca's late mother, Rosa, her rosary draped over one corner of the gilt frame.

Standing alongside the old photos was one of Francesca's brother Giovanni, in his Pioneer Corps attire, but the one that caught her eye was the photo of Cathy's brother Charlie in his Bombardier uniform, holding Patrick in one arm and Francesca in the other. Both were smiling and had love and happiness shining out of their eyes. It had been taken after their wedding, during the one day they'd had as a married couple before Charlie shipped out last June. One day and one very productive night, thought Cathy with a wry smile as she looked at her heavily pregnant sister-inlaw, who was tying a bib around her son. Francesca looked up as Cathy walked in.

'Just in time for dinner,' she said, lifting Patrick into his highchair.

'It's all right, we'll get something when we get to the rest centre,' said Cathy.

'You won't,' said Francesca. 'Not if I don't want your gran after me for letting you go hungry. It's beef stew.'

Cathy laughed. 'How can I say no?'

'You can't,' Francesca replied. 'There's a clean bib on the fireguard for Peter if you need it,' she called over her shoulder as she headed through the beaded curtain to the café.

Cathy took a couple of cushions from the sofa and piled them up on a chair. She covered them with a towel from the drying rack, plonked Peter on top and tucked him under the table opposite his cousin. She was just tying his bib on when Francesca returned carrying a tray loaded with four bowls and a plate of buttered bread.

Resting the tray on the table, she removed the two smaller bowls and placed them in front of the two toddlers.

'There we are, boys,' she said, handing them each a teaspoon. 'And try not to get it in your hair.'

Cathy laughed and took her bowl. 'How are your dad and brother?'

Between mouthfuls of dinner, Francesca gave Cathy a rundown of how busy the café was, how her dad doted on Patrick and how, thankfully, after almost a year building something for the army in the Outer Hebrides, her brother Giovanni had been transferred to Cambridge to build an airbase for the Americans.

'This is delicious,' Cathy said, scooping another portion of her stew on to her fork.

'Papa's wholesale butcher had a consignment of beef arrive from Canada a few days ago,' Francesca explained. 'So I guess every restaurant north of the Thames will be serving beef this week. Queenie brought Dad half a dozen eggs around the other day, so I put a couple of pounds of shin in the café fridge to take to your mum on my way back from seeing the midwives at Munroe House tomorrow.'

Jabbing a square of meat on to her fork, Cathy offered it to Peter. 'Everything all right?'

'Textbook stuff, according to the nurse I saw last week,' said Francesca, spearing a chunk of carrot. 'I had a letter from Charlie yesterday telling me yet again to put my feet up every afternoon and get a good night's sleep.'

Cathy raised her eyebrow. 'He's never had to look after a toddler all day, has he?'

Francesca smiled.

'No,' she said, guiding Patrick's spoon into his mouth. 'But I appreciate that he's worried about me.'

'I bet he said lots of other things, too,' said Cathy.

'Yes, he did.' Francesca gave her an innocent look. 'But nothing I'm going to repeat to his sister.'

Cathy laughed.

'I see you've taken Gran at her word,' she said, indicating the pink wool on her sister-in-law's knitting needles.

'Yes, I have,' said Francesca. Placing her hand on her bump, she looked down. 'I don't mind one way or the other but if Queenie says I'm carrying a girl, that's good enough for me. How did it go on Tuesday with your dad and the boys?'

'As you'd expect,' Cathy replied.

Francesca pulled a face. 'I'm sorry.'

Cathy swallowed another mouthful of her stew and shrugged.

'I've long stopped worrying about what my mother-in-law has to say about anything,' said Cathy, 'and what she says about me behind my back. Or to my face, for that matter. Now I've cleaned the front room from top to bottom, given the rug a good old beating in the yard and arranged the furniture in its place, I'm

180

ready to advertise the room.'

'Do you want me to put a card up in the café?' asked Francesca.

'Would you?' said Cathy.

Taking the spoon from her son, Francesca scraped the last of his meal on to it.

'Of course,' she said, popping it in Patrick's mouth. 'Are you doing full board?'

'I might if it's a mother with children, otherwise I thought just bed and breakfast,' Cathy replied.

'That's sensible,' Francesca said, tearing off a piece of bread and handing it to Patrick. 'After all, you don't want to have some stranger sitting at your kitchen table when you're having your evening meal.'

'No,' said Cathy. 'I'll point them in the direction of the British Restaurant at Redcoat School or the WVS canteen at the rest centre.'

'Then just put 'terms negotiable' on the postcard,' said Francesca.

'Good idea,' said Cathy, wiping Peter's face with the bib and letting him wriggle off the chair on to the floor. 'I'll let you have it on Sunday at church. Also' — she gave her sister-in-law an entreating smile — 'would you mind having Peter for a couple of mornings because . . . ' As her sister-in-law cleaned the gravy off her son's mouth, Cathy told her how her father was struggling with the paperwork. 'It's just until Mum can leave Victoria with Gran for a few hours.'

'I'd be glad to,' said Francesca, lifting Patrick out of the highchair and setting him on his feet. 'It'll give Patrick someone to play with.'

'Fight with, don't you mean?' said Cathy, looking across at the two toddlers as they started a tug of war with a rag doll.

Francesca sighed. 'Well, boys will be boys, I suppose.' She stood up. 'Tea?'

Cathy glanced at the clock on the mantelshelf and then placed her knife and fork together in her bowl.

She smiled. 'Need you ask?'

12

'Right, Chalky and Fred take the strain then winch the wee bugger up, gentle like,' shouted Archie, his eyes fixed on the bomb dangling from the gibbet on the back of D Squad's Austin.

It was the first Monday in January, just before four in the afternoon, and he and his six-strong team were in the middle of Hackney Marshes.

Defusing the bombs was all well and good, but of course that did leave Bomb Disposal with the problem of disposing of tons of high explosives. Sometimes they were able to do this on the spot by steaming the TNT into a non-explosive emulsion. However, Hexanite was much more volatile and had to be scooped out by hand, which wasn't particularly easy at the bottom of a fifty-foot pit. During the Blitz, when there were more bombs dropped in a night than the fledgling BDUs could deal with in a month, the Ministry of Defence had taken over open spaces within the capital. Hackney Marshes and Richmond Park were the largest, which is why Archie and the squad were having their balls frozen off by an icy wind that cut like an open razor across the wide expanse of the heathland.

Although 1943 was not yet a week old, thanks to the Bolsheviks pissing off Hitler by annihilating the best part of his Sixth Army in Russia and Monty forcing Rommel's Afrika Korps to jump in their boats and skedaddle back to Germany, the Führer had turned his attention back to London.

The wee bugger on the back of the lorry was, in fact, a 1,000-kilogram Hermann, which D squad had spent the past few days digging out.

It had fallen to earth during the seven-hour air raid on Saturday night and had landed just fifty yards from the main telephone exchange in Ilford. They'd finally uncovered it early that morning and had rung through to Wanstead to inform HQ the bomb was exposed and had been defused.

The German's armament factories were obviously having a New Year sale of old stock, as it was a straightforward number 17 fuse — Archie had been making them safe for the past two and a half years. To be honest, although King's regs stated only officers could defuse bombs, during the height of the Blitz he'd defused dozens, as had many other NCOs. They'd had to, firstly because there weren't enough officers to start with, and secondly because if they hadn't, they'd never clear one night's tally of bombs before the next lot were dropped. Although the regulations still stood, given that NCOs like Archie often had more experience than fresh-faced officers, the top brass turned a blind eye to it.

'Easy now, easy,' Archie said, as the block and tackle creaked under the weight of the explosive.

The cigar-shaped metal case inched higher.

'Easy,' Archie repeated. 'And put that bloody fag out, Mogg, before I put you on a charge! The fuse might have gone but there's still a thousand kilograms of TNT in that thing.'

The Welshman pinched out his roll-up and shoved it behind his ear.

Archie gave him a hard look then turned his attention back to the bomb, which was swaying a little as it

184

was hoisted higher.

'Right, that'll do it,' shouted Archie as the bottom of the case cleared the top of the truck sides. 'Swing it over and on to the trolley.'

The men manoeuvred the bomb on to the six-wheeled trolley beside the truck.

Archie looked at his watch. 'We won't have time to burn it out before the blackout starts so once we've dropped it off, you bunch of wee jessies can clear off.'

In the gathering January gloom there was a flash of white teeth as the squad realised they were dismissed for the day. Knowing the drill, the team quickly secured the bomb and then, stationing themselves on either side of the long handle at the front of the trolley, like a team of prize drays, they raced across to the safety area at the far side of the wasteland.

Archie watched them for a couple of seconds, then, satisfied that everything was in order, he turned his collar up, shoved his hands in his pockets, then trotted across to the guardhouse at the bomb graveyard's entrance.

Although you wouldn't think anyone in their right mind would want to go anywhere near thousands of tons of high explosive, after a couple of incidents with local villains helping themselves to the TNT left in defused bombs, the army had instigated hourly patrols.

Having signed for the bomb's delivery, Archie told the lance corporal and squaddie huddled over a paraffin heater in the guardhouse that he and the rest of the squad would be back in the morning to burn out the bomb. Retrieving his sheepskin jerkin from the store, he slipped it on, then, unchaining his bike, he shoved on his gloves, kicked the Triumph into life and

185

rode off.

What was left of the January sunlight was all but gone by the time Archie turned right at the bottom of Cambridge Heath Road.

Slowing down to let a mother with a bevy of children around her cross the road, Archie spied a café at the corner. His stomach rumbled, reminding him that it was almost five hours since he'd last eaten. Although the blackout blinds were down, as a couple of ARP wardens opened the door, Archie saw the inviting glow within. Waiting until there was a gap in the oncoming traffic, he turned into the side alleyway next to the café.

Having secured his bike to a lamp-post, he rubbed his hands together to restore the circulation and strolled around to the front. The bell over the door tinkled as Archie pushed it open and stepped into the warm fug. The unmistakable smell of home cooking made his mouth water.

As it was early evening the place was packed to the brim. People in various shades of navy and khaki, with the odd splash of airforce blue, were tucking into their meals before going on duty. There were also a couple of women in the forest-green uniform of the WVS, which instantly made him think of Cathy.

That, of course, was a complete lie. He didn't need anything to remind him of her because, in truth, apart from Kirsty, he thought of little else.

A few people looked up as he strolled in, the usual look of surprise on their faces, but their interest didn't linger and they returned to their meals.

Loosening his jerkin, Archie wandered across to the counter where a middle-aged man and a very pregnant dark-haired woman were serving. Spotting him waiting, she waddled over.

'Evening,' she said, giving him a friendly smile. 'You look like you could do with something hot and wet.'

'Aye, I most certainly could,' Archie replied. 'Tea, please, in the largest mug you have.'

'Coming up,' she said.

While she poured his drink, Archie studied the menu chalked on the blackboard fixed to the wall.

'Can I get you anything else?' she asked, placing a huge china mug in front of him.

'I wouldnae say no to a bowl of yon beef stew,' he replied.

She smiled again. 'Find yourself a seat and I'll bring it over.'

She shouted his order through the hatch then went to serve another customer. Picking up his mug, Archie turned and spotted a couple of auxiliary firemen getting up from a table at the back. He made his way over to the small table and sat down.

Slipping off his gloves and shoving them in his pocket, Archie hung his jerkin over the back of the chair. Cradling the mug, he pressed his icy hands around it, the heat bringing the blood painfully back to his fingers.

As he thawed, Archie glanced around and spotted a couple of paintings hanging on the wall behind the counter.

The pregnant young woman, carrying a tray with a steaming bowl and a plate of thickly cut bread and butter, squeezed her way between the tables to where he was sitting.

'One large portion of beef stew,' she said, placing it in front of him.

'Grand,' he said, as the meaty aroma wafted up. 'I

see you have a painter in the family.' He indicated the landscapes.

'My brother,' she replied. 'They are of the place in Italy where Papa and Mama's families are from. We've never been there but Giovanni painted them from a photo my mother brought with her to England.'

'They're very good,' he said.

'We think so.' She smiled. 'Although he's a bit fed up at the moment as he doesn't get much time to paint.'

'I know how he feels,' said Archie.

She looked surprised. 'You're an artist?'

He laughed. 'That's egging it a wee bit, but I dabble with the brushes. Mostly scenes of the bombing and the men in my squad up to their ears in mud at the moment. But portraits are what I really enjoy. Using light and shade to show the personality of the sitter.'

'I suppose you're too busy to get your brushes out,' she said.

'Aye, true enough, the Luftwaffe keeps me on my toes,' Archie replied. 'But my digs were bombed out the day before Christmas Eve and I've billeted with the team ever since. They're good lads, right enough, but . . . ' He gave her a wry smile. 'Let's just say my easel wouldn't stand a chance amongst a dozen squaddies.'

'Enjoy your meal,' she laughed.

She left and Archie tucked into his meal.

He was just scraping the last gravy from the bottom of the bowl when the young woman waddled towards him again with another steaming bowl in one hand and a mug in the other.

'Treacle pudding and custard,' she said, placing them both before him. She pointed at the embroidered badge of an inverted bomb on his uniform. 'On

188

the house.'

'That's very kind,' he said.

'It's just a small thank-you from all of us,' she replied.

She turned to leave him again when a young boy of about two dashed out from behind the counter and ran between the tables towards her.

He stopped next to his mother and stared at Archie.

'Hello, soldier,' Archie said, giving the toddler a friendly smile.

Hugging his mother's legs, the little lad continued to stare.

'Patrick,' said his mother, placing her hand on his curly black hair. 'Say hello.'

Patrick said nothing.

Colour flushed the woman's cheeks. 'I'm sorry.'

'Don't worry,' Archie replied. 'Lots of people are lost for words when they see my handsome face.' Turning in his chair, Archie bent forward and offered the boy his hand. 'Pleased to meet you, Patrick. I'm Archie.'

'Archie's a brave soldier just like your daddy, Patrick,' the young woman said.

The boy studied him for a moment or two then grabbed Archie's fingers.

'Pleased to meet you, Patrick,' Archie repeated. 'I've got a little girl a bit older than you back home.'

Patrick nodded then saluted.

Straightening up in his seat, Archie saluted back.

Patrick studied him for another moment or two then dashed back behind the counter.

'Your boy's a canny little lad,' Archie said, picking up the spoon.

'You're very good with children,' she said.

'Aye, I suppose I am, now you mention it,' Archie replied. 'But to my way of thinking they're who I'm fighting this bloody war for. It's their lives and futures that I have in mind when I'm lying with ma head inches from a five-hundred-kilo bomb, not Churchill.'

A thoughtful expression settled on the young woman's face. She studied him for a moment then she smiled.

'Enjoy your pudding,' she said and walked away again.

Archie made short work of the dessert and then slurped down the last of his tea. He stood up and, after donning his jacket again, took the empty bowl and mug back to the counter where the young mother was tidying away.

'Just like me ma makes,' he said, smiling at her as he placed the crockery on the marble surface. 'How much do I owe you?'

'One and three,' she replied.

Rummaging in his trouser pocket, Archie pulled out a handful of coins and handed over a shilling and six pence.

She gave him a silver thruppeny piece, which he dropped into the jar with a picture of a tank on it that stood next to the till on the counter.

'Thanks again,' he said, turning to go.

'Sergeant,' she called after him as he reached the door.

He turned back and she beckoned him back to the counter.

'Just a moment.' She waddled off into the back of the shop but returned almost immediately holding a postcard in her hand.

'My sister-in-law is looking for a lodger,' she said,

turning the card over in her hand. 'It's a clean house and just a stone's throw from here in Senrab Street, number twenty-four. She only gave me the card on Sunday, and I haven't had time to pin it up in the window . . . ' She glanced at the clock. 'If you're quick you could catch her before she leaves for the shelter.'

She offered him the card and Archie took it and put it in his pocket.

'Thanks,' he said. 'That's very kind of you.'

'I'm not promising, mind,' said the young woman. 'She's got a little boy too, so I know she was thinking of perhaps taking in a mother with children rather than a single man, but,' she smiled, 'as you're bomb disposal she might, well, take pity on you and your easel.'

'Senrab Street, is it?' he said, buttoning his jerkin.

'Straight down Sidney Street, opposite,' she said, indicating with her hand. 'Then left into Oxford Street and I think it's the third or fourth on the right; but there's a pub called the Clare Hall right opposite so you shouldn't miss it.'

'Much obliged, Mrs . . . ?'

'Brogan,' she said.

Archie touched his forehead, then shoving his hands into his gloves and setting the bell above the door ringing again, he strode out of the café.

★ ★ ★

'And the spitfire swoops down and . . . ' Cathy moved the potato-laden spoon around in an arch before offering it to Peter.

Peter laughed and opened his mouth.

'Back to the airfield,' Cathy added, popping another

191

portion of his evening meal between his cherub lips.

He swallowed it down.

'Good boy.' She loaded the spoon again. 'And now it's the Lancaster's turn to — '

The door opened and Violet, in her dressing gown, with her head full of curlers and a hot-water bottle under her arm, walked in.

The old woman's gaze flickered from Cathy to Peter and then back again.

'He should be feeding himself by now,' she said.

Cathy gave her son a bright smile as she wheeled the spoon in the air again. 'Circle around and land back home — '

'Stanley was feeding himself at that age and' — she glanced at the half a dozen nappies drying on the rack over the cooker — 'he was potty trained.'

'To the air base,' Cathy continued, holding the spoon out for her son again.

'You're making a mummy's boy of him,' continued the old woman.

Ignoring her, Cathy scraped up the last mouthful of the liver and potato casserole.

'And here's the last plane flying home safe and sound,' she said, as Peter gulped down the last morsel.

'I said — '

'You don't have to repeat yourself, Vi,' Cathy cut in. 'I heard you this time and every other time you've said the same thing.'

'Well, you are,' her mother-in-law added. 'From the time he could walk, I used to smack Stanley on the back of his legs every time he wet himself and he soon learned.'

'I bet he did,' said Cathy. 'And I bet you plastered his thumbs in mustard to stop him sucking them, too.'

192

'It's better than having a kid with buck teeth, isn't it?' said Violet.

Cathy ignored her and turned her attention back to her son.

'Say goodnight to Grandma,' she said, wiping his mouth with the end of the tea towel around his neck.

Peter gave Violet a little wave then looked back at his mother.

'Nanny and boys?' he asked.

'In a while.' Cathy lifted him down and set him on the floor. 'Go and fetch Mr Bruno while I clear away.'

Peter toddled off.

Cathy watched him for a moment then looked back at her mother-in-law.

'Don't let me keep you, Vi,' she said, giving the hateful old woman a syrupy smile.

Her curlers shaking with rage, Violet glared at her for a long moment, then with the pompoms on her tartan slippers bobbing, she stomped out of the back door, slamming it hard behind her.

Picking up the dirty crockery, Cathy placed it in the sink but as she reached out to turn on the tap, there was a knock on the front door.

Wondering if she'd perhaps left a light showing, she dried her hands and walked down the hallway. Throwing back the latch, she opened the door.

'I'm sorry about the — ' Cathy's eyes flew open. 'Sergeant McIntosh!'

'Mrs Wheeler!'

They stared wordlessly at each other for several moments as Cathy's heart thumped wildly in her chest.

'What are you doing here?' she asked.

Archie delved under the sheepskin jerkin and pulled out the postcard.

'I've come about the room,' he replied. 'Your sister-in-law in the café on Whitechapel High Street said you were looking for a lodger.'

'I am,' she replied as she studied his mouth.

'She thought that although you were looking to take in a family, you might consider me,' he continued, cutting across her speculation.

He gave her that quirky smile of his and Cathy's heart raced off again.

'Yes.' She blinked and scraped her scattered words together. 'Yes. I would. Consider you, that is.' She smiled. 'Why don't you come in?'

She opened the door and he strolled in, bringing the faintest hint of male aroma with him.

Cathy shut the door then turned to find herself staring at Archie's blunt and slightly stubbly chin. She raised her eyes and found his unbelievable blue eyes gazing down at her.

Turning away, she grabbed the door handle to the front room.

'This is the room,' she said, pushing the door open.

Archie walked in. Cathy followed and stopped by the bedside table.

He was standing on the other side of the bed with his back to her, his legs slightly apart and his hands on his hips. Before she could stop them, Cathy's eyes roamed across the breadth of his shoulders then down to his neat rear.

'All the furniture is new, as are the curtains,' she said, in a tight voice as her gaze moved on to his long legs, snugly encased in his khaki battle trousers.

Dragging her eyes away, she took a step forward.

'Well,' she said, straightening out a wrinkle on the patchwork bedspread, 'what do you think?'

Having tried and failed to get his pounding heart in check while studying the plaster architrave, Archie turned and smiled.

'It's a good size,' he said, acutely aware of the large double bed between them.

'Yes,' she replied, gazing across at him.

Archie looked at the window to stop the image of taking her in his arms and pressing his lips on to hers forming in his mind.

'And it's west facing.'

'The room keeps the light right through until ten o'clock in the evening during the summer,' Cathy added. 'So it's perfect for your painting.'

'It is.' Archie frowned. 'Sorry, I should have asked if you minded rather than just — '

'No.' Her gaze flickered on to the bed for a split second. 'I don't mind.'

They stared at each other across the multicoloured counterpane for what seemed like an eternity, then the door burst open.

'Bruno!' shouted Peter, dashing into the room clutching a well-loved brown teddy to his chest.

He saw Archie and stopped in his tracks.

Archie hunkered down. 'Hello again, young man. Who's that you've got there?'

'Bruno,' he announced, flourishing his toy bear at Archie and, in words understandable only to himself, Peter told him all about his teddy.

'Is that a fact?' said Archie when the lad had finished.

Cathy laughed.

'It's a bit chilly in here; would you like to have a

cuppa in the kitchen while we discuss things,' she said.

'I'd love one but only if I'm not putting you out, Mrs Wheeler,' he replied.

She smiled.

'Shall we make Sergeant McIntosh a cuppa, Peter?' she asked her son, stroking his sandy-coloured hair gently.

The lad nodded and trotted off towards the kitchen. Cathy moved to the door.

'It's just down the end of the hall,' she said.

Walking around the edge of the bed, he followed the boy out and Cathy closed the door behind them.

Although the temperature in the street was hovering just above freezing, the kitchen at the back of the house still retained the homely warmth and smell of the evening's cooking.

'Excuse the mess,' she said, indicating a couple of dirty plates in the sink as she filled the kettle.

Pulling out a chair, Archie sat down at the table and studied her womanly curves as she made the tea.

'It's five shillings a week in advance for bed and breakfast,' said Cathy, as she placed a mug in front of him then took the chair opposite. 'But for an extra three I'd be happy to do your laundry and have a hot dinner ready for you each night, as long as you can either bring your rations from your billet or let me have your ration book.'

Archie took a sip of his tea.

'A home-cooked meal at the end of the day instead of army canteen food sounds bonny,' said Archie, already looking forward to gazing across the kitchen table at her each night.

'And I know it was a little cold in there just now,' she continued, 'but as long as I've got the coal, I'll set

196

a small fire in there each night before you get back to take the chill off. And there's a lot of light-fingered tea leaves around here so if you want to make sure your petrol doesn't evaporate overnight, I'd park your bike in the backyard if I were you.'

'Thanks,' said Archie.

As he drank his tea Cathy told him she would give him a key so he could come and go as he pleased. Gas supplies permitting, he could have hot water for a drink or the washbowl in his room whenever he liked but he could also use the kitchen sink for a strip wash if he needed to.

'And,' she concluded, 'as long as you don't burn the house down, feel free to make yourself a slice or two of toast or something if you're a bit peckish.'

Archie laughed. 'I promise the house will still be standing when you get back home from the shelter each morning. I'm afraid King's regs mean that I have to tell HQ where I live so it is possible that there might be a copper banging on your front door in the middle of the night if top brass have a flap about something, just in case your neighbours start wondering what's happening.'

'I'll bear that in mind,' she said. 'When would you like to move in?'

'As soon as possible,' Archie replied.

'Would next Monday morning be all right?' she asked. 'It will give me time to get the room organised.'

'I'll speak to the duty officer and make sure I'm not rostered on duty until the afternoon,' Archie replied, still not quite believing what was actually happening.

Cathy took a sip of tea. 'Did you have a nice time at home at Christmas?'

'Aye, I did,' he replied. 'What about you?'

'Quiet,' she replied. 'Peter and I, we went to Mum's on Christmas Day and then round to my sister Mattie for Boxing Day. Did Kirsty like her present?'

'She loved it and wouldn't take it off,' he replied, pleased she'd remembered his daughter's name.

'I bet she loved having you home more,' she said.

'Not as much as I did seeing her,' said Archie. 'She'd sprouted up a good two inches, too.'

Cathy laughed. 'They grow up so quickly.'

'They certainly do.' Archie swallowed the last mouthful of tea. 'But now, Mrs Wheeler, I've taken up too much of your time and I must let you get to the shelter.'

Putting down his empty mug, he stood up and Cathy did the same.

'It's all right, you stay in the warm, I'll see myself out,' he said.

'It's no trouble,' she replied.

She headed off down the hall towards the front of the house with Archie, buttoning up his jerkin, following on behind.

'There is just one other thing, Sergeant,' Cathy said, as she put her hand on the front door latch. 'My mother-in-law, Violet, lives here with me and Peter. And well . . . the truth is, she's set in her ways so wasn't keen on taking a lodger. It might take her a bit of time to get used to having you here, especially with her son still missing in action.'

Archie nodded. 'I understand.'

He smiled, and Cathy opened the door.

He walked past her and stepped out on to the pavement.

'Until next Monday then,' he said, pulling his gloves from his pocket and shoving his fingers into them.

'Yes,' she said, giving that dazzling smile of hers. 'Until next Monday.'

They stared at each other for another moment then Archie walked to his bike. He rocked it off its stand, swung his leg over and kicked down on the starter pedal. Thankfully, despite the cold, his Triumph fired immediately.

Giving it a quick rev to clear the carburettor, Archie pulled on the clutch and nudged it into gear with his left toe.

He relaxed his grip on the clutch, but before the cogs bit together, Archie turned his head and saw that Cathy, now with Peter in her arms, was still standing on the doorstep.

He gave her a little wave and she waved in reply.

Archie turned back.

So, he's *her son*, is he, Cathy, and not your husband? thought Archie.

As his Tiger sped away, a smile spread wide across his face.

★ ★ ★

Carefully picking her way between the families already bedded down for the night in the shelter, Cathy guided Peter towards the family's three-tier bunk.

Her mother, who was sitting on the bottom bunk and balancing Victoria on her knee as she changed her nappy, looked up as Cathy approached.

'You're late, luv,' she said, through the safety pin clenched between her teeth.

'I was held up,' said Cathy, placing her basket on the floor.

Sitting on the bunk alongside her mother, Cathy

delved into her basket and pulled out Peter's nappy and fleecy pyjamas.

The ground around them shook as a bomb landed close by, sending a whoosh of air through the railway tunnel and causing the lights hanging overhead to dance wildly on their flexes. Babies and small children started crying as those sheltering in the arched dome of the underground station were showered with grit from above.

'And just in time,' her mother added.

'Bedtime, Peter,' said Cathy.

'Noooo,' he whined as she grabbed him. 'Mical and Bibby.'

'The boys are doing their homework,' Cathy said, as, sobbing, Peter tried to escape her grip. 'See them in the morning. Come on, Mr Bruno is very tired.'

Peter threw his teddy on the floor.

'Poor Mr Bruno,' said Ida. Pulling a sad face, she picked up the toy.

Peter stretched his hands towards her. 'Mine.'

'Only if you do what your mummy says,' Ida replied.

Peter stuck out his bottom lip but didn't fight as Cathy put on a double nappy to see him through the night and slipped him into his pyjamas. Wrapping him back in his coat, she sat him between her and her mother and then pulled out the smaller of the two flasks. Removing the Bakelite beaker, she popped off the cork then poured the warm milk into the cup and handed it to her son.

Taking the copy of *Noddy Goes on Holiday* that Mattie had bought him for Christmas out of the basket, Cathy opened it. As her son drank his nightcap, Cathy read a chapter to him while at the other end of the bunk bed her mother swaddled Victoria in knitted blankets and tucked her at the foot of the bottom bunk. Taking a rubber dummy from her pocket, Ida stuck it in her mouth for a couple of seconds then popped it into the baby's.

'Right, time for night nights, Peter,' Cathy said, when she reached the end of the chapter. 'Give Nanny a kiss.'

Her son handed back his cup. Going to his grandmother he puckered up ready. Ida gave him a kiss and handed him his ransomed toy.

'SargTosh,' he said, holding it up for her to see.

Cathy's mother gave her a questioning look and Cathy felt her cheeks grow warm.

'Come on, Peter, into bed,' she said, making a play of popping the cork back on the flask.

Standing up, she quickly removed his coat then hoisted him up and tucked him into his place at the foot of the single top bunk they shared.

Stretching up, she kissed his forehead. Holding Mr Bruno tight, her son snuggled under the covers and closed his eyes.

She watched him for a moment or two, then, feeling her mother's eyes on her, she turned around.

'SargTosh?' said Ida, as Cathy sat back on the bunk.

'Sergeant McIntosh — Archie. My new lodger,' she replied.

Another bomb came crashing down close by and the light fixed to the ceiling high above them went out. People screamed and shouted for help in the dark and someone along the way from them started praying for deliverance. The generator situated in the westbound tunnel started to hum and a yellow glow illuminated the shelter.

'Fancy a cocoa, Mum?' Cathy asked, as people

201

started to settle down again.

'I could murder for one,' Ida replied.

Having queued for ten minutes at the WVS canteen for their drinks, by the time Cathy returned, her two brothers were already top and tailed in the middle bunk. Billy reading a *Beano* at one end and Michael engrossed in a *Hotspur* at the other.

Her mother, who had retrieved the two deckchairs from under the bunk, was sitting beside it, knitting. Placing Ida's cocoa on the floor next to her, Cathy sat down in the other faded candy-striped chair.

Bombs still landed with monotonous regularity around them, rattling the ironwork in the shelter, but they seemed a little further away now as the waves of enemy aircraft targeted other neighbourhoods.

The faint sound of the BBC's nine o'clock pips heralded the Home Service's hourly news bulletin and Ida told the boys to go to sleep as people the length of the platform began to settle for the night.

Someone further down the platform started playing 'We'll Meet Again' on a harmonica and a few people joined in, their voices harmonising in the cavernous shelter.

Pulling her cloth knitting bag from the basket, Cathy took out the jumper she was making for Peter.

'Archie's a bit familiar for someone you've just met,' her mother said as Cathy started the first row.

'He's actually Sergeant McIntosh of the Royal Engineers,' she replied, slipping the stitch. 'He's in charge of a bomb retrieval and disposal squad and I haven't just met him, Mum, we met on the Sunday the bells rang for El-Alamein. Peter ran out of the church and Sergeant McIntosh stopped him ending up under a bus.'

'That was months ago,' said Ida. 'I'm surprised you remember his name.'

'Well, oddly, and just by coincidence, he popped into the rest centre for his midday meal a week or so later, and again at the Christmas Party, where Peter met him,' Cathy explained.

Her mother raised her eyebrow.

'Mum!'

'I didn't say anything,' Ida said.

'You don't need to. I know what you're thinking,' said Cathy.

Swapping her needles over, Ida looked down at her work. 'I thought it was only your gran who could read minds.' She raised her eyes. 'And . . . ?'

'Well, I have run into him at the evening institute once or twice,' said Cathy. 'And I did have a cup of tea with him at the children's Christmas party, but other than that, I hardly know him.'

'So how come he's your lodger?' asked Ida.

Cathy told her mother about the postcard she'd given to Francesca.

'So, what's he like this Sergeant McIntosh?' asked Ida.

'He's from Scotland, Glasgow, in fact,' said Cathy. 'I think he's probably about Charlie's age and he was married but his wife died in a tram accident five years ago, leaving him with a two-year-old daughter called Kirsty. She lives with his mother. And he paints.' She laughed. 'Portraits not walls.'

'You're right, Cathy,' said Ida, 'I can tell you hardly know the man at all.'

'Mum!'

Cathy gave her a hard look, which bounced right off Ida.

203

'Anything else?' she asked.

'Well, he's tall,' said Cathy, as the image of Archie standing on her doorstep materialised in her mind. 'Well-built but not beefy and . . . and he has the most startling blue eyes you've ever seen. Real sapphire blue they are, which is really surprising because . . . '

'Because?' asked her mother.

'Because Sergeant McIntosh is obviously either half African or half West Indian,' said Cathy. 'I didn't want to be rude and ask him which.'

'I should think not,' said Ida.

'Not that it matters,' said Cathy.

'Of course it doesn't.' Ida's eyebrow rose again. 'But does your mother-in-law know Sergeant McIntosh is moving in?'

'Not yet,' Cathy replied.

An amused expression spread across Ida's face. 'I'd like to be a fly on the wall when she finds out.'

'Well, if she and Stan hadn't worked a fast one with his savings then I wouldn't have even considered having a lodger, but now, as far as I'm concerned, she can like it or lump it,' said Cathy.

The lamps overhead went off and on again to warn people that lights out would be in ten minutes.

'You go first,' said Ida, finishing off her row.

Putting her knitting away, Cathy grabbed her sponge bag and pyjamas and then made her way to the washing cubicle and toilets at the very end of the platform.

Having got herself ready for the night, Cathy returned and, careful not to wake her brothers or Peter, climbed into bed as her mother trotted off to complete her bedtime ablutions.

Cathy was already under the covers when Ida

204

returned. Rocking the bunk a little, her mother climbed in to the bottom bunk just as the lights went out.

'Night, luv,' her mother whispered.

'Night, Mum,' Cathy replied in the same hushed tone. 'See you in the morning.'

Cathy pulled the covers up under her chin and listened to the now-familiar sounds of creaking beds, dry coughs and low voices as those sheltering deep beneath the pavement got ready for the long hours of night.

Closing her eyes, Cathy listened to the gentle sound of her son's breathing but, despite being up since six that morning, instead of feeling sleep steel over her, the image of Archie standing on her doorstep appeared in her head. Her mind shifted the scene to the front room and then showed her his mesmerising blue eyes. Not content with that, her subconscious invented an image of him lying on the bed. Then it conjured up things she'd never ever done. Like kneeling astride him, running her hands over his chest then ripping open his shirt.

She grew hot. Very hot.

Throwing off the sheet and blanket, Cathy opened her eyes. She tried to shove the images aside. Her traitorous mind laughed and let her imagine herself naked, with Archie's hands, his artist's hands, roaming over her body.

Cathy bit back a moan as a heavy yearning she'd barely felt before circled her navel a couple of times then settled lower, much lower.

'Cathy,' her mother whispered from beneath her.

'Yes, Mum?'

'Be careful. With Sergeant McIntosh, I mean.'

'I will,' Cathy replied. And she would. Well, at least until Easter, because until then, blue eyes or no blue eyes, she was still a married woman.

13

'That's the house,' said Archie, as he pointed to the house with the faded brown door on the east side of Senrab Street.

Mogg put his foot on the brake and then, turning the massive steering wheel, guided the three-ton Austin to a halt alongside the kerb.

Jumping down from the cab, Archie took two strides and reached for the lion's-head knocker but as he did the front door opened.

Although the dress she was wearing was a plain workaday dress with an apron over it, the colour, aquamarine, highlighted her tawny colouring perfectly. In fact, to his mind she couldn't have looked better had she been dressed in the finest silk but then, in truth, he thought the self-same thing every time he saw her.

'Morning,' she said.

He waved. 'Morning.'

She smiled that smile that kept him awake half the night. 'You're bright and early.'

'I'm not too early, am I?'

'No,' she said, shaking her head. 'The room's ready so bring your stuff in. I'm just giving Peter his breakfast, so I'll leave you to it.'

Giving him another pulse-racing smile, she went back inside the house.

Archie touched his forehead in a half salute then went to the rear of the lorry.

Chalky was already there with Mogg and Ron, who were unloading Archie's boxes.

'You lucky, bloody bugger, Archie,' said Ron, the roll-up between his lips moving about as he spoke.

'Jammy, that's what I call it,' agreed Chalky. 'Not only does all his gear survive when he's bombed-out, but then he gets himself digs with a little sweetheart who makes Rita Hayworth look like the Hunchback of Notre Dame.'

'Well now, lads,' said Archie, forcing an earnest expression on to his face. 'You'll find no argument from me on that score.'

'Sod off,' said Mogg, slinging Archie's kitbag at him.

Grinning, Archie caught it and swung it over his shoulder.

Grabbing the handle of his paint box, which Chalky had just set on the pavement, Archie strolled into the house. Placing his belongings on the Indian-style rug, he walked back outside to find Mogg and Ron unloading the last of his sketchpads and canvases.

'That's the lot,' said Ron, handing him the small suitcase with his personal paperwork and family photos in.

'Thanks, pal,' Archie said.

Chalky climbed back in the lorry and the lads drove way.

Archie went back in the house and was greeted by Cathy standing in the kitchen doorway.

'I've just put the kettle on — do you want a cuppa before you unpack?' she asked.

'That sounds grand,' said Archie.

Leaving the case just inside his room, Archie shut the door and followed her into the kitchen.

Cathy was standing by the dresser pouring milk into two cups while Peter was still in his highchair, eating his way through a plate of scrambled egg. He looked up and waved at Archie as he walked in.

'Hello there, young man,' said Archie, smiling at him. 'How's that ferocious wee bear of yours?'

Peter laughed and offered Archie the mangled bread and butter soldier in his hand.

'Thank you kindly, lad,' said Archie. 'But I've had my breakfast.'

Satisfied Archie didn't want it, Peter crammed the finger of bread in his mouth.

Pulling out a chair, Archie sat at the table, enjoying the Monday-morning scene. The clean crockery was upturned on the draining board, the family washing was soaking in the zinc bucket under the sink and the smell of toast filled the room, all with Cathy at its centre.

The kettle lid started to rattle as it let out a low whistle. Cathy flicked the switch to extinguish the blue and gold flames beneath the kettle then poured the steaming water into the pot.

'Oh, before I forget, I'll give you the keys.' Fitting the knitted cosy over the pot to let the tea brew, Cathy pulled two keys on a ring from the pocket of her apron.

'The larger one is for your room and the Yale is for the front door.'

She handed them to him.

'And in return' — Archie took his wallet out of his back pocket and flipped it open — 'here's this week's rent.' He pulled out the eight shillings he'd tucked away before he'd set out that morning. 'The pay clerk wasn't in when I left HQ this morning, but I'll be able to get my ration books from him when I go back to collect my bike.'

'That's fine,' she said. 'It's stuffed hearts tonight

and they're off rations anyway so tomorrow will do.'

She took the coins from him then turned and poured the tea.

'No sugar,' she said, placing a mug in front of him.

'You remembered,' he said, gazing up at her.

She gave him a shy smile. Moving over to the sink she bent down and grasped the handle of the washing bucket.

Archie jumped up.

'Here, let me do that,' he said, crossing the space between them.

Without thinking, he reached down and his hand closed over hers.

She looked up and, her face just inches from his, their gaze met.

Cathy's eyes darkened, which made his chest swell and sent his pulse racing.

The thought that he only had to move a little closer to taste her lips flashed through his mind but, as it did, Cathy let go of the bucket and stepped back.

Archie tore his eyes from her, lifted the brimming pail of washing from the floor and deposited it on the draining board.

'There you are,' he said, hoping only he could hear the gravel in his voice.

The golden curl that never stayed where she put it escaped again.

'Thank you,' Cathy said, tucking it back behind her ear.

She stared up at Archie for a couple of heartbeats then she placed her hand on the rim of the bucket.

'I ought to get on if I'm going to get this lot on the line before midday.'

'Me too.' He picked up his mug. 'Thanks for the tea.'

He smiled and she smiled back, then, to avoid doing something that would have him back on the street before he'd even unpacked his case, Archie turned and walked out of the room.

* * *

'She never did?' said Mary Weston, a look of complete horror on her fat face.

'She most certainly did,' said Violet, raising her voice for the benefit of those standing in the queue. "Vi,' she said, 'I'm taking in a lodger and if you don't like it you can sling your effing hook.'"

Mary's look of incredulity deepened.

'She actually swore at you?' she asked, as the dozen or so women lined up outside Empire and Country Grocery shop pursed their lips and tutted.

Violet nodded. 'And she threatened me with a knife.'

'You ought to get the police on to her,' said Mary.

Violet sighed. 'It's her word against mine.'

'And you say he's moving in today?' said Mary.

Violet glanced at the clock over the jeweller's shop, which was showing half past ten.

'Probably already got his feet under my kitchen table by now.'

'Still, it could be worse,' said Mary, as the queue shuffled forward.

Violet gave her a cool look. 'I don't see how.'

'Well, at least he's a soldier,' Mary replied. 'If he starts playing up, you can complain to the army.'

'Soldier!' sneered Violet. 'Someone who's wangled himself a cushy number away from the real fighting, don't you mean? My son Stanley is a real soldier. One

211

who's getting a medal for bravery in the face of the enemy,' she reminded her, 'while she's moving some coward into his home.'

The thin-faced woman in front of Mary turned around. 'I'm sorry, I couldn't help but overhear what you were saying and if it's any comfort I think the way you've been treated by your daughter-in-law is a disgrace.'

'Thank you, dear,' said Violet, giving the woman a plucky little smile.

'I agree,' said the grey-haired woman with a squint behind Violet, joining in the conversation. 'I'm not one to gossip but she's a Brogan and that family are nothing but a bunch of pikeys.'

'Bloody left-footers,' muttered another. 'Stick together like a dog shit on a shoe, they do.'

'They're as bad as the Yids,' said another woman, peering at Violet through gold-rimmed spectacles.

A squat woman with frizzy red hair rolled her eyes. 'Don't start me on them. Bloody racketeers.'

The crowd around Violet muttered their agreement.

'Of course,' said Violet, wanting to steer the conversation back to her many afflictions, 'you know where my daughter-in-law got her gutter language from, don't you?'

The crowd shook their collective heads.

'That mad old bat Queenie Brogan,' said Violet.

'Bloody bonkers she is,' said Mary as they all took a few more steps forward.

'Completely,' agreed the thin-faced woman next to her.

'Did I hear you mention Queenie Brogan's name?' asked a woman three people behind Violet in the

212

queue.

'Do you know her?' asked Violet as she turned and looked at the woman wearing an old-fashioned cloche bonnet pulled down over her ears.

'Know her! I should say,' the woman replied. 'I got in an argument with her about a year back and within a month this happened.'

She whipped off her hat and everyone gasped.

'A full head of thick brown hair I had until I crossed swords with Queenie Brogan,' she said, pointing at the little clumps of grey hair dotted across her bald head. 'So you want to watch yourself because your daughter-in-law could have the same powers.'

The crowd nodded their agreement.

Despite knowing she would have been six foot under long ago if Cathy had possessed such powers, a terrified expression spread across Violet's face.

'Don't worry,' said Mary. 'It's a known fact, Violet, that witchcraft don't work on good Christians like you.'

The queue moved forward again, and Violet stepped up to the marble-topped counter.

Willy Tugman, the owner of the Empire and Country, spotted her and before the young girl who served in the shop could step forward to take Violet's order, he intervened.

'It's all right, Polly,' he said, 'I'll serve Mrs Wheeler.'

He walked to the end of the counter and Violet followed.

'Now, what can I get you, Mrs Wheeler?' he asked.

Violet listed a handful of everyday items, including her tea and sugar ration plus a bar of soap and a tin of peaches that were on points that week.

He lined the items along the counter and Violet

handed over her ration and points book.

Willy crossed off the appropriate squares and handed them back.

'Anything else?' he asked.

'Just my usual order,' she replied. 'Would you put it in my bag?'

Slipping her shopping bag off her arm, she placed it at the end of the counter, out of the view of her fellow shoppers.

Willy turned his back on his young shop assistant and whipped out a package wrapped in newspaper from under the counter. He tucked it at the bottom of her bag then piled the rest of her shopping on top.

'That's one and a tanner,' said Willy.

Violet handed over half a crown.

Willy pulled open the cash drawer under the counter, took out thruppence and offered Violet her change.

Thinking of the jar of jam and packet of chocolate digestives sitting under the other items at the bottom of her basket, Violet smiled and took the money from him.

'Thank you,' she said, picking up her shopping bag. 'See you Thursday.'

Violet left the shop and glanced at the octagonal clock across the road again. Cathy would be hanging the washing up about now and then she'd be off to her mother's for a few hours, leaving Violet alone to enjoy a jam sandwich and a couple of chocolate biscuits in peace.

She frowned.

Well, not quite alone, but she'd be telling this battle-shirking lodger in no uncertain terms that other than for breakfast he was not to show his face outside his room.

Looking forward to sinking her dentures into a juicy layer of strawberry jam and sucking the chocolate off a couple of biscuits, Violet reached her house.

Turning the key, she pushed the door open but as she stepped into the hall, the door to the front parlour opened.

Violet's jaw dropped on the floor as a tall, West Indian soldier with a square jaw, wide flat nose and a crown of curly black hair stepped out in front of her holding a box.

His white teeth flashed into a smile.

'Good day to you,' he said, his alarmingly bright blue eyes boring into her. 'I dinna mean to startle you there, but I'm thinking you must be Mrs Wheeler senior. I'm Sergeant McIntosh,' his smile widened, 'your new lodger.'

Open-mouthed, Violet looked down at his hand for a moment then back to his brown face.

'You don't happen to know where my daughter-in-law is, do you?'

His smile widened. 'In the backyard.'

With a monumental effort, Violet managed to force a smile. 'If you'd excuse me.'

With the blood pounding in her ears and a scream trying to escape, Violet marched through the house, across the kitchen and through the back door into the garden, where Cathy was pegging up a nappy.

Storming across the paving stones, she glared across the washing at her daughter-in-law.

'I've just met your lodger,' she ground out between clenched teeth.

'Have you?' Cathy replied, taking another damp square of towelling from the bucket at her feet.

'Yes, I have,' snapped her mother-in-law. 'And he's

a bloody darkie.'

'He's a Scot, actually,' Cathy replied, jamming a peg down over the corner she was holding. 'From Glasgow, to be precise. And in case you didn't notice the badge on his arm, he's Royal Engineers, in the bomb disposal regiment.'

'I don't care,' Violet replied. 'They dress the chimps up in top hat and tails at London Zoo but they're still monkeys. And what will the neighbours say?'

'Whatever they like, as far as I'm concerned,' said Cathy.

'It's all right for you, but I have a respectable reputation,' said Violet. 'On top of which, I'm a member of the Church of England, so I can't have a heathen living under my roof.'

'He's not living under your roof, Vi.' Cathy gave her mother-inlaw a sweet smile over the top of the washing line. 'He's living under mine. Remember, I pay the rent.'

A throbbing started in Violet's right temple and little lights started to pop on the edge of her vision.

Imagining winding the washing line around her hateful daughter-in-law's neck and choking off her air, Violet glared at Cathy for a moment. Then she turned and marched back towards the house.

Stopping at the back door, she slowly counted to twenty before walking in. Her mouth pulled into a sour line at the sight of Cathy's lodger sitting at her kitchen table as bold as brass, holding a half-drunk cup of tea and a copy of that socialist rag the Daily Mirror in front of him.

He looked up.

'I'm just having a quick break before I tackle the last few bits,' he said, raising the mug.

Violet forced a sweet smile. 'Would you like a top-up, dear?'

'Naw, I'm fine thank you, Mrs Wheeler.'

Taking another slurp of his drink, he lowered his gaze.

As his eyes returned to the newspaper, Violet's smile disappeared.

He might have a Scottish name and accent and, granted, his mixed blood was less pronounced in him than some, but it was obvious Sergeant McIntosh was the by-blow of some passing darkie, thought Violet viciously.

'Did my daughter-in-law tell you her husband's missing in action?' she asked.

'Aye, she did. And I'm sorry to hear it and hope you hear some good news soon, Mrs Wheeler.' Sergeant McIntosh stood up. 'If you'd excuse me, I ought to get those last few things unpacked before I go to work.'

He went to pick up his dirty plate and cutlery. 'It's all right, Sergeant, I'll rinse those before I go,' said Violet. 'Thank you.' Picking up the paper, he folded it and tucked it

under his arm. 'And as I said earlier, it's nice to meet you.' He offered his hand again. This time Violet took it. He shook it once then turned and left the room. Violet waited until she heard the door to the front room shut

then she dashed to the sink.

Grabbing the bottle of Zal disinfectant and the bristle brush from the window sill, she poured the thick liquid over her hand and, heedless of the pain, scrubbed vigorously.

14

Cathy had just slipped the last paid invoice into the Dec '42 compartment of the filing cabinet when the rumble of a five-ton Bedford heralded her father's return from his morning's round.

Parking it by the wall, Jeremiah climbed down from the cab. Blowing on his hands and rubbing them together, he made his way towards the office, bringing a gust of icy wind with him but quickly shut the door.

Cathy closed the drawer and smiled. 'Coffee?'

'I could murder a cup,' he replied, holding his hands over the paraffin heater.

Cathy went over to the two-ring gas stove set up on a bench and relit the flame under the kettle that she'd boiled ready for his return.

'How're you getting on?' he asked, as she poured the hot water over the Camp coffee at the bottom of the enamel mug.

'Not too badly now I've figured out Mum's filing system,' Cathy replied. 'I've got all last month's accounts up to date and I'll make a start on this month when I'm next in. Plus, I've booked in three house-moving jobs. One for next week to Benfleet and two the following week to Hainault and Southend and' — stirring in a heaped teaspoonful of sugar, Cathy handed her father his coffee — 'I've written in all your local factory deliveries for next week.'

'Thanks, me darling,' he said. 'I don't know what I would have done these last couple of weeks without you.'

'Been buried under a mound of paperwork, I expect,' Cathy replied. 'And lost business, too, I shouldn't wonder.'

'You have the right of it there, and no mistake.'

Her father took a large swallow of his drink. Cradling the steaming mug in his massive hands, he raised his eyes and looked over the rim at her. 'And now tell me, how are you getting on with that new lodger of yours?'

'Oh, well enough,' said Cathy breezily. 'He's out from dawn until dusk most days so other than at breakfast and when I'm serving up his evening meal, I only see him in passing.'

'Except, of course, on a Wednesday night at your Cephas Street secretarial classes,' he reminded her.

Cathy nodded and forced a light laugh. 'Fancy both of us doing a class on the same night.'

Her father's mouth lifted in a little smile and he took another sip of his drink. 'Your mum says he's a widower with a little girl.'

'Yes, Kirsty. She's seven years old and he talks about her all the time,' she replied, thinking of the softness in Archie's voice as he spoke of his daughter.

'In passing,' said her father, his grey-green eyes scrutinising her face.

Feeling as if her father had received a letter from the headmaster about her bunking off school, Cathy glanced up at the old clock pinned on the wall above the filing cabinet.

'Oh, is that the time? I'd better get going.'

Taking her forest-green overcoat from the nail hammered into the wall, Cathy slipped her arms in.

'No point putting Mrs Paget's back up by being late,' she added, buttoning up the front.

'Francesca's keeping Peter this afternoon, so would you mind picking him up when you take Mum and the boys to the shelter? I wouldn't ask but I've got the practice test for my level-three Pitman exam in a few weeks,' Cathy said, tucking her scarf in around her neck, 'and I don't want to be late.'

Picking up her handbag, Cathy stood on tiptoe and planted a kiss on her father's bristly cheek.

Jeremiah opened his mouth as if he was going to say something but, after studying her for a moment or two, he smiled.

'Off you go then, luv,' he said, sitting in the chair she'd just vacated. 'See you tomorrow if I don't see you before.'

Walking back into the yard, Cathy smiled.

She'd thought for a moment her father was going to ask her if Archie was going to be at Cephas Street that night too. She was glad he hadn't. Glad because she didn't want to pretend she didn't know.

★ ★ ★

Cathy had just taken her seat in the small committee room alongside Dora, who oversaw the paper and cardboard salvage operation, when Mrs Paget swept into the room carrying a thick manila file.

'Good afternoon, ladies,' she said, giving them a tight smile as her cool eyes ran over each woman in turn.

The women muttered their acknowledgements as Mrs Paget took her seat at the head of the table.

'Now, ladies,' she said, opening the overflowing wallet containing the minutes of the centre's monthly meetings, 'as this is our first meeting of nineteen forty-three, we have a great deal to get through. So, are we all here?'

As Mrs Paget checked the women around the table against the list of section leaders, Cathy delved into her handbag and pulled out her notebook and pencil.

As the rest centre organiser ran through all the little deficiencies she'd noticed in the centre's operation, Cathy jotted it down.

Mrs Paget's complaints this month included squandering the centre's sugar allowance by putting icing on fairy cakes and using the canteen's condensed milk to make up babies' bottles instead of insisting nursing mothers bring their own.

Glancing at Cathy from time to time, the self-styled commanderin-chief of St Breda and St Brendan's Rest Centre ran through the good-hearted volunteers' many faults and Cathy scribbled it all down.

Mrs Paget concluded by reminding those around the table, yet again, that she would prefer them not to refer to each other by their Christian names while on duty but address each other as Mrs whatever they were. Thankfully, everyone, including Cathy, managed not to roll their eyes.

'Now,' said Mrs Paget, 'the penultimate thing that we need to discuss is the Christmas party.'

'Which was a great success,' chipped in Lottie.

'Thanks to our Cathy,' added Maureen.

The women around the table nodded their agreement.

A pinched expression tightened Mrs Paget's narrow features.

'Indeed,' she said. 'Although I thought the children were allowed to become a little too wild at times.'

'It was a party, Mrs Paget,' said Cathy, pausing in her note-taking and looking down the table at her, 'and the only bit of fun some of those kids have had for a long time.'

'Even so,' continued Mrs Paget, 'that doesn't excuse bad manners.' The hint of a sneer curled her upper lip. 'Of course, that's assuming that the children around here have been taught any manners in the first place.'

Cathy's mouth pulled into a hard line.

'Our children are taught manners, good manners, Mrs Paget,' she said, looking squarely at the other woman. 'But unlike children who are living in the country with their nursemaids and nannies, our children have had to sleep in a hole in the ground for the past three and a half years while everything they have is being destroyed. Therefore, to my way of thinking, if they want to stuff their faces with cake and run around like banshees for an hour or two, then I say let them.'

Mrs Paget's cheeks flamed bright red as mutters of 'Poor little mites' and 'God luv 'em' rose up.

Mrs Paget's gaze flickered on to the notepad on the table in front of Cathy then back to her face.

'Can I ask what you are doing, Mrs Wheeler?' she asked.

'Practising my shorthand,' Cathy replied. 'I've got a Pitman level-three test in a month.'

'Would you mind not?' Mrs Paget snapped. 'It is a little disconcerting having one's every word written down.'

Answering the other woman's enraged stare with a cool look, Cathy stopped writing .

'Thank you,' said Mrs Paget. 'Although, to be honest, I can't imagine why a woman such as yourself would bother with such a thing.'

'That's easy,' Cathy replied. 'Because I want to earn

my own living.'

'Earn your own living!' Mrs Paget laughed. 'Oh, Mrs Wheeler, what an amusing notion.' She put her hand on her chest as if she were struggling to speak through her merriment.

Although the pencil threatened to snap as Cathy's fingers tightened around it, somehow she managed to maintain her nonchalant expression as she laid it on the fresh page.

'Now lastly, ladies,' said Mrs Paget, beaming at the assembled women, 'HQ have asked that each WVS rest centre adopts a regiment or company and sends them letters and little gifts, like cigarettes or chocolate, just to keep up their morale and show them that the women at home appreciate their sacrifice.'

'I'd vote for that,' said Mary.

'Count me in,' agreed Olive, as others nodded in agreement.

'Splendid,' said Mrs Paget. 'Now, I propose we adopt 61 Squadron. They're based in Rutland, miles from anywhere, and could do with a bit of home comfort. I know it's a formality, but if I could have a show of hand — '

'What about the artillery division manning the ack-ack guns at Mudflat?' asked Dot.

'Or perhaps we could do what Old Ford WVS groups have done and link up with one of the Navy's ships, like HMS *Repulse* or HMS *Rodney*,' suggested Olive.

Mrs Paget gave a stiff smile. 'While both the ack-ack gunners and the Royal Navy's matelots are very worthy in their own way, I really think 61 Squadron, who tirelessly defend our skies against murderous Luftwaffe — '

'Isn't your son a member of the 61?' asked Cathy.

The flush returned to Mrs Paget's cheeks. 'Well, yes, he is, actually, but I don't see what — '

'I propose we adopt a regiment much nearer to home,' cut in Cathy. 'One that we see all the time in our streets and who risk their lives every day to keep our hospitals, schools and utilities running: the North East London Bomb Disposal Unit.'

'You're right, Cath,' said Lottie, sitting across the table from her. 'Those boys are always around. In fact, only the day before yesterday they defused a dirty great big bomb in Fairfield Road that would have blown the train lines into Liverpool Street, and the parachute factories, to kingdom come.'

'Yes, well,' said Mrs Paget, 'very commendable I'm sure, but — '

'And aren't they based somewhere around and about?' asked Mary.

'Wanstead,' Cathy replied. 'And they cover everything east of the city, right out as far as Barking Creek.'

'Well then,' said Polly, 'they're our own, aren't they?'

'Yeah,' added Maureen. 'We could adopt them as our cockney regiment.'

Dot laughed. 'The Pearly King of Stepney's own.'

'That's all very well,' said Mrs Paget, 'but I really — '

'Those bomb squad lads spend all their time in the cold and wet making Hitler's bloody bombs safe,' said Lottie. 'I reckon sending a packet of fags or a bit of cake now and again is the least we can do.'

'Well then, ladies,' said Cathy, sweeping her gaze over the committee, 'all those in favour of St Breda and St Brendan's WVS Rest Centre adopting the North East London Bomb Disposal Unit.'

224

She raised her right hand.

Everyone did the same, except the red-faced woman sitting at the other end of the table.

'Very well,' Mrs Paget said, through ridged lips. 'The North East London Bomb Disposal Unit will be our adopted company. Although, to be quite honest, with the monthly report to write and the catering accounts to check through, not to mention my parish duties, I'm not sure if I'll be able to inform them of their good fortune.'

Cathy's lips lifted in a sweet smile.

'Don't worry, Mrs Paget, I'm happy to write to them on the centre's behalf,' she said, raising the pencil in her hand. 'It will help me improve my typing speed.'

15

'It's looking good, Archie,' said Ted Inglis, as he studied the two-foot by three-foot canvas set up on the easel.

'Aye, I'm pretty happy with it myself,' Archie replied, noting a couple of places that would benefit from a bit more attention.

'Is it one of those you're putting into the exhibition?'

Archie nodded. 'The other paintings I'm entering in the 'Images of Defiance' feature the lads digging out and manhandling bombs. This one shows them having a break before descending back into the shaft again.'

The art instructor nodded. 'The human side of bomb disposal. What are you going to call it?'

'It's called *The Quick Brew*,' Archie replied. 'It's all but done; I just want to add a couple of dabs here and there to highlight the reflection of the winter sun on the kettle and shovels.'

'And your signature,' said Ted. 'Don't forget that.'

Grasping his hands behind his back, the tutor, dressed in oversized, paint-splattered overalls and with hair that would have set Archie's mother tutting, moved on to the next pupil, and Archie's gaze returned to his work.

If he said it himself, and he shouldn't, it wasn't half bad. It showed the men as they really were each and every day: dirty, wet and tired.

He and the squad had been sent out first thing to

deal with a bomb lodged alongside a granary on the River Lea in Leyton. Although it hadn't taken them long to clear the site around it, it had taken hours to get the fuse out, thanks to Lieutenant Monkman shilly-shallying about with various bits of equipment.

Archie had already released the charge on the old pre-15 fuse when Monkman arrived. The lieutenant had only needed to take a hammer and chisel to it, and then they could have all gone home. Instead, of course, he'd muttered about getting the clock stopper and then the steamer to extract the explosives in situ. In the end, when the senior officer stomped off to phone the boffins at Woolwich, Archie had bashed the fuse out himself.

By the time they'd got back to Wanstead, after ferrying the bomb to Hackney Marshes, it was almost five so, after stripping off his protective overalls, showering and gulping down a curling spam sandwich and a stewed cuppa in the squaddies' mess, Archie had slipped into the art class just as it started at six.

However, although his eyes now rested on his watercolour, Archie's heart quickened as the clock above the classroom door ticked away the seconds to eight thirty, which was when the class ended.

'Thank you, everybody,' said Ted. 'If you could leave the room tidy: the calligraphy class will be using it tomorrow afternoon. And I'll see you next week.'

Taking a last look at his work, Archie screwed the tops on the paint tubes and after stacking them in order, closed his paint box.

Satisfied the lock was secure, he slid the box into his old rucksack and pulled the drawstring tight. Setting it on the floor, he lifted his picture off the wooden tripod and carried it across to the drying rack.

Waving farewell to his fellow artists, Archie slung his knapsack over his shoulder and strolled out into the communal area between the second-floor classrooms.

He spotted Cathy standing by the stairwell, with a satchel over her shoulder. She was chatting to a young woman with red hair and glasses.

He studied her unobserved for a moment then, sensing his gaze on her, she looked across.

Joy flashed in her lovely eyes, setting Archie's heart off on a gallop.

She said goodbye to her companion and headed towards him.

'Sergeant McIntosh,' she called, zigzagging through the people who were making for the stairs.

'Hello,' he said, imagining swooping her into his arms as she reached him.

'Thank goodness,' she said breathlessly, stopping just in front of him. 'I was beginning to think I'd missed you, Archie. Have you got time for a quick cuppa?'

'Aye,' he said.

'Good, let's get a table downstairs before they all go.'

Trying to decide what he was most happy about: her waiting for him or the thought of gazing across a table at her for half an hour, Archie followed her down the stairs, shielding her with his body from people pushing past.

'Grab that table by the wall and I'll get us a tea,' she said.

'You will not,' Archie replied. 'You've been up since before I left, so you go and rest up a while and I'll fetch us our drinks.'

Leaving her to nab a seat, Archie went and queued up at the counter alongside a couple of ARP wardens who were getting something hot inside them before starting their evening blackout patrol.

Having ordered their tea and added a rock cake, Archie handed over a few coppers then carried the refreshments to Cathy, who was sitting at the table.

'I thought you might fancy one of these to soak up the tea,' he said, placing the plate in front of her.

'I would, if you'll share it with me,' she replied, as he placed the mugs on the table and sat down.

Picking up the knobbly lump with a handful of currants dotted on it, Cathy broke it in half.

'Now,' she said, offering it to him, 'you'll never guess what.'

Taking the portion of cake from her, Archie sat down and gave himself over to the pure pleasure of watching every tilt of her head, bob of her curls and the spellbinding movement of her mouth as she recounted the rest centre's meeting that afternoon.

'My goodness,' he said when she'd finished. 'I wish I'd seen you in action.'

'I was ferocious,' she said, pulling a stern face.

Archie laughed. 'I have no doubt about that, Mrs Wheeler.'

'Thankfully I remember you mentioning your commanding officer's name a little while back,' she continued. 'So I was able to type out the letter and envelope in class this evening. All I need to do is post it tomorrow and it'll be official.'

'Well now, the squaddies of the D are a fine bunch of men and they will be most grateful for your rest centre's consideration,' Archie replied.

'And extra cigarettes, cakes and socks,' said Cathy.

'Aye, that too,' Archie agreed.

She smiled and the warmth of it swelled his chest.

They stared at each other for a couple of heartbeats then her gaze shifted past him and she swallowed the last of her tea.

'I didn't realise the time,' she said, standing up. 'I ought to go and give Mum a hand.'

Archie rose to his feet. 'I'll give you a lift?'

'There won't be enough room on your bike, will there?' she said.

'Yes, if we juggle things a bit,' he replied.

Cathy looked unconvinced.

'I'm sure we can squash everything on,' added Archie. 'And it's only five minutes up the road, after all.'

'All right,' she said after a long moment. 'Come on then.'

Other than half a dozen Civil Defence lorries, Archie's motorbike was the only vehicle in the playground.

After strapping his rucksack on the rear parcel rack, Archie grabbed hold of the handlebars and got on his bike.

While Cathy buttoned her coat and wrapped her scarf around her, Archie kick-started the engine, revving it a couple of times to clear the carburettor.

'Just step on the footrest,' he said, raising his voice to be heard over the rumble of the engine. 'Then hold on to me and climb on.'

'All right,' she shouted back, securing her satchel behind her.

Placing her hand on his shoulder, she did as he instructed, the bike's balance shifting slightly as she did. However, as the Tiger's seat was no more than six or seven inches long, as she settled into the seat, her thighs pressed against his.

Archie swallowed hard.

'Ready?'

'Yes,' she replied.

'Hold on then,' he called back.

Shoving the bike off its stand, he opened the throttle and the bike rolled forward, but as it did two small hands closed around his hips, sending his already galloping pulse into a full-out stampede.

* * *

Up until the moment she sat down on the pillion space behind Archie, Cathy's experience of being on a vehicle with two wheels was the few occasions when she'd ridden crossbar on her brother Charlie's bicycle. However, as they shot forward, Cathy's initial fear of whizzing along the road at speed gave way to quite a different thought.

With her legs spread wide and pressed against Archie's thighs and her hands feeling the subtle movements of his body as he adjusted his position to balance them, her imagination, which seemed to constantly speculate as to what he might look like beneath his clothes, went into overdrive.

'Hold on,' he called over his shoulder as they stopped at the junction with Cambridge Heath Road to let a couple of army trucks pass.

Under the excuse of road safety, Cathy slipped her hands around his waist and tucked herself into him. Archie opened the throttle and swung the bike across the road to join a handful of cars and a bus travelling north.

231

With the wind whipping at her hair and her body pressing against his back, Cathy closed her eyes and just gave herself up to the sheer pleasure of it.

All too soon the bike rolled to a stop and Cathy looked across at the half-bricked-up entrance to Bethnal Green station shelter.

'Here we are,' said Archie, planting his feet on the tarmac either side of the bike to keep them upright. 'All safe and sound.'

Standing up on the narrow metal footrest, Cathy climbed off and stood next to him.

'Thank you, Archie.'

He smiled. 'My pleasure.' His eyes flickered up to her hair.

'I know, I must look a bit of a fright,' she said, trying to tug her windswept tresses into some sort of order.

'Not really,' he replied. 'But perhaps next time you might benefit from a scarf.'

Cathy laughed. 'I'll bear that in mind. Thanks again for the lift and I'll see you in the morning. Have a good night.'

'You too,' he replied.

Repositioning her satchel, Cathy crossed the road to join the small group of people making their way underground.

She stopped at the entrance and looked back.

Archie was still there, astride the bike, with his long legs holding it steady.

She waved and he waved back then he revved the engine, performed a U-turn across the street, and sped away.

She watched him for a moment then headed down into the shelter.

As it was now almost half past nine, people were

already bedding down for the night, so she wasn't surprised to see Peter fast asleep at the end of her bunk when she reached her mother's billet.

Ida was sitting in the deckchair breastfeeding Victoria, a tea towel draped across her to save her neighbours' blushes.

'I was beginning to worry,' said her mother, as Cathy reached her.

'Sorry, Mum,' Cathy said. 'I got chatting.'

Her mother's eyes flickered over her. 'You look a bit flushed. Are you all right?'

'I'm fine.' Cathy smiled. 'Never better.'

'And for goodness' sake,' her mother added, 'what on earth has happened to your hair?'

Cathy felt her cheeks grow warm.

'Oh,' she said, twiddling with a couple of curls, 'Archie gave me a lift on his bike. Lucky he did, or I'd have been even later.'

'Yes, well, at least you're here now,' said Ida. 'And you'd better get yourself sorted or you'll be brushing your teeth in the dark.'

Taking her pyjamas and toilet bag from the basket she'd left with her mother, Cathy grabbed her dressing gown from the end of the bunk and walked along the line of bunks until she reached the washing cubicles at the end of the platform.

Having washed, changed into her nightclothes and brushed out the tangles in her hair, Cathy poured her enamel bowlful of dirty water into the drain then stepped out of the plywood compartment just as the lights went off and on, signalling five minutes until lights-out.

Her mother was already in bed with Victoria snuggled in a multicoloured knitted blanket at her feet.

Cathy climbed up into her bed. After giving Peter, asleep at the other end, a light kiss on the forehead, she slid under the covers. As always, the rough cotton sheet was a little damp but that would soon go.

The lights went out and, apart from the odd baby grizzling, the shelter fell silent.

Cathy closed her eyes and although it was wrong, so wrong, she relived every nerve-tingling, heart-racing and need-inducing moment of hugging herself against Archie McIntosh's strong body.

★ ★ ★

Stroking the end of his mongoose-hair brush through the blob of Brown Madder on his palette, Archie ran the paint-loaded tip along the crooked line of Ron's back as he hunched over a 500-kilo bomb, then blended it into the dull brown of the squaddie's battle jacket.

It was Saturday and four days since he'd given Cathy a lift to the shelter. It was also his first weekend off since Christmas, thanks to the renewed bombardment of London by the Luftwaffe.

For once he was alone in the house: Mrs Wheeler senior was visiting her sister and had been gone since eight thirty that morning. This had allowed Archie the pleasure of watching Cathy make breakfast for him and Peter whilst all the time wishing she was doing it as his wife rather than as his landlady. Still, perhaps one day . . .

After she'd left, he'd donned the old boiler suit he'd worn at John Brown's shipyard and lace-less plimsolls, before setting out his equipment on the card table.

Swallowing the last mouthful of tea, Archie swirled

234

his brush in the water of the half-filled jam jar then wiped it on the rag lying on the newspaper-covered table.

He stood back and studied the canvas in the after-noon light streaming through the bay window of his room.

The image he'd been working on for the past few days was of the men bathed in the late-winter sun, unloading a bomb from their truck.

Although he was satisfied with the composition of the group, there was still work needed to convey the weariness of the men at the end of a long day's digging and the chill of the easterly wind cutting across Hackney Marshes.

But it was better. Much better.

Just because the colours of a bomb disposal crew's day were various shades of brown it didn't mean there wasn't the odd splash of brightness to be found, like the red glow of the setting sun glinting off their equipment, a purple buddleia flowering in the rubble or an ox-eye daisy clinging on at the edge of a crater.

Wiping his brush again, Archie was just about to smear it through the spiral of crimson on his palette when there was a knock on the front door.

Archie placed the brush, with the bristles upwards, back in the brush pot and, wiping his hands on his legs, he went to answer it.

Pulling the door open, he came face to face with a tall man, giving him the rare experience of looking someone almost straight in the eye.

Although the last time Archie had seen him he'd been heavily disguised as Father Christmas, Archie knew who the visitor was.

The man studied Archie for a moment then his

weather-beaten face lifted in an ingenuous smile. 'I'm thinking you must be Sergeant McIntosh.'

'Aye, I am,' Archie replied. 'And I'm guessing you're Mrs Wheeler's father.'

'I am indeed,' he replied. 'Jeremiah Brogan.'

He offered his hand and Archie took it.

Cathy's father had a strong grip, but Archie's handshake was its equal.

'I'm afraid she's not in,' said Archie.

Jeremiah looked surprised. 'Is she not?'

'No, she went out to the market just after ten,' Archie replied. 'She said something about dropping in on her sister Jo.'

An enlightened expression spread across the older man's rugged face. 'Now you mention it, I think she said something of the same yesterday.'

'And her mother-in-law is out also,' added Archie.

Smiling pleasantly, Jeremiah Brogan didn't move.

'Would you like to come in?' asked Archie, opening the door wider.

'Only if I'm not intruding on your leisure,' Jeremiah replied, stepping over the threshold and into the hall.

Archie closed the door.

'Would you like a cup of tea, Mr Brogan?' he asked, as the two men stood chest to chest in the narrow hallway.

'It's kind of you to ask, Sergeant, but no,' Jeremiah replied, his amenable expression at odds with his intense scrutiny. 'Cathy tells me you're an artist.'

Archie's mouth lifted in a wry smile. 'Well, an artist might be pushing it, but I do paint a bit. In fact, I was working on a new piece when you knocked. Would you like to see?'

'If it's no trouble,' Jeremiah replied.

236

Opening the door to the front parlour, Cathy's father strode in with Archie just a pace or two behind.

'She's done a grand job with this room,' Jeremiah, said, as his eyes skimmed over the colourful bedspread and heavy drapes.

'Yes, it's very comfortable,' said Archie. 'And there's plenty of space for my equipment.'

'I can see,' said Jeremiah as he stopped in front of the painting illuminated in the pool of winter sunlight streaming through the west-facing window.

'I'm just at the preliminary stage,' Archie said, indicating the bare sections of canvas where he'd pencilled in the truck and the team's equipment.

'It's very good,' said Jeremiah. 'It puts me in mind of Paul Nash's work.'

'I'm flattered you think so, Mr Brogan,' said Archie.

The older man raised an eyebrow. 'You don't seem surprised that a bog-trotting tinker should know about such a thing.'

'As a half-caste Jock I've learned never to judge a book by its cover,' Archie replied.

Jeremiah gave a short laugh then glanced around the room.

He spotted the image of Kirsty on the mantelshelf and wandered over.

'Your daughter?'

'Aye,' Archie replied, fatherly pride filling his chest. 'That's my bonny lass, right enough. She has her mother's looks, God rest her soul. That's her,' he said, indicating the other photo, a rosary draped over the frame.

'You're a Catholic, then?'

'I was christened as such, but to be honest I'm nae much of a church-goer,' Archie replied. 'I leave the

God-bothering to me ma.'

'Me too.' Jeremiah nodded. 'Our priest, Father Mahon, and my ma were children together back in the old country and sure you'd think he was kin the way she fusses over him.' His attention returned to the picture of Archie's daughter.

'It's a rare joy to be the father of girls, is it not, Sergeant?' Jeremiah said.

'It certainly is, Mr Brogan,' Archie agreed. 'And you more than anyone can know.'

''Tis true.' A sentimental expression stole across the older man's face. 'Blessed I've been with four sweet darlings.'

'They're a joy, right enough,' agreed Archie.

'And the first time they wrap their tiny fingers around yours, sure don't they capture your heart for all time?' Jeremiah added.

'You're nae wrong,' Archie laughed. 'You're nae wrong.'

Jeremiah nodded sagely then the shrewd spark returned to his eyes. 'As a father of a girl-child yourself, you'll understand me when I say they may be grown and have children of their own but they are still my little girls, and from the moment I took each of my darling daughters in my arms I swore that I'd have to be mouldering in my grave before I let anyone hurt any of them.'

'I would do much the same for Kirsty,' Archie replied, answering the other man's unwavering gaze with a forthright stare of his own.

He stood there, eyeball to eyeball with Cathy's father for a moment or two, then the smile returned to Jeremiah's face.

'Well, I shouldn't be keeping you from your work,'

238

he said. 'As I'm thinking between the digging them out and making bombs safe, you have precious little leisure.'

'You're nae wrong on that score either. This is my first weekend off for a month,' Archie agreed.

Jeremiah strolled back across the room and Archie followed him out to the hallway.

He opened the door and, with his hands deep in his worn corduroy trousers, Cathy's father stepped back into the street.

Archie offered his hand. 'Good to meet you, Mr Brogan.'

'You too, Sergeant McIntosh,' Jeremiah replied.

He went to release his grip, but Archie held his hand firm.

'And it's good to know we are of a mind in regard to daughters.'

16

With the rain dripping off the edge of his khaki water-proofs, Archie waited for Mogg to reel the bucket of soil clear, then he grasped the edge of the wooden parapet and leaned over.

'How's it going, lads?' he shouted, his voice echoing down the shaft.

Fred and Tim, who were wading about in a foot of filth at the bottom, looked up.

'Poxy London clay,' Fred shouted back, teeth flashing white in his mud-streaked face.

With mud all but covering their canvas boiler suits, Archie could understand his lance corporal's sentiments.

It was just after three on the last Wednesday of January, two weeks since he'd moved in as Cathy's lodger. He and the squad were down by the Thames in Beckton, where the River Roding drained into the Thames, and right by the two Victorian cast-iron gasometers belonging to the Gas Light and Coke Company's gasworks.

Archie had only just finished signing off the ARP paperwork and logging last week's work into the company's duty book when the cat-A yellow chit had arrived on his desk.

That was two days ago and they'd been trying to locate the ruddy UXB ever since.

'Aye, well, keep at it, lads,' Archie shouted back.

'What happens when we reach Australia, Sarge?' Tim shouted up.

'Catch me a kangaroo,' Archie replied. 'But until then just keep wielding those shovels, boys.'

The two men at the bottom of the shaft laughed and Archie straightened up.

Checking the safety ropes were still anchored to the parapet and had enough slack for the two squaddies to work, he turned to see Arthur, water also dripping from his camouflage poncho, coming towards him.

'Any sign of the bugger?' he asked.

'Not so much as a bloody tail fin,' Chalky replied. 'At this rate we'll be digging-out till the weekend.'

His corporal gave him a cynical look. 'If Lieutenant Monkman had listened to you, Archie, we wouldn't have wasted half a day tunnelling in the wrong place.'

As an NCO wasn't supposed to criticise officers in front of the men, Archie didn't reply.

Monkman had pulled up in his Rover 10 Tourer just after they'd arrived on site and, after having a bit of a poke around, had set them digging over the bomb's entry point.

In the ordinary way of things that would have been fine because most bombs entered the ground at an angle and continued along the same trajectory as they ploughed through the earth.

However, because London sat in a basin, the riverbanks on both sides of the Thames were made up of mud and slurry deposited over thousands of years. This meant that instead of ploughing through solidly packed earth, bombs landing here were apt to slither their way through the water-laden ooze unimpeded, which made their final resting point hard to detect. Archie had pointed this out to Monkman and had suggested that a disturbed mound of earth set

241

back from the river was a better place to start digging. Monkman had answered this suggestion with a hateful look and then set the men to dig on his original site before driving off, the mud spraying from his wheels as he accelerated away.

After two hours of digging in the new area, they'd discovered a collapsed channel, indicating that the bomb had swerved off to the left. After an hour of repositioning and redigging the shaft they had set-to again. That's when God, in his infinite wisdom, had seen fit to open the heavens above and it had been raining like a Presbyterian Sunday ever since, swamping the hole and churning up the ground.

'When do you expect him back?' added Chalky.

Archie cast his gaze around the lead-grey sky. 'Well, he'd better get here soon or it'll be too dark to see anything.'

As if he'd heard his name, the sound of wheels crunching over loose stones heralded the return of Monkman's car.

The lieutenant, dressed in his protective overalls and wellington boots, climbed out of his car and marched over.

'Have they found it yet?' he asked, as drops of water slid off the peak of his hat.

'The Thames mud doesn't make for easy digging,' Archie replied.

The lieutenant chewed the inside of his mouth, setting his thin moustache wriggling on his top lip.

'Have you checked the equipment?' he asked.

'Aye,' Archie replied. 'I wouldn't want to find myself face to face with a number thirty-five and find the clock stopper's leads were worn.'

'Sir,' Monkman snapped when it was clear that

242

Archie had finished his sentence.

'Sir,' Archie repeated, regarding his senior officer impassively.

Monkman studied him for a moment then fumbled under his waterproofs and took out his cigarette case.

Mogg heaved up another bucket of dirt from below and Archie, Arthur and the lieutenant stepped back as the squaddie manhandled it away from the top of the shaft.

Flicking his lighter into a flame, Monkman lit his cigarette.

'Bally weather,' he muttered as the wind threw sheets of rain against them.

'Worse still if you're soaked to the skin and frozen to the bone down the bottom of an eighteen-foot shaft. Sir,' Archie replied.

Monkman opened his mouth to speak but a two-tone whistle from below cut between them.

Archie went over to the parapet and looked over to see Tim and Fred's upturned faces.

'What is it, Fred?' he asked.

'We've found something like shrapnel mixed in with the gravel,' the lance corporal yelled back.

Archie straightened up and looked across at Monkman. 'Better have a look, don't you think, sir?'

The lieutenant held Archie's gaze for a moment, then, after taking a long draw on his half-smoked cigarette, threw it aside.

'Let's get on with it, then,' he barked, and stepped up on to the parapet.

'Hold fast, Fred, Lieutenant Monkman's coming down,' Archie shouted as Monkman descended, the smell of expensive brandy and cheap perfume lingering after him.

Swinging his leg over the top, Archie planted his foot on the first rung and followed his senior officer down.

His feet squelched as he stepped off the ladder on to the earth platform halfway down. The new shaft was below, and he continued down to where Monkman was standing beside the section's lance corporal.

Archie switched on his torch and shone it at the floor. Small fragments of metal glimmered back at him.

He chewed his lip.

It wasn't conclusive by any means, but it could be something that all bomb disposal squaddies dreaded: a camouflet. A pocket of deadly carbon monoxide caused by a bomb exploding beneath the surface.

Monkman hunkered down and scooped up a handful.

He directed the beam of light from his torch on to the contents of his hand then stood up.

'Just old nails and junk washed down the river,' he said, discarding them. 'Keep digging.'

Grasping his shovel, Fred stuck it in the earth.

Taking hold of the ladder, the lieutenant climbed back up to the platform.

'Stop digging, Fred,' shouted Archie.

The lance corporal stuck his shovel in a mound of earth.

'I said keep at it,' bellowed Monkman, glaring down from the platform six foot above them.

Tim and Fred looked at Archie.

'And that's a direct order, Soldier!' the lieutenant shouted, his voice booming around them in the damp shaft.

Archie, grabbing a handful of grit, climbed up to

244

join his senior officer on the earth platform.

'How dare you countermand a superior officer?' Monkman forced out between gritted teeth as Archie reached him. 'I could have you — '

'Look.' Picking out a fragment of twisted metal, he held it so Monkman could see it. 'It's not junk. It's from German armaments, sir.'

Monkman gave the fragments in Archie's hand a cursory glance. 'This is rubbish, nothing more.' He forced a laugh. 'Good God, man, this stuff is scattered all over London — '

'Aye, perhaps it's rubbish,' interrupted Archie. 'Or perhaps it's debris from a bomb that's exploded beneath the surface.'

The lieutenant gave him a mocking look. 'Don't be ridiculous — '

'If there is a camouflet down there,' said Archie, fixing his commanding officer with an unwavering stare, 'we need to bring down the rods to locate it before we let the men dig any further.'

Annoyance flickered across Monkman's face.

'Look, McIntosh,' the lieutenant forced out between tight lips, 'we've been days digging out this UXB and, for all we know, the bugger's ticking away ready to blow us all to kingdom come, so unless you want to be up on a charge of insubordination, I suggest you and your men get on with — '

'Right, men, out you come,' Archie shouted. 'Quick as you like.'

'Now you . . . you look . . . ' Monkman spluttered as his face went from pink to red to puce and he fought to get out his words.

Both men downed tools and hurried to the bottom of the ladder. Tim got there first, closely followed

245

by Fred. They started to climb but, halfway up, the youngster lost his footing on the sodden wood and fell back, taking the older man with him. They crashed, all arms and legs, on to the mud floor at the bottom of the shaft.

Tim rolled off and jumped up.

'Sorry, Fred,' he said, offering the other man his hand to help him up.

Fred scrambled to his feet but just then there was a low rumble below them. Both men looked down. For a split-second time stopped then the ground beneath the two sappers fell away, taking them with it.

Archie sprang forward and grabbed one of the safety cords.

'Help!' he screamed, as he wound the saturated rope around his forearms and took the strain of the fallen man.

He looked across at Monkman who, having flattened himself against the wall, was staring in horror at the gaping hole beneath them.

'Pull him up,' Archie yelled at him.

The lieutenant looked up.

'Pull the man up,' Archie bellowed. 'Grab the rope and pull him up.'

Yanked out of his stupor, Monkman fumbled around for a bit then caught hold of the other dangling rope. Someone above started tugging on the line Archie was holding. Tim, his face bright pink as he dangled like a puppet on the end of the rope, emerged from the chasm and was winched upwards.

Leaving the inert eighteen-year-old to be taken to the surface by other hands, Archie stepped over to where Monkman, with sweat running off his forehead despite the frigid temperature, was struggling to raise

Fred from the depths.

Ignoring the pain of his blistering hands, Archie grasped the damp hemp line just below Monkman's hands.

'Heave,' he yelled.

'I can't hold him,' moaned Monkman.

'You'll damn well have to,' Archie ground out between gritted teeth as the rope started slipping.

Using himself as a counterweight, Archie rocked back and hauled the squaddie at the other end of the line up a foot or two. Winding the rope around his arm, Archie heaved again, his boots sliding in the mud as he tried to get purchase.

Just as his arms felt as if they were about to come loose from their sockets, the rope grew taut as those above took up the slack. Exhausted, Archie released the rope as Fred, also bright pink and hanging like a sack of coal, was hauled to the surface.

Stepping back, Archie rested against the wooden planks of the shaft, his hands on his thighs as he regained his breath.

Opening his eyes, Archie looked across at Monkman.

'It was an accident,' the lieutenant said. 'No one could have known.'

Resisting the urge to smash his fist into his senior officer's face, Archie didn't reply.

Turning, he looked down into the gaping hole they had just dragged Tim and Fred out of. The bomb was sitting at the bottom.

Taking his torch, he switched it on.

'There you are, sir,' said Archie, directing the beam on to it. 'Looks like a 500-kilo to me.' Standing away from the wooden wall, he grabbed the ladder leading up to the surface.

'Where are you going?' asked Monkman.

'Up to see how my men are faring,' Archie replied.

★ ★ ★

''Toot, toot,' went Gordon the engine,' said Cathy, watching her son's eyes flutter down. ''Toot, toot,' Thomas replied, his big metal wheels rolling over the rails as he headed for the engine shed for a good night's sleep.'

Softly she closed the book. Placing it on her lap, she rested her hands on it.

In the mellow glow of the Noddy night light, Cathy gazed at her sleeping son and, as it always did when she looked at him, love filled her heart.

Although she still had vivid nightmares and often woke up in a cold sweat, the one thing she could never regret about her miserable, violent marriage was Peter. He was worth all the suffering she'd endured and, sin though it might be, she was counting the days, eighty-seven days in all, until she was officially free of Stanley Wheeler.

And then . . . An image of Archie smiling across the breakfast table at her that morning drifted through Cathy's mind and a little smile lifted the corners of her mouth.

Well, who knew?

Her mind was just about to conjure up a very pleasant fantasy of her life as a free woman when she heard the distinct sound of Archie's bike drawing up at the front of the house.

Leaning forward, she kissed Peter lightly on the forehead then stood up. Putting the book back with

248

the half a dozen others on his toy shelf, she made her way downstairs.

However, as she reached the last step, Archie, still dressed in his boiler suit and covered in mud, strode out of his room clutching a half-drunk bottle of Johnnie Walker.

'Ca— Mrs Wheeler,' he said, looking up at her. 'I thought you'd be at the shelter by now.'

'It's thick fog all the way up the Thames so I thought I'd treat myself and Peter to a night in our own beds,' she replied. 'But has something happened?'

Pain flitted across Archie's face and he covered his eyes with his free hand.

Cathy went over to him and put her hand on his shoulder.

'Come on, Archie,' she said softly. 'Let me get you something to go with your Scotch.'

He nodded and let her lead him into the still-warm kitchen, where he slumped on to the chair. Cathy fetched him a tumbler from the dresser and while he sat with his elbow on the table and his head on his hands, she poured him a stiff drink.

She nudged it against his hand. He took it and gulped it down then handed it back to her.

She went to pour him another, but he held up his hand. 'Thanks, but one will suffice.'

Resting his head back against the wall behind him, Archie closed his eyes.

Cathy put the cork back in the bottle and placed it on the table.

Feeling utterly helpless to ease his pain, Cathy drew up a chair and sat next to him.

Archie opened his eyes and glanced down.

'I'm sorry,' he said, grabbing the line of buttons

at the front of his muddy boiler suit and making to stand up. 'I shouldn't have — '

'It doesn't matter,' said Cathy, laying her hand on his arm. 'What happened?'

Pausing occasionally to master his emotions, Archie told her about Fred and Tim.

'Archie, I'm so sorry,' she said when he finished. 'Did you get them out in time?'

Archie shook his head. 'By the time I climbed up out of the shaft, someone had already draped Fred Wood's battle jacket over his face. Judging by the colour of him, my guess is he died instantly, so at least he wouldn't have known anything about it.'

'Has he got family?' asked Cathy.

'A wife and five kids; the youngest's but a few weeks old,' Archie replied.

'Poor woman,' said Cathy.

'Aye,' said Archie. 'Mercifully, although Tim had taken in a lungful of the deadly gas, the lads had managed to revive him up top. I had a couple of words with him before the ambulance carted him off to Plaistow Hospital. Of course, by then bloody Monkman, the lieutenant in charge, had buggered off back to his club or wherever officers go when they've caused a good man's death.'

'I thought you said it was an accident,' said Cathy.

'Aye, an accident that shouldn't have happened,' said Archie. 'All the signs were there indicating the possibility of a camouflet and I told Monkman as much. If he'd listened to me, Fred would be going home to see his new baby in a few weeks instead of lying on a mortuary slab and Tim would be chatting up girls in the Trocadero, not struggling for breath in an oxygen tent.' He gave a harsh laugh. 'The bloody

250

joke of all this is that when we got down to the bomb it was an old-type fifteen, so after pumping the fuse mechanism full of salt-saturated methylated spirits and waiting the obligatory thirty minutes for it to lose its charge, a quick flick of the wrist and it was out. All that was left to do was winch the bomb to the surface, load it on to the truck and whizz it off to Hackney Marches.' He sighed wearily. 'I know the CO will write to their families officially, but I'll pen a note to Fred's wife myself tomorrow when I have a moment or two. I always do.'

'Goodness, how many men have you lost?' she asked.

'Since we started in 'forty, eight officers and fifteen squaddies,' he replied. 'And that's only the ones in my unit. During the Blitz the company lost an officer almost every day because back then, to be honest, no one really knew what they were doing. First, we had straight forward fifteens and twenty-fives with the odd thirty-five thrown in. They were electrical fuses but then Fritz started dropping clockwork seventeens with unpredictable fuses, sometimes with the old electrical fuses in too to prevent you moving them. Each time we worked out how to neutralise a fuse, the bloody Germans would bring out another sort, then we'd lose more men until the boffins at Woolwich worked out how to beat it. For the past year things have settled down, but it's only the lull before the storm as I'm sure the Nazi engineers will be sending us another deadly puzzle to unravel soon enough.' He ran his hands over his face. 'I could ask for a transfer out, right enough, dozens do, but . . .'

'But?' asked Cathy.

'It's what I do,' he replied, giving her that quirky

251

smile of his. 'The Nazis try to kill people by dropping bombs on them and I stop them by defusing them. It's as simple as that.'

Cathy's heart ached for him.

'Have you had anything to eat?'

He shook his head. 'After I left HQ I needed to hear Kirsty's voice so I telephoned her, just to keep my bloody mind off all that'd happened, then I came straight here.'

'I've saved you some stew; shall I warm it through for you?' she asked.

'Please,' he replied, giving her a grateful smile.

Rising to her feet, Cathy went over to the stove and relit the gas under the pot on the back ring. Stirring the beef chunks and vegetables around in the thick gravy until they bubbled, Cathy then scraped the contents of the saucepan into a bowl. She placed it in front of Archie and handed him a spoon.

'Get that down you, Soldier,' she said, placing a plate with two slices of buttered bread at his elbow.

Leaving Archie to eat, Cathy refilled the kettle and put it back on the stove. By the time the whistle was starting to rattle, Archie had scraped the last smear of gravy from the bottom of the bowl.

Placing his spoon in his empty dish, he relaxed back in the chair and smiled at Cathy.

'Better?' she asked.

'Much,' he replied. 'And I'm sorry to have burdened you with it.'

'Don't be silly,' she said. 'I just wish I could do more.'

'You've done more than enough by just being here,' he replied. 'Now I should stop dirtying your kitchen and spruce myself up.'

'There's plenty of hot water in the kettle, so take a clean towel from the pile on the dresser and get yourself cleaned up,' she said. 'And while you're doing that, I'll fetch you a fresh vest and shirt.'

Leaving Archie to strip out of his dirty boiler suit she went into his room.

She picked a clean khaki vest from the top drawer of the dresser but as she reached into the wardrobe, a faint aroma of Archie drifted over her. Captured in the heady scent of him, Cathy gathered one of his shirts in her arms and pressed her face into it, inhaling deeply for a second then, remembering what she was supposed to be about, she hurried back to the kitchen.

Archie had stripped off his shirt, which lay discarded on the floor, and he stood at the sink in his vest.

Cathy stopped dead.

She'd guessed by the snug fit of his uniform shirt and trousers that Archie was in good shape, but never in her wildest dreams had she imagined just how muscular he'd be.

Although she knew she shouldn't, Cathy couldn't tear her eyes from the corded muscles of his back, shoulders and arms as he rubbed soap rigorously around his ears and through his hair.

His skin, too, fascinated her, so brown and, except for a light dusting of hair on his forearms, so smooth and sleek.

Dipping into the bowl again, Archie splashed water up and over his face, allowing tiny rivulets to trace along his arms as Cathy's fingers itched to do.

Sensing her behind him, he turned, giving Cathy's eyes a second helping of his strong, well-developed

253

body, including the muscles of his chest visible over the top of his vest.

'Sorry,' he said, smiling at her as he dabbed his face with the towel. 'I didn't hear you come back in.'

Swallowing, Cathy forced a casual smile.

'I have your clean clothes,' she said, somewhat needlessly as she was holding them in plain sight.

Not trusting herself to get any closer to him, Cathy draped them over the back of the chair.

Flicking the towel over his shoulder, Archie took two steps towards her and picked them up.

Now, just an arm's length from him, Cathy found herself gazing up into startling eyes. Except they weren't their usual icy blue, they were darker, much darker.

'I've put the kettle on again; shall I make us a cuppa?' he asked, in a low voice that shivered through her.

Although every bit of her wanted to say yes, Cathy shook her head.

'I'd better not,' she said. 'Peter will have me up at six and I'm helping Dad at the yard tomorrow.'

He smiled. 'You're always going somewhere and doing something.'

'Well, it keeps me out of trouble,' Cathy replied, the temptation to do the opposite tugging at her.

She stared up at him for a moment then dragged her mind back from its wandering.

'Well, I'll see you in the morning,' she forced out.

'Aye, you will,' he said, still looking down at her.

'And I am very sorry about your friends.'

'There is a war on, I suppose,' he replied.

'But that doesn't make it any easier.' Without thinking, she placed her hand on his arm.

As she felt the muscles flex under her fingers, an

emotion Cathy couldn't quite interpret flashed across Archie's face.

He glanced down at her pale hand against his brown skin, then his eyes returned to her face.

She forced a smile. 'Goodnight, Archie.'

'Sleep well, Cathy,' he replied.

Forcing her legs to move, she turned and walked to the door.

Shutting it behind her, Cathy leaned back against it. In the cool dark hallway, she took a deep breath to steady her tumbling emotions.

Sleep well! Some chance, she thought, as her heart thumped like a bodhrán in her chest.

Hardly surprising really because, although she couldn't explain exactly why, as he raised his gaze from her hand, Cathy had the oddest impression that she was about to be kissed.

And she wanted to be kissed by Archie. Very much so. And not just once but over and over again.

⋆ ⋆ ⋆

Pulling his battle jacket down at the front and raking his fingers through his unruly curls, Archie knocked on the half-glazed door that had been the headmaster's office.

'Come.'

Grasping the brass handle, he opened the door and walked in.

It was the following morning and as soon as he'd stepped over the threshold an hour ago at eight, Corporal Will had come scurrying out of the general office to tell him he was to report immediately to the Section Commander's office.

Major Williamson was sitting behind the oak desk with a pile of files and reports in front of him and with various charts and rotas pinned on the wall behind him. The officer in charge of No 8 Bomb Disposal Section had a sallow complexion and a face that seemed to be slipping off the bone beneath. His once ruddy red hair had long faded to cadmium orange, except for his overhanging moustache, which was stained mustard from the pipe permanently clenched between his teeth. As always, he was wearing his formal khaki jacket with the crown on his shoulder epaulettes and a string of campaign ribbons across his chest.

He'd seen service during the last war in the Royal Engineers and had spent most of his time on the Western Front. He'd volunteered to return to his old company as soon as war was declared and had been put in charge of the newly formed bomb disposal unit.

Having received his first command when the British Army still wore red jackets, Williamson was a bit of a spit-and-polish type of commanding officer. However, he was even-handed and fair when it came to the duty roster and time off, which is more than could be said for some Archie had served under.

He looked up from his tasks as Archie entered.

'McIntosh,' said Williamson, putting his pen back in the inkwell.

Archie marched across to the desk and executed a double step to attention. He saluted. 'Sir.'

'Stand easy.'

Catching his hands together behind his back, Archie took up a relaxed stance.

Making the chair creak with his movement, the major leaned back.

'Bad business about your two men,' he said. 'Wood

'Conner, sir,' said Archie.

'How is Conner?'

'Lucky to be alive,' Archie replied. 'Although I doubt he'll be returning any time soon.'

'Indeed,' said his commanding officer. 'Falling into a camouflet is usually fatal.'

'It was for Wood,' Archie replied, as the image of Fred's lifeless and mud-streaked face flashed in his mind.

'It's the carbon monoxide left after the bomb explodes that's the problem,' said the officer, puffing on his pipe.

'Aye, I know right enough,' said Archie. 'Your blood soaks up the gas and it clogs your vital organs.'

'Although Monkman tells me you acquitted yourself well.'

'Did he, sir?'

'He did,' said Williamson, his heavily lined face lifting into a rare smile. 'Quite the hero of the hour pulling young Conner out —'

'I just did what needed to be done,' Archie cut in.

'Even so, it was a bad business. Bad business all around.' The major puffed noisily on his pipe. 'Of course, no one could have known there was a damn camouflet just under the surface, could they, Sergeant?'

'With all due respect, sir,' Archie replied carefully, 'there was evidence that indicated there might have been one lurking under the surface, as I pointed out to Lieutenant Monkman at the time,' said Archie. 'And I'd like that noted in your rep —'

'Of course, McIntosh, but I think it's pretty clear that it was an accident and I'm sure when HQ review the incident they will find the same,' interrupted Major Williamson, his eyes studying Archie from beneath his shaggy brows. 'A terrible accident that was no one's fault.'

'I'm afraid, sir, with the greatest respect, I can't agree with that,' said Archie. 'In my opinion Lieutenant Monkman's nerve has gone and he is a danger to himself and to others, and I shall be putting in a complaint to that effect.'

Anger flashed across Williamson's face. 'Men who volunteer for Bomb Disposal know the dangers, Sergeant.'

'Aye, they do,' agreed Archie, 'but the men are in danger enough from the enemy's attempt to kill them without them having to risk the same from their officers.'

'Well, I suppose that's your right, Sergeant,' said Williamson, 'but I call it a bad show. A damn bad show.'

Archie held his commander's gaze but didn't reply.

The large clock hanging over the door ticked off a few seconds then Williamson sat forward.

'Very well,' said Williamson, taking up his pen again. 'Now, on to other matters. I believe D Squad are representing the Section next week at this WVS rest centre thing.'

'We are, sir,' Archie replied.

'Good, well, make sure your men behave themselves,' said Williamson.

'Don't worry, I will,' Archie replied.

'And as you've got to have an officer at this sort of thing, I'm sending Lieutenant Monkman too,' Williamson continued. 'He was shaken up in the mess last night after what happened yesterday, so this might cheer you all up. You know, remind him why we do this job.'

'Sir.'

Pressing his lips together, Archie's gaze returned to the point just above his commanding officer's head.

Williamson looked down and started scribbling on the paper in front of him.

'That'll be all.'

Archie stood to attention and saluted the top of his commanding officer's head, then he turned and quick marched out of the office.

★ ★ ★

With the soft lilt of the Manchester Light Orchestra drifting out of the wireless on the dresser, Violet sank her teeth into the second triangle of her mid-afternoon sandwich.

The strawberry jam between the slices of national bread oozed out on her tongue. Thinking it was worth every bit of the two shillings she'd slipped Willy Tugman, Violet closed her eyes and savoured its sweet fruitiness.

It was about three thirty in the afternoon and she had arrived back from the church's bric-a-brac fundraising sale for Jewish refugees some thirty minutes ago.

Surprisingly, instead of the usual tat there were a few nice items, like embroidered dressing-table doilies, wicker baskets and papiermâché waste bins. She hadn't bought anything, of course, because as Stanley always said Jews were money-grabbing enough without doling out charity to them.

However, she'd shown her face so, Christian duty

259

done, she was now sitting in the kitchen with a steaming cup of tea in front of her and her naughty little indulgence.

And it was no more than she deserved for being forced to live under the same roof as Cathy and her loathsome lodger.

A sour expression twisted Violet's mouth at the memory of the low murmur of her daughter-in-law and the darkie sergeant's voices in the kitchen that morning as she was getting dressed upstairs.

She couldn't hear what they were saying but when she came down she could see them smiling and laughing with each other. Disgusting!

Taking another bite of her sandwich, Violet licked a dollop of jam off her lower lip. As she rolled the sticky sweetness around in her mouth, she felt a little jab of guilt but brushed it aside because sugar was bad for children's teeth.

She took a sip of tea and was just getting ready to take another bite when she heard the back gate squeak open followed by heavy wheels rolling over gravel.

Cramming the rest of the sandwich in her mouth Violet threw a mouthful of tea after it then jumped up. She grabbed the plate and jam-covered knife and plunged them into the sink. Wiping her mouth on the tea towel she flicked it back over the drying rail above the stove.

The back-door handle rattled.

Lunging at the table, she just managed to grab the jar of Hartley's jam and put it behind her back as the door opened and Sergeant McIntosh, with a deep scowl on his face, strode in.

'Afternoon, Mrs Wheeler,' he said, looking at her from under his furrowed brow.

260

'You look like you've had a bit of a rough day,' she said.

'Aye, you could say that,' he replied, unbuttoning his sheepskin jerkin.

'Well then, I've just made a fresh pot and a cup of that will perk you right up,' she suggested.

He raised an eyebrow.

'It will take more than tea to do that,' he replied, raking his fingers through his hair. 'But if it's not too much bother it might help a bit.'

'It's no trouble at all.' She gave him her syrupiest smile. 'Could you pass me the milk?'

Hanging his tatty biking jacket on the hook behind the door, he turned towards the fridge.

Violet's kind expression vanished and she swiftly placed the pot of jam on the chair she'd just vacated.

Holding a bottle of milk in his hand, Archie turned back.

'Thank you,' she said, crossing the room and taking it from him. 'You sit yourself down.'

He pulled out the chair on the other side of the table from her and did as she suggested.

Satisfied that her secret was out of sight, Violet went back to the dresser and took a mug from the shelf.

'I thought Mrs Wheeler junior might be back from the rest centre by now,' Archie said, as she poured the tea.

I bet you did, thought Violet, remembering the shameful way he looked at her daughter-in-law.

'She's probably popped into her mother's,' Violet replied. 'Sugar?'

'No thank you.'

Violet turned back, only to find he'd slipped his battle jacket off and over the back of his chair. Her

261

eyes narrowed because not only had he loosened his tie but he'd unbuttoned his collar too, something Stanley would never have done in her kitchen. There was also a copy of that disgraceful Communist rag the *Daily Mirror* on the table.

Forcing a smile, she placed his drink in front of him.

'I hope it's how you like it,' she said.

'As long as it's wet and warm it's fine by me.'

Under the pretext of tucking her skirts under her, Violet took hold of the pot of jam and sat back down opposite him.

Wedging the jar between her thighs, she picked up her half-drunk cup of tea.

'How are you settling in, Sergeant?' she asked, placing both elbows on the table.

'Well enough, now I've got the lay of the land.' He took a sip of tea and then tapped the newspaper beside him with his finger. 'I don't know if you've seen the papers today, Mrs Wheeler, but Montgomery is poised to retake Tripoli.'

A pained expression formed on Violet's face.

'I'm afraid I can't read the newspapers any more, not since . . .' Taking her handkerchief from her pocket, she dabbed beneath her right eye.

'I'm sorry,' he said. 'Is there any news of your son?'

'Not yet.' She forced a plucky smile. 'But I'm certain there will be any day now.'

He smiled sympathetically but didn't reply.

She wasn't surprised.

Anyone with half an eye could see that he was after getting his feet right under the table, into Stanley's shoes and his bed.

Let him!

Because Sergeant McIntosh would be smiling on the other side of his face when Stanley came home. He'd sort him and that slut of a daughter-in-law out good and proper.

'It seems like only yesterday when he and dear Cathy got married.' Violet sighed. 'You should have seen her, Sergeant. She was such a lovely bride.'

'I'm sure,' he replied flatly.

'It was the day before war broke out.' A blissful smile spread across Violet's face. 'Such a happy day and such a tragedy that two people so much in love should have been torn apart so soon.'

'So many have,' he replied.

'Did my daughter-in-law mention that my Stanley was chairman of the British Peace League before war broke out?'

'No,' he replied. 'In fact, she doesn't mention her husband all that much at all.'

'I'm not surprised,' said Violet, slipping her hand beneath the table to adjust the jar between her aching thighs. 'She adored Stanley and it must be too painful for her to talk about him. Of course, with his asthma he could have had a medical exemption but not Stanley. Too patriotic, you see. He's no shirker, not like those bloody conchie cowards.' Pausing, Violet applied the handkerchief to her eyes again. 'Even if he does get the medal his commanding officer has put him forward for, it won't ease dear Cathy's broken heart, will it?'

Something flickered in the back of the sergeant's eyes, but his pleasant expression didn't falter.

Swallowing the last of his tea, he stood up. 'If you'd excuse me, Mrs Wheeler, I've a letter from my mother that is in need of a reply.'

263

'Of course.' She gave him her sweetest smile again. 'As we're living under the same roof it's nice to have the chance to get to know you a bit better, Sergeant.'

He picked up his cup and took a step towards the sink.

'It's all right,' she said. 'I'll do that.'

'It's no bother,' he said, continuing across the kitchen.

With her mind focused on the jammy knife in the sink, Violet started to rise but as she did the glass jar slipped from her grip and bounced on her foot.

She stood up and looked down just in time to see it roll out from under the table across the lino and come to a stop against Sergeant McIntosh's army boots.

With her eyes glued to her black-market jam, Violet watched as he reached down and picked it up.

He studied the jar for a moment then a contemptuous expression spread across his face.

He offered it to her and wordlessly Violet took it.

With his gaze still on her he lifted his jacket from the back of his chair.

'You're right, Mrs Wheeler,' he said, picking up the newspaper. 'I certainly do know you a whole lot better after our little chat.'

17

'All right, lads,' said Archie, striding into No 8 Section of North East London Bomb Disposal company's barrack room. 'Let me have a wee squint at you to make sure you're fit to be seen in decent company.'

The half a dozen men lacing their boots, knotting their ties and Brylcreeming their hair left their tasks and stood at ease at the end of their khaki-covered beds.

Archie, too, had recently emerged from the tiled shower room and had donned his freshly pressed uniform and parade boots in readiness for the squad's afternoon jaunt.

Pulling down the front of his parade jacket, he walked over to where his men stood ready for inspection.

Chalky snapped to attention as Archie stopped in front of him.

'Had your hair cut, Sarge?' he asked, as Archie gave him the onceover.

Giving the corporal a cool look, Archie moved on and the next man straightened up.

'Well done, Goodman,' he said, nodding approvingly at the squaddie.

Casting his eye over another couple of the team and finding them correct, Archie started down the other side.

'Tie, Mogg,' said Archie, stopping in front of him.

The private adjusted his knot then sniffed the air. 'Is that Old Spice you're wearing, Sergeant?'

There were a couple of sniggers.

Stony-faced, Archie flicked his gaze over Ron then stopped in front of Arthur at the end of the line.

Reaching out he straightened the soldier's collar.

'Ah, well,' said Archie, stepping back and giving an exaggerated sigh, 'I'm afraid there's nothing for it but to let you bunch of jessies spend the afternoon eating cake and drinking tea with the nice ladies at St Breda and St Brendan's Rest Centre.'

'That's nice,' said Mogg, placing his hand on his chest and trying to look offended. 'And after us being up all night darning our socks.'

The men laughed.

'But, Sarge, is it 'ladies' or is it one particular lady?' Arthur asked.

'With light brown hair?' added Mogg.

'And a figure like — '

'All right, lads,' interrupted Archie. 'You've had your fun, now get some dinner in the canteen because, reluctant though I am to inflict you bunch of savages on the genteel ladies of the WVS, we'll be leaving here at two, sharp. Dismissed!'

They saluted and half a dozen men stood to attention then peeled off right and trooped out.

'Don't worry, Archie,' said Chalky, seeing his apprehensive look, 'I'll make sure they're on the truck in good time.'

'Thanks, I'll — '

'McIntosh.' Archie looked around to see Monkman, wearing his regimental jacket with a pip on each shoulder, sauntering into the barrack room, his swagger stick in his hand.

Archie and his corporal snapped to attention and saluted as the lieutenant stopped in front of them.

'The old man asked me to be the officer at this

266

afternoon's little pantomime,' he said, brandy fumes wafting up as he spoke. 'Remind me, will you, where it is again?'

'St Breda and St Brendan's church hall,' Archie replied. 'In Sutton Street, E1. Just past the Blackwall Tunnel as you head west down Commercial Street. It starts at three.'

The lieutenant's thin face lifted in a condescending smile. 'I'm sure I'll find it eventually. I can't say spending the afternoon with a bunch of whiskery old biddies is my idea of soldiering, but we must

follow our superior officer's orders, mustn't we, Sergeant?'

Archie eyed the man in front of him coolly. 'Sir.'

Monkman turned as if to go but then he swung back again.

'Oh, by the way, McIntosh,' swinging his stick up, he rested it on Archie's chest, 'a little bird tells me that your landlady is a bit of a cracker.'

Archie didn't reply.

A leer spread across Monkman's face as Archie fought hard not to react.

'I can see she is.' He tapped Archie with his swagger stick. 'You *dark* horse, Sergeant. I look forward to making her acquaintance.'

Running his deep-set eyes over Archie a final time, he turned and strutted out of the barrack room.

'Corporal,' said Archie as he watched the lieutenant go, 'I don't want him causing any trouble for the lads, so can you remind them to watch themselves at the rest centre.'

'I will,' replied Chalky. 'But by the look on your face, Archie, I'd say you're the one who needs to keep a hold on your temper this afternoon.'

267

'What time are they coming?' asked Maureen as Cathy checked the row of cups lined up ready for the afternoon's proceedings.

'Any time now,' she replied, resisting the urge to look at the clock at the far end of the hall.

It was now ten past three and Archie and his men should have arrived ten minutes ago. There was still plenty of time for them to get in place for the ceremony but Cathy wished they would hurry up.

'I hope so, for everyone's sake, because Mrs Paget's temper's set to boil over any minute,' said Dora, nodding towards the kitchen's serving hatch where Mrs Paget was standing.

She, like Cathy, was wearing her WVS uniform but had three-inch-high court shoes on her feet instead of the stout lace-ups Cathy and her friends favoured.

'Yeah,' agreed Maureen. 'She's already got a face like a slapped arse and if the lads from the D Squad are late' — she sucked her teeth — 'all hell's likely to break out.'

'Like it hasn't already,' Dora remarked. 'She's been in a right mood since we voted down her suggestion of 61 Squadron.'

'Well, she'll have to lump it,' said Cathy. 'And I sometimes think she needs to be reminded that we're all supposed to be equals in the — '

The door swung open again and Cathy's heart went off at a thunder when Archie strode in with his squad a step behind him.

As far as Cathy was concerned, Archie always looked good, even when he was plastered with mud and grey with tiredness, but today, smartly dressed in his parade jacket, he looked utterly wonderful.

He glanced around the room until he spotted her and then, with his blue eyes focused on her, he strode over.

'Hello,' she said, feeling a little light-headed as he advanced towards her.

'Hello, yourself, Mrs Wheeler,' he replied, stopping in front of her.

They smiled at each other for a long moment then Maureen coughed.

'Sorry,' said Cathy, dragging her eyes from him. 'This is Maureen and Dora. Girls, this is Sergeant McIntosh.'

'Nice to meet you, Sergeant,' said Maureen, batting her lashes at him behind her spectacles.

'Likewise, I'm sure,' Dora added, giving him a lavish look.

He smiled and inclined his head. 'Ladies.'

He looked around. 'Is Lieutenant Monkman here?'

Cathy shook her head. 'I don't think so.'

Archie frowned and glanced at his wristwatch.

'Oh, oh,' said Maureen. 'Get your tin hats on.'

Cathy looked past Archie to see Mrs Paget, with a face like a fury from Hades, bearing down on them.

'What do you think you're doing, Mrs Wheeler?' she asked, barging past Archie.

'Welcoming our brave soldiers of the Bomb Disposal Unit,' Cathy replied.

'Well, as I'm in charge of this afternoon's proceedings you should have brought them straight over to me,' Mrs Paget snapped. She looked up at Archie. 'What are you doing here?'

'Me and my men are here to have a cuppa and a morsel of cake with the lovely lasses of the WVS,' Archie replied. 'And to thank them formally for adopting our section, Mrs . . . ?'

'Paget. And I'm the one in charge.' She looked pointedly at Cathy before she turned back to Archie. 'I thought your headquarters were sending an officer.'

'Aye, Lieutenant Monkman,' Archie said. 'And he should have been here well before now.'

Panic flashed across Mrs Paget's face.

'But don't fret,' he continued, regarding her coolly, 'if he doesn't arrive in time, I'll stand in for him.'

Like a goldfish with lipstick, Mrs Paget's mouth opened and shut a couple of times but before she could reply, the hall's door swung open again and Monkman, wearing his trench coat draped over his uniform, swept in.

'Thank God,' muttered Mrs Paget.

Raising his head, the lieutenant looked around, then, spotting them, he sauntered over.

'Mrs Paget, I presume,' he said, an urbane smile lifting his pencil moustache as he addressed her.

'Yes, indeed,' she replied.

He bowed.

'Lieutenant Monkman, at your service.' He gave her a considered look. 'You're not one of the Lincolnshire Pagets from Chesley Hall, are you?'

'Lord Paget is my husband Reverend Eustace Paget's uncle, and he spent many happy hours at the hall as a boy,' she simpered at him.

'Capital.'

The lieutenant's attention shifted from the vicar's wife to Cathy.

'And you are?' he asked.

'Mrs Wheeler,' she replied, remembering the two men injured — one fatally — and Archie's distress at

270

the hands of the arrogant officer.

His glance flitted on to Archie then back to her.

'And this is Mrs Morgan and Mrs Black,' Cathy added, indicating the two women either side of her to draw his attention away.

'Charming,' he said, his eyes running lazily over her.

'If you're ready, Lieutenant,' said Mrs Paget, extending her arm towards the stage.

Monkman studied Cathy for a little longer then turned away.

'Get your men in order so they don't disgrace us all, McIntosh,' he called over his shoulder as he followed Mrs Paget to the stage.

Archie's expression hardened for a moment then he turned away.

'Excuse me, ladies, but duty calls.' His eyes locked on Cathy's for a split second then he strode over to the refreshments area, where his squad were eyeing the cakes.

As Archie pulled his men into order on the stage and took up his position at the end of the line, the people in the hall, sensing the afternoon's proceedings were about to begin, stopped what they were doing and gathered in front of the stage.

With D Squad standing at ease behind their senior officer, Mrs Paget clapped her hands.

Other than the odd baby grizzling and a couple of people coughing and sneezing, the hall fell silent.

Mrs Paget stepped forward.

'Good afternoon, and welcome, all of you, to St Breda and St Brendan's Rest Centre,' she said, raising her voice so her strident, well-rounded tones could be heard by those at the back. 'But more particularly, I

271

would like to extend a warm welcome to Lieutenant Monkman and the brave men of . . . '

Of their own volition, Cathy's eyes moved from the woman talking to Archie and found him looking back at her.

Everything around Cathy faded until only Archie, with his dazzlingly blue eyes, filled her heart and mind.

★ ★ ★

'I think that went off well enough, don't you, girls?' asked Peggy, handing a mug of tea to an old man with a stick.

'Went like a dream,' said Cathy, as she splashed milk into another half a dozen cups.

'Yes,' added Maureen. 'Considering old face-ache over there was dead against it.'

The presentation had just finished and, after loud applause from everyone as Mrs Paget gave Lieutenant Monkman a framed letter formally adopting the Bomb Disposal Unit in exchange for a picture of their inverted bomb badge, Cathy and her two friends were now manning the refreshments table in the canteen area at the opposite end from the stage.

Because it was such a special occasion, the hall was jam-packed with not just the rest centre regulars but also local ARP personnel and WVS representatives from HQ and other nearby rest centres. Father Mahon was also in attendance, sitting in a seat Cathy had found for him, talking to Denis Topping, the councillor for the Wapping and Shadwell ward.

Despite the crowd of people around her, Cathy knew exactly where Archie was. Making a show of collecting up a handful of used cups and placing them on to the tray at the end of the table, she glanced across at him.

He had been cornered by a bevy of young women over by the shoe exchange benches on the other side of the hall. Although they were gazing adoringly up at him, Archie's gaze left his admirers and found Cathy.

He said something to the girls clustering around him and then, with his cup in his hand, walked across to Cathy.

'Can I get you another?' she asked.

'I wouldn't say no,' he replied, placing his mug on the table.

Cathy refilled it and handed it back.

'Your Mrs Paget looks happy enough now,' said Archie, indicating the centre's controller, who was still on the stage chatting to Lieutenant Monkman.

'It was him mentioning her husband's snobby family that jollied her up no end,' said Cathy.

He laughed.

'I can't look at him without thinking of your poor men, Archie,' Cathy said. 'Is there any news on the complaint you lodged?'

'It's been 'sent to HQ for consideration',' Archie replied. 'My eye! That's officer-speak for buried in a file somewhere.'

Studying the officer over the rim of his mug, Archie took a mouthful of tea.

'I don't suppose you putting in a complaint about him has endeared you to the lieutenant,' she said.

Archie shrugged. 'He and I weren't pals in the first place.'

As if he knew he was the subject of their conversation, Archie's senior officer turned and, from his vantage point above the crowd, let his gaze run slowly

273

over them.

Something caught Archie's eye to the side of Cathy and exasperation flashed across his face.

Looking around, Cathy saw two of his men trying to smooch a couple of giggly young women behind the rows of second-hand clothes.

'You know, sometimes,' he said, swallowing a last mouthful of tea, 'I think I'm more the men's nursemaid than their blooming NCO.'

Archie put the empty cup alongside the dirty ones she'd collected.

'If you'll excuse me,' he said with a sigh, 'I'd better go and make sure that D Squad's not banned from the rest centre they've just been adopted by.'

Cathy laughed. 'I'll see you later.'

He gave her that lopsided smile of his. 'Aye, you most certainly will.'

He marched off.

Cathy watched him for a second or two then she lifted the tray of used crockery and walked the couple of steps to the serving hatch.

On the other side of the opening, Sadie Lipman and half a dozen other women, red-faced and with their sleeves rolled up, were dashing from pillar to post boiling kettles, washing plates and drying cups.

Sadie, who was presiding over the organised chaos of the rest centre's kitchen, spotted Cathy. Wiping her hands on her apron, she hurried over.

'Ta, luv,' she said, as Cathy slid the tray through. 'You wouldn't do us a favour, would you? There's a box of spare cups on the table in the small committee room. Could you fetch them in for us as we're down to our last half-dozen?'

'Course,' said Cathy.

Wending her way around a group of well-dressed matrons tucking into their afternoon tea, Cathy made for the main door. Leaving the crowded hall, she stepped out into the cool corridor and hurried towards the last door on the right.

Turning the brass handle, she walked in. The box of spare cream-coloured cups were, as Sadie had said, sitting in the middle of the table. However, just as Cathy was about to lift them off the polished mahogany surface, the door creaked as someone opened it.

She turned. Seeing who it was, unease rippled through her but Cathy forced a sociable smile.

'If you're looking for the Gents, Lieutenant Monkman, they're down the corridor,' she said.

'Indeed they are,' the officer replied.

Closing the door, he ambled over.

'It's Cathy, isn't it?' he said.

'Well, I think Mrs Wheeler is a little more — '

'Sergeant McIntosh's landlady.' Stepping closer, his hooded eyes ran slowly over her face. 'His very pretty' — his gaze shifted down further — 'and full-bodied landlady.'

He grabbed her right breast.

Cathy went to slap him, but he caught her hand as it shot towards him.

Twisting it behind her back, he shoved her against the wall.

'Get off,' she shouted, struggling to free herself.

Pinning her against the oak panels lining the room, he forced her arm higher.

Pain shot across Cathy's shoulder and she gasped.

'Now, now. Don't be a prick teaser,' he whispered, as his fingers closed around her breast.

'Help — '

Monkman's hand clamped over her mouth.

Panic flared in Cathy's chest as the memory of Stan's hand doing the same, and more, surged into her mind.

'You know you want it,' he murmured, his breath hot on her skin. 'Your type always do. And if you let that half-caste Jock bastard into your knickers then you can let me have a poke too.'

Pressing on to her, Monkman ground his hardness against her.

Using the wall as leverage, Cathy tried to push him away but he just spread his legs wider and jammed into her harder.

With his hand still covering her mouth, his other hand reached between them and he grabbed the serge fabric of her skirt and hauled it up.

The lieutenant's fingers ran up and over her suspenders and on to her bare thigh.

Forcing aside the brutal memories of Stan that threatened to overwhelm her, Cathy compelled herself to take action.

As Monkman explored beneath the edge of her cotton drawers, Cathy let out a low moan and relaxed in his arms.

The lieutenant chuckled and, retracting his hand, reached down for his fly buttons.

As he arched back, Cathy forced a wanton look on to her face.

'Lieutenant,' she said huskily.

He looked up as Cathy jammed her knee into his crotch.

Gasping, Monkman staggered back, cradling his injured genitals.

'You cow,' he spluttered. 'You bloody — '

Cathy's balled fist smacked him across the face.

'No, you bloody bastard,' she replied.

Coughing, he staggered towards her. 'I'll show you, you — '

The door opened and Archie strode in.

Taking in the scene at a glance, and with fury flaring from his face, he started towards his senior officer.

Cathy met him halfway.

'Don't, Archie,' she said, blocking his path and placing a hand on his chest. 'He's not worth it.'

Archie's body tensed as his white-hot glare blazed across at Monkman.

Cathy held her breath but, after what seemed like an eternity, she felt him relax.

Picking up the box from the table, she handed it to Archie.

'Would you mind carrying these to the kitchen for me, Sergeant?' she asked.

With his eyes still burning into his commanding officer, Cathy felt Archie tense again, but then he adjusted the weight in his arms and stood aside.

Without looking at Monkman, Cathy turned and walked to the door with Archie no more than half a step behind her.

★ ★ ★

Carrying the box effortlessly in his arms, Archie walked with Cathy to the serving hatch.

'There you are, Sadie,' Cathy said, with a slight waver in her voice as Archie slid the box across the counter.

'Thanks, luv,' the jolly-looking woman on the other side replied.

Turning, Cathy looked up and gave Archie a too bright smile.

'And . . . and th . . . thank you, Archie, for . . . ' Her chin started to quiver.

Taking hold of her elbow, Archie guided her away from the bustling canteen and behind the book-exchange shelves in the corner.

Tears welled in her eyes as she started crying.

The image of Cathy's rumpled clothes and fearful eyes flashed through Archie's mind, igniting fury in his chest.

Balling his fists, Archie turned but Cathy caught his hand.

'Don't,' she said, holding his tight fingers in her soft ones. 'I said he's not worth it.'

Archie mastered his temper then stepped in front of her to shield her from prying eyes. He pulled out his clean handkerchief and handed it to her, then watched helplessly as she wept.

'I'm sorry,' he said, aching to take her in his arms.

Gathering herself together, Cathy looked up.

'It's not your fault, Archie,' she said, tears shimmering on her lower lashes. 'It's his. For being a pig.'

'But if I'd seen him disappear after you, I could have stopped him,' he replied.

She raised an eyebrow. 'I think I did that pretty well myself.'

The corners of Archie's mouth lifted slightly. 'You did that, bonny lass. But I hate that he's upset you so.'

'He hasn't,' said Cathy. 'To be honest, I've been dealing with blokes trying it on since I stopped wearing pigtails, it's just that when he put his hand over my mouth it reminded me of . . . '

Biting her lower lip, Cathy gave him a hesitant

glance.

'Your husband?' he said.

She nodded and anger again flared in Archie's chest.

'It's all right,' she said, seeing his expression. 'Lots of women have it worse than I did.'

'That doesn't make it right,' Archie replied.

She studied him for a moment then spoke again. 'You've never laid hands in anger on a woman, have you, Archie?'

'Never,' he replied.

Cathy gave a low laugh.

'I don't know why I even asked because I already knew the answer,' she said, dabbing the last few tears away. Her too-bright smile returned. 'I can't stand here chatting to you all afternoon. I have a rest centre to run.'

He placed a hand on her arm. 'Are you sure you're all right, Cathy?'

'I'm fine, honest,' she replied. 'I'll see you later.'

Letting his hand fall to his side, Archie stepped back.

Giving him another little smile, Cathy walked past him and headed into the main part of the hall.

Archie watched her go.

No woman deserved to be manhandled by the likes of Monkman or beaten and abused by her violent husband. What beautiful, clever, generous, open-hearted Cathy Wheeler deserved was to be loved and cherished for the rest of her life, and he just prayed she would let him be the man who would do just that.

18

As she gazed around the crowded hall, Marjory Paget had to admit that, despite her fury that Cathy Wheeler and her cronies had voted to adopt the bomb disposal squad instead of her dear son Reginald's squadron, the afternoon had gone very well. Very well indeed.

Even the appearance of that uppity sergeant and his rough soldiers hadn't marred proceedings. Well, not much.

And what good fortune, nay, divine intervention, that Lieutenant Monkman, an officer and a man of refinement, had been designated to represent the Section at the centre's little ceremony.

Of course, those of superior breeding recognised others of the same, and having established that the Monkmans and the Pagets were, albeit distantly, related, the whole afternoon had gone swimmingly. Especially when the lieutenant mentioned in passing that the Bishop of Banbury was his godfather and that he was looking for a new chaplain.

Her smile widened at the thought of exchanging the filthy streets and coarse people of East London for the lush fields and forelock-tugging yokels of the shires.

A gruff male laugh cut across her rural dream and Marjory looked around. She saw two of the bomb disposal squad with their arms around the shoulders of a couple of loose-looking young women.

Marjory's mouth pulled into a thin line. Typical!

And where was that sergeant of theirs who was supposed to be keeping them in order?

She glanced around and her mouth pulled even tighter when she spotted him tucked in the far corner with Mrs Wheeler.

Their heads were bowed and they looked deep in conversation.

She was just going to go over to give him a piece of her mind about his men's behaviour when the hall door swung open and Lieutenant Monkman walked unsteadily back into the hall.

He spotted his subordinate and loathing contorted his face.

Marching across to the edge of the stage, he grabbed his cap and swagger stick. Tucking the latter under his arm and jamming the former on his head, the commanding officer of No 8 Section marched back across the hall and practically swung the double doors off their hinges as he stormed out.

Seeing her dreams of a leafy parish in Oxfordshire leaving with the lieutenant, Marjory hurried after him.

He was just a few paces from the exit when she reached the corridor.

'Are you going, Lieutenant Monkman?' she called.

He spun on his heels and glared at her.

'I most certainly am, Mrs Paget,' he snapped back. 'And if I'd known —'

'Known! Known what?' she asked, her heart palpitating in her chest. 'What has happened?'

He paused.

'Please,' she urged. 'Whatever has caused you such distress, Lieutenant, at least give me the chance to make it right.'

He studied her for a moment then let out a long sigh.

'I'm sorry,' he said. 'I shouldn't blame you.'

'Blame me for what?'

'For the loose morals of . . . no.' He raised his hand. 'Perhaps better to leave the matter there.'

'I think not,' said Mrs Paget, striding down the corridor. 'If there is any immorality taking place in my rest centre then I need to know.'

'Very well,' he replied. 'I found that Wheeler woman in . . .' He shot her an uncertain look. 'Let's just say an intimate position no respectable married woman should be found in.'

'With whom?' asked Mrs Paget.

'Sergeant McIntosh,' he said.

'They weren't . . . ?'

'Not quite,' Lieutenant Monkman replied. 'But I'm sure she's as much at fault as him.'

'I'm sure she is,' agreed Mrs Paget. 'Her poor widowed mother-in-law is a member of our congregation, so I know exactly what the young Mrs Wheeler is like.' She pulled a face. 'She's from Irish stock.'

'That explains a lot,' he said. 'Of course, as a gentleman, I intervened and got this for my troubles.' He pointed to the red patch on his left cheek.

Mrs Paget's jaw dropped. 'He struck you?'

'Just a glancing blow.' Lieutenant Monkman frowned. 'And although it doesn't excuse her lapse in judgement, a man like McIntosh does seem to have a savage or animal appeal, if you will, that some women find hard to resist.'

'Common women, Lieutenant, common women,' Mrs Paget replied.

He nodded sagely. 'Of course, I should report the whole thing to HQ.'

'I should think so, too,' Mrs Paget replied with relish. 'I'm sure your CO would take a very dim view of you being assaulted by a subordinate.'

The lieutenant looked puzzled. 'Not my HQ, Mrs Paget, but yours.'

Something akin to ice water drained through Mrs Paget's veins.

'Is that really necessary?' she asked, hoping only she could hear the quiver in her voice. 'I mean, you've dealt with the unfortunate incident, so surely the WVS Area Committee need not be involved.'

The lieutenant's moustache moved back and forth a couple of times.

'Very well,' he said. 'I think we can let the matter rest. After all, I wouldn't want one unfortunate incident to disrupt the most excellent work you and your ladies do for the war effort.'

Mrs Paget let go of the breath she was holding.

'And even if there was some sort of inquiry,' he continued, 'it would be their word against mine.'

'Well, I know who I believe,' said Mrs Paget. 'And don't worry, from now on I'll be keeping a close eye on Mrs Wheeler.'

He pushed open the door.

'Of course,' he said, pausing on the threshold, 'what puzzles me is why they couldn't have just waited until they got home before they gave free rein to their passion.'

Mrs Paget stared at him.

'I'm sorry, Mrs Paget,' he said, seeing her bewildered expression. 'I thought you knew that Sergeant McIntosh lodges with Mrs Wheeler.'

★ ★ ★

With his elbow on the window frame and his fist supporting his chin, Archie scowled through the rain-splattered window as he thought of several very effective ways to inflict permanent injury on his so-called superior.

It was now nearly five o'clock and after thanking Mrs Paget, Archie and his men were heading back to base.

'Archie,' said Chalky, sitting next to him in the three-ton Austin.

'Huh?'

'Remember what you promised,' his corporal said, turning the wheel to avoid a pothole in the middle of Leytonstone Road.

'I didn't promise,' Archie replied.

'Come on, Archie!' continued Chalky. 'From what you tell me, your landlady had already made Monkman's eyes water before you arrived.'

'Aye, she had,' said Archie. 'But that doesnae mean I shouldnae follow her example and give him a good pasting, too.'

'For Gawd's sake, Archie!'

'Bloody gobshite,' continued Archie, as the image of Monkman manhandling Cathy raged through his mind again. 'I've a good mind to — '

'Find yourself up on a charge for assaulting a superior officer,' said Ron.

'Superior, my arse,' snapped Archie. 'The man's nothing more than a — '

'We all know what he is,' interrupted Arthur. 'And if you let that temper of yours get yourself a spell in the glasshouse, then he'll be able to call all the shots, and me and the boys will most likely end up lying on a mortuary slab like poor old Fred.'

Archie chewed the inside of his mouth.

'Listen, Archie,' continued Arthur, 'we can tell you've got a soft spot for your landlady, but after shrugging off all his ape and monkey jibes, don't let Monkman get under your skin about this. He's not worth it.'

Despite his rampaging temper, the side of Archie's mouth lifted in a wry smile. 'That's what Cathy said.'

'Well, then.' Arthur punched him playfully in the shoulder. 'You should listen to her.'

Archie sighed. 'Aye, I should.'

'And besides,' said Chalky, gripping the steering wheel again, 'if you get thrown in the can, some flashy Yank might move in while you're gone.'

Archie raised an eyebrow. 'Bugger off, Corporal.'

Chalky grinned. 'Bugger off yourself, Sergeant.'

Ten minutes later, and with Archie's temper more or less under control, Chalky turned the wheel and guided the front wheels of their lorry through the square brick-built gateway of Wanstead High School's playground.

There were only a handful of vehicles in the yard because, with another two hours until blackout, the other teams were still digging out whatever UXB they'd been allocated that morning.

Unfortunately, Monkman's Rover 10 Tourer was one of the few officers' cars parked alongside the side of the school building.

Archie jumped down from the cab and slammed the door.

'Right, lads,' he said as the men tumbled out of the tailgate, 'you've had a doss of a day today but you'll be hard at it again tomorrow so have a drink —'

'Or two,' someone shouted from the back.

'Or two,' Archie agreed. 'But have a good night's kip as I'll be wanting to see you keen and ready because with Jerry visiting us again tonight there'll be no tea and cakes tomorrow.'

'No, just poxy mud,' shouted Mogg.

Archie grinned. 'Aye, poxy mud. And lots of it.'

Laughing and jostling each other, the men of D Squad trudged towards their billets.

After helping Arthur and Chalky secure the tailgate and awning, Archie, with his corporal and lance corporal alongside him, followed the rest of the team into the building.

Raucous laughter from the officers' mess greeted Archie as he passed through the entrance and into the main corridor.

His jaw tightened but, fixing his eyes on the company offices at the far end of the corridor, he marched on.

Without glancing to the side, Archie strode on past the open door of the officers' drinking hole.

'Sergeant McIntosh!'

Archie stopped, as did his two men.

'A moment of your time, if you please.'

'Remember what Cathy said,' Chalky told him softly.

Taking a deep breath, Archie turned around. Pulling down the front of his jacket, he walked back and stopped at the door.

Monkman, with a drink in hand, was lounging by the fire in one of the leather button-backed chairs. Lieutenants Streetly and Paltock, also clutching glasses of spirits, reclined in a similar manner opposite.

'Sir,' Archie said, standing to attention and fixing his eyes on the faded portrait hanging over the mantelshelf.

'Come in, man,' smirked Streetly, a sallow youth who struggled to grow a moustache.

'Yes,' belched Paltock, sloshing the drink in his chubby hand as he spoke.

Archie stepped over the threshold, and despite every nerve in his body being as tight as a Yarrow gangmaster's fist, he stood at ease.

'Lieutenant Monkman here has been telling us all about the little circus you attended this afternoon, McIntosh,' said Streetly.

'Has he, sir?' Archie replied.

'Indeed,' said Paltock. 'And all the tempting cake on offer.'

Streetly sniggered. 'Moist, too, wasn't it, old chap?'

'Very,' said Monkman, his eyes fixed on Archie.

Attempting to keep the red mist at the edge of his vision at bay, Archie returned his gaze to the oil painting above the fire.

He snapped to attention. 'If that's all, sir, then — '

'He was also enlightening us as to the outstanding qualities of your landlady, Mrs Wheeler,' said Paltock. 'Both of them.'

'Didn't you say they were a full handful, Monkman?' asked Streetly.

'I most certainly did,' Monkman replied, leering. 'But better still was the soft feel of her . . . ' He winked. 'Isn't that right, Sergeant?'

Blazing fury shot through Archie.

Crossing the room in two strides, he grasped the officer's lapels and heaved Monkman out of his chair, dangling him like a rag doll.

'Now steady on,' said Paltock, rolling out of his chair and struggling to his feet.

'Yes, steady on, Sergeant,' agreed Streetly. 'We were

just having a bit of fun, that's all, man to man, you know.'

Hands grabbed Archie's arms.

'Let him be, Archie,' said Chalky, from what seemed like a long way away.

'Do what Chalky says, Archie,' Arthur added.

Archie's grip tightened.

'Come on, Archie, lad,' repeated Arthur. 'Think of Cathy.'

As an image of her smile floated into his mind, Archie released his grip.

Monkman fell back. Regaining his balance, he stood.

Giving Archie a murderous look, the officer pulled his jacket straight.

'Do you think after your bit of common fluff opened her legs for a half-bred animal like you, McIntosh, I'd touch her with a barge pole,' he spat out.

Balling his right hand into a fist, Archie drew his arm back but, as he stepped forward, his two men grabbed him again.

'What on earth is going on here?'

Monkman and the two other senior officers snapped to attention and saluted as sharply as the almost empty bottle of brandy on the table between them allowed.

The two men holding Archie let go immediately and he looked around.

'I said — '

'Just a bit of high spirits, sir,' Lieutenant Streetly replied, attempting to stand up straight as he saluted No 8 Section's commanding officer.

Major Williamson looked Archie over then fixed his eyes on the three lieutenants.

'Well?'

288

'Ye-yes, sir,' spluttered Paltock. 'As Streetly said: just high spirits.'

The CO's hooded eyes shifted to Monkman.

Monkman, who held his superior officer's gaze for a few moments, gave a curt nod.

'Good,' said the major. 'Because we've got a bloody crisis on our hands. We've had three squads blown up in the past two days. They were dismantling what was, on the face of it, a straightforward number seventeen, so the top brass and boffins at Woolwich suspect that Jerry has developed a booby trap specifically designed to kill bomb disposal personnel.'

'Bastards,' muttered Archie.

'My thoughts exactly, Sergeant,' Major Williamson replied. 'But until we have figured out how to get around whatever it is they've concocted, no one touches a bomb. Do you hear? No one.'

* * *

'It's not your rations you're using, Mrs Day, so I'll have a bit more milk in my tea if it's not too much trouble,' said Violet, giving the woman behind the refreshments table a tight-lipped smile.

Bette Day's nostrils flared a little as she topped up the cup.

It was Wednesday at about eleven thirty and the midweek service had just finished. The curate, Father Silas, had taken the service under the direction of the vicar and he'd given them a homily about forgiveness, which was all well and good but not when you had to live with the likes of Cathy Brogan.

Picking up her drink and taking a biscuit from the plate alongside, Violet turned and surveyed the room to find a free chair.

She spotted Winnie Master sitting at a table in the corner so, in anticipation of finding out whose husband was sneaking through which back door in the blackout, she started towards the part-time ARP warden.

'Mrs Wheeler!'

She turned to see the vicar's wife, not a hair out of place and impeccably dressed as always, homing in on her.

Violet smiled. 'Good morning, Mrs Paget, and can I say what — '

'May I have a word?' she cut in. 'In private.'

Grabbing Violet's elbow, she propelled her across the room and back into the church.

The verger and his team were straightening the kneelers and collecting stray service books so, without pausing, Mrs Paget headed for the rear of the side chapel.

'Is anything wrong?' asked Violet, as they stopped at the back of the pews.

'Wrong!' snapped the vicar's wife. 'Yes, Mrs Wheeler, something is very wrong. Why wasn't I informed that the sergeant from bomb disposal is your lodger?'

'He's not my lodger,' Violet replied. 'If it were up to me, he'd be out on his ear.'

'Well, be that as it may,' continued the vicar's wife, 'I will not have him and your daughter-in-law dragging down the reputation of my rest centre.' Her eyes narrowed. 'And after yesterday's little incident — '

'What incident?' asked Violet, her ears pricking up.

The vicar's wife frowned. 'Can I rely on your discretion, Mrs Wheeler?'

'Totally, Mrs Paget,' said Violet.

290

Mrs Paget glanced around. 'They were discovered . . . together.'

Violet's eyes stretched wide. 'No! Not . . . '

'I'm afraid so,' said Mrs Paget. 'Not by me, thankfully.' Her eyes narrowed. 'I had my suspicions when he started hanging around the rest centre before Christmas. I didn't want to seem uncharitable, so I told your daughter-in-law to direct him to one of the other centres nearer to the dock where others like him hang out. But now it seems rather than do as I instructed, she's his— I'm sorry, I'm so appalled I can't even say the word.'

Despite heavily hinting the same to everyone in the market and beyond, Violet was pretty sure nothing was going on — she would have heard — but nonetheless . . .

'I had heard rumours,' she said. 'But I didn't want to believe that even she would sink so low.' She covered her eyes with her hand.

'Oh, my poor Stanley,' she continued in a faltering voice. She looked up. 'I imagine you're going to throw her out of the WVS.'

'If I had proof, I would,' said Mrs Paget.

'I thought you said someone found them together,' said Violet, imagining the field day she could have telling everyone in the market tomorrow.

Mrs Paget pulled a regretful face.

'It's their word against his.' Her plucked brows pulled together. 'But believe me, Mrs Wheeler, the moment I have irrefutable proof of your daughter-in-law's immoral behaviour, her feet won't touch the ground and she'll be out of the WVS.'

19

'Quick, Cathy,' said Jo, 'before the lights change, or we'll have to walk back from the bus garage.'

Holding on to the upright pole on the number 25's platform, Cathy glanced behind her. Seeing no bicycles coming up on the inside, she jumped on to the pavement.

'Goodness,' said Cathy as she adjusted her hat. 'That was a bit of a mystery tour around Bethnal Green, wasn't it?'

'Well, better than disappearing into that crater we saw opposite the almshouses on Mile End Road,' said Jo. 'I bet Francesca felt that one fall last night in the café cellar.'

It was about five thirty on the first Wednesday in March and almost a month since the incident with Monkman.

Cathy and her younger sister were standing on the south side of Whitechapel High Street, just down from the pile of rubble that had, until last year, been St Mary's Church.

The bus pulled off and people hurried past on their way home at the end of the working day. Cathy's eyes focused on the building opposite. Its doors were wide open and a small well-heeled crowd were making their way inside the Whitechapel Art Gallery.

Her heart did a little double step as expectation bubbled around in her stomach.

'Jo,' said Cathy, 'perhaps we should — '

'Don't you dare,' said Jo, slipping her arm through

her sister's.

'Dare what?' asked Cathy.

'Bottle out,' Jo replied. 'I've been looking forward to this all week.'

'I didn't know you were interested in art,' said Cathy.

'I am.' Jo winked. 'But I'm interested in seeing this Sergeant McIntosh of yours more.'

'You have,' said Cathy. 'When you came out to fetch me back into church.'

'That was months ago,' Jo replied. 'And I only just glimpsed him. So stop shilly-shallying about and let's go.'

Jo looked both ways. Satisfied the coast was clear, she frogmarched Cathy across the road.

They handed over their coats to the girl in the cloakroom and were given a two-page black-and-white programme listing all the exhibits in return.

'I must just spend a penny before we go in,' said Cathy.

After doing what she had to do, Cathy studied herself in the mirror as she washed her hands.

She'd tried on and discarded three outfits before she'd settled on her navy dress with pencil skirt, three quarter-length sleeve and scoop neckline with a white Peter Pan collar.

'You look fine,' said Jo, joining her at the sinks.

'Are you sure?' said Cathy, twisting to look at her rear in the reflection.

'I am,' Jo replied. 'And, before you ask, yes, your seams are straight. Now come on.'

After wiping their hands on the towel roll hanging next to the sinks, they headed out, but as they reached the entrance to the exhibition, Cathy caught her sister's arm.

'And just so you know,' she said, giving her a firm look, 'Sergeant McIntosh isn't my anything.'

Jo grinned. 'If you say so, Cathy.'

She trotted off into the main gallery.

Sighing and wondering if the whole evening was going to be a total disaster, Cathy followed her in.

She saw her sister gazing up at a large canvas entitled *We Will Fight Them*.

It depicted a platoon of rather elderly Home Guards standing on the White Cliffs of Dover, brandishing their bayoneted rifles across the Channel.

'I bet Hitler spotted that lot through his binoculars and called off the invasion,' whispered Jo, as Cathy joined her.

'Behave,' said Cathy, in the same hushed tone, suppressing a smile.

They moved on to the next painting entitled *The Land Thanks You*, which was an image of a farmer on his tractor surrounded by Land Girls in tan jodhpurs and green woollies, waving at a squadron of Spitfires overhead.

'Cathy!'

She looked around to see Archie, dressed in the uniform she'd steamed and pressed for him the day before.

To be honest, since the day of the presentation Cathy had taken it upon herself to do lots of little things for Archie. Things like darning a threadbare sock she'd found in the washing or making his favourite meal if he had been out in the rain all day. However, no matter how small they were, Archie always noticed and rewarded her with his thanks and that sideways smile of his. Now he strode across the central space towards her.

'Hello,' he said, his eyes warm as they rested on her.

She smiled. 'Hello, Archie.'

'Have you just arrived?'

'Yes, I'm not late, am I?' she asked, as her gaze ran over his face.

He laughed. 'Of course not. They aren't doing the presentations for a while yet.'

His attention shifted and Cathy remembered her sister.

'This is my sister Jo,' she said.

'Nice to meet you,' he said.

'Jo, this is Sergeant McIntosh,' Cathy said.

'Nice to meet you, Sergeant McIntosh,' Jo replied. 'Cathy's told me a lot about you and how brilliant your paintings are.'

He raised an eyebrow. 'That's kind of her to say, but perhaps I should show you them so you can judge for yourself. They're on the far wall with the rest of Cephas Street entries.'

He led them past the displays of paintings, sketches and even the odd sculpture to the rear of the gallery, where the evening class's artwork was displayed across the back wall.

'These are mine.' He indicated the five large boards in the middle of the display. 'So, what do you think?' he added, his nonchalant tone at odds with the anxiety in his eyes.

Open-mouthed, Cathy stared at Archie's five paintings, unable to speak as she took in the dirty, back-breaking, dangerous work of the bomb squad that Archie had brought so vividly to life in his work.

'Oh, Archie,' she said, running her gaze over the paintings yet again. 'They are truly wonderful.'

He gave her a bashful smile. 'Och, it's kind of you

to say, Cathy, but — '

'My sister's not being kind,' interrupted Jo, her expression sober as she studied the works. 'Your paintings are wonderful, Sergeant McIntosh. And they ought to be in the National not the Whitechapel Gallery.'

Jo stepped forward to take a closer look and Archie took her place beside Cathy.

'I'm really glad you came, Cathy,' he said in a low voice.

She looked up into his blue eyes and smiled. 'I'm glad you invited me, Archie.'

'Sergeant McIntosh,' her sister's voice cut between them, 'do you know that three of your paintings have a highly commended card on them?'

She pointed at a red square tucked in the bottom left-hand corner of the frame.

'Aye,' he replied. 'I saw as much when I arrived. Even though I doubt any of my paintings will get put forward, at least I won't go home empty handed.'

'I didn't know this was a competition,' said Cathy.

'Well, it's not really,' Archie replied. 'But 'Images of Defiance' is part of a series of art exhibitions being put on all over the country. Any works judged good enough will become part of a national exhibition that will be shown in town halls up and down the country as a bit of a morale booster for the Home Front.'

Something caught his eye across the other side of the room and exasperation flitted across Archie's face.

'I'm sorry, Cathy,' he said, 'Ted, who runs my art class, is beckoning me over.'

'Don't worry,' said Cathy. 'You go.'

Giving her a regretful smile, he sauntered off. Cathy's eyes followed the roll of his shoulders and hips as he went.

Jo slipped her arm through Cathy's and guided her along the rows of artwork.

'For goodness' sake, Cathy,' she said, as they stopped in front of a series of sketches featuring bombed-out churches, 'why on earth didn't you tell me about your Sergeant McIntosh?'

'I've only seen the odd glimpse of his work and I didn't know how good he was,' Cathy replied, as they moved on to stand in front of a watercolour of barrage balloons.

Jo rolled her eyes. 'Not his painting, you daft item. Him! What he looks like.'

Cathy's gaze shifted from her sister over to where Archie was chatting to a scruffy individual with long hair and two men in pinstripe suits.

'He is a bit good-looking, isn't he?' she said, as they moved on again.

''Good-looking'!' said Jo. 'He's blooming gorgeous. Those eyes! And saints in Heaven, doesn't he fancy you or what?'

Excitement fluttered in Cathy's stomach.

'Don't be silly,' she replied, pretending to concentrate on the drawing in front of her.

'I'm not, but you will be if you don't grab him with both hands.' Jo winked.

'Jo!'

Her sister laughed. 'Don't tell me you haven't thought about it.'

She strolled on to look at the next exhibit.

Under the pretence of looking at the catalogue, Cathy stole another glance at Archie.

He was standing with his legs apart, the snug fit of his combat trousers showing his flat stomach and muscular legs clearly. There was little room for movement in his battle jacket either, as his chest and shoulders stretched the off-the-peg uniform to its limits.

Yes, she had thought about it, and a whole lot more.

Leaving her sister, who was several exhibits ahead of her by now, Cathy walked back to where Archie's paintings were displayed.

As she stopped in front of them again, Archie came over to join her.

'Sorry,' he said. 'Ted wanted to introduce me to the Ministry of War fellas who are choosing the pieces for the round-Britain shindig.'

'Well, I wouldn't want their job as there are lots of good pieces on display,' said Cathy. 'But I think yours should be among them.' She looked at his five entries again. 'And I'm not just saying that, Archie.'

They stood in silence for a moment then he spoke again.

'Which one do you like the most, Cathy?' he asked.

'I couldn't rightly say,' she replied.

A group of people walked past. Archie's arm brushed hers lightly as he moved forward out of their way.

'But if you had to choose, which would it be?' he asked.

Thinking of the conversation she'd just had with Jo, Cathy's heart fluttered at his nearness.

Trying to get her tumbling emotions back on to an even keel, Cathy studied his exhibits again.

'That one' — she pointed to the one at the far end — 'because of the way we're at the bottom of the dark shaft looking up at a sunny blue sky. And that one,' she indicated the middle one of the five. 'Because the way the men are bent over means you can really feel the weight of the bomb they're lowering on to the truck. But I suppose if I had to choose, I'd say my favourite is the one of your squad having a cup of tea together. There's destruction all around them and an unexploded bomb to find, but, like the rest of the nation in the middle of their fight against evil, they've stopped to have a cup of tea. Ordinary life carrying on regardless.'

Archie raised an eyebrow. 'Keep calm and carry on?'

'Isn't that what we've been told to do?' Cathy smiled up at him.

'It's yours,' Archie said in a low tone.

'Mine?'

'Yes,' he replied. 'I'm giving it to you.'

'But you can't,' she said. 'I mean, it's so good, much too good to just give away.'

'Well, I have, to you, Cathy,' he said. 'And if by some miracle I become a famous artist, you can sell it for a fortune.'

'But — '

'Please, Cathy,' he said, in a low voice. 'I want you to have it.'

Open-mouthed, she stared up at him.

His expression changed, setting Cathy's emotions tumbling again.

An ear-splitting buzz cut across the room as a man, standing beside a sculpture made from empty food cans, switched on the microphone.

'That's Mr Gillespie, from the Ministry of War,' Archie whispered.

Cathy looked around and spotted her sister on the other side of the room. Jo indicated she was going to stay where she was rather than try to push through the crowd, and Cathy nodded.

Realising the speeches and presentation were about to start, those still wandering around appreciating the artwork returned to the main part of the gallery. To prevent her from being jostled, Archie took up position behind her.

'Am I on?' asked the man from the ministry. His voice stretched around the high ceilings of the gallery and people covered their ears.

Someone twiddled a knob somewhere and the noise disappeared.

'Right,' he said, taking a breath. 'Good evening, everyone, and thank you for coming to support our Home Front artists. For those of you who don't know ...'

Cathy tried to concentrate as Mr Gillespie explained the reason behind the exhibition and the proposed nationwide tour, but with the faint musk of Archie behind her and the feel of his chest skimming the tips of her shoulder blades, she barely took in a word.

'And now, without further ado,' Mr Gillespie concluded after almost ten minutes, 'I would like to hand over the microphone to Mr Winterton, who is the permanent under-secretary to Sir Alistair St John at the Ministry of War. Mr Winterton, a world-renowned expert in the seventeenth-century Flemish school of painters, has been instrumental in getting the Home Front Art initiative off the ground. I therefore call upon him to announce the pieces of artwork chosen from the Shadwell, Stepney, Wapping and Whitechapel exhibition. Mr Winterton.'

As the audience clapped loudly, the man from the ministry stepped up to the microphone.

'Thank you,' he said as the applause died away. 'Firstly, let me say what a pleasure it is to be here and what a magnificent display of creativity surrounds us, so much so that any one of the artworks shown here today would be worthy of being included for display in the country-wide Home Front Exhibition. Sadly, I can choose only a handful and they are as follows.'

He cleared his throat.

'*The All-clear* by A. Hanson.'

Someone gave a whoop at the back of the gallery and there was a ripple of applause.

Cathy's heart jumped up into her throat.

'*Watching the Skies*, D. L. Mills.'

A cheer went up followed by mute hand clapping.

Another name was read out, which Cathy didn't hear because of the blood hammering through her ears.

She looked up and gave Archie an encouraging smile.

'And lastly . . .'

Cathy's mouth lost all moisture as everything surrounding her moved away then came shooting back.

'Three works, *Digging Out*, *Blue Sky Above* and *The Quick Brew* by A. J. McIntosh —'

Cathy gasped and spun around.

'That's you, Archie,' she cheered, bobbing up and down on the balls of her toes.

'Aye, it is, right enough,' he replied, grinning down at her.

'It's you,' she repeated.

Without thinking she threw her arms around him.

He didn't move for a moment then his arms wrapped around her.

Raw need surged through Cathy so strongly she felt faint and, although she knew she shouldn't, she closed her eyes and revelled in the smell, the feel, the manliness of him.

301

He held her there for a second, or perhaps a minute or perhaps it was an eternity, she didn't know, but then he released her.

Struggling to get the air moving in her lungs again, Cathy stepped back.

They stared at each other for a moment then others crowded between them. Archie smiled as they slapped him on the back and shook his hand, but his eyes returned constantly to Cathy.

'Your handsome sergeant did it, then,' Jo whispered, as she squeezed her way through the crowd of people surrounding Archie.

'Yes, he did,' said Cathy, wanting to shove Archie's well-wishers aside and lose herself in his embrace again. 'Perhaps we ought to leave him to it.'

She started towards the main door.

'Cathy!'

She turned back to see Archie pressing through the crowd towards her.

'You're nae going, are you?' he said. 'I mean, there's a spread being laid on and you and Jo are welcome to stay for it.'

'I'd love to, but Jo's meeting a few friends for a drink,' Cathy replied.

'Will I see you at home later?' he asked.

'No, it's been lively the past few nights, so I said I'd meet Mum at the shelter,' she replied. 'But I'll be back as usual to make your breakfast before you go off to work. Congratulations again, Archie, and enjoy the evening.'

Fighting the urge to throw herself into his arms again, Cathy turned to go, but he caught her arm.

She looked around.

'I'm really glad you came, Cathy,' he said, dropping

his hand back to his side.

She smiled. 'So am I.'

He gave her that crooked smile of his. 'Until tomorrow, then.'

Cathy smiled back. 'Yes, until tomorrow.'

★ ★ ★

'Well, here we are,' said Jo.

'At last,' said Cathy. 'The blooming bus was packed.'

'We were lucky to get on that last one,' said Jo.

Having got off a number 25 outside Whitechapel station, they'd walked with the narrow beams of their pencil torches lighting the pavement in front of them to Cambridge Heath Road. They were now standing outside the Blind Beggar at the corner.

'Mum'll be in the shelter by now,' said Cathy. 'Are you on duty Friday?'

'I'm afraid I am right through until Saturday,' said Jo.

'Well, I'll see you in church, then,' said Cathy.

'You will,' said Jo, her face just discernible in the dimly lit street. 'And I hope by then you will have taken my advice.'

Cathy gave her sister a puzzled look. 'What advice?'

'To grab that handsome Sergeant McIntosh and let him put a smile on your face,' said Jo.

Cathy rolled her eyes.

'For goodness' sake, Jo,' she said, trying to stop her imagination conjuring up images of her and Archie entwined.

'Well, you are almost a free woman,' said Jo.

'Not until Good Friday, I'm not,' said Cathy. 'And besides, I can't just go and jump on him, can I?'

303

'I don't see why not,' said Jo. 'That's what I did to Tommy.' She kissed her sister on the cheek. 'Say hello to Mum and I'll see you Sunday.'

Jo continued on towards Stepney Green.

Tucking her collar up, Cathy walked around the corner and, keeping her torch pointed downwards, continued up the road towards the Bethnal Green shelter. Although it was dark and the street was unlit, small pinpricks of light darted across the pavement as people made their way along the street. As she passed the Queen's Arms, where Archie and his fellow artists had a swift half after class each week, the memory of his embrace flooded back. Thinking perhaps she should take her courage in her hands and do as Jo suggested, Cathy walked under the railway arch. As she emerged, she spotted a familiar figure pushing a pram on the other side of the road.

'Mum!' she shouted.

Ida stopped and looked around as Cathy hurried over to her.

Peter, who was sitting on the toddler seat across Victoria's pram, spotted her and stretched out his arms.

'I thought you'd be down in the shelter by now,' said Cathy, kissing her son's soft cheek as she hugged him.

'I would have been,' her mother said. 'But when the boys got home from school, your dad needed them to help him on a delivery to Plaistow and they didn't get back until gone seven. He was on duty at eight, so he dropped us off ten minutes ago at the top of the road.'

'Where are the boys?' asked Cathy.

'They ran on ahead,' her mother replied. 'But I told them to wait for me by the entrance. Did you and Jo have a nice evening?'

As they strolled past Bethnal Green Gardens and library, Cathy told her mother about her evening at Whitechapel Art Gallery.

'And the best of it was that Sergeant McIntosh had three pictures chosen for the national exhibition,' Cathy concluded.

'I'm not surprised,' said her mother. 'Dad said his painting were very good.'

'Did he?' said Cathy, raising an eyebrow.

'You can't blame your dad for dropping by to make sure your sergeant is on the level,' said her mother. 'You may be all grown up now, but you'll always be his little girl. Now, let's get along to the shelter so we can get these little 'uns to bed. I'm dying for a cuppa.'

Smiling, Cathy hooked her arm in her mother's and squeezed. 'Me too, Mum.'

The clock on St John's Church opposite the Bethnal Green shelter was showing a quarter past eight by the time Cathy and her mother reached the junction with Green Street.

'There's a bit of a crowd tonight, isn't there?' said Cathy.

'I expect that's because the cinema down the road has just finished for the night,' Ida replied. 'Plus, as it's a clear night, people know there's likely to be a raid.'

'Well, in that case, you'd think there'd be a warden around and that they would have opened both gates,' said Cathy as they reached the square brick-made entrance.

'I expect they're here somewhere.' Ida looked around. 'Where are those boys?'

'There they are,' said Cathy as she spotted them

loitering with a couple of other lads. 'Billy! Michael!'

Her brothers ran over.

'Right, you two, carry these,' said Ida, unloading the basket and blankets from under the pram and handing them to the two boys, 'while me and Cathy carry the babies.'

Tucking the pram alongside the railing next to a dozen or so others, Ida lifted out the sleeping baby while Cathy unclipped Peter from his seat and settled him on her hip.

'We nearly lost Mr Bruno last night,' she said, handing him his teddy. 'So make sure you hold him tight, Peter.'

With the two boys laden with their shelter provisions walking in front of them, Cathy and Ida joined the dozens of people streaming into the shelter.

Squeezing through the narrow entrance, they entered the half-lit interior.

Adjusting Peter, and with her mother holding Victoria close, Cathy started to make her way down the stairs. As always, warm breath and damp clothes had caused condensation to form on the cold walls, and the stone steps were slippery under foot.

They were nearly at the bottom when, above their heads, the air raid siren let out a mournful wail. People behind them pushed forward and a woman carrying a child and her shelter provisions stumbled. She swung out to grab the side rail, knocking the old man next to her off his feet. Both were just righting themselves when a series of ear-bursting explosions swallowed up all sound and the earth shook like the devil's hordes were breaking through.

People screamed and surged forward into the packed stairwell. The woman holding the child went down again and others behind her tripped and piled on top of her.

Someone fell against Cathy and she almost toppled over but managed to step down on to the next step. Someone cannoned into her, propelling her closer towards the tiled wall at the bottom of the stairs. She caught sight of the boys, pushing through the tumbling people and disappearing around the corner on to the next set of stairs.

The earth rattled again as people pressed in on her. Trying to shield Peter from the crush, Cathy stood on tiptoes and drew breath. A woman, her mouth gasping and the whites of her eyes bright with fear in the gloom, pressed into Cathy, thrusting her forward.

Holding Peter tight, Cathy turned as she crashed into the wall. People piled on top of her, squeezing the air from her body and pinning her against the damp tiles.

In the half-light cast by the single 25-watt bulb, Cathy looked around. Like a grotesque medieval painting of hell, all around her were the tangled, lifeless bodies of men, women and children. The gruesome scene in front of her eyes was amplified by the piercing screams and pleading voices echoing around the tiled walls of the staircase.

Peter stretched out for something. Cathy looked around and saw Mr Bruno had been snatched from his hand in the squash and was now trapped under a booted foot.

As the weight pressed in on her, panic pulsed through her. Suddenly, the memory of Archie smiling down at her with those lovely blue eyes of his and saying 'see you in the morning' flashed through Cathy's mind.

Her head started spinning as blackness crowded her vision. Forcing her mind to think, Cathy dug in her elbows. Hugging Peter tight, she summoned every ounce of strength and twisted out of the suffocating crush around her. Pain tore through her as she gulped in air, her lungs aching as they expanded again.

As the dizziness subsided and her breathing eased, Cathy frantically searched among the contorted faces and mangled bodies for her mother. She spotted Ida, clutching Victoria to her, trying to squeeze herself free from the wall of people around her and on her.

'Mum!' Cathy called out.

'Take the baby!' Ida shouted.

Swinging around, Cathy thrust Peter at Billy who, mercifully, had come back to see what was keeping them. Now, his eyes wide with horror, he snatched Peter from his sister.

Stepping over a woman lying white-faced and unmoving beneath an old man, Cathy dug her shoulder into someone's back and pushed them out the way. Planting her feet wide, she reached across and took Victoria from her mother's outstretched arms.

Swinging around, she found Michael standing ready. She thrust the infant at him then turned back to her mother, but as she reached for Ida, the column of people around her mother toppled over as others piled on from above.

Ida gasped and her eyes rolled up into her head.

'Mum!'

Shoving people aside and treading on arms, legs and unresponsive bodies, she reached her mother, whose head hung motionless as she lay trapped.

High above them, the air raid wardens' whistles pierced the air and the sound of people shouting joined the moans of those people jammed in the stair-well.

Scrambling up to her mother, Cathy shoved an ash-en-faced woman off Ida then grasped her mother's floppy hands. Putting her foot on someone's hunched shoulder to give her leverage, she strained back and pulled. Nothing. She pulled again and Ida slid for-ward. Letting go, Cathy grasped her around her elbow. Someone else grabbed Ida's arm and Cathy looked around to see Michael beside her.

'On three.'

He nodded.

'One, two, three.'

Straining every muscle, Cathy and Michael heaved, their faces contorted with effort.

Nothing happened for a moment, then suddenly Cathy and Michael staggered back as Ida slipped out from under the pile of the dead and dying.

Others from below had now joined them, trying to unravel the limbs of those packed on top of each other.

Between them, Michael and Cathy dragged Ida down the few steps to where Billy sat with Victoria in his arms and Peter between his outspread legs.

Loosening her mother's coat and scarf, Cathy rubbed her chest. Ida didn't move, so, taking her arms again, Cathy pulled her upright and propped her against the wall.

'She's not dead, is she, Cath?' asked Billy.

Praying to every saint in heaven, Cathy leaned for-ward and put her face close to her mother's. She felt Ida's breath on her cheek.

'Thank God, no,' she sobbed, rubbing her mother's hands. 'Come on, Mum.'

Ida coughed.

'That's it, Mum,' said Cathy. 'Take a deep breath.'

Ida's eyelids fluttered a little then were still again.

Resting her hand on her mother's shoulders, Cathy hung her head.

Other people were now running up the stairs from below and pushing past Cathy, desperate to reach those poor suffocating souls who could be heard begging for help as they lay among the dead.

'Right, boys,' said Cathy, stirring herself back into action. 'We're going to have to move her. Billy, you take Victoria and Peter to our bunk while me and Michael carry Mum.'

* * *

'Well done again, Archie,' said Ted, as they stepped out of the Whitechapel Art Gallery.

'Thank you,' said Archie, 'for being such a good teacher.'

'I may have taught you about paints, brushes and techniques, Archie' — the art instructor's long face lifted in an ironic smile — 'but you were born with an artist's eye for shape, form and colour.' He looked at his watch. 'Is it half ten already?'

'Aye,' said Archie. 'With free sandwiches and cake, no one wanted to leave.'

Ted laughed. 'Well, I'd better get a move on or I'll miss the last train. Are you on your bike?'

Archie shook his head. 'My billet's only a short stroll away so I think I'll walk.'

'I expect you could do with a bit of a walk to help you calm down after the excitement of the evening,' said Ted, tucking his woolly scarf across his chest.

310

Archie smiled and thrust out his hand. 'Goodnight, Ted.'

'And you,' Ted replied as they shook.

Turning, he walked swiftly away toward Liverpool Street station.

Archie watched him for a while, then, ensuring his field cap was set at the correct angle, he shoved his hands in his pockets and headed off in the opposite direction.

Ted was right, it had been an exciting evening and although he was overjoyed to have had three of his works chosen for the national Home Front Exhibition, what had really made his evening was holding Cathy in his arms.

Of course, it was only a spontaneous gesture on her part to congratulate him, but at least he now knew the pleasure of her body against his, even if the memory of it wouldn't help him sleep.

With a grin on his face, Archie crossed Osborne Street. He passed the bombed-out ruins of St Mary's on his right and carried on down the High Street past the Salvation Army hostel and Whitechapel Bell Foundry.

However, as he reached Whitechapel station, Archie heard the sound of bells cutting through the silence of the night. Two ambulances, their bells echoing between the buildings, screeched around the corner and into the front of the London Hospital on the other side of the road.

Puzzled because he'd heard no air raid sirens, Archie picked up his pace. As he reached Cathy's sister-in-law's café, he spotted an auxiliary constable using the police telephone box outside the Blind Beggar.

He marched over.

311

'You all right, pal?' he asked, as the officer replaced the receiver. 'Or is there something I can do for you?'

The constable, an older man with a fulsome moustache and unruly eyebrows, looked him over then spotted the Bomb Disposal badge on his uniform.

'Not for me, son,' the policeman replied. 'But for those poor souls in the Bethnal Green shelter caught in the accident.'

An icy claw closed around Archie's heart. Cathy!

'We're not sure exactly how many fatalities there are yet, but —'

Turning on the balls of his toes and with his heart pounding, Archie dashed off down Cambridge Heath Road.

Dodging around an ambulance, and with the blood thundering through his ears, Archie tore across the road, then belted along the pavement, past the shrubs bordering Bethnal Green Gardens, towards St John's Church at the end of the road.

With his lungs on fire after the half-mile sprint, Archie swung around the corner into Green Street. He skidded to a halt as the full horror of what had happened was laid out before him.

Ambulance crews were stretchering people away from the scene while wardens, their arms supportively around them, led people away. A couple of auxiliary policewomen were gathering a group of wide-eyed and white-faced children away from the people sitting head in hands on the kerb. However, what set his mind screaming was the row of two dozen or more mauve-tinged bodies, with small children dotted among them, lined up along the railings with coats thrown over their faces.

No, please God in Heaven, no!

Raking his fingers through his hair and with his heart beating wildly in his chest, Archie's eyes darted along the row of bodies.

Seeing none that remotely resembled Cathy or Peter, Archie closed his eyes for a second then turned towards the shelter entrance. Next to it was a haphazard pile of baskets, handbags, blankets and other personal effects, which the rescuers had thrown aside. His gaze wandered on but then Archie caught sight of something tucked beneath a battered briefcase.

With fear gripping his chest, Archie skirted around a first-aider holding an oxygen mask over a child's face as they lay on a stretcher, and hurried over to the case.

A chasm opened at his feet as he stared down at Peter Wheeler's teddy.

Forcing his mind into action, Archie looked around and spotted a member of the rescue team who seemed to be directing the operation. Gripping the toy in his right hand, he strode over.

'Do you know where the owner of this might be, pal?' he asked, holding up the bear.

The warden shook his head. 'Sorry, mate. The heavy rescue just dumped the stuff there as they cleared it out.'

Raking his fingers through his hair again, Archie looked back at the row of corpses he'd just passed.

'Are they all the fatalities?' Archie asked, as a weeping ARP warden carrying the lifeless body of a child walked past.

'I wish they were,' the warden replied, 'but they've already taken away dozens to the London and we've got at least another fifty still down there.' He pointed his torch into the stairwell where rescue workers were retrieving the bodies of those who had been crushed to death. 'You got loved ones down there?'

Unable to speak, Archie nodded.

The warden placed his hand on Archie's arm. 'I'm sorry, son.'

'I need to find them,' said Archie. 'They've been taken to the London, you say?'

'Yeah, but before you go racing off there, you'd better check to see if they're in the church over there,' said the warden. 'We're using that to store them, because the hospital morgue's full.'

★ ★ ★

With the low hum of voices echoing around the vaulted ceiling and galleries of St John's, Archie dropped the coat back over the face of a young woman with dark brown hair, her red lipstick still bright on her grey lifeless lips. He walked slowly past a couple of men and an older woman with a built-up sole on her left surgical shoe whose heads and shoulders were covered with their coats, before stopping in front of another young woman with a mac over her upper body.

Archie studied the mud-spattered coat for a moment then reached down and lifted the corner.

It was a young woman of about Cathy's age but with bobbed strawberry-blonde hair and a plump face.

Letting out a long breath, Archie dropped the fabric back over her. Turning his head, he looked up at the cross on the side altar for a moment then looked back down at the row of corpses lined up along the south aisle of the church.

Every age of man was represented: from the baby whose feet peeked out from under its mother's coat

314

as it lay tucked into her arms, through to the old man who'd survived poverty and disease to reach his three score years and ten, only to have the life squeezed out of him in the East End equivalent of the Black Hole of Calcutta.

Archie wasn't alone in his search. Several men and women, relatives he guessed, were also making their way slowly along the line of bodies, lifting up the coats to see the faces of the dead, praying each time, as he did, that it would be a stranger beneath.

As far as he could tell, the victims laid out in the cold calmness of the church had all suffocated, as the mauve tinge of their skin testified. They were also soaked as the rescuers, desperate to revive them, had doused them with cold water in a vain attempt to shock them into breathing again.

'Have you found them?'

Archie turned to see a young woman in a white coat wearing a matching tin hat with 'M' stamped on the front.

Archie shook his head. 'They're nae here. I'd better away to the hospital and look there.'

The doctor glanced at the bear in Archie's hand. 'I hope you have a fruitful search.'

Giving him a compassionate smile, she moved on to where an elderly couple clung together sobbing.

Gripping Peter's teddy firmly, Archie made his way back past the thirty or so bodies lying side by side and out of the church's main entrance.

Archie's face tingled as the chill of the night whirled around him. Taking a deep breath, he gazed up at the handful of stars punctuating the clear black sky above.

If, as his mother asserted, there was an all-powerful being overseeing the universe, what part of any great eternal plan required Cathy, the woman he would love until the last breath left his body, the woman he dreamed would have his children, to be snatched away from him so cruelly, yet again?

20

'Mind how you go now, there might still be stuff on the stairs,'

said Bob Mitchel, his face drawn and grey in the dim light.

'Ready, Mum?' Cathy called over her shoulder.

'Yes, let's just get out of here,' Ida replied.

'Just go slow,' Bob said, shining his torch up the staircase to the landing where, just two hours ago, Cathy had saved her mother from certain death.

Now they, along with everyone else trapped on the platform, were making their way to the surface.

Mercifully, as she and Michael had half carried, half dragged their mother away from the stairwell, Ida had begun to regain consciousness and when they'd reached the family sleeping area, the cold air whistling out of the tunnels had fully revived her. Her first thought had been for Victoria who, oblivious to all around her, was niggling for her evening feed.

Having been reassured that the boys and Peter were all right, Ida had settled down to feed the baby, which had seemed to bring her back to the here and now.

It was just as well, because they'd had to sit huddled together as something close to hysteria swept through the shelter. It was hardly surprising given that so many people had friends or loved ones who were still unaccounted for. Many, too, forced to walk between the platforms to go to the toilet or get a cup of tea, had seen the piles of bodies wedged at the top of the staircase.

317

Cathy had averted her eyes but that hadn't cut out the sound of the rescuers' cries of distress as they'd removed dead babies and children from the stack of bodies.

'It won't be long, Mum,' said Cathy, adjusting a sleepy Peter in her arms. Her mother and the two boys followed her up the steps to the shelter's entrance.

As they reached the top of the first flight of stairs, Cathy gagged as the smell of ammonia and faeces clogged her nose.

'Those poor souls,' muttered her mother, crossing herself.

Cathy did the same, then, holding her breath, she walked across the wet landing and started up the final flight of stairs leading to the street.

A waft of icy night air whooshed down the stair-case, stirring Cathy's hair and chilling her cheeks.

The image of Archie smiling at her floated through her mind again and she drew in a long breath, enjoy-ing the sensation of it filling her lungs.

She was alive and so was he. Nothing else on earth mattered now, because she loved him.

With thoughts of Archie filling her head, Cathy put her foot on the final step but Peter struggled in her arms.

'Mr Bruno,' he said, stretching behind her.

'We'll find him later,' said Cathy.

'Noooo!' He tried to twist out of her arms, but Cathy held him tight and continued towards the entrance.

Ted Tweedy, red-eyed and grey-faced, was standing outside the shelter as she emerged.

'Are you all here?' he asked, looking behind her.

'Yes,' said Cathy, as her mother and then Michael and Billy, carrying the baskets and blankets, emerged from the entrance. 'Me, Peter, Mum, Victoria and the two boys.'

'Thank God,' he said, crossing their names off the list on his clipboard.

Cathy spotted ambulance crews ferrying bodies to their vans.

'How many, Ted?'

'No one's too sure, just yet,' he replied. 'But I'd guess it's over a hundred. We've already had word from on high not to talk about it, so you won't be reading about it in the newspapers tomorrow, that's for sure.' His weary features lifted in a smile. 'But at least you and yours aren't amongst them.'

'No, thank God,' said Cathy.

They moved aside as others came out of the shelter. All around them the ARP emergency services were packing up, as the last few victims were stretchered across the road to rest in the church.

'The pram's where I left it, so I suppose we'd better get home,' said Ida. 'Come on, boys, let's make tracks.'

Weaving their way past the queue of people lining up to quiz the shelter's chief ARP warden, Cathy and her mother walked to the line of prams. She couldn't help but wonder how many would have to be taken away by the council in the morning.

Peter wriggled in her arms, trying to look behind her. Feeling her aching shoulder muscles protest, Cathy lowered him to the ground.

'I think you're getting a bit big for me to carry —'

'Bruno!' he shouted, then shot off.

Cathy spun around. 'Pe —'

Her words evaporated and joy and love burst through her as she watched her son run to Archie,

319

the only man she would ever love, who was standing in the road holding her son's teddy in his right hand.

* * *

As Peter dashed along the pavement towards him, Archie's world fell back into place. Bending down as the little lad reached him, Archie scooped him into his arms and handed him his toy.

Peter hugged him and, with love and happiness filling his chest, Archie looked over the boy's shoulder at his mother.

Cathy stared back at him with an expression on her face that set his heart, which had only just returned to a steady beat, racing again.

He wanted to dash to her, take her in his arms and tell her he loved her and that she filled his mind and heart and would do for ever. Then he wanted to kiss every inch of that beautiful face and when he'd finished, do it again. Of course, he couldn't, not yet.

Peter wriggled out of his arms and trotted off towards his mother.

Archie followed, crossing the space between them in half a dozen strides, reaching her as she settled her son on her hip.

Smiling, she tilted her face up to him and it was all he could do to stop himself from taking her in his arms and pressing his lips on to hers.

He placed a hand on her arm.

'Cathy,' he said, his gaze running over every inch of her lovely face.

'Archie,' she replied breathlessly.

Of its own volition, his free hand moved forward to encircle her but just as the tips of his fingers brushed the fabric of her coat, he caught the older woman, who he guessed was Cathy's mother, looking at him.

Dragging his gaze from Cathy, he shifted his attention to the woman beside her.

'Your pardon, Mrs Brogan, I should have introduced myself,' Archie said. 'I'm Sergeant McIntosh and I'm your daughter's lodger.'

'I guessed as much,' the older woman replied. 'But what are you doing here? I thought you were at your exhibition.'

'I was walking home...' He told her how he'd rushed to Bethnal Green after he'd found out. 'I was afraid for Mrs Wheeler and Peter, so I came straight here.'

'I'm very glad you did,' said Cathy, gazing up at him.

Archie lost himself in her eyes for a moment or two, then a lorry with 'Brogan & Son' painted on the side screeched to a halt alongside them. The cab door burst open and Cathy's father, dressed in his auxiliary fireman's uniform, jumped down.

His eyes darted over Archie and Cathy and then fixed on his wife and children.

'Ida!'

Archie and Cathy stepped aside as Jeremiah caught his wife and sons in a bear hug.

'Holy mother of God,' he said, kissing them each in turn. 'When I got back from Canning Town and heard what happened, I...I...' He looked up, his eyes bright with unshed tears.

Cathy's mother started to cry and then Billy and Michael joined in. Jeremiah hugged them close. Archie understood the depth of the older man's emotions as they perfectly matched his own.

'Let's get you all home,' said Jeremiah, his arms still firmly around his wife's shoulders. 'It'll be a bit of a squeeze, Cathy, but if — '

'I'll be happy to take Mrs Wheeler and her son home, Mr Brogan,' Archie said, looking Jeremiah square in the eye.

'Well, that's mighty kind of — '

'Sergeant McIntosh can see us home, Dad,' Cathy cut in, shifting Peter on her hip and moving closer to Archie. 'And then you can take Mum and the boys straight back.'

'I'll make sure your daughter and Peter get home safely, Mr Brogan,' Archie continued.

'He's going there anyway, Dad,' added Cathy.

Jeremiah looked from Archie to Cathy and then back again.

'All right, Cathy,' said her father. 'As long as you think you're up to it, but I'll be coming by first thing.'

'Thanks, Dad.' Cathy gave him a kiss on the cheek. 'See you tomorrow.'

Jeremiah gave Archie another considered look, then he gathered Ida and the children together and helped them into the lorry.

The engine shuddered into life and then, with a crunch on the gears, the vehicle sped away.

As her father's van disappeared around the corner, Cathy turned and put her hand on Archie's arm. 'Let's go home.'

21

The kettle's whistle started to rattle, so, rising from the kitchen chair, Archie went to the stove and turned it off. Splashing a little hot water into the brown earthenware teapot, he swilled it around then emptied it down the sink. Taking the tea caddy from the shelf above, he'd just spooned in a couple of measures when the floorboards overhead creaked.

Archie looked up briefly and, thinking of the woman above, he smiled.

As he took the milk out of the refrigerator, the kitchen door opened and Cathy came in.

'You didn't have to do that,' she said.

'It's no trouble,' he replied. 'Did Peter go down all right?'

'Yes. Let me do that.' She took the bottle of milk from him. 'It was lucky that taxi came along when it did,' she said, putting milk into the two cups he'd placed ready, 'or you'd have had to carry him all the way home.'

'Aye, it was,' said Archie. 'But I wouldnae have minded.'

Giving him a too-bright smile, Cathy stirred the pot. 'I thought I'd try to get some beef out of Ray at the butcher . . .'

Archie stepped back and listened as she chattered on about tomorrow's dinner and getting the washing out early. He understood why, so he waited.

'And I meant to thank you for saving the day by finding Mr Bruno.' Giving a light laugh, Cathy picked

323

up the teapot. 'Where on earth was he?'

'Among the pile of personal effects beside the shelter's entrance,' Archie replied softly.

Cathy stopped moving for a moment then tea splashed out of the spout as she started to shake.

In two strides he was with her.

'It's all right, Cathy,' he said, taking the pot from her hand and placing it on the dresser.

She stood motionless for a moment then turned and looked up at him.

'So many people,' she whispered, tears welling in her eyes.

He placed his hand on her arm. 'I know.'

'So many people all . . . all . . . just pressing in.' A large tear rolled down her cheek. 'I couldn't stop them. And there was Peter. He was going to die if I didn't get him free, and Mum, too. But I was trapped and couldn't breathe and . . . and . . . ' Her eyes, wide with horror, locked with his. 'Oh, Archie . . . '

Gathering her into his embrace, Archie held her tightly as she sobbed out the nightmare she'd just lived through.

After a while she fell silent and reluctantly Archie released her.

'Sorry for blubbering all over your uniform,' she said, lightly brushing the damp patch on his chest and setting his senses on fire.

He cleared his throat. 'It's all right.'

She raised her head.

'When I walked out of the shelter and you were there, Archie, I . . . '

Cathy's gaze was warm and inviting as she looked at him.

Archie's head told him she was in shock and to take

it slow, but as love and desire swelled his chest, his body wasn't listening.

Reaching out, his arm encircled her waist and he drew her to him again, savouring the feel of her soft body as it moulded itself into his.

Her eyes opened wider and her lips parted slightly.

Lowering his head, Archie covered her mouth with his own. She hesitated for a moment then her lips yielded to his and her hands slid around him and up his back. Widening his stance, Archie's arms tightened around her as his kiss deepened.

With raw need pulsing through him, Archie anchored her to him with one hand while the other smoothed over her hip and upwards. However, as his hand brushed over the pleasing fullness of her breast, the honourable part of his brain reasserted itself.

Releasing her, Archie stepped back.

'I'm sorry,' he said, mastering his raging passion.

'It's all right, Archie,' said Cathy breathlessly, looking at him with half-closed eyes.

'It's not,' he said, pulling down the front of his battle jacket. 'You've had a terrible shock. And I shouldn't have taken advant — '

'I said it was all right.'

Her hands went to the front of her blouse and, looking him square in the eyes, she started unfastening her buttons.

'What are you doing, Cathy?' he asked, as she freed the last one and slipped the garment off her shoulders.

A wide-mouthed smile spread across her face. 'Just taking my sister's advice.'

★ ★ ★

Raising his head from her shoulder, Archie kissed her gently then rolled with a satisfied sigh on to his back.

Blinking, Cathy stared wondrously up at the ceiling. So that's . . .!

She lay there contemplating for a moment more the unknown mysteries she'd just discovered, then, without bothering to pull the rumpled sheet over her, she lifted herself on to her left elbow.

Archie, the hint of a smile playing across his lips, had his eyes closed and a tranquil expression on his face.

He, like her, was naked. Truthfully, other than in the bath, she couldn't remember the last time she'd been completely bare. But she was now, and with Archie's warm skin against her, she had no desire to change her nude state.

She snuggled closer. Archie acknowledged her movement by sliding his arm around her and hugging her to him.

Cathy's gaze ran over the hard curves of his broad torso, shoulders and arms before moving to his taut stomach, with just a narrow trail of hair tracking down from his navel. Her gaze drifted lower for a moment before returning to his face.

Unable to resist, she placed her hand on his chest, enjoying the contrast of her pale fingers against his smooth brown skin.

Turning his head, Archie opened his eyes.

'You do know I love you, don't you?' he said, in a low voice that vibrated through to her fingers. 'And I want you to marry me.'

Stretching up, she kissed him. 'And I love you. And I will. In seven weeks and two days.'

'You're counting?'

She gave Archie a sad smile. 'You'd be counting, too, if you'd been married to Stan.'

Anger darkened Archie's face and he gathered her into his arms and kissed her forehead.

Resting her head on his chest, Cathy listened to the steady beating of his heart for a few moments, then got up on to her elbow. Stretching over him, she pressed her lips briefly on to his. 'Tell me about Moira?' she asked.

'Her family lived in the same tenement as us and we went to the same school,' he replied.

'You were childhood sweethearts?'

He gave a rumbling laugh. 'I wouldn't say that. All I can recall of our schooldays together was her punching me in the chest one time when I pulled her pigtails. When we left, I started work in the shipyard and she went to one of the carpet factories in Bridgeton, but we would see each other in the pubs and dancehalls and, although her parents weren't keen, we got married when we were both twenty-one. Kirsty was born two years later. We had four happy years together before she died.'

'You were very lucky,' said Cathy, as scenes from her marriage flickered across her mind.

'Aye, I was.' Reaching up, Archie ran his index finger lightly along her cheek. 'And now I'm lucky again.'

In the dim glow of the bedside lamp, Cathy studied his face for a second or two, then, leaning over him again, she pressed her lips on to his.

His mouth opened under hers, setting the low rhythmic pulse below her navel throbbing again.

Cathy raised her head.

They gazed wordlessly at each other for a couple of heartbeats then Cathy got up and sat on her heels.

Although his posture remained relaxed, Archie's blue eyes darkened.

His gaze roamed slowly over her and then, in one swift movement, he caught her around the waist and rolled her on to her back.

With his weight pressing down on her, Archie smiled briefly then captured her lips in his. Closing her eyes, Cathy gave herself up to the pleasure of his dexterous hands as they started their magic journey over her again.

22

'Sorry, luv, but we're out of sugar,' said Mrs Hawkes, a matronly woman resplendent in her Sunday-best hat, as she handed Cathy her cup of tea.

'That's all right, I've given it up,' she replied with a yawn.

It was just after eleven on the first Sunday in March and she was in the small hall behind St Breda and St Brendan's Church. Cathy, along with most of the congregation, had made her way into the hall after Sunday Mass, which had finished ten minutes before.

Picking up a digestive biscuit, Mrs Hawkes offered it to Peter, who was hanging on to Cathy's skirts.

'Here you are, my little sweetheart,' she said.

'What do you say?' Cathy said, as her son took the biscuit.

'Fank oo,' he replied.

Mrs Hawkes's expression shifted from kind-hearted to sentimental. 'Ah, bless his little cotton socks.'

Cathy yawned again.

'I know,' the middle-aged matron continued, 'I've hardly had a wink of sleep meself for the last three nights, what with the bloody Luftwaffe dropping bombs until dawn.'

Cathy smiled. Mrs Hawkes was right, she'd hardly slept for the past few nights, but not because of the Germans.

Taking her tea, Cathy turned.

As her mother, who was rocking Victoria's pram over by the store cupboard, was in deep conversation with a couple of her friends, and Francesca was admiring someone's new baby by the noticeboard, Cathy made her way over to Jo, who was sitting at a table in the far corner.

Spotting his aunt, Peter trotted off and by the time Cathy had reached her sister, he was firmly ensconced on Jo's lap.

'Hello, you,' she said, sitting down on the chair next to her.

'Oh, Cathy,' said Jo, placing her hand on her arm. 'Thank goodness. I've been working fourteen-hour shifts all week, so I only heard what happened to you and Mum yesterday. Are you all right?'

'Just about.' Cathy yawned again. 'Every now and then it comes back to me and I can feel myself getting panicky again. Especially when I think of Peter.'

'I'm not surprised,' her sister replied, giving him a quick kiss on the head.

Twisting on her lap, he offered her his half-eaten biscuit.

Jo pretended to take a bite and Peter stuffed it back in his mouth. 'Mum says you're not going to the shelter any more.'

'I can't face it, not after what happened,' Cathy replied. 'Dad's going to get me a Morrison shelter this week for the front room and Peter and I will sleep there from now on.'

'What did old misery guts say about that?' asked Jo.

'I haven't told her yet,' Cathy replied, suppressing another yawn. 'But she can say what she likes. I'm paying the rent.'

'Francesca's looking well,' said Jo.

Cathy took a mouthful of tea.

'Yes,' she replied, studying her sister-in-law's

massive stomach. 'I reckon, by the size of her, it could be any day now.' She looked across at Jo. 'I'm guessing there's no news.'

Pain flitted across Jo's face and she shook her head. 'I got my hopes up last month when I was a week late but . . . ' Jo planted a kiss on Peter's sandy-coloured hair. 'You're so lucky to have him, you know.'

Cathy gave her a sympathetic smile. 'It's still early days. And I'm sure you'll find yourself throwing up down the bog soon enough.'

'That's what Mattie said,' Jo replied.

'Well, you should listen to her,' said Cathy. 'After all, she's supposed to be the brainy one of the family.'

Jo laughed. 'According to her.'

'I thought she'd be here today,' said Cathy, glancing around.

A serious expression replaced her sister's merry one. 'I think Daniel might be off again soon, so they've gone to visit his parents this weekend.'

The last time Daniel went 'off ' it was undercover to France behind enemy lines for three months, and although the whole family knew, it was never spoken about.

'Poor Mattie,' said Cathy. 'I'll pop around to see her before I go to the centre on Tuesday.'

They both took a mouthful of tea. Peter, who'd spotted his cousin Patrick with a couple of other toddlers on the other side of the room, wriggled off Jo's lap.

'At last,' said Jo, looking beyond Cathy to the door.

Cathy followed her sightline to see their gran walking into the hall with Father Mahon.

'Goodness, he looks a year older every time I see him,' said Cathy, watching the old priest, walking

331

stick in hand, shuffle in with Queenie.

'Do you think Mattie's right?' said Jo.

'I'm not sure,' said Cathy, as Queenie helped the good father into a chair. 'When she said it, I thought, 'Don't be ridiculous', but since then there's been a couple of times when I've looked at Dad and Father Mahon standing together and I'm not so sure. There is something about the shape of their faces and some of their gestures that makes me wonder.'

Cathy yawned again.

'Not keeping you up, am I?' asked Jo. She placed her hand on Cathy's arm again. 'I'm sorry. I suppose you've been having nightmares.'

'I've had a couple. But that's not what's keeping me awake at night.' She glanced around and then leaned closer to her sister. 'I took your advice.'

Jo looked puzzled for a moment then her eyes flew open.

'Oh my goodness,' she said, drawing her chair nearer. 'You actually — '

'Yes.'

'And?'

Cathy frowned. 'I'm not telling you all the details.'

Jo rolled her eyes.

'But I will say' — a smile spread across Cathy's face — 'Archie might be a painter, but he's got sculptor's hands.'

'You hussy,' laughed Jo.

Memories of the past nights entwined in Archie's arms flashed through Cathy's mind.

'I know,' she said, as the thought of him ignited her desire again. 'In fact, I make myself blush thinking of some of the things I've done to him that I've never even dreamed of before.'

332

Jo shook her head and tutted.

'Well, I hope you're not going to go and confess all this to Father Mahon,' she said.

'I wasn't planning to,' Cathy replied.

'Good, because it would probably finish him off,' said Jo.

They both laughed.

'You are being careful, aren't you?' said Jo.

'Yes, of course we are,' said Cathy.

Which was almost true.

Archie had bought some French letters, but it wasn't often in the forefront of their minds, if she were honest.

'But, it's not just a fling, Jo,' said Cathy. 'I love him.'

'And even a blind man could see that he loves you, too,' said Jo. 'But what are you going to do?'

'Well, Stan will be declared officially dead on Good Friday,' said Cathy. 'Once I have the formal letter, Archie's going to fetch his daughter and mother down, find somewhere to live, and then we'll speak to Father Mahon about getting married.'

Jo grinned. 'Can I be a bridesmaid?'

'It's not going to be a big — '

Something crashed on to the floor and Cathy and her sister looked around.

Father Mahon was slumped on his chair, his face grey and his eyes closed.

'Patrick!' shouted Queenie, rubbing his hand briskly as others gathered around. 'For the love of God, Patrick, wake up!'

'Someone call an ambulance,' shouted Jo, standing up and running across. 'Stand back,' she said, waving people aside. 'Give him some air.'

The crowd shuffled back but looked on anxiously,

as Jo removed Father Mahon's stiff dog collar and unfastened his top button.

Rising to her feet, Cathy went over to Peter. She picked him up and hurried over to where Francesca was.

'Do you think the ambulance will be here soon?' asked Francesca, as she joined her.

'I hope so,' said Cathy.

'So do I,' replied Francesca, 'because I thought the backache I woke up with was from lifting Patrick, but now I think it's because I'm in labour.'

* * *

Acknowledging the odd acquaintance as she passed, Queenie Brogan, her basket gripped firmly in her hand, marched down Sutton Street towards the wrought-iron gates.

Well, truthfully, it was the space where the ornate wrought-iron gates used to be as they, along with the railings encircling the small rectory garden, had been donated to the war effort two and a half years before.

Passing between the square-capped columns, she headed up the path towards the black-lacquered door. It, like the rest of the solid three-storey Victorian house, had seen better days.

When she'd arrived in the parish as a new bride over forty-five years ago, there had been three priests living in St Breda and St Brendan's rectory, with five servants to look after them. Now it was just Father Mahon, his assistant, young Father Riley, who looked as if he should still be wearing a school uniform rather than a cassock, and Mrs Dunn, the resident housekeeper.

Queenie climbed the three steps to the door, grasped the lion's-head knocker and rapped it against the brass stud beneath.

It echoed through the cavernous house beyond for a moment then the door opened.

Queenie's face lifted in a genial smile.

'Good morning to you, Mrs Dunn.'

Bridget Dunn was a vinegar-faced woman who, although widowed over a decade ago, still wore the widow's weeds of the newly bereaved.

Although her breasts barely troubled the front of her blouse, their lack of substance was made up for by her hips that, if they got any wider, would probably force her to walk sideways through doorways.

Standing on the coconut mat in the doorway, she gave Queenie an acerbic look.

'Mrs Brogan. It's yourself again.'

'It is,' Queenie agreed. 'And a blessing it is that your faculties are still sharp enough to remember.'

The housekeeper's pale lips pulled into a tight bud. 'Father Mahon is resting.'

'Glad I am to hear it,' said Queenie. 'For hasn't the poor man worked his fingers to the bone tending his flock.'

Mrs Dunn didn't move.

'As I said, the good father's resting, so perhaps it would be better if you came — '

'And before I forget,' Queenie interrupted, 'Fast Jimmy asked me to tell you that he has what you were asking him for.'

Two splashes of red coloured the housekeeper's sallow cheeks. She chewed the inside of her mouth for a moment then opened the door wider.

'You'd better come in and I'll see if Father Mahon

is awake.'

Queenie stepped into the bare-board hallway.

Mrs Dunn shut the door and then hurried off. Listening to the wind whistling through the all but empty house, Queenie gazed around at the old prints that had hung in the hall for as long as she could remember.

As always, her eyes rested on the small picture to the right of the heavy oak hall mirror.

It was a panoramic landscape of Kinsale's riverfront, town and hills. A scene she and Father Mahon knew well. Although the bright green of the fields and crystal blue of the river had faded, the memories of the wet meadow grass between her toes and the icy chill of the sparkling water were still vivid in Queenie's mind.

The door at the far end of the hallway opened and Mrs Dunn appeared again.

'Father Mahon said he will see you,' she said.

Taking off her coat, Queenie hooked it on the hall stand, then, smiling, she walked towards the door.

Pulling out a paper bag, she handed it to the housekeeper.

'There's half a dozen eggs for the good father's breakfast,' she said, handing it to her. 'And when you fetch the tea, Mrs Dunn, I'll have two sugars.'

Giving her a filthy look, the rectory's housekeeper stomped off to the kitchen.

Queenie walked through into the south-facing parlour that had once been the housekeeper's office.

Father Mahon was sitting in a winged chair next to the hearth with his slippered feet up on a scuffed footstool, a tartan blanket over his legs and a knitted shawl around his shoulders.

It was five days since he'd collapsed in church. The doctors had kept him in hospital for observation until Monday but with bombing casualties filling every bed and trolley, they'd sent him home on Tuesday and Queenie had visited him every day since.

He had his eyes closed and as her gaze ran over him, she didn't see a frail old man, with wisps of grey hair and bony hands. Instead, she saw the strapping youth who'd chased her through the long grass on a sunny Irish afternoon.

His hair had been thick and curly then and his arms strong, strong and tender as they held her away from prying eyes in the bluebell wood half a century ago.

Sensing her presence, Father Mahon opened his eyes and smiled.

'Queenie,' he said, straightening up a little, 'I wasn't expecting you.'

'I was passing, so I thought I'd pop by and see if the syrup I left for you on Tuesday has shifted that cough, Patrick,' she said, coming into the room.

'It did.' He chuckled. 'It was just like the one my mother used to make for us when we had a touch of damp on our chests.'

'Was it now?' Queenie frowned. 'And bejesus, what in the name of all goodness is that in the grate? Because if it's supposed to be a fire, it's a poor excuse for one.' Bending, she grabbed a lump of coal. 'I've a good mind,' she said, throwing it on the smouldering embers, 'to write to that bishop of yours and tell him what poor care that woman who styles herself as a housekeeper gives you.' She added another black nugget to the grate.

'Easy now,' he said. 'She does her best.'

Queenie pulled a face and amusement sparkled in

his still-clear black eyes.

There was a knock on the door.

'Come,' called Father Mahon.

Mrs Dunn walked in carrying a tray with a tea set and a plate of arrowroot biscuits on it. She placed it on the coffee table next to the priest's chair and picked up the teapot.

'Sure, I can do that,' said Queenie.

Mrs Dunn looked at Father Mahon.

He smiled. 'Thank you, Mrs Dunn.'

Giving Queenie a furious look, the housekeeper left.

Queenie poured them both a cup of tea. She handed one to Father Mahon and then took her own and sat down in the chair opposite his.

'So, how are the family?' he asked.

'They're keeping well, and blessed I am, to have them sitting in the pews beside me every Sunday,' she replied.

He took a sip of tea and a fond smile lifted his wrinkled face.

'And fine they look, too.' He raised an almost invisible eyebrow. 'Although I'd like to see Jeremiah more often alongside them.'

'Ah, well now,' said Queenie, 'after working from dawn to dusk six days a week, sure even the Almighty wouldn't begrudge him a lie-in now and again.'

Father Mahon nodded slowly. 'He's a good father, for sure. Though God only knows where he learned to be because, if you'll pardon me for saying it, Fergus was none such.'

'You speak but the truth, Father,' she said, 'God rest his soul.'

Queenie crossed herself and Father Mahon did the

338

same.

He chuckled. 'You know, sometimes when I look down from the pulpit at Jeremiah's brood, I'm still surprised that none of them inherited Fergus Brogan's fiery red hair.'

Queenie didn't comment.

'Now,' he said, holding his cup poised in front of him, 'apart from filling up two pews every Sunday, what else have they been up to?'

Between mouthfuls of tea and biscuits, Queenie told him the latest news from Charlie in North Africa. She updated him on Mattie and her two and told him how little Victoria had put on three ounces the week before. Jo, like everyone else in the Civil Defence, was working twelve-hour days, which she didn't mind at the moment because Tommy had been sent back to Bletchley for a couple of weeks, and Billy and Michael were making good progress at Parmiter's. He didn't ask her if she was still reading the tea leaves, which was a good thing because it saved her from lying and him from having to pretend he believed her.

'And blessings upon blessings,' she concluded, 'Francesca had a darling little girl, just as I said she would. Six pounds three ounces, which is a good weight for a first born.'

'Are they both well?'

Queenie nodded. 'Ida and Mattie are pitching in, looking after Patrick and doing a bit of housework. Francesca's named her Rosa after her mother.'

'And what about Cathy?' he asked, when she'd finished.

'Sure, she's been down too, with Peter, to do the washing,' Queenie replied.

'I meant with her husband still missing,' said Father

339

Mahon.

'She's holding up,' said Queenie.

He studied her for a moment then spoke again.

'I know it's not the happiest of marriages, but she should be praying for his return. After all, he is her husband,' he said.

''Tis true enough, Father, but you saw yourself what her face looked like after the last time he was home, so, wicked though it is to say, I'd be glad to dance on his grave. And don't look at me like that, Patrick,' she continued, seeing the old priest's shocked expression. 'You can give me a hundred Hail Marys until eternity, but I'll never say different. Having endured the same myself, I'd suffer the fires of hell if I stood by and let it happen to one of mine. And if it wasn't for respect for yourself and the Holy Virgin, I'd have summoned up the fairy folk and spirits from the old country to curse Stanley Wheeler's devil soul before now.'

Patrick Mahon, being a man worthy of his calling, tried to maintain his censorious expression but, after a moment or two, he let out a long sigh.

'Again, Queenie, you probably have the right of it.' Placing his empty cup back on the tray he looked across at her. 'And though I'd never tell the Pope should I ever meet the man, after almost fifty years of ministry, I've found that right and wrong isn't as easily identified in everyday life as we're taught it was in the Seminary.'

Leaning back, the old priest's still bright eyes studied her for a moment then he spoke again.

'It's strange, isn't it, how as you get older you forget what you had for breakfast but can remember things from years ago as clear as if they happened yesterday?' he said.

'That you do,' she agreed.

'This time of year, there would be sweet new grass growing in the meadow along the edge of the Brannon,' he said, his gaze growing misty as he spoke.

'And old man Finnigan's herd feeding on it,' Queenie agreed.

'And the bluebells,' he continued. 'Do you remember the bluebells?'

'That I do,' Queenie replied, remembering them bobbing above her head in the soft spring breeze as she lay in the shade of a crab apple tree.

Father Mahon smiled and then his almost transparent eyelids fluttered down. She waited but after a few moments, thinking perhaps he'd dropped off to sleep, Queenie swallowed the last mouthful of tea and put her cup down on the tray next to his.

He opened his eyes and looked across at her.

'It's funny, isn't it? God and his flock have filled my life for almost fifty years and, other than the monthly letters from my sister Bernadette back home, I've rarely thought of the life I left behind.' Father Mahon's grey-green eyes, so like Jeremiah's, became soft as he looked across at her.

'Do you ever think how things might have been, Philomena?' he said softly. 'The family we might have had?'

'Now and again, Patrick,' she replied. 'But we can't go back.'

'No, we can't go back.' He gave a breathy little chuckle. 'You know, talking about my sister, a couple of times recently your Cathy has put me in mind of Bernadette at the same age.'

341

23

'Sleep tight,' said Cathy, kissing Peter on the forehead. 'Mummy will come to bed later.'

Peter stuck his thumb in his mouth and, hugging Mr Bruno to him, closed his eyes.

Straightening the covers over him again, Cathy crawled backwards out of the Morrison shelter. Rocking back on her heels, she stood up and straightened her skirt.

It was the first Thursday in April, April's Fools day, in fact, and four weeks since the horrific night in Bethnal Green shelter. The signature tune of 'Rhapsody in Blue' was drifting through from the kitchen, making it just before seven o'clock.

Cathy had just finished her new bedtime routine of putting Peter to bed in the Morrison shelter, which her father and Jo's husband Tommy had spent all of one Sunday afternoon putting together for her. It was a reinforced steel box with mesh sides, into which she'd squeezed the double mattress from her bed for her and Peter to sleep on.

It now sat squarely in the middle of the back parlour and during the day, as the accompanying leaflet advised, she draped a flowery tablecloth over it and used it as a table.

Turning down Peter's night light, Cathy walked back into the kitchen. Violet, who was filling her hot-water bottle from the kettle, looked around as she walked in.

As always at this time of night, she was wrapped in

her dressing gown with her hair full of curlers.

'I don't know why you don't just let Stanley come down to the shelter with me,' said Violet as she forced the stopper in.

'If you don't know that by now, Vi, then there's not much point in me explaining it,' Cathy replied.

Cathy walked across to the dresser. Reaching up to the wireless on the shelf above, she turned the volume knob to full.

'And you've got a bloody cheek having that great monstrosity in the middle of my parlour,' shouted Violet, as the Airforce Band blasted out 'The Six Five Special' through the wireless's woven grille. 'You wait until my Stanley hears about this. And he will.'

Lifting the lid of the saucepan, Cathy threw a pinch of salt into the chopped cabbage she'd prepared earlier and then did the same to the peeled potatoes.

'Don't think I don't know you're counting the days until Easter,' her mother in-law bellowed.

Cathy didn't deny it. It was twenty-two days to be precise!

Singing along, she took the kettle her mother-in-law had just emptied and refilled it under the tap then placed it back on the gas ring.

Violet gave her a sour-faced look and then her eyes shifted to the two chops sitting on the plate beside the cooker.

'I suppose that's for you and him,' she said.

'If you mean Sergeant McIntosh, yes, it is,' Cathy replied, feeling a little ripple of excitement pass through her.

'How come he has pork chops and all I got for supper was a couple of grizzly bangers with a scrap of potato?' asked Violet.

343

'Because Sergeant McIntosh pays eight shillings a week, that's how come.' Cathy gave her a sweet smile. 'If you fancy a couple of chops, why don't you ask Willy Tugman to slip a couple into your basket alongside the rest of the stuff you get from him under the counter.'

Giving Cathy a look that could have sliced stone, her mother-in-law stormed through the back door.

Reaching up, Cathy turned the music down and glanced at the clock as she lit the gas under the vegetables.

Five past seven.

With the clocks going forward a couple of weeks ago, the evenings were getting lighter and spring was well and truly around the corner.

Although it was half an hour until blackout, Cathy stretched up and closed the blinds then turned on the light.

The 40-watt bulb dangling from a cord overhead spluttered into life, filling the kitchen with a mellow light.

She glanced at the back door her mother-in-law had just stormed out of. Knowing very soon Archie would be walking through it, Cathy felt a little ripple of excitement run through her again.

It was also four weeks since Archie had first taken her in his arms and into his bed and she'd almost lost count of the number of times he'd done so since.

Water spilled over one of the saucepans with a hiss and as Cathy turned down the gas to a simmer, she heard the squeak of the side gate opening.

Taking a knife, Cathy scraped a knob of lard on to the blade and flicked it into the frying pan on the front ring. She watched it melt for a moment then

344

laid the chop in it.

The door opened and Archie, wearing his sheepskin jerkin over his battle dress, strolled in. Cathy's heart did a little double step.

Truthfully, it always would because she had a love for Archie that would last a lifetime and beyond.

'Just in time,' she said, placing the second chop into the sizzling fat.

'Good, because I'm starving,' he replied, hooking his outer jacket up on the back of the door.

She laughed. 'That's what you say every night.'

Taking off his riding gauntlets, Archie locked the door. He hooked the key on the nail hammered into the wall next to it and strolled over.

'That's because I am.' Standing behind her, his arms wound around her waist, he drew her close. 'And not just for food.'

He kissed the sensitive spot just behind her ear and planted feathery kisses down her neck.

Cathy leaned into his hard chest for a second then straightened up and pushed him away.

'Archie McIntosh,' she said, 'will you nae control yourself, mon, and sit doon?'

Grinning, he gave her a noisy kiss on the cheek and let her go.

'I see you've been working on your Scottish accent, then,' he said, pulling out a chair and sitting down.

Cathy pulled a face and turned the chops over.

'Good day?' she said, moving them around in the fat with the slicer.

'Not bad, I suppose,' he replied, as he unbuttoned his jacket and eased back in the chair.

As she dished up their supper, he told her about what he'd been up to.

'Of course,' he concluded as she put their plates on the table, 'it's all very well waiting for the scientists at Woolwich to come up with a fix for this new Y fuse, but if the Germans start hitting cities again before we know how to deactivate it then all hell will break loose.'

'Is there no sign of it being figured out?' she asked, sitting down opposite him.

'I think someone might have come up with something,' he replied, picking up his cutlery. 'Someone from HQ is coming down to give us a briefing next Wednesday.' He cut off a portion of meat. 'What about you? What have you and Peter been up to?'

As they ate their meal, Cathy ran through her afternoon at the rest centre and how Peter was learning his colours, then, as they worked their way through their bread-and-butter pudding, she told him about her visit to Francesca to see her newest niece, Rosa.

An odd smile spread across Archie's lips when she'd finished.

'What?' asked Cathy.

'I was just thinking this is how it's going to be,' he said, scraping the last of his pudding from the bowl. 'You and me, sitting across a table at the end of the day.'

Cathy raised an eyebrow. 'Boring old Mr and Mrs McIntosh.'

Leaning across, he took her hand.

'Aye, perhaps, but happy,' he replied, his eyes full of love.

Cathy smiled. 'Yes. Happy. Very happy.'

They gazed at each other for a long moment then Cathy withdrew her hand.

'Tea?' she said.

'I wouldnae mind,' he replied.

Cathy stood up and reignited the gas. She went to take two mugs from the dresser but before she could reach up for them, Archie's hands encircled her waist. Turning around within his grasp, she looked up and saw the now-familiar glint in his blue eyes.

'I thought you wanted tea,' she said, giving him a look from under her lashes.

'I did,' he replied, in a low voice. 'But now I fancy something else.'

He nudged her with his hardness and a slow smile spread across Cathy's lips.

'Well, then,' she said, reaching across and flipping off the gas switch, 'the tea will have to wait.'

★ ★ ★

A chill roused Cathy from wherever it was she'd drifted off to and her eyes blinked open. Sitting up, she looked around. Archie was sitting stark naked on the chair with his sketchpad in hand.

'What's the time?'

'No more than ten thirty,' he replied. 'I had a wee peek at Peter not ten minutes ago and he's fast asleep.'

Cathy relaxed back on to the pillow. 'I thought for a moment I'd overslept.'

He grinned. 'Don't worry. We've hours yet.'

His gaze returned to his drawing pad.

'What are you doing?' she asked.

'Just a wee doodle,' he replied, skimming his pencil across the paper. 'Now put your arm back behind your head.' Raising his eyes, Archie smiled. 'Please.'

Cathy adjusted her position as requested.

Archie's gaze ran slowly over her again before his

347

attention returned to his work.

Without moving her head, Cathy looked across at Archie.

Well, after all, what's good for the goose is good for the gander.

He was sitting with his right ankle resting on his left knee with the drawing pad leaning against his thigh, which gave her an interesting view of things. The soft light from the standard lamp above him accentuated the muscular curve of his shoulder and arm as his hand moved across the paper.

The desire that had been sated only a while before bubbled up in Cathy again.

She had to be honest. The thought of posing naked for Archie had crossed her mind more than once in the past couple of weeks, but imagining it was just a pale imitation of the emotions pulsing through her at the moment.

'I was thinking,' he said, pausing to study his work for a moment, 'I might start looking for a place. Unless you want to wait until . . .'

'No,' she replied. 'He will have been missing for six months in just over three weeks.'

He smiled. 'If you're sure —'

'I am,' Cathy cut in.

If the Red Cross hadn't located Stan by now, they never would.

'Where are you thinking of looking?' she asked, shoving all niggling thoughts of her loathsome husband from her mind.

'I thought the other side of the Mile End Road,' he continued, his eyes returning to his work. 'I spotted some nice little houses just off Globe Road.'

'Well, as soon as you find somewhere, we'll move

in,' said Cathy. 'And then you can bring Kirsty down to join us. I can't wait to meet her.'

Pausing in his work, Archie looked up.

'I'll be fetching Ma, too,' he said, studying her closely.

'Of course you will, Archie,' said Cathy, smiling back at him. 'And I look forward to meeting her, too.'

His shoulders relaxed a little. 'You do know how much I love you, don't you?'

A lazy smile spread across Cathy's face. 'I think you might have mentioned it.'

They gazed at each other for a couple of heartbeats, then Archie's pencil returned to the paper.

Cathy settled back again and studied the man she loved as, with a slight frown across his brow, his skilled hand moved the pencil across the paper.

Three weeks and a day and it would be Good Friday: she would be free. Free to marry Archie and start her life over again.

A slither of cold air from under the door rippled over Cathy and she shivered.

'There's a draft in here,' she said.

Archie's eyes flickered on to her breasts and he grinned.

'I can tell.'

Looking over at him, Cathy's mouth lifted slightly at the corners and his blue eyes changed from being an artist's to a lover's in an instant.

'Do you want to take a look?' he asked, lifting the drawing pad and putting his foot back on the floor.

Swinging her legs off the bed, Cathy strolled across to where he sat.

'What do you think?' he asked, holding the sketch so she could see it.

Tilting her head, Cathy looked down at the drawing and studied herself through Archie's eyes.

It was her but not as she thought of herself, a tired mother running from pillar to post just to keep food on the table and a roof over her head. Here, she was a desirable woman who was loved.

'Do I really look like that?' she asked, noting the heavy shading of her nipples and pubic hair.

Throwing the pad on the floor, Archie's arms wound around her and, in one swift move, he sat her astride his lap.

'Better,' he replied, as his hands ran over her stomach and cupped her breasts. 'Much better.'

Arching her back, Cathy closed her eyes, ready to give herself up to Archie's embraces, but as she did, the chair beneath them creaked.

Rocking forward, Archie rose to his feet and, with Cathy's legs firmly wrapped around him, he took her back to the bed.

★ ★ ★

Waking with a start, Violet Wheeler's eyes flew open and the dark dream at the edge of her consciousness disappeared before she could focus it in her mind. But, in truth, she didn't need to because it was the same one that had brought her awake with a start ever since the letter informing her that her Stanley was missing in action had arrived.

But he wasn't dead.

She knew that, as sure as breath still moved in and out of her body, but in just a few weeks, as far as the world was concerned, he would be, and then her hateful daughter-in-law would get off scot-free.

350

Scot-free, despite the callous way she treated her, despite christening little Stanley Peter, a popish name if ever there was one, despite installing a lodger in the front room of her house, but most of all, despite being the reason her Stanley was in the army in the first place.

Contemplating the brutal retaliation her son would inflict on his worthless wife when he returned, Violet relished the raw hatred swirling around in her mind for a moment longer and then she switched on the bedside lamp.

Placing her hands on her chest, Violet took a couple of deep breaths and gazed up at the corrugated metal of the Anderson shelter above her head.

Many of her neighbours only took shelter in their back-garden bunkers when the air raid siren sounded, however, air raid or no air raid, Violet trundled down to her refuge each night regardless.

It was no hardship because, as thoughtful as ever, her Stanley had kitted it out with her comfort in mind. He'd installed a pipe chimney so she could use the paraffin camping stove by the door to make herself a brew. In addition, he'd run an electric cable from the house for the bedside lamp and wireless to keep her company.

Violet's gaze shifted to the photo of Stanley, surrounded by a silver frame, hanging on the wall opposite. Unlike most mothers, who displayed images of their male offspring dressed in their uniform, Violet had chosen a picture of her Stan dressed in his best suit with his hair slicked back as he smiled out of the picture at her.

Well, not her, but the photographer who'd taken his wedding-day photograph just over three and a half years earlier on 2 September 1939. The day everything went wrong. The day he'd tied himself to Cathy Brogan.

The rage that simmered constantly at the thought of her daughter-in-law started to bubble in Violet, but she damped it down.

Stanley wasn't dead and when he came home that bitch of a wife of his would be laughing on the other side of her face.

Feeling her heart beating beneath her hand and knowing it would be a good half an hour before she could settle back again, Violet swung her legs out of the bed.

The midnight news summary would be on soon so, putting on her candlewick dressing gown, Violet turned the dial on the small Bush radio.

As the valves warmed into life, Violet lit the gas under the half-filled kettle on the camping stove and spooned tea into the pot. However, as she picked up the milk bottle, she misjudged the distance and knocked it over instead.

Pressing her lips together, Violet glared at the milk as it disappeared into the crack at the edge of the shelter. Stepping into her shoes and wrapping her dressing gown around her, she unhooked the back-door key from the nail and opened the shelter door.

Although chilly, the night air was clear, with a hint of spring in the twinkling stars above. After making use of the lavatory and wondering why, given it was such a perfect night, there hadn't been an air raid, Violet unlocked the back door and walked into the kitchen.

Going to the refrigerator, she opened it and was just about to head back to her garden shelter when she heard the faint sound of Cathy moaning.

Putting the bottle of milk on the table, she opened the door to the hallway and listened. Her daughter-in-law moaned again but this time a deep male voice groaned too.

With her heart beating wildly in her chest and stepping carefully around the loose floorboards, Violet crept forward, the gasps and grunts echoing around the empty hallway.

Stopping in front of the front parlour, Violet's mouth pulled into a hard line as she listened to her slut of a daughter-in-law and her sergeant fornicating.

Rage and hatred flared up so ferociously that black spots exploded around the edge of Violet's vision. Her hand went to the door handle but just before she grasped it, she paused.

In the dark hallway, a malevolent smile spread across Violet's face and she withdrew her hand. After all, there was more than one way to skin a cat.

24

'Eat your breakfast, Peter,' said Cathy, pulling the grill out and turning over the four slices of national bread. 'We're off to see Auntie Muriel soon.'

Picking up a blob of scrambled egg, her son placed it in his mouth.

'Good boy,' Cathy said, smiling across at him as he sat in his highchair.

Like every other Tuesday, she was dressed in her WVS uniform ready for a long day manning the second-hand clothes section. And if Friday was anything to go by, she'd be rushed off her feet.

With the arrival of warmer spring days, there had been a flurry of mothers swapping their children's winter clothes for summer ones. On top of which, thanks to the efforts of the Royal Navy, many more merchant ships were making it across the North Atlantic, so the supply of parcels from the generous citizens of Canada and America had almost doubled.

But then, today wasn't like any other Tuesday and tomorrow wouldn't be like any other Wednesday. In fact, no day was the same any more because of Archie.

He had changed her days and her future.

With a small smile lifting her lips, Cathy pulled out the grill again and, using the tips of her fingers, removed the toast. Dropping it on a plate, she moved the frying pan from the back of the stove to the front. As she lit the gas, the kitchen door opened and Archie walked in.

'Morning,' she said, her heart doing a little dance

at the sight of him. 'Did you sleep well?'

'Aye,' he replied, his blue eyes capturing hers. 'After a bit of rolling about. You?'

'I had a very satisfying night, thank you,' she replied, cracking an egg into the frying pan.

He blew her a kiss then turned to Peter.

'Good morning, General,' he said, snapping to attention and saluting the lad.

Giggling, Peter put his hand flat on his forehead in response.

'You're looking a bit dapper this morning,' said Cathy, adding a rasher of bacon to Archie's plate.

Archie pulled down the front of his battle jacket that she'd pressed for him the day before.

'I thought, as the captain and scientist from HQ were coming to tell us how to deal with the new fuse, I'd better make an effort,' he replied.

A chill trembled through her.

She knew what his job involved and, like every other woman whose love was putting their life on the line to keep them safe, most of the time she could deal with it, but sometimes, just sometimes, when she lay in his arms, the fear of losing him was almost unbearable.

Damping down her bubbling fear, Cathy gave him a bright smile. 'Well, you look very smart.'

Giving her a look that sent her pulse racing, he dropped his jerkin over the back of the nearest chair and strolled over.

'And you,' he said, placing his hands around her waist, 'look utterly beautiful.'

Archie's right arm wound around her while his left hand smoothed up her spine.

Placing her hands on his hard chest, Cathy glanced at the back door. 'Archie, you shouldn't, what if old face-ache walked in?'

'Let her,' he replied, drawing her into his embrace. 'I don't care. She'll know soon enough and so will everyone else and then,' he kissed her again, 'you won't have to slip away in the wee small hours.

And I'll be waking up with you beside me every morning.'

'Yes, you will,' she said, yearning for the day.

'And anyway,' he added, 'we'll hear the key.'

'But —'

His mouth stopped her words and Cathy gave herself up to the magic of his lips and embrace for a moment, then, remembering the sizzling frying pan, she pushed him away.

'Stop it,' she said half-heartedly.

'You didn't say that last night, as I recall,' he said, drawing her back into his arms. 'Quite the opposite, in fact, because I distinctly heard you tell me to —'

'Archie!' Suppressing a smile, she gave him a hard look.

'All right,' he said, raising his hands and stepping back. 'That's the look that any sensible man would take heed of.'

Turning off the gas under the frying pan, she left the stove but as she reached up to collect their plates, Archie grabbed her again and turned her around.

'But unfortunately, I'm no a sensible man.'

'Archie, I said —'

His mouth covered hers again.

She yielded for a moment then she shoved him away, giving him another exasperated look.

He raised his hands again but this time he backed away properly.

'That's better,' she said, straightening her clothes.

She smiled. 'And there's tea in the pot.'

She turned back to the stove but as she man-oeuvred Archie's fried eggs on to the buttered toast, she caught a whiff of fried fat, causing the bitter taste of bile at the back of her throat.

Cathy swallowed it down and, taking a deep breath, dished up Archie's breakfast.

Archie had just finished pouring them both a cup of tea as she returned to the table.

'Thanks, that looks delicious,' he said, smiling up at her as she placed a plate with two fried eggs on toast and a rasher of bacon in front of him.

She kissed his forehead then sat in the chair next to him. 'Then eat it before it gets cold.'

He picked up his cutlery. 'Aren't you having any?'

'I had a bit of toast when I made Peter's before you came through,' she replied.

Archie nodded. Spearing a chunk of fried bread on his fork, he dabbed it in an egg yolk. 'I meant to say — '

The sound of the key rattled in the back door.

It opened and Violet, wrapped in her dressing gown and with curlers in her hair, walked in.

Her gaze flitted from Cathy to Archie and back again.

'Good morning, Mrs Wheeler,' said Archie, scraping the last of his egg up with the remaining wedge of fried bread and popping it in his mouth.

She didn't reply, but instead stood clutching her water bottle to her chest.

Downing his last mouthful of tea, Archie placed his cutlery together on his empty plate and pushed it away.

'Well now, bombs and fuses wait for no man,' he

357

said, standing up.

Taking his sheepskin from the back of the chair, he shrugged it on. Then, pulling a serious face, he saluted the toddler again.

Peter waggled his spoon at him, flicking a blob of egg into his hair in the process.

Archie looked across at Cathy. 'I'll see you tonight, Mrs Wheeler.'

'Yes, have a good day. Oh, I managed to get my hands on a couple of onions yesterday,' Cathy said, bringing him back to the present. 'So it's liver and onion casserole tonight.'

'That sounds grand,' he replied, pulling his cycle gauntlets from his pocket. 'See you tonight.'

Cathy smiled. 'Yes, see you tonight.'

With a last look at her, Archie opened the door and stepped out of the house.

Ignoring her mother-in-law, Cathy started clearing away Archie's used plate and cup.

With Violet's hateful stare boring into her back, Cathy laid them in the enamel bowl and sprinkled soap flakes on them.

'Hurry up, Peter,' she said pleasantly, pouring water from the kettle into the bowl. 'Then we can go to see Auntie Muriel.'

Taking Peter's old vest that served as a washing cloth from behind the tap, Cathy wiped it over the plates.

Behind her she heard the catch of the door to the hallway click shut as Violet left the room.

Resting her hands on the edge of the sink, Cathy's shoulders sagged for a moment.

The opening bars of Vera Lynn's 'It's a Lovely Day Tomorrow' drifted out from the wireless.

Cathy raised her head and gazed out of the window at the early-morning sunlight.

It wouldn't be a lovely day tomorrow but as soon as she had the letter declaring Stanley officially dead, she could start her new life with Archie, the man she would love into eternity. She smiled. Just seventeen short days.

* * *

'So as you can see, gentlemen,' said Captain Newitt, tapping the chart hanging on the wall beside him with the end of the pointer, 'a Y fuse is a real beauty and it's only thanks to one being recovered intact from a bomb on the Bakerloo Line a few weeks ago that we know how they work.'

It was just before twelve thirty and Archie was sitting in one of the classrooms in the Bomb Disposal School at the Duke of York's HQ on the King's Road.

The officers and other NCOs like him were scribbling away in notebooks, all desperate to get back to their job of saving British lives and infrastructure but also to avoid blowing themselves up in the process.

However, despite being squashed in a room with forty others for the past three hours, as an engineer, Archie couldn't help but admire Germany's latest invention. It was, as the captain said, a real beauty. With three mercury tilt switches in gyroscope formation, which would trigger the detonator at the slightest move, it was genius, except for the fact that it was specially designed to blow bomb disposal personnel to kingdom come.

'So, we've told you the bad news,' continued Captain Newitt. 'After lunch we'll be looking at how you're going to defuse the little blighters. Dismiss.'

Archie rose to his feet and stood to attention as those around him did the same. They stood silently until the officer and his assisting lieutenant had left the room and then the men stood easy and started milling about.

The officers, who had commandeered the best seats by the window, pushed past the NCOs and headed out to the officers' mess on the top floor of the building. Monkman was among them. As he passed, he looked across at Archie and his eyes narrowed.

Since they had clashed on the day of the presentation, when Monkman had molested Cathy, Archie had done his best to keep out of the lieutenant's way. This hadn't been difficult given they'd been more or less stood down until the scientists at Woolwich figured out how to deal with these new Y fuses. However, now Archie and the rest of the company would soon be back digging up and defusing bombs, avoiding his senior officer would prove more difficult.

Archie matched his hostile stare.

Monkman held his unwavering gaze for a couple of seconds then looked away and walked on.

'Cor blimey, if it ain't that miserable old haggis,' a voice said from behind.

Archie turned.

'Stormy,' said Archie, offering his hand to the ruddy-faced Londoner with wiry ginger hair. 'So the Boche haven't got you yet, then?'

Sergeant Ernest Gale, who like Archie had been tinkering with bombs from the start of the Blitz, held up his left hand minus a little finger.

'They tried.' He took Archie's hand. 'Where're you stationed now?'

'Wanstead. You?'

'Hackney, just up from Shoreditch church,' Ernie replied. His eyes flickered on to Archie's sergeant's stripes. 'I see we've both moved up in the pecking order.'

'Aye,' said Archie. 'But then if you've survived six months tinkering about with thousand-kilo bombs with hair-trigger fuses, you've got more experience than some of these wet-behind-the-ears officers they churn out in this place.'

'Too right,' said Ernie. 'But never mind all that, how are you?'

'I'm fair,' Archie replied.

'Still painting?'

Archie told him briefly about his three works touring in the Home Front Exhibition.

'And yourself? How are you and the family faring?' asked Archie. 'You've three boys, I recall?'

'I did have,' Ernie replied. 'But me and Ethel have got four kiddies now. Just before Christmas. Little Linda. And she's already got me wrapped around her little finger. What about your . . . ?'

'Kirsty,' said Archie. 'She's a fine young lass. At school now and writing her old dad a letter a week.'

Ernie whistled through his teeth. 'They do grow fast, don't they?'

'Too fast,' Archie agreed, as the familiar ache for his daughter made itself known.

Ernie gave him a sympathetic look. 'Must be hard with her up there and you down here.'

'It is, but she and Ma are joining me soon.' A wide smile spread across Archie's face. 'I'm getting married.'

'You old dog, Archie,' Ernie said, slapping him on

the upper arm. 'When?'

'In about six weeks. To Cathy,' Archie added, the sound of her name swelling his chest.

'Well, good luck to you both.' Ernie glanced at the door. 'I'd better catch up with my lot before they scoff everything.'

'Aye, but it's good to see you, Ernie,' said Archie.

'You too,' said Ernie, slapping him on the arm again. 'And good luck again.'

Ernie turned and joined the sea of khaki making its way towards the door.

Feeling ready for whatever it was on the canteen menu, Archie picked up his notebook and followed but as he stepped into the corridor, he noticed Monkman loitering at the bottom of the stairs.

Archie strolled towards the double doors of the canteen but as he came abreast of him, Monkman stepped into his path.

'What do you think you're bally well playing at, McIntosh?' Monkman forced out between his teeth, looking up at Archie.

'I don't know you're meaning, sir,' he replied.

'Don't you?'

'No.'

'No, sir!' barked Monkman. 'And stand to attention when a superior officer is addressing you.'

Archie pulled himself up to his full six foot two inches.

'No, sir,' he replied, looking coolly down at the lieutenant.

'I'm talking about this bloody complaint you had the nerve to put in about the unfortunate camouflet accident,' Monkman said, blowing smoke from the side of his mouth.

'With all due respect, sir, it wouldn't have happened if you'd taken note of — '

'I know what this is about,' the lieutenant cut in. 'It's about that business with your bit of skirt. It's your way of getting back at me.'

Mastering his temper, Archie's eyes bored into him

'If you'd bother to check the date of my complaint, you'd know I lodged it a full week before you molested Mrs Wheeler, sir,' said Archie as the corner of Monkman's left eye started to twitch. 'And it was an accident that should never have happened. A good man with a wife and family died and another who'd not yet reached his majority is crippled for life because of your actions.'

Monkman took a long draw on his cigarette.

'Very sad I'm sure, but there's a war on. Men die. It's as simple as that, which is why it was thrown out,' he said, smoke escaping from his mouth and nostrils as he spoke. 'And I don't know what you're bellyaching about, McIntosh. The men have been replaced.'

Pressing his hands to his thighs to stop them grabbing the lieutenant by the throat, Archie gave him a glacial look. 'Will that be all, sir?'

'N . . . n . . . no it will not,' Monkman stuttered, the twitching nerve working overtime. 'In the army, men should know their place, especially' — he looked Archie up and down — 'damn half-breeds, even if they've got stripes on their arm.'

Although his jaw clenched, Archie's expression remained impassive as he counted slowly to ten in his head.

Monkman's angry eyes studied him for a minute or two then he spoke again.

'Dismiss.'

Standing to attention, Archie saluted then turned on his heels to march to the canteen, but after a couple of steps, he stopped.

'By the way,' he said, turning back to face Monkman, 'if I had my way, I'd be dealing with a man who attacked a woman by offering him a square-go before pasting the pavement with him, *sir*.'

25

Fastening Peter's top button, Cathy gave him a quick kiss and then straightened up.

'Say bye-bye to Auntie Muriel,' she said, taking his hand.

Peter waved at the matronly woman helping a little girl put a dress on her dolly. She waved back and Cathy walked him out of the nursery and through into the playground.

As it was just after four thirty, there were already a number of Cathy's fellow WVS volunteers putting their toddlers and babies into prams ready to set off home after their stint at the centre. Older women without dependent children were just arriving to man the canteen and, if there should be an air raid, stand ready to receive people bombed out during the night.

Locating her pushchair under the bike shelter, Cathy lifted Peter in and fastened his blue leather straps.

Kicking off the brakes, she leaned on the handle and manoeuvred the pushchair on its back wheels past the tangle of prams and out through the Catholic Club's gate.

Picking up her pace, Cathy mingled with the other people heading home after a long day. She caught sight of the clock above the jeweller's shop showing ten to five. Just three hours and Archie would be home. Of course, now she didn't head off to the shelter each evening at five, she had to suffer Violet for a few hours each night, but it wouldn't be for much longer.

Archie had already found them a little house off Globe Road and was just waiting for her to see it and say yes before he sought permission from his HQ to move in. It was a guinea a week, a bit steep for a three-up three-down house, and it would take a big chunk out of Archie's four pounds, ten shillings wages. However, it had a basement, which could be reinforced, and a small garden, and although she'd lose the Army's widow pension, once they were married Archie could claim the married man's allowance for two dependent children and a wife.

Cathy turned into Senrab Street. As she approached the house, she noticed a huddle of her neighbours chatting excitedly and laughing, with Violet at their centre, as they milled around outside her front door.

'Here she is!' shouted Mrs Jolliffe, the red-faced woman who lived opposite, as she spotted Cathy approaching.

From among the bevy of women, her mother-in-law's eyes fixed on Cathy and a smug smile lifted her thin lips.

'Tell her, Violet,' said Ethel Basset, who lived two doors down.

'Tell me what?' asked Cathy, as her mouth went dry.

Like the Red Sea before Moses, the crowd of neighbours parted as her mother-in-law glided through the small crowd.

Violet held up a telegram. 'Stanley's been found.'

Cathy gripped the handle of the pushchair to steady herself as the ground beneath her feet threatened to rise up and meet her.

'Can you believe it?' said someone.

'And after so long,' added another, as Violet's words

366

screamed around her.

A hand rested on her shoulder. 'It's a miracle.'

'Isn't it marvellous, Cathy?' asked Mrs Sutton from across the road.

Cathy stared at them, open-mouthed, unable to think or speak.

A sentimental expression spread across Violet's face.

'I think she's a bit overwhelmed.' Stepping forward, her mother-in-law placed a hand on Cathy's arm. 'But you can stop worrying now, dear,' she said, her artless expression giving way to a smug one. 'You're not going to be a widow after all.'

★ ★ ★

The last rays of April sunlight were tinting the west-facing upper window pink when Archie steered his Triumph around the corner and into Senrab Street. Slowing the bike to a halt, he put his feet to the ground and cut the engine.

It was now almost eight and a little later than he'd anticipated as the training session had run over. Understandable, really, because the German's new Y fuse was nothing like they'd encountered before so the boffins had had to develop the technique for disarming it from scratch. And after what he'd seen today, Archie hoped he wouldn't be encountering one any time soon.

Yawning, he stepped off the bike. Grasping the handlebars, he rolled it down the side alley and through the back gate. Pulling it on to its stand, he pulled the tarpaulin cover over it and headed across the small yard to the back door.

367

Imagining Cathy waiting for him, Archie opened the door and found only Mrs Wheeler senior in the kitchen.

He glanced at the clock.

'I know I'm usually tucked up in my little bunk by now but . . . ' She gave him a sweet smile. 'Would you like a cup of tea?'

'Er, no, thank you,' he replied. 'Where's Mrs Wheeler?'

'She's just settling little Stanley down for the night,' she replied. 'She'll soon be —'

The door opened and Cathy walked in, hollow-eyed and with the colour all but gone from her face.

'What's happened?' he asked.

Looking bleakly across at him, Cathy opened her mouth but didn't speak.

'She's a bit emotional,' said Violet chirpily. 'And who can blame her after getting such happy news?'

Archie looked puzzled. 'News?'

Mrs Wheeler's smile went from sweet to syrupy and she looked at Cathy.

'Do tell him, dear,' she said.

With her gaze locked with his, Cathy found her voice. 'The Red Cross have found Stanley.'

Archie looked at her incredulously. 'What?'

'Yes, isn't it marvellous?' Violet chipped in. 'Of course, they aren't sure exactly where he is just now, but as soon as they locate him and inform the Ministry of War what POW camp he's being held in' — her eyes narrowed as they slid from Archie to Cathy and back again — 'I'll be writing to him to tell him all about everything that's been going on.'

Somewhere about a mile or so away an air raid siren went off.

'Oh,' said Violet, her bright smile returning to her face. 'That's my cue to get into the cosy little shelter.'

She went to the stove. Archie and Cathy stared wordlessly across the room at each other as she filled her hot-water bottle from the kettle. Jamming the stopper on, she turned to face them.

'Well, that's me done,' she said, smiling at them both. 'Have a nice evening.'

Tucking the rubber bottle under her arm, she opened the back door and left.

As the key turned in the lock, tears welled in Cathy's eyes and her face crumpled.

'Archie,' she sobbed, reaching out for him.

Throwing his gloves on the kitchen table as he passed, Archie crossed the space between them and gathered her into his arms.

★ ★ ★

Archie woke with a start. Finding the space beside him in the bed empty, he sat bolt upright.

He looked around and saw Cathy naked and standing by his easel in the bay window.

She was holding his sketchpad and looking at the drawing of her he'd done a few days before. She opened the curtains, allowing the mellow April sunlight to flood into the room.

He glanced at the clock on the bedside table. Five thirty!

She'd usually slipped in beside Peter in the Morrison shelter long before now.

Hearing him move, she turned and smiled.

She was still a little red around the eyes but as they rested on him, they were filled with happiness and love.

'Morning,' she said, turning to face him as naturally as Eve in the Garden of Eden. 'Isn't it a lovely day?'

'Yes, yes, it is,' he said, taking note of the pattern of the sunlight on her body. 'When did you wake up?'

'About an hour ago, I suppose; it was still dark,' she replied. 'I couldn't sleep.'

'Are you all right, sweetheart?' he asked.

She hadn't been and had sobbed for a full fifteen minutes after her mother-in-law had left them. Feeling helpless and as if someone had ripped out his innards, he had just held her close.

Rather than give voice to their feelings, they'd expressed them by making love with such desperation it had left them both drained of every emotion. The last thing he remembered was holding her in his arms, studying every inch of her beloved face as she slept, after which he too had fallen into a fitful but dreamless sleep.

Cathy's smile widened. 'Never better. I lay there watching you sleep for a while then I got up and opened the curtains to see the sun rise. I also thought I'd see how you're getting on with this.' She turned the image towards him.

'And what do you think?' he asked.

'I think you're very talented to have created something as beautiful with just a pencil and a sheet of paper,' she replied.

'Aye, but I had a beautiful subject,' he said, running his gaze appreciatively over her. 'And I've been working on it.'

'I can see,' she replied. 'You've added in shading to show the curves and roundness of my legs and hips,

370

and the way you've caught my likeness is . . . well, it's as good as any photo.'

'I'm glad you like it,' he said. 'I was thinking of using it as a basis for a watercolour portrait.'

He waited for her to object; after all, it had started as just a doodle between themselves, but now the colours he would need to create Cathy's fair skin tone, the golds, reds and browns he could employ to bring out the myriad tones of her hair and the berry blush of her mouth, kept flashing into his mind.

Cathy's eyes returned to the sketchpad.

'You know, Archie, it doesn't matter,' she said, still studying his work. 'Stan being alive, I mean. And it doesn't matter either that we can't be married. I don't care. I don't care what people say or what they call me. I don't care about any of that as long as you love me.'

Letting the bedcover fall from him, Archie stood up.

'I do, Cathy.' He raked his fingers through his hair. 'God in heaven knows, I do.'

Cathy raised her head, her eyes locked with his.

'I know, and I love you just as much,' she said. 'As far as I'm concerned, I'm your wife, Archie. And we're going to move into the house off Globe Road with Kirsty and your mother. In time, please God, instead of just the four of us we'll be six or seven, or even more. We'll be married in all the ways that matter and if someday we can sign a bit of paper that says we are, then we will, if not . . . ' She shrugged. Her gaze returned to his drawing for a moment then she turned it around so he could see his own work. 'I love this sketch. I really do. And do you know why?'

'Tell me,' he said, walking over to her.

'Because this is me,' she replied, looking up at him as he stood before her. 'Not the stupid little girl who was so intent on being the prettiest bride and getting one over on her elder sister by walking down the aisle first that she was blind to the violent brute she was marrying. But me now, Catherine Celia Brogan, who loves and is loved by you, Archie James McIntosh, a man worth ten of any other. So, if you want to make this sketch into a painting six foot high and display it in every gallery in the land then I'd be glad to stand beside it. As I'll be glad to stand by you for the rest of my life.'

Feeling as if his heart was going to burst with love, Archie stared down into Cathy's stunningly beautiful face for a moment.

Taking his sketchpad from her he dropped it on the floor, then, with his eyes locked on hers, his arms wrapped around her slender waist.

He drew her to him as desire and need pulsed through him, mingling with overwhelming love.

In one swift movement, he swept her into his arms, intent on taking her back to the bed, but his second stride kicked his sketchpad under it.

'Your drawing,' Cathy said, looking over his shoulder at it.

'Don't worry,' he said, lowering her on to the bed and covering her with his body. 'I'll get it later.'

26

'And this is the kitchen,' said Archie, as Cathy, holding Peter's hand, followed him out of the back parlour and into the rear of the empty house. 'I know it's not as big as the one you're used to, but — '

'No, it's fine, Archie,' said Cathy, looking around. 'It's about the same size as my parents' and there's a larder. Plus, there's room for a table and a nice view of the garden, which is east facing. It will have the sun all morning so I can dry the washing.'

It was just about ten thirty in the morning and the Monday after they'd found out Stan was alive, and they were standing in a three-up three-down house in Alderney Road around the corner from Stepney Green station.

As Archie had been working all weekend, they had taken advantage of his first day off in two weeks to look over the house he'd found for them. Although he was off duty, he was still on active service, so he was wearing his uniform. However, Cathy had discarded her WVS uniform for a red sweater and tartan slacks, and was a little disconcerted to find she'd put on weight since she'd last worn them — it had been a struggle to fasten the button.

The house Archie had found for them was in a row of Victorian terraced houses, so it was almost exactly like her childhood home, but the layout was the mirror image of her parents' home. Facing the road and with the stairs immediately in front, to the left was the best parlour with a bay window and its original

Victorian wrought-iron fireplace. Behind this room was the everyday parlour with French windows opening on to the concrete patio at the side of the kitchen. However, at the end of the hall there was an additional scullery with a window that looked out on to the square of yard.

After passing through the scullery you reached the kitchen that ran down the side, where they were now standing.

Peter wriggled in her grasp, so she let go of him and he stomped around, punching his arms back and forth and making chuff-chuff sounds.

Going over to the sink, she looked down into it.

'It could do with a bit of a going-over with a Brillo Pad and some Vim,' she said, glancing at the brown rings around the plughole. 'But there's an Ascot.' She indicated the white enamel cylinder fixed to the wall beside her. 'So no more boiling water to wash.'

'And plenty of hot water to bath the children in front of the fire on Fridays,' Archie added. 'Of course, we'll have to buy a cooker before we move in, but I thought we could have a dresser there.' He indicated the space next to where the gas fittings jutted out from the wall. 'And maybe a couple of cupboards there.' He pointed at the gap below the small side window.

'Good idea,' Cathy replied.

Taking a step forward, she gazed around the room again. 'Shall we look upstairs?'

Archie smiled. 'After you, madam.'

'Let's go and look at your new bedroom, Peter,' she said.

Peter stopped racing around the empty space and ran back into the hallway.

'Wait for us!' she shouted, as she and Archie hurried

374

after him.

Peter was already on the bottom step, picking at the loose wallpaper, when they reached him.

'Up we go, lad,' said Archie, taking his hand.

As her son hung on to Archie and took big strides up the stairs, Cathy followed behind until they reached the square landing at the turn of the stairs.

'I thought this could be Peter's room,' said Archie, pushing open the door to reveal a small box room.

Peter thundered in and Cathy strolled after.

'Peter, how would you like to have this as your bedroom?' she asked.

Her son rushed to the window and jumped up and down to see out, raising dust under his Start Rite shoes.

Cathy smiled at Archie. 'I think he likes it.'

'And the other two are up top,' said Archie, striding out of the room.

Peter went to run after him, but Cathy caught his hand and followed.

Taking the half-dozen stairs two at a time, Archie went to the top landing.

'I thought Kirsty could have the back room,' he said, as Cathy reached him.

Letting her son run into the empty room she poked her head around the door and inspected the second bedroom.

'We'll have to get an electric fire for her and Peter's rooms, but both are more than big enough to take a single bed and wardrobe.'

'And this,' he said, taking her hand and leading her into the large room at the front of the house, 'is ours.'

This room sat over the front parlour and it, too, had a bay window. Also like the lower room, the old-fashioned

375

wrought-iron fireplace was still in place. However, unlike downstairs, floor-to-ceiling cupboards were fitted into the alcoves on either side of the chimney breast.

'Mind, we'll have to make do with a few sticks of furniture and no rugs for a while as the beds have to be bought first,' he said.

'Well, at least we can furnish this room,' Cathy said. 'Everything in Senrab Street is Violet's, other than a couple of pots, pans and a bit of crockery, and the handful of linen I had in my bottom drawer, but I'm sure Dad will be able to help us with furniture.'

Archie frowned. 'Aye, your father. I've been thinking about him.'

'Don't worry, I'll talk him around,' she said. 'Jo already knows, and my gran will be no problem at all, so once I get Mum on side, Dad won't be able to say no.'

Archie opened his mouth to speak but Cathy got in first. 'Where's your mum going to sleep?'

'In the back parlour,' Archie said. 'It's the same size as the room next door and bigger than the one she's squashed into now.'

Peter came running into the room and Cathy scooped him up and on to her hip. Taking a step back she gazed around at the bare windows, peeling paint and ripped wallpaper, then up to the flex dangling, without a light bulb, from the ceiling rose.

Archie raked his fingers through his hair. 'I know it needs a dab of paint — '

'And a going-over with a scrubbing brush and bleach,' said Cathy, noticing the mouse droppings in the hearth. 'And it's a guinea a week?'

'Aye,' he replied. 'I'll concede it's a bit over the

odds, but I've been all over it and there's no damp or wood rot. Plus, I'd be happier with you all sleeping in a proper basement shelter rather than in a metal box all night. And I know it's a bit sparse after Senrab — '

'It's perfect,' said Cathy, swinging around and smiling at him.

Peter wriggled to get down and Cathy set him on his feet.

Archie raised an eyebrow. 'It's certainly nae that.'

Crossing the floor to where he stood, she rested her hands on his chest.

'It is,' she said, sliding them up and around his neck. 'Because you're here.'

Archie's eyes darkened as his arms wound around her.

'You're a bit heavy with the swank today, aren't you, missis,' he said in a low voice as he drew her into his embrace.

'Perhaps,' she replied, tilting her head back. 'And I grant you this is no palace, but it's where we can start out life together.'

'So, shall I tell them we'll take it?'

Cathy nodded.

'We'll take it,' she said, pulling Peter away from where he was swinging on the cupboard handles.

'Grand.' Archie strode over to the window. 'I'll drop by the office tomorrow and pay them two weeks' rent in advance. I'll request a day off on Monday and we can move in. Then Ma and Kirsty can come on Thursday so we're all together for Easter.'

'We should be able to sort out some furniture by then,' said Cathy.

He nodded.

'And finally this' — he stretched his arm across the

empty space of the bay — 'is where I'll set up my easel and paints to take full advantage of the afternoon and evening light.'

Cathy laughed. 'That's why you're so keen on this house: for your precious paintings.'

Sidestepping Peter, who'd returned to being a train and was chugging around the room, Archie crossed the space between them in two strides and took her back into his arms.

'I'm keen on this house because it means we can start living the rest of our lives together.' Kissing her, his hands slipped down her back and on to her bottom. 'Also,' he said, tucking her against him, 'even with a wardrobe, chest of drawers and a double bed, there's enough room in here for a crib to tuck down the side.'

'You're running ahead of yourself, aren't you?' Cathy said, giving him a saucy look from under her lashes. 'We've not moved in yet.'

'Well, you know what the old women say, don't you?' he asked, the promise in his blue eyes sending excitement through her. 'New home. New bairn.'

Cathy gazed up at him for a moment then Peter took off out of the room again.

'Hold up there, young fella,' shouted Archie, letting her go and tearing after her son.

Pondering if she'd like a boy or a girl first, before deciding she didn't really care, Cathy glanced around the empty room that would soon be their home and followed them out.

★ ★ ★

Cathy, pushing her son in his pushchair, and Archie arrived back at Senrab Street just before noon. The handful of neighbours still out polishing windows and loitering on their doorsteps studied them as they walked towards Cathy's front door.

Thinking how glad she was that this time next week she could wave all of Violet's gossipy neighbours goodbye for ever, Cathy guided the front wheels of the pushchair down the side alley.

However, Archie caught her arm and she stopped.

'Do you think your dad's back from his morning rounds yet?' he asked.

'I should think so,' said Cathy. 'He only had a local delivery this morning and he's got an unclaimed possessions auction at St Paul's council depot this afternoon. Why?'

'I thought I might take a stroll down and have a chat with him,' Archie replied.

Cathy looked puzzled. 'But I've already said I'll talk him around.'

'So you did, pet.' He kissed her. 'I'll be back in a while.'

Shoving his hands in his pocket, Archie strolled off down the street in the direction of Commercial Road and Jeremiah's yard.

* * *

Ten minutes later, having negotiated his way through the prams and shopping trolleys of the midday bargain hunters, Archie reached the end of Watney Street Market and turned right into Chapman Street.

Strolling past the coopers' arched doorway and the garage, he came to the double green gates with 'Brogan

& Sons Home Clearance, Removals and Deliveries' painted in bold fairground-type lettering across them.

The gates were open, and parked inside the enclosed space was an empty five-ton Bedford lorry with the same insignia painted on the side.

A goods train rattled past on the viaduct above and Archie paused.

Straightening his tie, he strolled in.

Walking between the bedsteads, washstands, sideboards and chairs stacked along one side of the arch, he headed for the space at the far end of the cavernous railway arch.

Reaching the office at the back, Archie found Jeremiah in his workaday cords and collar-less shirt hunched over a ledger on the desk.

He looked up as Archie stopped in the doorway.

'Sergeant McIntosh,' Jeremiah said, a broad smile lighting his face as he turned in the chair to greet him.

'Good day to you, Mr Brogan,' Archie replied. 'I wonder if I might take a moment of your time.'

'Certainly,' Cathy's father replied, stowing his pen behind his ear. 'Is it some furniture you're looking for?'

Archie gave him a half-smile. 'In a while perhaps, but first I'd like to talk to you about Cathy.'

Although Jeremiah's jovial expression remained, a sharp glint crept into his eye. 'Would you now?'

'Aye, I would,' Archie said.

Jeremiah leaned back on the chair. 'Perhaps I'm being a mite fanciful, but I have the feeling I'll not be too happy when you have.'

'You may not,' said Archie. 'I thought Cathy a bonny lass as soon as I met her, but living under the same roof as her these past months, ma feelings for

380

her have changed. Knowing she was married I held myself back but on that terrible night at the Bethnal Green shelter, when I thought I'd lost her, I told her I loved her. She said she felt the same about me, so we decided to marry as soon as she had the official notification of her husband's death. I had planned to come and speak to you once that had happened, to ask you formally for

your blessing, but now I can't.'

'Because Stanley Wheeler's been found,' her father said flatly.

'Aye,' said Archie, feeling the weight of the other man's eyes on him. 'We'd planned to wed on the first of May but as we can't we've decided to set up home together anyhow.'

Jeremiah gave him a hard look. 'Have you now?'

'We have,' Archie replied, matching the other man's forthright stare. 'We've just been to look at a house at the back of Stepney Green station and, as Cathy likes it, I'll be dropping by the rent office tomorrow. We plan to move in next Monday and I'm bringing my daughter and Ma down from Glasgow next week.'

Jeremiah gave him a wry look. 'I have an understanding now as to why you might be in need of some furniture.'

'I'm not best pleased about the situation we're in as I'm wild to marry Cathy,' Archie continued. 'You and I both know the names Cathy will be called when she moves in with me, with or without a ring on her finger, but neither of us are prepared to live apart for one day longer than we have to, which is why I'm standing before you now. I'm sure you wanted more for Cathy than to be the common-law wife of a half-caste bastard, but I love Cathy and I swear I'll spend every day

381

of the rest of my life looking after her.'

Jeremiah studied him for a moment.

'Now, as I recall, the last time we spoke on the matter, I said that it's a rare joy to be the father of girls,' he said, rising from his seat.

'You did,' said Archie. 'And I agreed with you.'

'And correct me if I'm wrong but didn't I also say I'd have to be mouldering in my grave before I let anyone hurt any of them?'

Archie drew himself up and looked the older man square in the eye. 'I remember you saying the very same.'

'Well, I tell you now, Sergeant,' said Jeremiah, taking a step nearer, 'I haven't yet fulfilled that oath as far as my darling Cathy is concerned because the police and the Secret Service got their hands on Stanley Wheeler before I did. Now, I won't lie and say the situation between you and Cathy is exactly as I'd like it to be, but I tell you this and tell you no more: all I've ever wanted for my darling girls is that they find someone who loves them as much as I do. Now, I don't care if you're sky blue with green spots, Sergeant, if you're that man for Cathy —'

'I am, Mr Brogan,' Archie said firmly. 'I promise you, I am.'

The older man scrutinised him for a moment or two longer then offered him his hand.

Archie took it. 'Thank you, Mr Brogan.'

They shook, then Archie gave him a querying look. 'The Secret Service?'

'It's a long tale best told over a pint.' Jeremiah punched him lightly on the upper arm. 'And I'm thinking, Archie, it's your round.'

27

'It's going to be a beautiful day,' said Cathy, looking at the first few rays of spring sunlight streaking across the sky as she filled the kettle with water again.

'It's always a beautiful day, waking up next to you,' Archie said, winding his arms around her waist and kissing her just below her ear.

It was the Wednesday before Palm Sunday and, as the Reveille on the Forces Service had just started, it was just after six thirty. It was also just over a week since the news arrived that Stanley had been found.

Cathy had woken up about fifteen minutes earlier to find Archie already up and having a strip wash at the sink. She was bare-footed and wore just her dressing gown wrapped around her. Archie, on the other hand, was now fully dressed except for his battle jacket, which was draped over the back of a kitchen chair.

Closing her eyes, Cathy revelled in Archie's loving embrace for a moment then as his hand slipped between the front of her robe and across her skin, she reluctantly wriggled free.

'You'll be late,' she said, putting the kettle back on the hob.

'I've got five minutes yet,' he said, drawing her back to him for a brief kiss, then letting her go.

'Peter still not awake?'

Cathy shook her head. 'Not yet. I'll get him up when you've gone. There's no rush. I'm popping around to Mum's before I head off to the centre.'

Picking up his dirty breakfast crockery from the table, she slid the cup into the washing bowl in the sink. However, as she scraped the bacon rind into the pig swill bucket under the sink, the pungent

smell of rotting vegetation wafted up and turned her stomach.

Cathy took a deep breath and the nausea subsided.

'I'm expecting the official thumbs-up from HQ today,' Archie said, sitting down and pulling on his left boot. 'So I'll drop by the Bancroft Estate offices and get the rent book for the house tomorrow and we can move in next week.'

'Good,' said Cathy. 'I can't wait. And I don't care if you, me and Peter have to sleep on a mattress until we can get the furniture and before your mum and Kirsty arrive.'

'It's worked out well as the school's closing for the Easter Holidays next week, so it'll give me a chance to speak to the headmaster at Wessex Street School a few streets away from us too,' he said, tugging his bootlaces tight.

'Jo already knows, but it's all happened so fast I haven't had a chance to speak to mum, Gran or . . . 'Cathy glanced at the clock. 'I didn't realise the time. You'd better get a move on.'

'I should.'

Standing up, Archie took two strides, slipping his arm around her waist.

'See you later, sweetheart,' he said, his ice-blue eyes hot as they gazed down into hers.

Reaching up, she smoothed her hand over his freshly shaved cheek. 'Be careful, Archie.'

He smiled and pressed his lips on to hers for a moment then released her. However, as he did, the smell of his aftershave drifted up and Cathy's stomach churned again.

Grabbing his jacket from the chair and opening the back door, Archie strode out.

Cathy watched him through the window as he wheeled his motorbike through the side gate then she returned to the stove. She reached for yesterday's national loaf sitting on the bread board and her stomach heaved. She gagged. And then gagged again.

Covering her mouth with her hands, she stumbled to the back door and, headless of her bare feet, dashed across the flagstones. Yanking the lavatory door open, she stepped in. A wave of nausea rose up and Cathy planted her hands on either side of the scrubbed wooden seat and threw up.

She took a deep breath then vomited again.

She waited until her stomach had quietened then raised her head. Taking her handkerchief from her dressing-gown pocket, she wiped her mouth and straightened up.

Retying her dressing gown across her, Cathy put her hand on the rough planking of the outhouse door.

She pushed it open to find Violet, also in her dressing gown, standing on the other side.

'Well,' she said, giving Cathy the sweetest smile. 'That's something new to put in Stanley's next letter, isn't it?'

* * *

Archie pulled on the brake and slowed his Tiger to a stop. Planting his feet firmly on the tarmac playground, he switched off the engine.

He stepped off and heaved his bike on to its stand

385

and then turned and raised his head. Archie studied the sun lighting the eastern sky above the rooftops. Cathy was right: it was going to be a beautiful spring day. It perfectly reflected his mood.

Satisfied his bike was securely balanced, Archie padlocked it to the railings then, grinding gravel under his boots, he strolled across to the main building.

Pushing open the door, Archie walked in and was greeted by the sound of telephones ringing, male voices and stomping feet from the floor above where the sappers were billeted.

'Morning, Sarge!'

Archie turned.

'Aye, so it is,' he replied, acknowledging Smudger the clerk in the dispatch office. 'A very good morning indeed.'

Glancing up at the blackboard where the allocations were marked up, Archie yawned.

'Anything in yet?'

'Not yet,' replied Smudger from his seat behind the line of telephones on his desk. 'But it's still early and, after the night we had last night, it won't be long, and D Squad are on first call.' He grinned. 'Looks like the Boche kept you awake all night, too.'

Archie smiled as he remembered why he was tired.

'Well, I'm away to grab myself a brew so tell any of my bunch of jessies who might be looking for me I'm in the canteen,' Archie replied.

Turning, he headed towards what had been the school dining hall, but just as his hand touched the brass plate on the door someone called his name.

'Sergeant McIntosh!'

Archie turned to see the clerk puffing down the corridor waving a yellow report slip in his hand.

'What is it?' asked Archie, meeting him halfway.

'The ARP control room in Shadwell have just sent this through,' Smudger said, handing him the report.

Archie read quickly then looked up. 'Who's first-call officer?'

A sympathetic expression lifted the stout corporal's round face. 'Lieutenant Monkman.'

★ ★ ★

Twenty minutes later, with the sun now bursting over the tops of the riverside wharfs, the police officers moved aside the yellow cordon strung across the road and waved through D Squad's lorry. Careful not to drive the truck's tyres over the jagged glass and nails scattered across the road, Mogg pulled hard on the steering wheel and drew up alongside the kerb in Glamis Road.

Opening the cab's door, Archie jumped down and surveyed the scene.

The southern end of the road that ran off Cable Street was a mix of warehouses and small factories, while at the northern end of the street, by St Mary's Church, there were residential dwellings.

Although the three-up three-down houses were still standing, their windows gaped like toothless mouths; their glass panes had been shattered in the previous night's air raid. At the Cable Street end of the cobbled thoroughfare a heavy-rescue team was just packing up, having finished their early-morning search for survivors among the rubble. Behind them, towards the river and docks, a pall of black smoke billowed upwards, the aftermath of a bomb that wouldn't need Archie's attention.

The tailgate banged as the men inside scrambled out. Chalky came forward to join him.

'We seem to have a bit of an audience,' Chalky said, indicating the large crowd of people on the other side of the ARP cordon.

'Aye,' said Archie, studying the anxious-looking men and women huddled together. 'And to my way of thinking they're a mite too close.'

'My very thoughts,' said Chalky.

Archie turned to the men gathered behind him.

'Arthur, set up the safe place around yon corner,' he said, pointing to a side passage fifty yards away.

'Right you are, Sarge,' the lance corporal replied.

As the men set about the task, Archie turned back to Chalky. 'Let's go and see what the Luftwaffe have sent us this time.'

With glass crunching under his boots, Archie strolled across to the half a dozen ARP wardens milling about by a damaged wall.

'Sergeant McIntosh,' said Archie, addressing the grey-haired warden sporting a sky-blue badge with two broad yellow stripes on his chest. 'What have you got for us?'

'Captain Cox, Royal Transport and Chief Warden,' he replied, giving Archie the usual curious look through his metal-rimmed spectacles. 'And I'd rather wait for an officer before proceeding.'

'He's on his way,' Archie replied.

He was hoping that was true. Despite being rotated on duty since o-seven hundred hours, there'd been no sign of Monkman when they left the depot at seven thirty-five.

'So if you wouldn't mind showing what we're dealing with I — '

'I served in the last war, Sergeant,' interrupted Cox, puffing out his chest. 'Although I'm now civilian defence, technically, as chief warden of the Shadwell and Wapping area, I outrank you so — '

'For Gawd's sake, Dick,' snapped a matronly woman in the same ARP uniform and wearing a tin hat with a white 'W' on it. 'Unless you want to go down and sort the bugger out yourself, show the sergeant where the bomb is.'

Through the lenses of his glasses, the warden's eyes bulged. 'Mavis, I was just pointing out — '

'Well, don't,' said Mavis.

'All right, all right,' said Cox, giving her a testy look. 'This way, Sergeant.'

Archie looked at Mavis.

'Do you think you and your warden pals could disperse the crowd?' he asked. 'I'm not planning to end up at the Pearly Gates today, but if I do, I'd rather be there alone.'

'We've tried,' she replied. 'But their kids are in there.'

'In where?' asked Archie.

'The hospital,' the youthful warden alongside Mavis said.

'But the chit I was given said it was located near a gas pipe,' said Archie.

'It is,' said the young warden. 'It runs under the bottom of the street.'

'But the bomb lodged itself in the stairwell of the East London Children's hospital,' said Mavis, 'trapping a dozen children and nurses on the top floor.'

'Can't you evacuate them down the fire escape?' Archie asked, as images of Kirsty and Peter flickered through his mind.

The wardens exchanged an uneasy look and then Cox spoke.

'We would have, but . . . ' The chief warden cleared his throat. 'Well, it's like this. It's an old building and the wrought-iron fire stairs at the back collapsed a month or so back in an air raid. The hospital board were supposed to have replaced them but — '

'I hope you're nae going to point out that there's a war on,' cut in Archie.

The chief warden lowered his eyes.

Stepping forward, Mavis put her hand on Archie's arm.

'You will be able to stop the bomb going off, won't you?' she asked, looking anxiously up at him.

'I'll do my best,' Archie replied. His attention shifted back to Cox. 'After you, Chief Warden.'

★ ★ ★

After climbing over the bricks and mortar of the gutted northwest corner of the hospital, Archie and Chalky stood in what had been the hospital's main corridor. They looked down into the basement.

'It's a big bugger, ain't it?' said Chalky.

'They don't come much bigger,' Archie replied, studying the 1,000-kilogram Hermann lying among the shattered storage shelves and displaced medical equipment.

The corporal pointed to the narrow concrete stairs at the side. 'At least they look sound enough.'

'Aye.' Archie looked up. 'Which is more than can be said for that lot.'

Chalky followed his gaze up to the shattered beams and twisted girders above them.

390

'Shall I get the Heavy boys to put some props in before we start?' Chalky asked.

Archie shook his head. 'Not until I've seen what we're dealing with.'

Chalky raised an eyebrow. 'We? Shouldn't that be Lieutenant Monkman?'

'It should but as he's not here and we have a dozen women and children above us about to be blown to kingdom come, I'll make a start,' Archie replied. 'You go back and tell Colonel Blimp to move those civilians back and to make sure all the children on the upper floors move to the east end of the building and to barricade themselves with mattresses.'

Chalky hurried off.

Stepping back from the edge, Archie navigated through the wreckage wrought by the bomb crashing through three floors of concrete, wood and steel, and made his way to the corridor running off the main entrance.

Most of the office doors had burst open, scattering paper everywhere. However, the first door on the right was shut.

Trying the handle, Archie found it was locked. Stepping back he launched himself, shoulder first, at the doorway. It gave way, revealing the stairs to the basement.

Taking them two at a time to the bottom, he stepped through to the basement. To avoid a soaking, he gave the jet of water gushing from a burst water pipe a wide berth and looked up.

Relieved to see that there was no overhanging debris that could drop and trigger the bomb, Archie made his way over. Mercifully, the black metal cylinder, which would have topped him by twelve inches standing upright, was lying on its side in a nest of splintered wood and brick dust, with its circular fuse clearly visible.

Staring at it, Archie knew. He just knew.

Taking a deep breath to steady his pounding heart, he took the torch from his pocket. Creeping within inches of the inanimate object of death and destruction, he hunkered down.

He switched on the torch and shone the light on the metal disc sitting slightly proud of the bomb's casing. Taking out the handkerchief Cathy had given him that morning, Archie wiped off the dust to reveal the letters and numbers beneath.

He studied them for a moment then straightened up and took a step back.

The sound of feet above told him Chalky had returned.

'Is it?' his corporal shouted, his voice echoing.

'Aye,' Archie replied, his eyes fixed to the bomb. 'It's a Y.'

* * *

As the announcer introduced the ten-fifteen Morning Service on the wireless, Violet's eyes narrowed.

'I shall check, you know,' she said, sipping her tea. 'And if you take anything that belongs to me or Stanley, I'll call the police.'

'Don't you worry,' her daughter-in-law replied, buttoning little Peter's coat, 'other than the furniture in the front room, the only thing I'll be taking with me when I go next week is a suitcase with our clothes in it.'

Turning her back on Violet, her daughter-in-law,

who was dressed in her WVS uniform, took her own coat from the back of the door.

It had been just over a week since the telegram had arrived confirming what Violet had known all along: that her dearest and most precious son was alive.

And she wished Stanley had been there to see the look on his pretty wife and her fancy man's faces when they'd heard the news. However, her pleasure was short lived because now their secret was out: they'd been carrying on shamelessly. She'd even come face to face with Cathy walking out of the front room in just her dressing gown the day before, while behind her stood her bit of fancy knotting his tie in front of the wardrobe mirror while little Stanley played on the bed.

'It's disgusting,' continued Violet, as the memory of the guttural sounds she'd heard through the door flashed through her mind. 'I don't know how you can bear his hands all over you let alone . . . his

thing inside you.'

Slipping on her coat, Cathy didn't reply.

'You know what women like you are called, don't you?' Violet continued. 'Women married to one man and living with another? A tart, that's what.' She answered her own question. 'A tart!'

Completely ignoring her, Cathy lifted her son from the floor.

'Up we go, Peter,' she said, sitting him in the push-chair and fastening his harness. 'Let's visit Nanny and Gran for a while, then we'll go to nursery.'

'That's what you are, Cathy Brogan, a tart!' Violet hissed. 'And I'm sure Stanley will be pleased to hear you've got yourself up the duff with his sprog while he's been fighting for King and Country.'

'Do what you like, because in four days' time I'll be gone. Oh, but in case I forget,' grabbing her left hand with her right, Cathy twisted the ring off her third finger, 'you can have this now.'

Slamming it on the table in front of Violet, she opened the back door and, pushing Peter in front of her, walked out.

Violet leapt to her feet.

'Tart!' she screamed. 'And I 'ope you bloody well lose it.'

Pacing to the door, she glared at the door for a moment. Spotting Cathy's cup on the table, she grabbed it and hurled it across the room, sending a dozen fragments of broken china skidding across the lino.

A roar filled her mind and loathing surged through her so violently that a pain shot across the back of her eyes and a red mist crowded into her peripheral vision.

Violet took a deep breath and the pain subsided a little.

She picked up the ring and hurried upstairs to her bedroom.

Pulling open the top drawer of her dressing table, she dropped it in. Fumbling around among the handkerchiefs, hairnets and rollers, she pulled out a key attached to a Devon pixie keyring.

Gripping it tightly, she hurried back down and stopped by the front-parlour door.

Jamming in the key, she turned it and walked in.

The faint aroma trickled into Violet's nose, and her top lip curled into a sneer.

Revolting!

Looking around, she spotted the pictures stacked by the window next to the easel. She walked over.

Violet flipped through the paintings for a moment and then moved on to the half-finished painting on the tripod stand. Toying with either punching a hole through the canvases or dousing the whole lot with a bucket of water, she studied the image of men doing something with a bomb. She went to walk away but as she turned, her elbow knocked over the brushes pot.

Bending down to gather up the scattered brushes, she spotted what looked like a corner of a book poking out from under the bed.

Returning the brushes to the pot, she set it back on the table and walked across the room.

Resting her hand on the bed, she reached under and pulled out a drawing pad. Holding it in one hand, she flipped over a couple of pages. After various sketches of men with bombs she found something very different.

A smile spread wide across Violet's face.

Closing the pad, she hurried back into the hall. Propping it against the hallstand, she grabbed her coat and put it on while stepping into her shoes. Securing her second-best hat in place, she tucked the sketchpad under her arm then walked out of the house and turned in the direction of St Philip and St Augustine's vicarage.

* * *

'I think we're just about done, Sarge,' said Ron Marchant, as he tightened the wingnut on the tripod lamp.

'I think you are,' Archie replied, glancing around the basement where he and the men had spent the past three hours clearing rubble and setting up the equipment, including a thick canister of liquid oxygen and a chunk of modelling clay.

As the brainboxes at the BD experimental section in Woolwich had discovered by studying a Y fuse
recovered from the intact Bakerloo Line bomb, the
one weakness of the ingenious fuse was that if you
froze the battery to -30c then it was as dead as a dodo.
Unfortunately, the only way to achieve this was by
dripping liquid oxygen on the fuse. Which meant that
not only were the bomb disposal crew trying to keep
thousands of kilos of TNT from blowing up, but they
were also trying to ensure they didn't create a spark
that would ignite the gas.

'Right, you lot, get yourself back outside and head
to the safety point while I fetch the lieutenant,' said
Archie.

Picking up their tools and battle jackets, the six-
strong squad headed for the stairs, relieved, no doubt,
to put some distance between themselves and 1,000
kilograms of TNT.

'And make sure you can hear the call-rope bell from
the safety point, Chalky,' Archie called after them.

Wiping the beads of sweat from his forehead with
the back of his hand, Archie stood up and followed
his men back to the hallway.

Walking out of the building, he was pleased to see
that the crowd had remained at the end of the street.
They'd agreed to move back but only after Archie had
gone and talked to the worried parents himself. The
ARP, too, were now at a safe distance and, as always,
bless them, a mobile WVS canteen had turned up and
was supplying those waiting with hot sweet tea to help
their nerves.

Archie looked around and, seeing no sign of Monkman, walked over to where Mogg was helping the

men load the last of the equipment into the back of the lorry.

'Where's the lieutenant?' Archie asked, as the squad's driver coiled a rope around his arm and hand.

'Last I saw of him, he was going towards the park,' Mogg replied, indicating the bottom end of the street.

Picking up his pace, Archie headed towards the river. Reaching Cable Street, he spotted Monkman sitting on one of the park benches taking a swig from a hip flask and staring aimlessly at the ack-ack guns on the lawn of the Edward VII Memorial Gardens.

Archie's mouth pulled into a hard line.

Ordinarily, and although it was only officers who were supposed to tackle a bomb, Archie would have just got on with it, as he had before, but as this was the first Y they'd encountered, he thought for once he'd let Monkman take the lead.

Waiting for a couple of trucks to pass, Archie marched over and through the stone portals on either side of the park gate.

Seeing Archie crunching over the gravel path towards him, Monkman shoved the silver flask into his pocket.

'We're ready for you now, sir,' said Archie, standing to attention.

Monkman stood up. 'About damn time.'

Swinging his swagger stick as he went, the officer strode off. Thankful that at least his senior officer wasn't unsteady on his feet, Archie followed.

★ ★ ★

A few minutes later Archie stood alongside the lieutenant as he studied the bomb.

397

'Are you sure you've got all the equipment, Sergeant?' asked Monkman, taking off his hat.

'Aye, sir,' Archie replied. 'And I've checked it, twice.'

'Well then, let's get on,' Monkman replied, stripping off his brown gloves.

Dropping them in his cap, he handed it and his stick to Archie.

Putting his senior officer's possessions on a block of concrete, Archie unwrapped the grey block of clay and handed it to him.

Monkman's hands shook as he took it.

Giving Archie a jaundiced look, Monkman started softening the clay between his palms but after a moment or two a bit broke off.

'Where did you get this from?' he barked, pummelling the piece back into the lump.

'The storeroom at HQ,' Archie replied.

'Well, it's no bally good,' Monkman said, as another bit broke off. 'How am I supposed to mould the bloody stuff into a cup?'

Archie said nothing as the officer, his hands shaking, grappled with the clay until finally, after a minute or so, he managed to make it into something resembling the illustration in the training manual.

Crouching down, Monkman placed the misshapen container over the fuse but as he pressed it on to the bomb case it fell apart.

'For God's sake,' said Monkman, staggering back as he stood up.

'Would you like me to have a go?' asked Archie.

'If you must,' said Monkman.

Archie hunkered down and, after rolling the clay between his hands, fashioned it into a bottomless bowl. Laying it over and around the fuse, he gently but firmly pressed the reservoir on to the metal casing of the bomb.

Satisfied that it was tightly sealed, he straightened up.

'I think that's done it, sir,' he said.

Giving him a resentful look, Monkman squatted down to inspect it.

'Cotton,' he said.

Archie reached into the tool case to retrieve the reel of thick white buttoning thread.

'Come on, come on,' barked Monkman, clicking his fingers. 'We haven't got all day. This bloody thing could go up at any minute.'

Archie handed him the cotton and Monkman bit off two strips. Pulling the threads through his mouth to wet them, he laid them on either side of the fuse.

'That's not an inch,' said Archie.

'Of course it is,' the lieutenant replied.

'Begging your pardon, sir,' said Archie, trying to keep an even tone, 'but the frost ring has to be a foot wide on either side of the fuse before the battery is inert. As it says in the instruction manual, and Captain Newitt took great pains to point out, the most effective way of monitoring the effects of the liquid oxygen on the fuse is to make sure the cotton is laid at intervals an inch apart.'

Delving into his top pocket, Archie pulled out a six-inch ruler and offered it to the other man.

Monkman snatched it from him. Then, measuring the space, he adjusted the cotton a little further along. Biting off another length of cotton, he continued until there were twelve evenly spaced lengths of cotton on either side of the fuse head.

Picking up the two pairs of goggles and heavy-duty

399

welders' gloves from the metal toolbox, Archie handed Monkman his equipment then put on his own.

'Right, let's get started,' Monkman said, the large Perspex lenses of his goggles making him look like some oversized insect.

Stretching his fingers in his gloves, Archie picked up the canister of liquid oxygen and unscrewed the lid. A wisp of chilly vapour spiralled out. Monkman crouched down again and Archie handed it to him.

Grabbing it between both hands, Monkman tipped the canister and dribbled the freezing liquid into the clay reservoir that Archie had secured around the fuse.

A frozen cloud gushed up.

Monkman coughed as it caught him in the back of his throat and a drop spilled on the bomb's casing.

Archie held his breath, but mercifully nothing happened. Monkman resumed trickling the freezing fluid on to the deadly fuse.

With his eyes fixed on the lieutenant, Archie stepped carefully around to the other side of the bomb. He hunkered down, knowing it was going to be a long afternoon.

28

'There we are, Peter,' said Cathy, as he wriggled out of his jacket. 'You're just in time for Afternoon Storybook.'

She indicated the half-circle of children sitting cross-legged in front of Mrs Morgan, one of the nursery helpers, who had a book open on her lap.

Peter trotted off to take his place with the other children, but as Cathy went to hang his coat up on his allocated hook, Sally Mullens, a mother of two whose husband was in the Merchant Navy, hurried over.

'I hope you've got your tin hat with you, Cath,' she said. 'Mrs Paget arrived about an hour ago with a face like a smacked arse, and she's been biting people's heads off ever since.'

'What's happened to bring her in on a Wednesday?' said Cathy.

Sally shrugged. 'Search me, but she's been on the phone to Regional HQ ever since. I expect you'll find out at the meeting.'

'Meeting?'

'Yes, she wants to see all the heads of department in the small committee room at eleven,' Sally explained.

Cathy glanced at the clock on the wall, which showed ten fifty.

'Well, I'd better go and get myself a cuppa before it starts,' she said.

Leaving the nursery, Cathy crossed the corridor to the main hall, where the smell of boiled cabbage filled the air. Thankfully, since her early-morning visit to the outside bog, her stomach had behaved itself. However, after doing a quick bit of arithmetic, she'd realised that the last time she'd seen Aunt Flo was over two months ago and as she and Archie had been lovers for six weeks, her mother-in-law was right. There was something new to write to Stanley about.

Smiling at the possibility of Archie's baby growing within her, Cathy got herself a mug of tea from the canteen and then made her way down to the small committee room as the clock in the hallway started to chime the hour.

Turning the door handle, Cathy walked in.

Mrs Paget, dressed in her tailored WVS uniform, was sitting in her usual place at the head of the table and Sally was right. She did indeed have a face like a smacked arse. Her eyes narrowed and her mouth pulled into a tight bud when she saw Cathy standing in the doorway.

Taking a sip of tea, Cathy squeezed herself into a seat at the opposite end of the table between Lena Wilcox, who was in charge of the laundry, and Milly Pearson, the overseer of the home dinner deliveries to the elderly.

Cathy gave them a querying look as she sat down and they both looked blank.

As the last couple of section supervisors settled themselves around the table, Cathy acknowledged her friends with a smile. Then Mrs Paget cleared her throat and stood up.

'Thank you all for coming at such short notice and I'm sure you're wondering why I'm here on a Wednesday morning instead of celebrating mid-week Eucharist,' she said. 'Well, I wouldn't be if it wasn't for the fact that this morning a very grave matter was brought to my attention. A matter so dire that if not dealt with firmly now, it would destroy all the much-needed war work we're doing here. A matter,' Mrs Paget's hard eyes ran around the table, 'of immorality and depravity.'

There were gasps and whispering around the table as the blood in Cathy's veins seemed to drain to her feet.

Mrs Paget let the muttering die down and then fixed her gaze on Cathy.

'One of our number, who you regard as a respectable wife like yourselves, has been carrying on an adulterous relationship with — '

'Are you talking about me, Mrs Paget?' asked Cathy, rising to her feet.

'I am, Mrs Wheeler,' she replied.

Somehow, despite her rising temper, Cathy managed to maintain her cool expression.

'I wouldn't listen to gossip, if I were you,' she replied pleasantly. 'Certainly not when it comes from my mother-in-law's mouth.'

A triumphant smile slid across Mrs Paget's face and, bending over, she retrieved Archie's sketchpad from beside her chair. With her gaze fixed on Cathy, she flipped over a few pages and turned the pad around.

'But it isn't just gossip, is it, Mrs Wheeler?' she replied, holding the pad so everyone could see Archie's drawing of Cathy.

Again there were gasps and mutters as people recognised the nude subject, then a dozen pairs of eyes went from the sketch to Cathy and then back to the sketch.

There were giggles and a few furtive glances cast Cathy's way as she stared at the arrogant woman at the opposite end of the table.

Fury burned through her and for a couple of seconds the urge to run and hide swept over her, but she shoved it aside.

Pulling her shoulders back, she raised her head and matched the other woman's bald-faced stare.

'You do know it's a criminal offence to handle stolen property, don't you?' she said, giving the vicar's wife a glacial look. 'And that sketchbook you're holding belongs to someone else.'

'So, you don't deny it?' said Mrs Paget. 'You don't deny that you are in an adulterous relationship with that sergeant who lodges with you?'

'No, I'm not denying it,' Cathy replied. 'In fact, I'll tell you straight, seeing how you seem to be making my business your own: I'm setting up house with Archie McIntosh and although it's a little early to be sure, I hope I'm also carrying his baby.' She smiled. 'But I'm sure my dear mother-in-law has already told you that.'

Mrs Paget's eyes bulged as an unhealthy flush crept upwards from the white bow tied at her throat.

'We're fighting this war to preserve England and its values,' the vicar's wife hissed. 'One of those values is the sanctity of marriage. You took a vow, a sacred vow, to forsake all others, and you have broken that vow to both God and your husband.' Mrs Paget's eyes narrowed to pinpricks of malice. 'I've spoken to HQ and they agree with me: in view of the circumstances, you are no longer welcome as a volunteer helper at this rest centre.'

The women around the table again looked shocked but this time there were angry faces among them and murmurs of 'no', 'that's not fair' and 'you can't do that'.

Stepping out from behind the table, Cathy walked past the wide-eyed, open-mouthed women to where Mrs Paget was standing.

Looking into Mrs Paget's flushed face, Cathy held out her hand.

The vicar's wife held Cathy's unwavering gaze for a moment then threw the sketchpad on the polished surface of the committee table.

'You should hang your head in shame for this,' she sneered.

Cathy picked it up.

'Well, I'm not,' she said, carefully closing the pages. 'Quite the opposite. I'm proud of the picture and to be loved by Archie McIntosh, and I don't care what you or anyone thinks.'

Tucking the sketchpad under her arm, Cathy turned and, under the sympathetic eyes of her friends and fellow section leaders, walked out of the committee room.

★ ★ ★

'If you could have seen her face, Mum,' said Cathy. 'For all her pious talk about the 'sanctity of marriage' and 'vows', she was just relishing the chance to get back at me.'

'For what?' asked Ida, deftly securing the nappy around Victoria's nether regions while balancing her on her lap.

'For stopping her giving the good toys that had been donated to our children to rest centres in 'better areas', for getting the centre to adopt Archie's bomb disposal company instead of her son's RAF base. And

405

because of Archie's colour; she hated him on sight,' said Cathy.

It was now just after one thirty and in the same way she'd needed her mum when she'd fallen out with Deirdre Toomey in the playground, or the time she'd found out that Alfred Burnett was walking out with Olive Looker, Cathy had come straight around to her mum's after marching out of the rest centre.

Having fed her and Peter with Spam sandwiches and made copious cups of tea, Ida had patiently listened for three-quarters of an hour while Cathy sobbed out the whole story of her and Archie and what had happened that morning. They were now sitting under the window at either end of the sofa while on the wireless BBC 'Workers' Playtime' boosted morale from somewhere in Britain.

'I'll tell you, Mum, it was horrible,' said Cathy, remembering the scene in the small committee room. 'There were at least a dozen women in that room.'

'Never you mind about that,' said her mother, turning Victoria the right way up and propping her up on a couple of cushions. 'As your dad always says, if it wasn't for the Brogans, the neighbours wouldn't have anything to talk about.'

'Even so,' said Cathy.

Reaching across, her mother placed her work-worn hand on Cathy's and squeezed. 'It doesn't matter, I tell you, and after everything you've been through with Stanley and his cow of a mother, all we want is for you to be happy.'

'Jesus, Mary and Joseph!'

Cathy and her mother looked around to see Queenie, wearing her everyday coat and hat, standing in the kitchen door.

'What in the name of Heaven has happened to you, Cathy?' her gran asked.

'It's that bloody woman,' said Ida.

Queenie's eyes narrowed. 'What's she done now?'

Cathy told her gran a cut-down version of the meeting.

'Also,' Cathy concluded, looking from one to another, 'I should tell you about —'

'You and your handsome sergeant?' her gran cut in.

Cathy looked incredulous at her grandmother. 'How did you know?'

Queenie rolled her eyes. 'Sure, didn't I see him as plain as day in your tea leaves? And the baby —'

'Baby!' gasped Ida, looking at Cathy, who gave her a shy smile.

Queenie waved away her words and picked up Archie's drawing pad off the sideboard. 'And is this the sketch?'

'It is,' said Cathy, looking squarely at her grandmother.

Queenie flipped over a few pages and then her eyebrows rose.

'Your sergeant's got a fair eye for detail, so he has,' she said. 'But I wouldn't advise you to show it to your father.'

Closing it, she put it back where she'd found it. Queenie's wrinkled cheeks lifted in an amiable smile. 'Now, me darling girl, where might that cow of a mother-in-law of yours be found just now?'

★ ★ ★

'So, Violet, a few of us are thinking about going to the matinee of the new Stewart Granger film at the

407

Paragon on Saturday, do you fancy coming too?' asked Dot Tomms, looking at Violet through the thick lenses of her spectacles.

'I haven't felt like enjoying myself these past five months but now . . .' Violet gave a little tinkling laugh. 'I think I feel like a bit of a treat.'

'Good for you, Violet,' said Ruby Wagstaff, a smile beaming out of her round face. 'I think I'd feel the same if my son had just been found alive.'

Violet smiled.

She was pleased. Not only because Stanley had been found but because of her little discovery.

It was shameful. And Mrs Paget had said the same when Violet had turned up at the vicarage and shown it to her.

Oh, how she would love to have been a fly on the wall when Mrs Paget raised that item on the morning meeting. And finding her slut of a daughter-in-law puking up down the toilet was just the icing on the cake.

'Any news of where he is?' asked Joan Robinson, who, despite the altar flowers looking like a patch of weeds each week, was in charge of the church flower rota.

Violet shook her head.

'But I imagine the Germans will have put him in one of their most secure jails. After all, my Stan was never one to hold back from a fight,' said Violet, imagining her son single-handedly fighting off dozens of Germans. 'Did I tell you he was the East London heavyweight cham — '

The double doors at the end of the hall burst open and Queenie Brogan, her coat streaming behind her and her hat askew on her white hair, marched into the room.

She stopped a few feet in and, with her feet apart and her hands on her hips, the old woman's flint-like eyes scoured the sea of faces until they reached Violet.

'You!' she shouted, jabbing her finger at her. 'You fecking gobshite, Violet Wheeler.'

With their teacups poised in their hands, the women in the hall stared open-mouthed at Queenie as, hands clenched at her side, she marched over.

With a face tight with fury, the old woman stopped in front of Violet.

She glared at her for a moment then smashed her fist down on the table, rattling crockery and spilling tea.

A couple of women screamed, while those sitting around Violet shrank back.

Fighting the urge to jump up and run, Violet gave her a cool look.

'This meeting is for Mothers' Union members only,' Violet said, forcing herself to hold the old woman's piercing stare.

''Tis as well then, isn't it, that I'm not here for a cup of tea,' Queenie replied.

'It was my Christian duty to tell Mrs Paget about your granddaughter's shameful behaviour — '

'Christian duty, is it? You fecking hypocrite. Well, you enjoy your moment of triumph, because when your dear friends hereabouts find out the truth about your darling son, and be sure they will, you'll find no hole deep enough to hide yourself in.'

Queenie's eyes lost their focus for a moment and, raising her hand and looking heavenwards, she muttered something. Her gaze returned to Violet.

Some of the women in the hall grabbed the crosses

hanging around their necks as the old woman stretched out her gnarled hands.

'I'll tell you this and tell you no more, Violet Wheeler,' she said in a voice that carried to the back of the hall. 'You will see your son's face again, and soon, but it will give you no pleasure.'

Her eyes bore into Violet for a moment longer, then, straightening her battered hat, she turned and marched back to the entrance.

Grasping the brass handle, Queenie Brogan pulled the door open but then she stopped and looked back at Violet. A chilling smile spread across her ancient face. 'No pleasure at all.'

29

'What time is it now?' Monkman asked Archie.

Resisting the urge to say five minutes since you last asked me, Archie glanced at his wristwatch.

'Twenty-five past four,' he replied, looking at the officer through his goggles and a haze of icy steam.

'It should have worked by now,' snapped the lieutenant.

He was right, but then, as Archie was happy to concede, disarming a Y fuse was still very much in the learning phase.

However, oddly, considering he was crouched next to a bomb that had the potential to obliterate him from the face of the earth, what concerned him more was Monkman.

'We're almost there, sir,' said Archie calmly, as he studied the frosty ring that was just a quarter of an inch from the last length of cotton.

'That's all very well for you to say, but you're not holding this bloody canister,' Monkman replied.

'I'll take over if you need a rest,' said Archie for the third time.

Monkman ignored him and, with shaking hands, tipped the flask further.

'Gentle, now,' said Archie as the icy liquid spurted out. 'You don't want to split the — '

'Bloody shut up, will you? Just shut up,' shouted Monkman, his eyes fixed to the glowing fluid trickling into the clay cup.

Archie clamped his mouth shut and prayed the

liquefied oxygen would complete its task soon.

A couple more minutes dragged by and then, finally, the ring of hoar frost, glittering on the dull grey metal of the six-foot-long bomb, reached the last cotton marker.

'At last,' said Monkman, wiping the beads of sweat from his forehead. 'Tools!'

Reaching into the toolbox, Archie was about to hand him the narrow jemmy when there was a metallic squeak followed by a heart-stopping crack.

Monkman screamed and sprang up. With his eyes wild, he staggered back, stumbling over the bricks and mortar scattered around him. He started for the stairs, but Archie stepped in his path.

'Out of my way,' Monkman shouted, shoving Archie in the chest.

Archie stood his ground. 'We have twenty minutes — '

'I said, get out of my way,' yelled Monkman, ripping off his mask and gloves and throwing them aside.

Archie grasped the officer's lapels and shook him.

'Pull yourself together,' he said, fixing the lieutenant with a glacial stare. 'If the fuse was going to blow, we'd already be in heaven. If we don't defuse it, and soon, a dozen women and children will — '

'I don't care,' bellowed Monkman, pulling himself out of Archie's grip. 'Do you hear? I don't care.'

Regaining his balance, Monkman scrambled again for the stairs, shoving mangled debris aside. He wrenched a filing cabinet out of his path and pushed it to one side. It crashed against the bomb, sending sparks into the air as it scraped down the side of the casing.

Archie stepped forward and grabbed the officer's

412

shirt and tie with his left hand then, balling his right hand into a fist, pulled back his arm and landed the lieutenant a blow square on his chin.

Incredulity flickered across Monkman's face for a split second before his eyes rolled up into his head and his knees buckled.

Archie released him and he crumpled on to the floor.

Stepping over the unconscious lieutenant, Archie grabbed the tool bag and returned to the bomb.

He looked at his watch again.

Dealing with Monkman had taken five minutes. Five minutes he didn't have to spare.

Hunkering down again, Archie ripped the clay reservoir away. He grasped the jemmy and eased the edge under the narrow rim of the fuse. He exerted pressure but the edge of the tool couldn't get purchase and pinged off. Archie tried again but the same thing happened.

Wiping his forehead with the back of his hand, he stood up and dug the edge of the jemmy in deeper, forcing it between the casing and the fuse. This time it bit and the fuse lifted slightly. With sweat trickling down his back and his heart thumping in his chest, Archie moved the jemmy's flattened metal edge and prised the fuse up a little until it was an inch clear of the casing. Curling his fingers, he grasped the frozen fuse and gently pulled it out, but after raising it another few inches, it stuck on the jagged edge of the split casing.

Archie glanced at his watch, then, grabbing the jemmy, he tapped the fuse on alternate sides to nudge it out of the obstruction. He took hold of the barrel of the fuse again.

413

Staring unseeing at the far wall, Archie took a deep breath and then drew the fuse out of its pocket in one even movement.

Looking down at the eight-inch cylinder of precision engineering designed to kill anyone who touched it, Archie let out a long breath. But he wasn't done.

Holding it firmly, Archie unscrewed the gane, the deadly firing charge that would still blow him to kingdom come if ignited by the fuse's firing trigger.

In a series of steady motions, he unscrewed it, popped it in his pocket and then, holding the fuse tight in his left hand, Archie straightened up.

Stepping backwards away from the bomb, he placed it in the purpose-built padded box ready to go to the lab at Woolwich.

Heaving a huge sigh, and rolling the tension out of his shoulders, he yanked on the call-rope and within a minute Chalky and Ron peered over the gaping edge of the floor above.

'What happened to him?' asked the corporal, indicating the unconscious Monkman sprawled across the floor.

'He fainted,' Archie replied. 'Now, Ron, go and get the boys to rig up a block-and-tackle set-up so we can winch this bloody thing up. Chalky, you come and help me clear up.'

Ron disappeared whence he'd come while Chalky clattered down the stairs.

Bending down, Archie dragged Monkman upright and rested him against a pillar.

'What really happened?' asked Chalky, as he joined him.

'What was bound to happen eventually,' Archie replied. 'He lost his nerve.'

'So you landed him one?' said Chalky.

'Aye.'

'And he went down in one?'

Archie gave him a wry smile.

'You wouldnae survive a Saturday night on Sauch-iehall Street if you didn't floor 'em with the first blow.' He kicked the officer's boot. 'Monkman!'

Monkman's eyes fluttered a little then closed again. Archie crouched down and lightly tapped his face. 'Monkman!'

The lieutenant jerked and his eyes flew open.

With confusion written across his face, his pale eyes darted around, then as they rested on the bomb, panic gripped him again.

Screaming and with his gaze riveted to the bomb, he scrambled backwards away from it. Archie bent down, seized him, and dragged him to his feet.

Wide-eyed, Monkman struggled to free himself.

'It's safe!' Archie shook him. 'The fuse is out. The fuse is out!'

Monkman blinked. 'Out?'

'Aye. It's out. Safe,' Archie repeated. 'We're just getting set to lift it out.'

He indicated above to where the squad, who'd just returned, could be heard clattering about.

The wildness left the lieutenant's eyes, so Archie let him go.

Leaving Monkman to tidy himself up, Archie looked up.

'If you sling a couple of stout beams across here,' he said, indicating a place between two untouched concrete basement pillars, 'I reckon we can roll it across and —'

Archie caught a movement out of the corner of his

eye. He looked around to see Monkman lighting his cigarette with a match.

'No!' he screamed, launching himself at Monkman as the lieutenant casually flicked the still-flaming match towards the canister of liquid oxygen.

Time seem to slow but as Archie's hands connected with the other man's chest, a fierce flash of searing white light stabbed like a stiletto through his eyes for a split second. Then everything went black.

★ ★ ★

'Have you finished, Peter?' asked Cathy, lifting a mixing bowl from the sudsy water and stacking it on the draining board.

Peter, who was sitting up at the table eating his tea, lifted his plate by way of reply.

'Good boy,' Cathy replied, smiling at him. 'Would you like pudding?'

Her son nodded his head and picked up his spoon.

She cut a slice from the apple tart she'd made after she'd returned from her mother's house an hour ago and set it in front of him.

She glanced at the clock on the dresser.

Four thirty. Just three hours and Archie would be home.

And from next Monday he would be returning to their home, not this house of misery and hate that she'd been imprisoned in for over three years. It would be full of love and . . . Cathy put a hand on her stomach and smiled.

Of course, she wouldn't tell Archie for a few weeks yet. Not until Kirsty and his mother Aggie came to join them and they'd all settled into a rhythm as a family.

However, just because she was moving out of the area didn't mean she was going to let this business with Mrs Paget lie. In fact, once she'd cried it all out at her mother's, she'd pulled herself together and, while Peter had taken a late-afternoon nap on the sofa, she'd sat at the kitchen table and written a letter to the WVS's regional HQ complaining about Mrs Paget's treatment of her. She'd also mentioned the coordinator's sneering attitude towards the very people she was supposed to be helping. She'd posted it on the way home from her mother's and, although it might not change anything, Cathy felt a great deal better for writing it.

Turning back to the oven, Cathy whipped a tea towel off the rack and winding it around her hands, she opened the door.

The mouth-watering smell of lamb stew billowed out from the casserole on the top shelf.

Reaching in, she lifted the lid and, satisfied that her and Archie's evening meal wasn't drying out, put it back and closed the oven door.

She refilled the kettle. She had just relit the gas beneath it when the back door opened and Violet walked in with a face like a gargoyle with a wasp stuck up its nose.

To be honest, as the Wednesday-afternoon church tea had wound up over an hour ago, she'd expected Violet to already be at home when she'd returned. The fact that she hadn't been was a thin silver lining on what had otherwise been a very cloudy day.

Cathy smiled. 'I'm guessing Gran had a word with you then, Vi.'

'I've never been so embarrassed,' snapped Violet.

Cathy gave her a confused look. 'What, not even when MI5 turned up and arrested your Stanley as a traitor?'

'My Stanley was led astray, but he's a hero now and will be

getting a medal to prove it,' Violet snapped. 'And when he gets — 'The crack of the front-door knocker cut across her words. Giving Cathy a hateful look, Violet left the room to answer it. Taking the spoon from her son, Cathy fed Peter the last couple

of scraps of his dessert. She was just wiping his face with his bib when the door opened. A fair-haired soldier with a bomb disposal badge on his sleeve and a forlorn expression on his face entered the kitchen.

Staring across at him, Cathy's blood turned to ice as her heart

crashed in her chest. 'Mrs Cathy Wheeler,' he said, twisting his field cap in his hand. 'Yes.' 'I'm Corporal White, and there's been an accident.'

30

With her coat streaming behind her, Cathy grasped the handrail and swung herself from the stairs on to the second floor of The London Hospital.

Like the rest of the hospital, the green-tiled corridor she was standing in was busy with nurses in lilac pinstriped uniforms and starched frilly caps, as they hurried between wards and white-coated orderlies pushing hospital gurneys.

Looking up at the noticeboard pinned to the wall, Cathy's eyes ran swiftly down the list of wards, then she hurried along the corridor.

The distinct smell of detergent and surgical spirit wafted up as she pushed open one of the double doors and burst into Charrington Ward.

The ward, like the others in the eighteenth-century block, was set out in the classic Nightingale formation, with beds lined up along each wall. The kitchen and sluice were at one end of the room and the patients' day room at the other.

As it was now just after five thirty, the nurses were busy giving out supper to the men, who were sitting in their beds or in chairs alongside.

A stout nurse in a navy puffy-sleeved uniform, a ridged white cap and silver belt buckle, spotted Cathy and waddled over.

She stopped in front of Cathy.

'I'm Sister Torrance. Can I help you, my dear?' she asked, her rosy face lifting in a friendly smile.

'I believe a Sergeant McIntosh was brought in a

little while ago,' said Cathy.

'Are you a relative?' asked the ward sister.

'I'm his . . . wife,' Cathy replied. 'What happened to him?'

'He was caught in an explosion,' said Sister Torrance. 'And while he's stable, breathing . . . ' She gave Cathy a sympathetic look. 'I'll ring the doctor so he can explain it to you fully.'

'Can I see him?' said Cathy, her imagination flicking through images of Archie burnt and with limbs missing.

'Yes, of course. He's been sedated, so he might be a little drowsy.' The ward sister placed a hand on Cathy's arm. 'I don't want you to be too alarmed about the bandages. They are just a precaution. Follow me.'

Sister Torrance turned, and when they reached the side room she stood aside.

Cathy walked in and her gaze fell on Archie's long body as he lay flat on the bed. He was covered with a blue counterpane, which had been folded back to just above his waist. He was wearing his army vest, and his bare brown arms and muscular shoulders contrasted starkly with the crisp white sheet beneath them. There wasn't a mark or injury on him and she could see the outline of his legs and feet beneath the bedcovers.

However, as her gaze reached his face, Cathy covered her mouth with her hand to stifle a scream as she saw the bandages covering his eyes.

Sensing her presence, Archie's head turned in her direction.

'Is that you, Nurse?' he asked.

'No, Archie, it's me,' Cathy said, putting her handbag on the locker beside the bed. She sat down in the chair next to him then slipped her hand in his.

'Cathy,' he said, his long, dexterous fingers closing around hers. 'How did you hear — '

She cut off his words by covering his mouth with hers and putting her arms around him. His arms encircled her as he crushed her to his chest, his lips pressed on her forehead in a series of hard kisses. Tears gathered in her eyes.

Not wanting to let him know she was weeping, she disentangled herself from his embrace and sat up.

'Your corporal came to tell me on his way back to base,' Cathy replied. 'He gave me a lift to my sister Mattie's. I left Peter with her. He also told me to tell you that the heavy rescue got all the children and nurses out.'

'Thank God,' said Archie.

From nowhere, despondency surged up in Cathy. 'Oh, Archie, I . . . '

A tear escaped and fell on to his arm.

'Now, now,' he said, taking her hand and pressing it to his lips.

Cathy ran her hand across his stubbled cheek but didn't speak as tears streamed down her face.

Sister Torrance appeared at the door and beckoned to her.

Cathy wiped her eyes again and forced a laugh.

'You know, I've been in such a hurry to see you, I forgot to spend a penny.' She squeezed his hand. 'I won't be long.'

Standing up, Cathy hurried out and followed the ward sister into an office. Inside, an elderly doctor wearing a white coat and with a stethoscope around his neck was standing by the desk.

'Mrs McIntosh, I'm Dr Alder,' he said, offering her his hand.

'Why are my husband's eyes bandaged?' Cathy asked, as she shook his hand.

'It's a precaution, until we can ascertain the extent of the damage,' the doctor replied.

Cathy's jaw dropped as the word 'damage' screamed around in her head.

With tears once again distorting her vison, Cathy looked from the doctor to the nurse then back again.

'But he will get better, won't he?'

Sister Torrance gave her a little chin-up smile but didn't reply.

'We have an ophthalmologist coming from Moorfields to examine your husband tomorrow,' Dr Alder replied softly. 'We will have a better idea then.'

Cathy took her handkerchief out of her pocket and dried her eyes.

'Thank you, Doctor,' she said.

With her feet feeling as if they'd turned to lead, Cathy retraced her steps to the side room. Archie turned his head in her direction as she walked in.

'Cathy?'

'Yes,' she said, resuming her seat next to him and taking his hand again. 'I bet you thought I'd fallen down the pan.'

'Or run off with a handsome doctor,' he laughed.

She laughed, too.

'I suppose the house will be gone by the time I get out of here,' he continued.

'Don't worry about the house,' she said. 'We'll find another. The main thing is to get you fighting fit again.'

Cathy shifted on to the bed, and finding her hand again, he squeezed it.

They sat in silence for a long while then from outside on the ward came the faint sound of the seven o'clock pips.

'You should be getting back to your sister, Cathy,' he said softly. 'The blackout will be starting soon.'

'No, but I — '

'I don't like to think of you walking through the streets alone or getting caught in an air raid,' he said.

She opened her mouth to speak.

'Please. For me.'

'All right, if you insist,' she said, desperately wanting to say otherwise. 'But I'll be back first thing.'

'I'm counting on it.'

He gave her that quirky smile of his and tears sprang into Cathy's eyes again.

'Do you want me to phone your mum?'

'Not yet,' he replied. 'Wait until we hear what the consultant says tomorrow but take my wallet. There's money in it if you need it.'

Taking it from the locker drawer, she dropped it in her handbag, then, stretching over him, she pressed her lips on his. Archie's arms wound around her, holding her close, his mouth opened under hers.

Tearing herself from his embrace, Cathy stood up.

'Until tomorrow,' she said.

He blew her a kiss. 'Until tomorrow.'

Although she just wanted to throw herself back into his arms, she hooked her handbag over her arm and walked around the bed. As she reached the door, a tear escaped and rolled down her cheek.

She turned back to the bed.

'I love you, Archie,' she said, wiping it away with the heel of her hand.

The corners of his mouth lifted in a smile. 'And I love you, too, Mrs McIntosh.'

Cathy had just turned into her sister Mattie's road when the air raid siren went off.

Picking up her pace, she reached the front door as the first humming overhead started. Turning the key, she went in and through the blackout curtains and found Mattie, wearing her slippers and dressing gown, standing in the hall.

'Thank goodness,' her sister said, helping her off with her coat. 'I was beginning to worry.'

'How's Peter?' asked Cathy.

'Absolutely fine,' Mattie replied. 'He and Alicia were tearing around pretending to be aeroplanes after supper, so he was almost asleep on his feet by the time I put him to bed. Now what's this about Sergeant McIntosh?'

Cathy opened her mouth to speak but instead she covered her face and burst into tears.

Mattie's arms closed around her and, resting her head on her sister's shoulder, Cathy wept uncontrollably for a moment or two and then, as the bombs started falling on Limehouse Basin half a mile away, Mattie spoke again.

'Come on,' she said, giving Cathy a hug. 'Let's go downstairs to the shelter and you can tell me all about it over a cuppa.'

Half an hour later, with bombs shaking the earth around them, and having told, or more truthfully sobbed, the whole story about her and Archie, Cathy blew her nose.

'I know I should have said something to you before now, Mattie, but we were waiting until we'd got everything sorted out . . . ' She gave her sister an apologetic smile. 'Sorry.'

Mattie, knitting needles in hand, was sitting opposite Cathy in one of the two comfy chairs in her basement shelter. They both had a cup of tea courtesy of Mattie's primus stove, and the soft sound of a string quartet drifted over them from the Pye wireless that was sitting on an old dresser at the other end of the room.

To her left, in her sister's Morrison shelter, tucked up in a sleeping bag and with his thumb in his mouth, slept Peter. Next to him was Mattie's two-year-old Alicia with baby Robert snuggled in his collapsible canvas cot alongside.

All three of them, having known nothing but bombs dropping around them since they were born, slept peacefully in their metal cage while German armaments crashed to earth above them.

'It doesn't matter,' said Mattie, pulling a length of pink three-ply from the ball on her lap. 'To be honest, Cathy, you've had such a blooming smile on your face for the past month, I'd pretty much guessed. But what are you going to do now?'

Cathy's mouth pulled into a determined line.

'I know it will be hard if . . . if . . . Archie's sight is permanently damaged,' she said, forcing her words over the lump in her throat.

'But I don't care. I love him and as soon as he is out of hospital, we're going to set up house together as husband and wife. And if I have to scrub floors like Mum did to pay the rent and put food on the table then that's what I'll do.'

Her chin started to tremble.

Setting aside her knitting, Mattie reached across and squeezed her hand.

'I know you will,' she said. 'In the same way I would if it were Daniel lying in that bed. But if you need anything then you only have to ask.'

'Actually,' said Cathy, giving her sister a pleading look, 'is there any chance I could borrow a fiver? I'll pay you back and I wouldn't ask but — '

'Of course.' Mattie smiled. 'That's what family's for, isn't it?'

'Thank you, Mattie.'

They exchanged an affectionate look then Cathy yawned.

'You'd better get some rest.' Her sister pointed to a set of candy-striped pyjamas on top of the Morrison shelter. 'I've brought you a set of mine, and there should be enough water in the kettle for you to have a wash. Then you can snuggle in alongside me in the hamster cage.'

'What about Daniel?' asked Cathy.

'He got a call from Whitehall this afternoon and has had to go somewhere north for a couple of days, so I'm not expecting him back until Monday,' Mattie replied.

Rising to her feet, Cathy picked up the nightwear and crossed the room. She poured the remaining water from the kettle into the enamel bowl on an old washstand.

'It'll be like the old days with me, you and Jo all squashed into that old double bed,' she said, yawning again as she unbuttoned her blouse.

'And giving you both a cuddle when you had a nightmare,' Mattie called across.

'Yes,' she called back over her shoulder as she slipped off her blouse.

Turning back, Cathy placed her hands on her still

426

flat stomach and looked bleakly at the mirror on the wall.

Yes, just like the old days, except now her nightmare was real.

31

'The doctor should be here soon,' said Cathy, who was sitting in the chair next to his.

Entombed in his world of blackness, Archie smiled. 'Aye, I'm sure he will be.'

Cathy had been at his side since eight thirty, arriving just after the nurse had finished helping him with his breakfast. He guessed it must be gone eleven by now. It was hard to tell without the changing daylight to give you a clue and because, with wild thoughts driving sleep away all night, he'd nodded off to sleep mid-morning. He'd woken up in a panic, but finding Cathy there beside him had calmed him instantly. In truth, having her beside him was the only thing anchoring his sanity at the moment.

'Would you like another cup of tea?' she asked.

'Thanks, but I'm fine,' he replied. 'But you pop out and get one if you want.'

'No, I'm fine too,' she replied.

Manoeuvring her hand in his, he entwined his fingers in hers. 'I'm going to be all right.'

'Of course you are,' she replied chirpily.

He knew she was lying, but then so was he.

They were both pretending that his unseeing eyes were akin to a broken leg or a burnt arm.

And although she'd tried to disguise the fact, Archie also knew she'd been crying. He didn't blame her. He wanted to cry himself.

'It was good of Corporal White to pop in first thing to see how you were getting on,' said Cathy.

'Chalky's a good fella,' Archie replied, happy to change the subject. 'I'm glad to hear that HQ are going to send someone down to investigate the incident fully.'

'So your blooming commanding officer won't be able to cover up for Monkman,' Cathy added. 'It's a pity it took — ' She stopped. She didn't need to say it because Archie was thinking the same.

Thinking to steer the conversation into relatively safer waters, he spoke again. 'Is Mrs Wheeler behaving herself?'

'Of course,' Cathy replied in a tone that said otherwise.

'What's she done?' asked Archie.

'Nothing, nothing really.' Cathy forced a little laugh. 'You know, just being her old spiteful self.'

She was a terrible liar but at the moment he didn't have the strength to press her. She and Peter were safe and just now that's all that mattered, so whatever it was could wait.

Cathy's fingers tensed as the sound of footsteps heralded people entering the room.

'Good morning, Sergeant McIntosh,' said a man's voice.

'Good morning, Dr Alder,' said Archie. 'I think we met briefly yesterday.'

'We did indeed,' the doctor replied. 'Good morning, Mrs McIntosh.'

'Morning, Doctor,' she replied, her grip on Archie's hand tightening.

'And this is Sir Mungo Henderson,' said Dr Alder, 'a fellow countryman of yours, Sergeant, and the senior ophthalmic professor at Moorfields, which, as you may know, is the world's foremost eye hospital.'

429

'Indeed, I am,' the professor replied, in a voice that would have made a BBC announcer sound like a cockney barrow boy.

'Sergeant McIntosh is a hero,' said a female voice.

'So I hear, Sister,' Henderson replied.

Cathy relinquished his hand and it was grasped by a rougher, hairier one.

'Good to meet you, Sergeant.'

Archie shook the professor's hand.

Henderson cleared his throat. 'Now, to business. Dr Alder has asked me for a second opinion.'

'I'm sorry, Sir Mungo, I'll take off the bandages,' said the sister.

'That's not necessary, thank you, Sister,' the professor replied.

Cathy reclaimed Archie's hand. 'Aren't you going to examine my husband's eyes?'

'No need to, my dear,' Sir Mungo replied, 'because it will tell me nothing more than I can read in his notes. According to Dr Alder, the white and iris of both your husband's eyes are clear and undamaged, and are apparently unusually blue for someone of his racial mix. However, the problem isn't in the part of the eye we can see, but rather the area we cannot.'

Archie's mouth lost all moisture. 'What do you mean?'

'I understand from what you told Dr Alder of the accident when you were admitted that you were in close proximity to an intense burst of light, after which you lost your sight,' said Sir Mungo.

'Aye,' Archie replied, as the incident flashed across his mind.

'And in doing so you've damaged your optical nerves and the special cells at the back of your eyes,'

430

said the professor. 'Much like a roll of camera film if you exposed it to sunlight.'

'But it's only temporary, isn't it?' asked Cathy, the hope in her voice palpable.

There was a telling pause and then Sir Mungo spoke again. 'It's too early to say, Mrs McIntosh.'

Archie's heart thumped painfully in his chest as the urge to scream rose up in him. He heard Cathy's handbag clip open, he guessed to retrieve her handkerchief.

Archie swallowed and took a breath.

'How long before you do know, Sir Mungo?' he asked, hoping only he could hear the waver in his voice.

'A week,' the professor replied. 'I'll come back next Wednesday to supervise personally, if you don't mind, Dr Alder.'

'Not at all,' the ward doctor replied, sounding relieved.

'What are your instructions for Sergeant McIntosh's care?' asked the sister.

'The old tried-and-tested, Sister,' replied Sir Mungo. 'Rest and plenty of it, plus three square meals a day.'

'What about dressings?'

'Change them when you have to but only if you have to,' Sir Mungo replied. 'And tell your nurses no bathing them with anything, and Sergeant . . .'

'Sir?'

'When your dressings are changed, although it might be very tempting, you must keep your eyes tight shut. If you repeatedly picked off a scab, eventually the skin would become coarse and ridged. The same may be true of your eyes if they are exposed to light

431

again before they have a chance to heal. It may cause irreparable damage. Do you understand?'

'I do,' Archie said.

'Well, I'll leave you in Dr Alder and Sister's capable hands and I'll see you next week.'

'Yes, sir,' Archie replied.

'Thank you, Sir Mungo,' said Cathy.

Rubber soles squeaked on the lino as Sir Mungo and his retinue left their position at the foot of Archie's bed.

'Cathy?'

The chair scraped along the floor.

'I'm here,' she said, close to his ear. 'I'll always be here, Archie.'

He opened his mouth to speak but the enormity of what might be his future life overwhelmed him. With Sir Mungo's words circling around his mind, Archie put his hand over his unseeing eyes.

'Oh, Cathy, I can't — '

'No!' she said. Her hands gripped his biceps, her nails biting into his flesh. 'Whatever you were going to tell me you can't do, you bloomin' well can, Archie McIntosh. *We* can. From now on we face everything life might throw at us together, do you understand?' She shook him. 'Do *you* understand?'

He let out a long sigh. 'I do.'

'Good,' she said, releasing her grip a little. 'You're alive. And soon we're going to be a family, with me and you, your ma, Peter and Kirsty and the . . . and that's all that matters.'

She was right, of course she was, and he had to hang on to that because, just now, the thought of never being able to see Cathy's face, or his daughter's, or to be able to pick up a brush again made him almost wish the white light that had robbed him of sight had been the 1,000-kilo bomb detonating.

★ ★ ★

'Well, I don't know about you, Violet, but I thought that was a load of old cod's wallop,' said Elsie, who was sitting alongside her in the nine pennies.

'The B pictures always are, but at least they're only half an hour,' Violet replied, looking at her friend in the dim silver light from the cinema's screen.

Violet and the dozen or so other Mothers' Union members were sitting downstairs in plush, garret-coloured theatre seats, roughly halfway back from the screen.

With seating for three and a half thousand people, the Troxy was billed as the largest cinema in England and this afternoon nearly every seat was filled, thanks to the fact that the film Violet and the others had come to see featured Stewart Granger, a rising star and a bit of a heart throb amongst the matrons of East London. In fact, Violet had spotted several of her neighbours and a number of market acquaintances in the audience.

People who'd already sat through the Saturday special matinee programme filed out and others took their places. As always, in the lull between the end of the short supporting film and the main feature, the Government's Ministry of Information took the chance to remind people what was expected of them as part of the war effort. And, as always, people responded by totally ignoring what was on screen and chatting amongst themselves.

'Your lodger was the talk of the market this morning, Violet,' said Minnie, sitting beside her.

'Was he?' Violet replied.

'I'm not surprised,' said Dot, the images from the screen flickering across her lenses. 'Defusing that big bomb and saving all those little kiddies.'

'He's a real hero,' added Ruby.

Others around her muttered their agreement.

As a jolly trumpet heralded the start of an information film encouraging people to dig for victory, Violet's mouth pulled into a tight line.

'He might have dug it out, Ruby,' said Violet, 'but I think you'll find it was the officer who did the actual defusing of the bomb.'

'Not according to Sadie Cohen, he didn't,' said Eliza Benton, sitting in the row behind. 'Her Sammy was one of those trapped. She was outside when the officer was brought out dribbling and shaking. One of the squaddies told her he'd gone to pieces and the sergeant had taken over.'

'Like we said, Violet,' added Minnie, 'that Jock sergeant's a real hero.'

Elsie's thin face took on a sad expression. 'It's a pity, though, isn't it?' she said. 'You know, about his eyes . . .'

Matching Elsie's sombre features, the women around Violet nodded.

A little smile lifted the corner of her lips. Yes, what a great pity.

A pity the ruddy bomb didn't go off and blow him to kingdom come.

The opening bars of Pathé News blasted out and Violet settled down to watch. In strident British-bulldog tones, the commentator showed how the Royal Air Force were harrying the last remaining scraps of Rommel's army in North Africa and how the grubby

Arabs were cheering the British troops. There was another tedious piece focusing on a bunch of Land Girls using a horse-drawn plough, followed by a couple of shots of over-paid American GIs somewhere in England undertaking ground-assault manoeuvres.

The news reel moved on.

'But while Britain stands firm against Nazi evil,' continued the commentator as the film showed a clip of soldiers, bayonets in hand, running across the sands, 'our brave boys . . .'

A cheer went up in the auditorium and the women around Violet screamed and shouted with the best of them.

Elsie blew a kiss at the screen. 'God bless 'em.'

'Give the bloody Krauts some cold steel, boys,' shouted Minnie, her hands cupped around her mouth.

'. . . are putting a spanner in Hitler's evil plan with every inch of ground they take back. But Goebbels . . .'

As an image of the studious-looking head of German propaganda came on the screen the applause was replaced by boos and jeers.

'Bloody pig,' muttered Ruby, shaking her bony fist.

'. . . is dreaming up new ways to sabotage our efforts with his propaganda,' continued the report. 'He tried to drain our island spirit with Lord Haw-Haw . . .'

William Joyce's face replaced Goebbels' and the shouts of fury grew louder.

'String him up,' shouted Elsie.

'Hanging's too good for him,' a man bellowed to the side of Violet.

'Knowing we English are too wise to fall for his lies, German High Command has come up with something else,' said the reporter, his voice taking on a

435

graver tone.

Before their eyes, the picture of Lord Haw-Haw was replaced by a line of German soldiers standing to attention as an SS officer inspected them.

'They look like just another line of Hitler's lackeys, don't they? But look closely, ladies and gentlemen,' continued the commentator. 'Look closer at the insignia on their arms.'

The camera closed in on a shield-shaped badge with a Union Jack at its centre, below which was embroidered the words 'British Free Corps'.

'Yes, I know, you can hardly believe your eyes,' the reporter added. 'This is Hitler's latest effort to make our great nation cringe with fear.'

'Traitors,' shouted Dot.

'A bunch of simple-minded misfits . . . '

The camera scanned along the line of faces and then focused on the man at the end.

Blood pounded in Violet's ears, blotting out the commentator's modular tones. She rose to her feet and stared at Stanley in an SS uniform as the image filled the fifty-foot-wide, thirty-foot-high screen.

'Hang on,' said Ruby. 'Isn't that your Stan, Violet?'

Staring blindly at the screen, Violet didn't reply.

'It is, you know,' agreed Dot. 'It's your lad.'

'You're right, Dot,' Elsie agreed. 'That's Violet's boy, Stan Wheeler. I'd know him anywhere.'

A man sitting in front of them turned around.

'You're saying you know that bastard?' he asked.

'Yes,' piped up Minnie. She pointed at Violet. 'It's her son, Stanley.'

People all around them were standing up and glaring at her.

'But he's a hero,' Violet muttered, her eyes glued to

436

the screen. 'He stayed behind to save his comrades. He's getting a medal.'

'Medal!' shouted the man in front, his face contorted with anger.

'Medal! What he's going to get is six foot of rope when our boys

get their hands on him!'

The shouts of 'traitor' got louder as people all around stood up.

'He's a ruddy coward, that's what he is,' shouted someone a few rows away.

A man climbed over a couple of seats and glared in Violet's face. 'Our lads are dying to save this blooming country while those bastards turn their coats and volunteer to fight for Hitler.'

Averting her eyes from the disgusted sneers on her friends' and neighbours' faces, Violet stumbled her way to the end of the row, only to find the stairs leading up to the foyer crowded with people.

Holding her handbag close, she lowered her head and hurried through the jostling and jeering crowd towards the exit.

* * *

'Not long now, Peter, and we'll be home,' Cathy said to her grizzling son as she turned into Commercial Road.

It was now coming up to five and she'd just picked him up from Mattie's. Many of the shops lining the main thoroughfare from Aldgate to Limehouse were already putting up their shutters ready for a well-earned day off tomorrow. After passing a couple of roads running off to her right, Cathy turned into

Head Street then right again into her own road.

However, instead of just a few children playing on the cobbles in the peaceful residential street, there was now clusters of women outside some of the doors. If that wasn't odd enough at this time of day, at the far end of the street there were a couple of policemen loitering about and a van parked outside her own house.

Mary Tyler, who lived across the road from her, spotted Cathy and said something to the three women, standing with their arms folded, next to her. They all looked at Cathy then one of their number waved to another huddle of women, who also turned in her direction. Several other groups did the same, all muttering and giving her the once-over.

Gripping the pushchair handle firmly, and with every pair of eyes riveted on her, Cathy continued towards her house.

As she made her way down the street she heard murmurs of 'traitor', 'turncoat' and 'Nazi'. And when she drew closer to her house, she noticed someone had daubed 'traitor scum' in red paint across the brickwork.

Weaving her way through her neighbours, she headed for her open front door, but just before she reached it, a portly middle-aged man with thinning hair and a gloomy expression on his face came out of her house carrying a box.

Balancing it on his knee, he opened the back of the Morris van and shoved the box inside.

'What are you taking out of my house?' Cathy asked, as she reached him.

'Are you Stan's wife?' he asked, shutting the van.

'I am.'

'Oh, I'm sorry,' he said, looking genuinely sad. 'I

didn't recognise you. I'm Frank Appleby, Violet's brother-in-law. We were at your wedding.'

'Nice to meet you again,' said Cathy. 'But that still doesn't explain why you're carrying boxes out of my house.'

'The wife got a frantic phone call from her sister about an hour ago saying she needed us to come and pick her up urgently,' Frank replied. 'The two of them are in there supposedly packing a couple of cases.' He rolled his eyes. 'Couple of cases! I've already loaded four full boxes of junk in the van.'

'But why?'

Frank moved closer.

'It's Stan,' he said, in a low voice with just a whiff of halitosis. 'Violet was at the flicks with her pals and her precious bloody son was on Pathé News during this afternoon's matinee.' He glanced over his shoulder at the open door. 'He was in the German Army's British Corps. As bold as brass on the full screen wearing a German uniform and giving a heil Hitler salute for everyone to see. Someone recognised him and then, well . . .You know how these things get around.' He raised his eyebrows. 'Still, best get on or I'll have both of them on at me.'

He went back inside the house.

Putting her foot on the back axle, Cathy leaned on the pushchair handle and, clearing the doorstep with the front wheels, followed him. As she did, she came face to face with a tight-faced stick of a woman who could only have been Violet's sister Ivy.

Dressed in a tweedy suit and unadorned brown hat, she was standing at the bottom of the stairs with a suitcase in either hand. Her husband was just behind her, carrying another brimming box.

'Where's Vi?' asked Cathy.

'*Violet* is in the kitchen,' Ivy replied.

Cathy continued down the hallway and into the kitchen, where she found Violet putting a news paper-wrapped plate into a wooden fruit box.

'Well, it seems that the truth will out, eh, Vi?' said Cathy.

Her mother-in-law shot her a hateful look but said nothing.

'Your 'hero' son has excelled himself this time,' Cathy continued. 'I just wish I'd been there to see your face.'

'I suppose you're enjoying this,' Violet said, her face contorted with hate as she grabbed another plate from the dresser.

'Not particularly,' Cathy replied. 'It's bad enough being married to your precious son without everyone knowing he's betrayed his country, too.'

'Well, I'd take that self-satisfied look off your face if I were you,' said Violet. 'Because the army will stop his pay and then where will you be? And in case you're thinking this will get you that divorce you're desperate for, remember you're the one committing adultery with that darkie sergeant, so no court in the land will grant you one, not when my Stanley is the innocent party.'

'Innocent!' laughed Cathy. 'I don't think that's what most people would call fighting for the enemy. But don't worry, Vi. I'm not going to bother try-ing to divorce Stan because I'll be a widow soon enough — when the army catches up with him your precious son will be dangling from the end of a rope. So, scurrying off to hide at your sister's, are you?' said Cathy. 'You might as well because you won't be able to show your face around here for a while.'

Shoving a saucer in the box, a malicious glint sparked in her mother-in-law's eye.

'You can take that smug look off your face,' she said. 'Because you're his wife and people will be talking about you, too.'

Cathy shrugged. 'People already are, thanks to you. And I'm sure I'll give them more to talk about before I'm done. But I'm a Brogan and we're used to it.' She glanced at the china bowl in her mother-in-law's hand. 'Is that your grandmother's tea set?'

'It is,' Violet replied. 'You don't think I would leave all my good china here for you to use, do you?'

'Good,' said Cathy, unclipping Peter and lifting him out. 'Because it's the bloody ugliest set of crockery I've ever set eyes on.'

Shoving the bowl in the box, Violet shot Cathy another withering look then snatched the box from the table and marched out of the kitchen towards the front door.

Putting Peter on her hip, Cathy followed her.

'There she is,' shouted someone, as Violet stepped over the threshold.

A yell rose from the crowd as a rotten apple landed at her mother-in-law's feet.

'Bastard traitor,' screamed someone else, as a tomato mashed into the wall beside the door.

Clutching the box, Violet tucked her head in her collar just as a lump of mud thumped into the back of her head, knocking the wash-and-set she'd had at the hairdresser's that morning askew.

'Clear off,' bellowed a gruff voice, as Violet dashed for the van where her sister and brother-in-law were already in the front seat.

441

A whirl of dog dirt sailed over the heads of the crowd and splattered across Violet's light grey coat. A cheer went up and sensing their quarry was getting away, the crowd surged forward as a volley of gutter mud and spoilt fruit rained down on Violet.

Seeing the change in mood, the two police officers ambled forward and ushered Violet towards the waiting vehicle. The crowd followed them all the way until the constable bundled Violet in the back seat then jeered as it sped off.

Then Cathy's neighbours turned and trudged back to where she was standing.

Sticking his thumb in his mouth, Peter held her tightly as they approached.

The crowd stopped in front of her and Cathy raised her chin. Despite her mouth feeling like a bone in the desert, she studied them coolly.

'Did you know?' ask Lenny Willis, who lived three doors down, jabbing his finger at her.

'Of course I didn't,' she replied, her heart thumping wildly. 'I'm not surprised that my husband threw his lot in with the Nazis at the first opportunity, but I'm puzzled why you lot are.' She cast her gaze over the sea of angry faces. 'After all, everyone in this street knew Stan was the top man in Mosley's thugs in the so-called British Peace League. And it wasn't me who swallowed Violet's lies about her 'hero son' and how hard done by she was because of her 'wicked daughter-in-law', so don't you come the high and mighty with me.' With slow deliberation Cathy's hard gaze ran over the crowd. 'Anyone got anything else to say?'

Those gathered outside her house, unable to look her in the eye, shuffled on the spot and studied their feet.

442

'Good.' Cathy shifted Peter's weight in her arms. 'Now if you don't mind, I have a very tired and hungry son who needs his supper.'

She turned to go back in the house but then she looked back at the gathered crowd again.

'And I'd be obliged if whoever did that,' she indicated the red paint splattered across the brickwork, 'would scrub it off, because there's no 'traitor scum' living here.'

Turning her back on them, Cathy carried Peter back into the house and slammed the door.

32

Listening half-heartedly to the plummy voice on the radio informing the audience of the programmes for the rest of the morning, Archie marvelled at how quickly the body adapted.

This time last week he doubted he could have identified more than half a dozen voices with his eyes closed but now, after six days living in his black world, he reckoned it would be at least double that number. And it wasn't just people's voices. He could distinguish Sister Torrance's brisk footsteps from Staff Nurse Carmichael's lighter ones. He also knew that there were two dinner trolleys used on this ward: one had a squeaky wheel while the other's door rattled.

In fact, it was that one, with the crockery and waste from breakfast, that the orderly had just trundled past his side-room door towards the ward's main doors.

Until one of the nurses had mentioned it earlier, he'd forgotten that it was, in fact, the Wednesday of Holy Week so, along with the usual morning service, there had been an extra Bible reading. As that had just finished, it meant that it was now ten fifteen.

It was also a week since the accident and the day Sir Mungo Henderson would be returning.

Unable to sleep more than an hour or two in a stretch, Archie had been awake well before the chattering nurses had arrived for the morning shift at six thirty.

He'd nabbed one of them straightaway and had asked them to bring him a bowl for a wash. He'd just wiped the soap from his face when the hospital's barber, a chatty fella called Joe, arrived on the ward. Archie had collared him, too, and so by the time Matron did her rounds at eight, Archie was up, washed, shaved and sitting in the chair beside his bed dressed in his uniform. He might be in hospital but he wasnae going to act like an invalid.

She'd protested as usual, telling him yet again that patients should wear pyjamas and be resting in bed. In response, Archie had given her a half-hearted apology, which had sent her away tutting.

As the early-morning bustle of breakfast and bed baths subsided, Archie had resumed his morning occupation of listening to the wireless.

However, although his eyes were covered, Archie's mind was forever conjuring up images. The soft spring breeze from the window brought the blue of a summer's sky vividly to mind, along with the ethereal texture of swollen white clouds. The whiff of flowery perfume as a nurse made the bed had pinks, yellows and lilac popping in his mind.

It wasn't just colours. It was the shape of his daughter's cheeks as they lifted in a smile and the curve of his mother's sinewy arms as she kneaded bread; but the images that returned again and again were the colour, texture and form of the woman he would love for eternity: Cathy.

None of which he could now see and it was possible he would never see again. He knew he was alive, and had a loving family, but the thought of spending the rest of his life in utter darkness threatened to overwhelm him.

He wouldn't see Kirsty grow into a young woman; and would she, as a bride, have to lead him down the aisle rather than the other way around? And before that day came, how could he support her and his mother if he couldn't work?

And then there was Cathy. The woman he loved so much that being apart from her was a physical ache. The woman he'd dreamed of building a future and a family with. How could he burden her with a blind husband? And not even a real husband, because they would be man and wife without the benefit of a wedding certificate.

How could he do that to her? In fact, if he loved her, truly loved her, he should send her away, let her get on with her life and find someone new.

A wry smile lifted the corners of Archie's mouth.

He should do just that, but selfishly he couldn't.

Truthfully, it would be a bitterly hard battle to face a life lived in darkness with her, but it would be an impossible task without her.

Footsteps sounded outside and he recognised Cathy's light tread as she walked into his small side room.

'It's only me, Archie,' she said.

He felt her hand on his shoulder, and a faint smell of gardenias drifted up as a pair of warm familiar lips pressed on to his.

His arm wound around Cathy's shoulder and he gathered her to him, savouring her kiss for a long moment.

'How are you?' she asked softly when he finally released her.

'All the better for having you here,' he replied, in the same hushed tone.

The signature tune of *Music While You Work* started, and foreboding gripped Archie.

Shoving away the black cloud that hovered over him, Archie squeezed her hand. 'How are you and Peter getting on at your sister's?'

'Peter loves it with his auntie and cousins. It's such a change to get home and be greeted by a friendly face. I got there just as the air raid siren went off last night,' she said. 'Peter was asleep but . . .'

Archie forced his turbulent mind to concentrate on Cathy's voice as she recounted the events of the previous night, but as she started to tell him about Peter's fight with his cousin at the breakfast table, the sound of footsteps coming to a stop outside his room sent Archie's heart hammering in his chest again.

There was the rustle of starched fabric as two pairs of heavy feet marched into the room.

Cathy fell silent.

'Good morning, Sergeant McIntosh,' said Sir Mungo's well-modulated tones.

'I hope so, Sir Mungo,' said Archie, forcing the words out.

'As do we all,' replied the ophthalmic specialist. 'Good morning to you.'

Somewhere to the left of him, Cathy murmured a reply.

'The chart, if you please, Sister.'

'Of course, Sir Mungo,' Sister Torrance replied.

Metal rattled on metal as she took the observation chart from the end of Archie's bed.

There was a moment of silence then the consultant spoke again.

'Now, Sergeant, can you tell me . . .'

Sir Mungo ran through a couple of mundane questions which Archie did his best to answer over the choking lump in his throat and the roar of blood

447

through his ears. Finally, after what seemed like an eternity, the consultant addressed the Sister.

'If I could have the blinds down, please?'

There was a rattle behind Archie as she closed the Venetian blinds.

'Thank you,' said Sir Mungo. 'Now, Sergeant McIntosh, Sister here is going to take off the bandages, but you must keep your eyes closed until I ask you to open them. Do you understand?'

Archie nodded.

He heard feet shuffling and chairs scraping on the floor. As gentle fingers touched his forehead, fear gripped Archie's chest, squeezing the air from it.

In the past day he'd been telling himself that he was going to be fine, that he'd soon be seeing the world again in all its bright colours, but once the bandages came off . . .

The final layers were peeled away.

With his eyelids pressed tightly together and hardly daring to breathe, Archie waited.

There was a pause and then Sir Mungo spoke again. 'Whenever you're ready, Sergeant.'

* * *

Cathy held her breath in a vain attempt to steady her wildly beating heart as she silently prayed, *God, let him be able to see.* Feeling sick, she waited for what seemed like for ever, but then slowly Archie opened his eyes. He gazed around for a moment then his face crumpled. Raising

his right hand, he covered his eyes. 'Archie?' said Cathy. He looked up, and his eyes, glistening with unshed tears, ran slowly over those in the room before coming to rest on her. 'Aye,' he said, his ice-blue eyes filled with love. 'I can see.' Suppressing the urge to jump up and down with joy, Cathy

smiled, and Archie returned her smile with that quirky one of his. 'Splendid,' said the consultant. Archie watched as the middle-aged consultant, with a full head

of steel-grey hair and a stout figure, took an ophthalmoscopy from his jacket pocket.

Moving closer, Sir Mungo pressed the instrument to his own eye then peered into Archie's. Seemingly satisfied with what he found, the ophthalmic specialist stood up again.

'There's still some residual damage,' he said, pocketing his instrument. 'But the injured cells at the back of your eyes seem to be healing well. Is your vision clear?'

Archie looked around the room again then studied his hand. 'It is.' 'What about this?' The consultant took the chart from the end of

his bed and handed it to him. 'Can you read the print at the bottom?' Archie's eyes skimmed down the sheet. 'Aye, well and fine,' he replied, handing it back. He squinted.

'Mind you, everything seems a mite bright.'

'It will do for a while,' the consultant replied. 'You'll have to wear dark glasses for a few weeks but only until your eyes are fully healed.'

'And when will I be able to return to duty?' asked Archie.

'I'd say a couple more weeks after that,' Sir Mungo replied. 'By then your sight should return to normal. But I'd like to see you myself at Moorfields before you return to duty. Sister will arrange the appointment.'

'When can he come home, Doctor?' asked Cathy.

'I'll get the limbs and appliance chap to sort him out a pair of dark glasses, but we'll be kicking him out tomorrow.' Sir Mungo's round face lifted in a jovial smile. 'Unless you'd like us to keep him out of your hair a little longer.'

Cathy laughed.

'No, tomorrow's grand. I don't want him cluttering up your ward any longer.'

'Well, then, as that seems to be settled, I'll wish you all a good day. Sergeant.'

He offered his hand and Archie took it.

'Thank you, Sir Mungo,' he said, as they shook.

'Mrs McIntosh.' The consultant nodded at Cathy then swept out of the room with Sister Torrance half a step behind.

They looked at each other for a moment, then Archie stood up. Crossing the space between them, he took Cathy's hands and drew her into his embrace. As his arms enfolded her, Cathy burst into tears.

'Oh, Archie,' she sobbed.

'Hush, hush,' he murmured into her hair. 'It's done.'

'I know,' she said, as she freed herself from his arms and retrieved a handkerchief from her handbag.

'I bet I look a mess,' she said, wiping under her eyes carefully so as not to smudge her mascara.

Archie kissed her forehead. 'You've never looked better. Now, woman, will you at last tell me what you've not been telling me this last week.'

Enjoying the feel of his arms around her, Cathy looked up into his mesmerising ice-blue eyes and smiled.

'Well, first off, Archie McIntosh, I think you ought to know that I've thrown up down the toilet each morning for the past week.'

33

Sliding the page he'd just read behind the next, Archie reread the letter from his mother that Cathy had brought to hospital the day before.

She'd given it to him along with another one that had arrived on the day of the accident. As well as all the usual news and an update on Kirsty, his mother had said that she guessed he was busy as she hadn't heard from him. He usually wrote a couple of times a week and phoned when he could, so he knew that after a week of silence she would be worried.

Promising himself he would ring her later, Archie continued reading, but as he got halfway down the page, Chalky strolled through the door into the side room.

'Here he is, Mogg,' said the corporal, 'skiving as always.'

'Me, skiving?' said Archie, putting aside the letter and rising to his feet. He shook his corporal's hand. 'Shouldn't you two be digging up a bomb somewhere?'

'Just taken some equipment to another team in Shoreditch, so we thought we'd drop by and annoy you for ten minutes,' said Mogg as he joined them. 'That pretty redheaded nurse making the bed said it would be all right.'

'Well, it's good to see you both,' said Archie.

'And the boys 'ad a whip-round and bought you these.' Lowering his kit bag to the floor, Chalky opened it. Pulling out four bottles of Guinness, he

452

put them on the side locker.

'Thanks.' Archie smiled. 'I'm touched.'

'See,' said Mogg, tapping the side of his head with his index finger. 'I always told you he was.'

Archie gave them a long-suffering look and resumed his seat as the two men pulled the upright visitors' chairs forward.

'To be honest, we thought they might have already kicked you out,' said Chalky, sitting astride his chair with his elbows on the backrest.

'They have,' Archie replied, indicating his packed haversack in the corner. 'Doc came around ten minutes ago and gave me the all-clear. I'm just waiting for Cathy to arrive. I told her she didnae have to fetch me but she said she wanted to.'

'It's always a good idea to do what the little woman says,' said Chalky.

Mogg picked up the pair of dark glasses on the side locker. 'These yours?'

'Aye,' Archie replied. 'I have to wear them for the next week or so whenever I go outside.'

'When will you be back?' asked Chalky.

'The specialist from Moorfields wants to see me in two weeks,' Archie replied. 'So I expect he'll sign me fit then. Do you think you can manage not to get yourselves into trouble until then?'

'Probably not,' Chalky replied, looking hard at the squaddie sitting alongside him.

Mogg looked indignant. 'I was just looking through the window for the other blooming tail fin, so how was I to know that woman was having a strip wash at the kitchen sink?'

Archie laughed.

'Seriously, mate, you gave us a right scare,' Chalky

said.

'No more than I gave myself,' Archie replied. 'I can't tell — '

The terror of being imprisoned in utter darkness rose up again, but Archie cut it short and shifted his mind on to the new little McIntosh who would be joining them just before Christmas.

'Still,' said Chalky, cutting across his fatherly thoughts, 'at least you'll have some free time to paint while you're off.'

'That I will,' he replied. 'But I imagine I'll be spending a good few days looking for another house for the family.'

The corporal looked puzzled. 'I thought you'd found somewhere near Stepney Green station.'

'We did, and it was perfect, but because of everything that's happened it will have gone by now,' Archie said.

'Pity,' said Mogg. 'Decent accommodation's like blooming hen's teeth.'

'Aye, it is, and more's the pity, because I was planning to bring Kirsty and Ma down this week and now it'll be more like Whitsun before I can.'

Frustration niggled but Archie damped it down, reminding himself that at least when they did get to London, he'd be able to see them standing before him.

'Anyhow,' he said, pushing the setback aside, 'what else's been going on?'

'Well, firstly,' said Chalky, pulling a copy of the *East London Advertiser* from his jacket and placing it on the hospital's blue counterpane, 'you're officially a blooming hero.'

Archie opened the newspaper and saw the picture of himself, cropped from the squad's photo the previous summer, and above it was the headline 'The Hero of Shadwell'.

He read down the page, which told how he, Sergeant Archibald McIntosh, at great personal risk to life and limb, had saved twenty-six children and nine nurses from being blown to smithereens.

'You'll be needing those blooming dark goggles,' said Mogg, 'to avoid being mobbed by admirers when you walk down the street.'

'There's even muttering in the CO's office about a George Cross coming your way,' added Chalky.

Archie skimmed through the article again then looked up. 'There's no mention of Monkman.'

'I guess the reporter thought it would be bad for morale if they had a picture of men in white coats escorting the lieutenant away in a straitjacket,' said Chalky. 'Well, perhaps not an actual straitjacket,' he continued, seeing Archie's shocked expression, 'but he was a blubbering wreck by the time we got him out.'

'He's gone, then,' said Archie, putting the newspaper back on the bed.

'Gone, and good riddance,' said Mogg.

'It was all hush-hush, like, from the top brass,' said Chalky. 'Put it around he's gone for some R&R, but the world and his wife know he's been sent to an asylum.'

'I wonder who HQ will send to replace him?' said Mogg.

'By rights, seeing as how he knows more about dismantling German fuses than half of the top brass, it ought to be Archie-boy here,' said Chalky.

'Well, I thank you for your vote of confidence,' said Archie, 'but I doubt there's many with pips on their shoulder in Whitehall who look like me.'

A flash of red caught Archie's eye and he turned to see Cathy, illuminated in the spring sunshine as she stood in the doorway with Peter, also in his Sunday best, by her side.

The red that had caught his attention was the cropped Rose madder jacket that she wore over a flowery dress. Her golden-brown hair was loose under her perky summer hat and fell in bouncy curls on her shoulders.

He stood up and so did Chalky and Mogg.

Cathy's gaze fixed on him, and Archie's world came together like the perfect combination of tones and hues on a masterpiece.

'Morning,' she said.

'Morning, Mrs Wheeler,' they said in unison.

Spotting Archie, Peter slipped out of his mother's grip and dashed towards him.

'Arrie,' the little lad said as he hugged Archie's knee.

'Hello there, pal,' he said, scooping the little boy into his arms. 'I hope you've been a good boy for your ma while I've been away.'

'He's been very good,' said Cathy, smiling as she walked across to join them.

'I'm pleased to hear it,' said Archie. 'It's never too early to get into Father Christmas's good books.'

'Well then,' said Chalky, retrieving his kitbag from the floor and slinging it over his shoulder, 'we'd best be about our business. And, Mrs Wheeler, see if you can keep this great loon in one piece so he can come back and make sure D Squad do the same.'

Cathy laughed. 'I'll try, Corporal, but I can't promise.'

'I'll be seeing you, lads,' said Archie, putting his free arm around Cathy. 'And from now on, it's Mrs

456

McIntosh.'

The two squaddies gave him a casual salute and left.

Cathy turned, and with her eyes filled with love, she stretched up on tiptoes and kissed him briefly, then the smile that had captured his heart spread across her face. 'Let's go home, Archie.'

★ ★ ★

Five minutes later, having gathered his kit together, thanked the nurses and put on his protective glasses, Archie, carrying Peter and with Cathy on his arm, strolled out of the hospital's main entrance.

However, as he reached the bottom of the hospital's wide Portland stone steps, Archie stopped.

Gazing through his sepia-tinted glasses, he scanned the clear blue sky above him and then looked across to the crowd of people bustling through the market opposite.

He took a deep breath to still the emotions gathering in his chest.

'Are you all right?' asked Cathy.

Archie shifted his attention down to the woman who was, and always would be, standing beside him.

'I am,' he said. 'And thankful. Very thankful.'

She smiled that lovely smile of hers. 'Me too.'

They gazed at each other for a moment then Peter started wriggling.

Putting the little boy on the pavement, Archie adjusted his kitbag strap across him. His gaze ran along the dozen or so prams parked under the rain shelter to the right of the door.

'Where's the pushchair?'

'I didn't bring it as Dad dropped me off,' she replied.
'Well, it's nae far; Peter can perch on my shoulders,' he said.

He went to lift the boy up again, but Cathy caught his arm.

'There's no need, Archie,' she said, with barely concealed excitement brimming out of her lovely eyes. 'Because we're catching the bus.'

★ ★ ★

Half an hour after leaving the hospital, and with his arm stretched along the seat behind Cathy, Archie roared.

'I can't believe you did that,' he laughed, as the bus whizzed past the almshouses on Mile End Road.

'It wasn't just me, but Dad and the boys, too,' Cathy said, shifting Peter on her knee. 'It took them the best part of the day to load all her junk on the lorry.'

After leaving the hospital, as they waited for a bus on the Whitechapel Road, Cathy had told him about Violet stealing his nude sketch of her and the meeting at the WVS. She'd also explained how she'd secured the house they'd wanted to rent by borrowing the money from her sister.

And when they'd finally boarded a number 25 a quarter of an hour later and settled themselves in one of the downstairs seats, Cathy had revealed, in hushed tones, how Violet had discovered that Stan was a signed-up member of Hitler's British Free Corps, not a POW. Now, as they reached the end of their journey, she'd been running through how she'd cleared the house in Senrab Street before handing back the keys.

'But dumping the lot on the pavement outside her sister's house,' chuckled Archie, pushing the dark glasses back up his nose.

Cathy shrugged. 'She ought to be thankful I didn't just leave it in the house.'

'I wish I'd seen her face,' said Archie, thinking that retribution for the spiteful old woman's behaviour was long overdue.

'So do I. It was a real picture. But as she was forever going on about her expensive furniture and pictures, I thought she might like to have them. Mind you . . .' A mischievous smile lifted Cathy's full lips. 'I didn't let Violet have everything.'

Amusement flickered in Archie's ice-blue eyes. 'You kept the fridge.'

'I certainly did,' said Cathy as the bus slowed down at a stop. 'And the cooker and the linen, plus the washing tub and everything in the kitchen, Peter's bed and the front-room furniture.'

Archie smiled. Hugging her to him, he pressed his lips on her hair.

'Do you think your father will be able to get another couple of beds so I can tell Ma to bring Kirsty down next week?' he asked.

'I'm sure he'll try,' she replied. 'What day were you thinking?'

'Perhaps Wednesday or Thursday?'

Amusement sparked in Cathy's eyes. 'I can't wait to meet them.'

Archie was just wondering what he'd said that was so entertaining when he caught sight of the municipal washhouse and Stepney Green station through his sepia-tinted lenses.

Rising from his seat, he reached up and yanked on

the bell-pull that stretched the length of the bus.

Lifting his kitbag from the floor, his slung it across him again then held out his hand.

'This is our stop, lad.'

Peter hopped off his mother's lap and took Archie's hand.

The bus drew to a stop outside the Farmer's Arms. Archie guided Peter between the passengers on the bench seats towards the platform at the back of the bus, then scooping the little boy in his arms, he stepped off.

'Be careful now,' he said, offering his free hand to Cathy.

She gave him an exasperated look. 'I have got off a bus before, Archie.'

'Aye, you have,' he replied, as the bus pulled away. 'But I nae want you taking a tumble in your condition, woman.'

Archie set Peter on his feet. As he did so, he caught sight of the red telephone box next to the station's entrance.

'Perhaps I should telephone Ma,' he said, thinking of her two letters tucked in his inside pocket.

Cathy looped her arm in his. 'Why don't you have a cuppa first?'

'It'll only take a moment,' Archie replied, his fingers sifting through the loose change in his trouser pocket.

'I know, but . . . I need to spend a penny.' Cathy smiled apologetically. 'Sorry.'

'All right,' Archie replied. 'I suppose thirty minutes won't harm one way or another.'

Archie took one of Peter's hands while Cathy took the other and they headed towards their new home.

Ten minutes later they were standing on the front step of number seventy-two Alderney Road.

Stepping forward, Cathy grabbed the iron ring of the lion'shead knocker and rapped on the door.

Archie gave her a curious look.

'It's an old Irish custom.' Delving into her pocket, Cathy pulled out a key with an enamel Mackeson keyring attached and offered it to him. 'You go first.'

Letting go of Peter's hand, Archie took the key.

He unlocked the door, stepped inside, and stopped dead.

Time seemed to stand still for a moment as he stared at his mother, wearing her best dress, and his daughter, all pigtails and freckles in her school uniform, before they rushed towards him.

'Da,' screamed Kirsty, throwing herself into his arms.

Dropping his kitbag on the floor, Archie's arms closed around her. Lifting her off her feet, he hugged her tightly to him. Almost overwhelmed with joy, Archie savoured the feel of her in his arms after so long. Then a hand rested on his upper arm, and he looked up to see his mother's grey eyes.

Putting Kirsty down, he reached out and drew his mother into the family embrace. They hugged for a moment longer, then Archie lifted his head.

'But how are you both here?' he asked, still finding it hard to believe they were standing before him.

His mother's face lifted in a soft smile, then she turned and glanced down the hall.

'You've got your bonny lass to thank for that, son,' Aggie said.

Raising his eyes, Archie looked over his mother's head at Cathy, who was still standing in the doorway.

461

'Well, you did say you wanted us all to be together for Easter,' she said, looking justifiably pleased with herself. 'So now we are.'

'She telephoned yesterday so Kirsty and I caught the mail train from Glasgow Central yesterday evening,' his mother explained. She pulled a face. 'An experience ma old back is in no hurry to repeat, I might add. Cathy and her father kindly collected us from Euston just after six and brought us here. And . . .' She whacked his arm.

'What's that for?' asked Archie.

'For no letting her telephone me sooner,' his mother replied.

★ ★ ★

As she watched Archie's joyful reunion with his mother and daughter, weariness washed over Cathy. She wasn't surprised, for she had spent the past week between hospital visits washing down cupboards, scrubbing floors, polishing windows and hanging curtains. Thankfully, Jo and Mattie had rolled up their sleeves and pitched in, as had her father, who'd found not only beds for Kirsty and Aggie, but wardrobes and dressing tables. He'd also brought the Morrison shelter from the old house and, with the help of her two brothers and Jo's husband Tommy, manhandled it down into the basement. At the end of each day of rushing around after her son and trying to set up a home, Cathy had collapsed exhausted in it alongside Peter. However, last night, for the first time since Corporal White had turned up on her doorstep a week ago, and despite an air raid going on above, Cathy had slept the whole night through. In fact, she was only just up and ready when her father had called for them at six.

And to be honest, as she'd waited for Archie's mother and daughter to emerge out of the billowing steam on the platform, Cathy's heart had been in her throat. In contrast to her towering son, Archie's mother was a few inches shorter than Cathy, and probably a size smaller than Cathy's size twelve.

The girl walking alongside her down the platform and wearing a green school uniform was unmistakably Archie's daughter. And not just because of her milky-coffee-coloured skin. She had her father's height, and although her hair was tied back in two long plaits it was the same rich brown. Her eyes, too, were Archie's, and she would be a beauty when she was grown.

Mrs McIntosh was carrying a suitcase while the young girl beside her had her satchel over her shoulder and clutched a small weekend case. They had stood looking along the platform at each other for a moment and then, just when Cathy thought her heart was about to burst from her chest, Archie's mother had smiled.

A moment later they were embracing as if they'd know each other for years. Everyone was introduced to everyone else. Cathy nudged Peter into giving Kirsty the ration-size bar of Cadbury's Dairy along with a latest copy of *School Friend* she'd bought as a present. In return, Kirsty handed Peter a *Ladybird Book of British Trains* and a packet of Fruit Pastilles.

Jeremiah, who had been waiting a little way away until the introductions were done, came over to take Aggie and Kirsty's luggage to the lorry. A few minutes later Cathy and Aggie, with Kirsty between them and Peter on Cathy's lap, were in the driver's cab of the Bedford. With Peter sucking his sweets and Kirsty nibbling her chocolate, she and Aggie chatted all the way as Jeremiah drove them to Alderney Street.

They'd arrived home an hour ago and Cathy had set off to fetch Archie, leaving Archie's family to settle in. So eager was she to see his face when he walked in and found them waiting for him, she'd nearly let the cat out of the bag when they'd got off the bus and he'd spotted the telephone box. She was glad she'd stopped herself just in time as seeing his tearful happiness now brought a lump to Cathy's throat.

After several rounds of hugging and kissing in the hallway, Archie lifted his head and his blue eyes returned to Cathy.

Untangling himself from his womenfolk's embrace, he took a step towards her but as he did, Kirsty grabbed his arm.

'Da, Da,' she begged, dragging him to the stairs. 'Come and see ma room.'

'Kirsty, where are your manners, child?' remonstrated her grandmother.

'No, it's all right,' Cathy said, smiling at the young girl, who looked a little crestfallen as she stood beside Archie. 'Go ahead, Kirsty. I'm sure your dad will want to see it.'

Taking her father's hand and chattering ten to the dozen, Kirsty practically dragged Archie up the stairs, leaving Cathy and his mother standing in the hallway looking at each other.

'You mustn't mind her,' said Aggie. 'It's been such an age since she's seen him and — '

'I don't mind at all,' Cathy replied, bending down to take off her son's coat. 'I know how much she must have missed him, and I'd have been the same at that

464

age if I hadn't seen my dad for months.'

Free of his outer clothing, Peter toddled off into the front room.

Cathy glanced at the hall clock.

'Goodness, is it midday already? The dinner must be almost ready,' she said.

'I'll see to it,' said Aggie as Peter returned carrying his toy train.

'That's good of you,' said Cathy, 'but you don't have to —'

'Aye, I ken,' said Aggie comfortably. 'But I'm not one to sit idle while there's chores need doing.'

The sound of running footsteps clattered above their heads and Aggie glanced up then looked back at Cathy.

'You go up and I'll put a light under the carrots. And, Peter . . . ?' The boy paused rolling his train back and forth on the floor and looked up. 'Shall we see if there's a wee biscuit in the barrel?' Aggie asked, smiling at him and Cathy in turn.

Scrambling to his feet and clutching his train, Peter followed the older woman into the kitchen.

Leaving Aggie to potter around in the kitchen, Cathy made her way upstairs and found Archie and Kirsty standing in front of his easel and art equipment, set up and ready to go in the bay of their bedroom.

He was gazing fondly at his daughter as she flipped through his canvases stacked under the window sill.

'Dad's showing me his pictures,' said Kirsty, as Cathy walked into the room.

'They're very good, aren't they?' said Cathy.

Kirsty nodded, her long pigtails bobbing up and down her back as she did.

'Did he tell you that three of his paintings are in

465

an exhibition, travelling around the whole country so lots of people can see them?' Cathy asked.

'Are they, Da?' asked Kirsty, looking up at her father with wide-eyed adoration.

'Och, well,' Archie replied, looking oddly boyish for a six-foot-two man with size-eleven shoes.

Turning back to her father's artwork, Kirsty looked at a couple of others then her face lit up. 'Aunt Cathy, there's a drawing of you.'

A look of horror flashed across Archie's face.

'Look,' said Kirsty, pulling out a small head-and-shoulders line drawing from among the canvases and sketchpads.

Archie took it from her, and his relief was palpable.

'I was surprised to find it when I packed up your work,' Cathy said, not bothering to conceal her amusement. 'As I'd never seen that one before.'

'I drew it just after I met you at the rest centre the first time,' he said.

'Da does that all the time,' giggled Kirsty, handing it to her. 'Draws you when you're not watching. He did one of Gran asleep once when her top teeth had slipped.'

'Well, luckily I haven't got dentures, but thanks for warning me,' said Cathy.

'Kirsty!' shouted Aggie from the bottom up the stairs.

Archie's daughter walked across the room to the door.

'Yes, Nana.'

'Come and set the table.'

'But I'm with Da,' Kirsty called back.

'I know full well where you are, child,' her grandmother shouted back.

Kirsty looked at Archie.

'You heard your gran,' he said. 'Me and Aunt Cathy will be down presently.'

The corners of Kirsty's mouth turned down.

'Kirsty,' said Cathy, 'I was thinking of getting a few chickens, so perhaps after dinner you could help your dad decide where to build the coop.'

Kirsty's face brightened immediately.

'Can I, Da?'

'I was counting on it.' Putting his arm around his daughter, Archie kissed her on the forehead. 'Now go and help Nana.'

'Kirsty!' shouted Aggie.

'Coming,' Kirsty shouted back, tearing out of the room.

'Honestly, Cathy,' said Archie as his daughter's footsteps faded, 'when she dived in to get that picture, I nearly had a heart attack.'

'Don't worry,' she laughed. 'I'm not going to be caught like that twice. I've tucked the other one away for now on top of the wardrobe.'

'It seems to me you've been busy while I've been away,' he said, taking her hands and drawing her into his embrace.

'I wanted you to have a proper home to come back to,' Cathy replied, placing her hands on his hard chest then sliding them up and around his neck.

'Well, you've certainly done that, Cathy, and more.' He kissed her. 'Because I've come home to a family.'

He placed his hand on her still flat stomach. 'A growing one, too.'

'Archie, don't tell Kirsty about the baby just yet.'

He looked concerned. 'Is there something wrong?'

'No,' she laughed, 'nothing at all. In fact, I'm going

to book in with the midwives at Munroe House next week. But Kirsty's obviously missed you very much. I don't want her to feel pushed out by me or the baby. She's going to have to adjust to lots of new things, so let's wait a few weeks until we've all got to know each other a bit and she's settled into her new school.'

Archie's arms tightened around her.

'You know, Cathy,' he said, his captivating blue eyes filled with love as he gazed down, 'every morning I wake up and think I can't possibly love you any more than I do, and each day you do something that makes me love you even more.'

His gaze locked with hers for a moment then, lowering his head, Archie's lips pressed against hers. His splayed hands anchored her to him as Cathy moulded herself into the hard contours of his body.

His kiss deepened and her mouth opened under his, igniting want and desire deep within her.

The sound of feet thumping up the stairs cut through the thoughts swirling in Cathy's mind.

Tearing her lips from Archie's, Cathy stepped back just as Kirsty ran into the room.

'Dinner's ready, Da!' she said breathlessly.

Archie cleared his throat.

'Is it now?' he said, straightening his tie.

Kirsty nodded.

'It's on the table.' She grabbed his arm. 'Come on, Da.'

He shrugged and looked across at Cathy.

'I'll follow you down,' she laughed, as his daughter dragged him to the door.

Alone, Cathy looked around. Seeing her sketched portrait lying on the bed, she picked it up.

She was wearing her WVS uniform and her hair was

468

pinned back and, even though done from memory, Archie had captured the shape of her mouth and the tilt of her nose exactly. He'd even caught the sadness in her eyes.

She had hoped that tomorrow, Good Friday, would be the day she'd finally be free of Stanley. Sadly she wouldn't be, and the saints above only knew when she would be, but although legally she was still tied to him, her heart and soul were free.

As a still-married woman living with another man, and a man of a different colour, Cathy knew life wouldn't be easy. She knew what people would call both her and their children born out of wedlock.

In the years to come, Archie would probably sketch and paint her from time to time, but this small line drawing would be the only one showing her looking sad. Because Archie had replaced that sadness and emptiness within her with a love that would last all of this life and the next. He'd given her a happiness that she'd never even imagined existed.

So let the gossips do their worst. With Archie's love surrounding her, she could face anything and, as her dad always said, if it wasn't for the Brogans, people would have nothing to talk about.

Acknowledgements

As Always, I would like to mention a few books, authors and people, to whom I am particularly indebted.

In order to set my characters thoughts and world-view authentically in the harsh reality of winter 1942 and spring 1943, I returned to *Wartime Britain 1939–1945* (Gardiner), *The East End at War* (Taylor & Lloyd), *The Blitz* (Gardiner), *Living Through the Blitz* (Harrison) and *The Blitz* (Madden).

As before in the Ration Book series, I've dipped into *Wartime Women: A Mass-Observation Anthology* (Sheridan), *Voices from the Home Front: Personal Experiences of Wartime Britain 1939–45* (Goodall) and *The Wartime House: Home Life in Wartime Britain 1939–1945* (Brown & Harris), plus this time, to give me the right feel and context of Cathy's work in the WVS, I used *Women at the Ready: The Remarkable Story of the Women's Voluntary Service on the Home Front* (Malcolmson & Malcolmson).

As always I like to return to primary sources if possible, and so I was delighted to discover *My London Bomb Squad* by Captain C. Nevil Newitt to help me bring to life Archie's role in the Bomb Disposal section of the Royal Engineers. In addition, *Danger UXB* (Owen) provided me with much of the technical details around the fuse types, explosives and the equipment developed to deal with unexploded bombs. I also took copious notes while I watched the whole 1970s ITV series *Danger UXB*, starring a very young Anthony Andrews. I also found 'Cyberwar

Before there was Cyber: Hacking WWII Electronic Bomb Fuse' as a PowerPoint presentation by Peter Gutmann from University of Auckland online, which was very helpful.

The first-hand account of the Bethnal Green Tube disaster by Dr Joan Martin, https://bbc.in/3jU0UM2, vividly describes the events of 3 March 1943. In addition, I had my mother's memories of being trapped underground as a sixteen-year-old caught up in that terrible night and how she and her sister were finally brought to the surface.

For Stanley Wheeler and the background of Hitler's British Free Corps, I delved into *Renegades: Hitler's Englishmen* (Wheale), and I will be returning to it again for *A Ration Book Victory*, the last in the Ration Book series.

I would also like to thank a few more people. Firstly, my very own Hero-at-Home, Kelvin, for his unwavering support, and my three daughters, Janet, Fiona and Amy, who listen patiently as I explain the endless twists and turns of the plot.

Once again, a big thanks goes to my lovely agent Laura Longrigg, whose encouragement and incisive editorial mind helped me to see the wood for the trees. My lovely editor Susannah Hamilton, who again turned my 400+ page manuscript into a beautiful book, and last, but by no means least, a big thank-you to the wonderful team at Atlantic Books, Karen Duffy, Poppy Mostyn-Owen, Jamie Forrest, Patrick Hunter, Sophie Walker and Hanna Kenne, for all their support and innovation.